Demon Box

Ken Kesey lives in Oregon, USA, with his wife, Faye. An old painted bus is still on the farm. His novel *Sometimes a Great Notion* is also available in paperback from Methuen.

Also by Ken Kesey

One Flew Over the Cuckoo's Nest
Sometimes a Great Notion*
Kesey's Garage Sale

* available in Methuen Paperbacks

Ken Kesey
DEMON BOX

A Methuen Paperback

A Methuen Paperback

DEMON BOX

British Library Cataloguing in Publication Data

Kesey, Ken
   Demon box.—(A Methuen paperback).
   I. Title
   818'.5408   PS3561.E667

   ISBN 0-413-40510-9

First published in Great Britain 1986
by Methuen London Ltd
This edition published 1987
by Methuen London Ltd
11 New Fetter Lane, London EC4P 4EE
Copyright © Ken Kesey 1986

Some of the essays in this collection were previously published,
in slightly different form, as follows:
'Tranny Man Over the Border' under the title 'The Thrice-thrown Tranny
Man or Orgy at Pallo Alto High School', and 'Good Friday' in *Spit in the
Ocean*; 'Abdul and Ebenezer' and 'The Day After Superman Died' in *Esquire*;
'The Search for the Secret Pyramid' (a revised edition later appeared in *Spit in
the Ocean*), 'Finding Dr Fung', and 'Now We Know How Many Holes It
Takes to Fill the Albert Hall' in *Rolling Stone*; 'Run Into Great Wall, under
the title 'Running Into the Great Wall' in *Running*; 'Killer' in *Playboy*; and
'Little Tricker the Squirrel Meets Big Double the Bear' in *Wonders* published
by Straight Arrow Press.

Printed and bound in Great Britain
by Richard Clay Ltd, Bungay, Suffolk

To Jed
across the river
riding point

TARNISHED GALAHAD . . . *what the judge called him at his trial*
– written later, on the run, in Mexico:

Down to five pesos from five thousand dollars
Down to the dregs from the lip-smacking foam
Down to a dopefiend from a prizewinner scholar
Down to the bush from a civilized home.

What people once called a promising talent
What used to be known as an upstanding lad
Now hounded and hunted by the law of two countries
And judged to be only a Tarnished Galahad.

Tarnished Galahad – did your sword get rusted?
Tarnished Galahad – there's no better name!
Keep running and hiding 'til the next time you're busted
And locked away to suffer your guilt, and shame.

– pretty much what happened.

Demon Box

D Tank Kickout

I check in at the SM County facilities dressed in my usual stuff – leather jacket, striped pants and shoes, silver whistle hanging around my neck. They allow you to wear street business up at camp. The bulls here at County Slam hate the policy. Lt Gerder looks up from his typewriter sees my outfit and his already stone-cold face freezes even harder.

'All right, Deboree. Give me everything.'

'Everything?' Usually they let the Honor Camp prisoners check through, trust them to give up their watches, pocketknives, etc.

'Everything. We don't want you blowing your whistle at midnight.'

'Make me out a complete property slip, then.'

He gives me an unwavering stare through the mesh as he takes a triplicate form from a waiting stack and rolls it into the typewriter.

'One whistle,' I say, pulling the chain over my head. 'With a silver crucifix soldered to the side.'

He doesn't type.

'One blues harp, E flat.'

He continues to look at me over the keys.

'Come on, Gerder; you want everything, I want a property slip for everything – whistles, harps, and all.'

We both know what I'm really worried about are my two Honor Camp notebooks.

'You just slide everything into the trough,' he says. 'In fact, I want you out of that Davy Crockett costume, Jackoff. Peel it.'

He comes out of the cage while I take off the fringed jacket Behema made me from the hide we skinned off the cow elk Houlihan ran over coming down off Seven Devils Pass that All Souls' Eve with the brakes gone and the headlights blown.

'Stuff it in the trough. Now, hands on the wall feet on the line. Spread 'em.' He gives the inside of my ankle a kick. 'Deputy Rhack, back me while I examine this prisoner.'

They frisk me. The whole shot, flashlight and all. Taking

sunglasses, handkerchief, fingernail clippers, ballpoint pens and everything. My two notebooks are wrapped in the big farewell card Fastinaux drew for me on butcher paper. Gerder rips it off and stuffs it in the wastebasket. He tosses the notebooks on top of the other stuff.

'I get a property slip for this stuff, Gerder. That's the law.'

'While you're in my tanks,' Lt Gerder lets me know, 'you go by my law.'

No malice in his voice. No anger. Just information.

'Okay then' – I take my two notebooks out of the trough and hold them up – 'witness these.' Showing them to Deputy Rhack and the rest of the men waiting in the receiving room. 'Everybody? Two notebooks.'

Then hand them to Gerder. He carries them around into his cage and sets them next to his typewriter. He hammers at the keys, ignoring the roomful of rancour across the counter from him. Rhack isn't so cool; a lot of these guys will be back up at camp with him for many months yet, where he's a guard without a gun. First he tries to oil us all with a wink, then he turns to me, smiling his sincerest man-to-man smile.

'So, Devlin . . . you think you got a book outta these six months with us?'

'I think so.'

'How do you think it'll come out; in weekly instalments in the *Chronicle?*'

'I hope not.' Bonehead move, giving those three pages of notes to that Sunday supplement reporter – pulled my own covers. 'It should make a book on its own.'

'You'll have to change a lot, I'll bet . . . like the names.'

'I'll bet a carton I don't. Sergeant *Rhack?* Lieutenant *Gerder?* Where can you come up with better names than those?'

Before Rhack can think up an answer Gerder jerks the papers out and slides them under the mesh. 'Sign all three, Deputy.'

Rhack has to use one of the pens from my pile. When Gerder gets the signed forms back he scoops all the little stuff out of the trough into a pasteboard property box with a numbered lid. He puts my wadded jacket on top.

'Okay, Deboree.' He swivels to the panel of remote switches. 'Zip up your pants and step to the gate.'

'What about my notebooks?'

'You'll find stationery in Detain. Next.'

Rhack hands me my ballpoint as I pass, and Gerder's right: there is paper in D Tank. Sixo is still here, too, after coming down for his kickout more than a week ago. In blues now instead of the flashy slacks and sports jacket, but still trying to keep up the cocky front, combing his greasy pomp, talking tough: 'Good deal! The pussy wagon has arrived.'

One by one the other guys that rode down on Rhack's shuttle show up. Gerder has had to give them each the same treatment, taking cigarettes, paperbacks, everything.

'Sorry about that,' I tell them.

'Steer clear of Deboree,' Sixo advises them. 'He's a heat magnet.'

Just then keys jangle. 'Deboree! Duggs is here to see you.'

Door slides open. I follow the turnkey down the row of cells to a room with a desk. Probation Officer Duggs is sitting behind it. My two notebooks are on the desk beside my rapsheets. Duggs looks up from the records.

'I see you made it without getting any more Bad Time tacked on,' Dugg says.

'I was good.'

Duggs closes the folder. 'Think anybody'll be here for you at midnight?'

'One of my family, probably.'

'Down all the way from Oregon?'

'I hope so.'

'Some family.' He looks at me: caseworker look, conditioned sincere. Sympathetic. 'Sorry about the report on your father.'

'Thanks.'

'That's why Judge Rilling waived that Bad Time, you know?'

'I know.'

He lectures me awhile on the evils of blah blah blah. I let him run out his string. Finally he stands up, comes round the desk, sticks out his hand. 'Okay, Short-timer. But don't miss the ten-thirty hearing Monday morning if you want to get released to an Oregon PO.'

'I'll be here.'

'I'll walk you back.'

On the walk back to D Tank he asks what about this Jail Book; when will it be coming out? When it's over, I tell him. When might that be? When it stops happening. Will this talk

tonight be in it? Yes . . . tonight, Monday morning, last week –
everything will be in it.

'Deboree!' Sixo calls through the bars. 'Put this in your fucking
book: a guy – me – a guy shuns his comrades, plays pinochle five
months with the motherfucking brass up there – five and a half
months! When he musters down, one of those bulls misses a
pack of Winstons and calls down and asks, "What brand of
cigarettes did Sixo check in with? Winstons? Slap a hold on
him!" I mean is that cold or what, man? Is that a ballbusting
bitch? But, what the fuck; Sixo will survive,' he crows. 'Angelo
Sixo is Sir Vivor!'

Some dudes can snivel so it sounds like they're crowing.

They lock me in and Duggs leaves. Sixo sits back down. He's
doing Double Time, on hold like this – Now Time along with
Street-to-come Time. You can even be made to serve Triple
Time, which adds on Street-gone-by Time and that is called
Guilt. A man waiting for his kickout is on what's called Short
Time. Short Time is known for being Hard Time. Lots of Short-
timers go nuts or fuck up or try a run. Short is often harder than
Long.

The best is Straight Time. That's what the notebooks are
about.

More guys check in. Weekenders. D-Tankers. Some Blood
hollers from the shadows, 'Mercy, Deputy Dawg . . . we done
already *got* motherfuckers wall to wall . . .'

> Drunk tank full to overflowing
> Motherfuckers wall to wall
> Coming twice as fast as going
> Time gets big; tank gets small.
>
> Dominoes slap on the table
> Bloods play bones in tank next door
> Bust a bone, if you be able
> Red Death stick it good some more.
>
> Three days past my kickout time
> Ask to phone; don't get the juice –
> Crime times crime just equals more crime
> Cut the motherfuckers loose.

Will I make the Christmas kickout?
Will commissary come today?
Will they take my blood for Good Time
Or just take my guts away?

Some snitch found my homemade outfit!
They've staked a bull up at the still!
They've scoped the pot plants we were sprouting
At the bottom of the hill.

They punched my button, pulled my covers
Blew my cool, ruint my ruse
They've rehabilitated this boy
Cut this motherfucker loose.

The fish that nibbles on the wishing
Let him off his heavy rod
The gowned gavel-bangers fishing
Cut them loose from playing God.

Back off Johnson, back off peacefreaks
From vendettas, from Vietnam
Cut loose the squares, cut loose the hippies
Cut loose the dove, cut loose the bomb.

You, the finger on the trigger
You, the hand that weaves the noose
You hold the blade of brutal freedom –
Cut all the motherfuckers loose.

Eleven forty they take me out give me my clothes whistle and
harp put me in this room with a bench and one other Short-
timer, gray-pated mahogany-hued old dude of sixty years or so.
'Oh, am I one Ready Freddy. Am I ever!'
He's pacing around the little room picking up and putting
back down and picking back up one of those old-fashioned
footrest shoeshine kits, full of personals. He has on a worn black
suit, maroon tie and white shirt. His shoes have a sensational
shine.
'What you in for, Home?'
'Weed. What about you?'

'I pull a knife on my brother-in-law . . . my old woman call the cops. Wasn't no *actual* goddamn fight whatsoever. But I don't care. Just let me on my mother *way!*'

Putting down his kit sipping his coffee picking his kit back up.

'Yessir, on my *way!*'

'Good luck on it,' I say.

'Same to you. Ah, I don't care. I even lost some weight in here. Met some nice folks, too. . . .'

A young black trusty stops in and gives him a number on a slip of paper.

'I hope you writ where I can read it,' the old man says.

'Plenty big, Pop. Don't forget. Call soon as you hit a phone, tell her her *Sugardog* still be barkin'.'

'I'll do it, I sure will!'

'Thanks, Pop. Be cool.'

As soon as the kid is gone the old man wads the paper and drops it in the pisser.

'Damn fool tramp. Met some real motherfuckers, too, as you can see.' He puts the kit down so he can rub his hands as he paces. 'Oh, that ol' city be just right, Saturday night still cookin'. If I can get me to a bus, that is. What's the time?'

'I got twelve straight up. I should have some family waiting; we'll give you a lift.'

'Appreciate it,' he says. 'Straight up you tell me? Ah well, I don't care. We got nothing but time to do, wher*ever* we be. What you say you been in on?'

'Possession and cultivation.'

'If that ain't a shame – for the good green gift of the Lord. He hadn't wanted it to grow, there wouldna been seeds. How much they give you?'

'Six months, five-hundred-dollar fine, three-year tail.'

'If that ain't the shits.'

'It's done.'

'I reckon. Nothin but time – ' He starts to take a sip of his cold coffee, stops – ''ceptin, oh, I am *ready*.'

He puts the cup down, picks the kit back up.

'Franklin!' a voice calls. 'William O. – '

'In the wind, Boss. On my *way!*'

I'm alone on the bench, sipping what's left of his cup of coffee, spoon still sticking out. The plastic bag his suit was in hangs from the conduit; his blues are right where he left them,

6

on the floor. Ghost clothes. I'm ready too. This stationery is finished both sides.

'Deboree! Devlin E. – '

'On my way!'

*Red Death. What they call the glop of strawberry jelly comes with breakfast coffee and toast – makes, among other things, quite a powerful glue.

**Never did get those two notebooks back.

Joon the Goon was What

. . . she used to be called on the beat scene. Shows up this A.M. with her old man who turns out to be the guy in jail with me called Hub, the dude that did two for two. Famous for stretching a two-month Disturbing rap to two years by not standing for any shit. Proud of his rep in the slam, on the streets now he's vowed to change his violent ways – no more red meat, red wine or white crosstops.

Joon drove him up from Calif this morn for the sake of our soothing farm influence. Their Nova quit on the road before it made it into our drive. They explained everything in a bashful stammer, Joon blushing, Hub wringing his huge tattooed hands together like mastiffs in a pit.

We talked some about the early frost, the green tomatoes, how some of them might ripen inside the sun on windowsills. I told them they better use our car and jumpers to get their rig off the road. They head off, Joon in the lead, her purse knocking against her knobby knees. Made me think of Steinbeck and the thirties and the hand-scrawled warnings that are turning up taped to all the cash registers in the area: NO CHECKS CASHED FOR MORE THAN AMOUNT OF PURCHASE!

The first school bus slows and stops by the frost-gilded corn, lets Caleb off just in front of where Hub has my clunker mouth to mouth with his. The kids at the windows flash peace signs; the look of Joon's tie-dye wraparound, I guess.

A neighbour goes by and honks – our ritzy neighbour, the one with rich relatives and a 'ranch' instead of a farm. He's driving a new maroon metallic-flake Mustang.

Sounds like they got the clunker clunking again; I hear it pulling into my drive below.

Caleb brings up the mail – bills, broadsides, and a hardbound tome called *Love of Place*, authored by a famous holy man I've never heard of. You can't learn love of place from those above or below you, it don't seem to me . . .

Lotsa action, banging, clunking, as the sun seeps through hazy

September. A plane mumbles by and the corn goes golder and golder.

The second, bigger-kids' bus. Quiston and Sherree get out. Caleb goes loping through the rows to greet them, swinging a golden ear around his head.

'Hey I bet you didn't know Joon and her Goon was here!'

Mother's Day 1969:
Quiston's Report

I think she's out of the woods I think she's made it to where she ought to have a name.

Dad thinks.

I think a good name is Feline, Sherree says, *ree*-ally. . . .

Sherree and Caleb and me we're in the orchard feeding her warm water out of one of Sherree's Tiny Tears bottles. We're outside because Dad wants to get some footage. He's moving the tripod all over, worrying about shadows. I think she looks perfect, hopping around in the soft yellow mustard and sunshine. I been thinking about the softness of things, and time going by, and how it will be good to have pictures of her growing up with us all, all the cows and the dogs and ducks and geese and pigeons and peacocks and cats and horses and chickens and bees, with Rumiocho the Parrot and Basil the Raven and Jenny the Donkey, and all these people.

The camera is going. Dad shoots me and Caleb feeding her and Sherree making a garland and putting it around her neck: Princess Fe-*line*. Then Dobbs shows up in the dumptruck full of his kids and the mint compost mix that Mom ordered.

We all ride out to Mom's garden smelling like a million old Life Savers, and Dad shoots us shovelling and sweeping it out. Then us standing with our shovels and brooms on our shoulders. He shoots the chickens all already lined up at the fence like for class pictures, and Stewart making a big show out of beating up on Frank Dobbs's dog, Kilroy. Then he wants to finish the roll shooting the horses out in the far field.

Quiston, he says, you lock all these damn dogs in the paint-room. So they won't go bothering the fawn.

When the dogs are all shut in the paintroom we climb in the back of the dumptruck that's never dumped since Dobbs fixed it, and ride out to the pasture. Me and Caleb and all the Dobbs kids, and Sherree with her nose wrinkled at the smell. When we go by the orchard she's still nested right where we left her, in

10

the tall mustard behind the flat-tyred tractor. Her head is up like a princess all right, showing off her necklace of daisies and bachelor buttons.

The horses are excited to have all these people come visit. Dad shoots them prancing around on their green carpet, fat and feisty. He shoots until he finishes the roll and puts the camera in its suitcase, then gets out the grain bucket. He shakes it so they can hear there's something in it and then heads for the side gate. He wants to get them off the main pasture so it will make hay. They don't want to go. The colt Wild Snort and Johnny bump and nip at each other. Horsing around like kids in the locker room Dad says. Wild Snort's a young Appaloosa stud dropped off by Deadheads passing through last fall, and he's mine if I demonstrate I can take proper care of him.

His mother the white-eyed mare hangs back, watching. She's watching her kid sow his wild oats Dobbs says. Then she goes through the gate where Dad is shaking the bucket. Wild Snort follows in after, then Jenny the Donkey. Johnny the Gelding is last, being ornery and nearsighted. We have to chase him and chase him until we finally drive him close enough he sees the other horses getting the grain poured out of the bucket; then he goes through in a gallop.

Dad says Johnny is like a proud old silver-haired Texas Ranger, *always* got his man *never* took a bribe, but he's older now . . . has to finally go for the bucket.

Jenny the Donkey goes sidling up to the poured-out grain, rump first. And Jenny's like a Juarez hooker Dobbs says . . . she has to do what she has to do, too.

Sherree walks back to the house. Caleb and Dobbs's kids are all off in the clover, chasing gardener snakes. I ride back in the cab between Dad and Dobbs. At the corral fence there's Joon the Goon in her nightgown, standing right alongside Abdul the Bull. Both of them are frowning out across the pasture, to make sure nothing's being mistreated. Such *barbarism*, Hubert, Dad says, like he's being Joon talking to her boyfriend Hub standing alongside, not the bull. Cruel, carnivorous *barbarism!* Makes me shudder.

Dobbs answers, I know what you mean, Joonbug – being the bull being Hub – but it's the only free accommodations available, here in carnivore country.

Dad laughs. People on food trips are funny to him. We drive

through and I get out and shut the gate behind us. Joon is stepped up on the bottom rail so she can frown at Johnny prancing around where Wild Snort is jumped up on Jenny the Donkey from behind. Jenny's huffing and twisting this way and that. You *guys*, Dad says. I don't know who he's being.

We fix the pipe and turn on the pump and drive back in through the orchard past the beehives. Yesterday's new swarm is still there in the blossoms, drooping from a branch, like a big cluster of peach grapes, buzzing and working in the low light. The sun is slid nearly down the naked chin of old Nebo. Dad stands out on the runner board of the dumptruck and hollers for everybody to come in from the field: *Star Trek* in town at Uncle Buddy's in less than an hour!

From the garden where she's been raking, Mom hollers, An hour? More like less than *half* an hour!

Dobbs goes to put some bales in the back to sit on and roust up Mickey. Sherree goes to get tomorrow's homework to take to Grandma and Grandpa's. Caleb and Louise and May go to let out the dogs. I run on ahead of Dad back out to the orchard, to bring her in for the night.

Something is wrong. She is just where we left her, but her head is tilted wrong. Her garland has fallen off and there's a look in her tilted face. It isn't drowsiness and neither is it loss of moisture like from her diarrhoea two days ago. I run to lift her and the head flops: Dad! He comes running.

Shit! The goddamn dogs got her.

I locked the dogs in the paintroom.

Maybe it was the neighbour's dog. *Shit!*

She feels – ah Dad, her back feels broke! Do you think she got run over when we came in from the pasture?

I don't think so, Dad says. I saw her when we drove through the orchard. She was fine then.

It was the sun! Mom warned us. It was too much sun!

Naw . . . you think? She wasn't out in the sun that long, it didn't seem . . . really.

It really didn't. Dad took her and carried her out of the orchard around the barn to the concrete grain storage, not because it was where Hub was living with Joon but because it was the coolest room on the place. The room looked cramped and little, with ten times the clutter that all of us used to make when we lived in it, and we were six! Dad cleared a spot and

12

found a half-blowed-up air mattress and laid her on it. I saw everybody coming so I climbed up on the cement shelf that used to be my bed. Everybody crowded in and fussed over her. Her breath was getting raspy and she was starting to twitch. I saw twitches begin, first at her spotted tail, then pretty soon they were running up her spine, then over her shoulders and around to her chest. Mom came and gave her some more of the clorzum milk she'd froze from when Floozie's calf died, and I tried to pray. But all the time I could see the life twitching against the little ribcage like it wanted out.

Hub came in from work and yelled a cussword. She was really his. He found her up where they were logging, no mother in sight. Orphaned by a sonofabitch poacher, was what he figured, poor thing. When he saw her in a wad on the rubber mattress, he yelled and threw his plaid lunchbox against the concrete wall and dropped to his knees. He started rubbing his huge rough hands up and down his pantlegs and cussing in a whisper. It was all raspy. He reached out to touch her. She arched backward into his hand when he stroked her neck, then flopped limp. He cussed and cussed and cussed.

She got worse. Her breaths came harder. Even up on my old shelf I could hear the stuff gurgling in her. Mom said she was afraid that she was drowning. Fluid in her lungs. Pneumonia.

Dad and Hub took turns holding her up with her head down, so they could get on their knees to try and suck that stuff out. Jelly stuff, silver grey, out of her nostrils. The blackbright shine was going away in her eyes, and the twitch against her ribs was getting calmer. Once, bowing backwards, she gave out a call, thin and high. It reminded me of the sound of Grandpa's little wooden varmint caller that he blows in the dark when he wants to lure in a fox or a cougar or a bobcat. Or says he does.

Hub kept sucking and puffing. She was getting bloated. Dad let him do it for a long time before he said, Give it in, Hub. She's dead. When Hub stopped and Dad put her down, the air coming out made a sound, but not an animal sound. It was a kind of silly honk, like Caleb's Harpo horn he got a long time later.

Sherree and Joon filled an apple box with rose petals and clover blossoms. Mom found a piece of silk from China. Out at the pump the cows and horses all stood around and watched. We put a round stone on top, a fine big stone Mom found on a

13

river called Row. Before we were born, she said. Dad played his flute and Dobbs blowed his mouthharp and Joon tinkled on that old Fisher-Price xylophone Great-grandma Whittier gave me that still works. Hub blew once on a blade of grass – it made that same thin sound – and the funeral was over.

So we missed *Star Trek* at Buddy's and Sunday supper and Grandma and Grandpa's and everything. Dad cut our hair instead. Everybody went to bed early. Then, this morning, still foggy before the schoolbus comes, there's a loud bunch of barking from the pond. Mom says, Never you kids mind finish your breakfast and get things ready. She'll go see what it's all about. She goes out the sliding kitchen window and heads down through the mist. Hub gets up and watches, sipping his coffee, then the barking stops and he comes back to the table. Joon puts his lunchbucket on the table next to his plate and Hub grunts. I think for a minute he's going to go to cussing again. But then here comes Mom back, Stewart and Lance jumping all over her! She's carrying our five-gallon minnow-catching bucket held high from the dogs, and she's red with excitement.

I thought it was a frog a *bull*frog that the darned old heron had crippled but couldn't carry off, she says. Except when I got closer I saw it was *hairy*. It was swimming like anything out where Stewart was barking, round and round and around in the pondweeds. I told Stewart, No! Leave it alone! Hush! And as soon as he hushes, I swear, *here it comes right up the bank at us!* I scooped it in the bucket before I knew *what* it was. . . .

It's a big old bull gopher, mean-looking as the devil. His front teeth are terrible, like two rusty chisel blades. He's up on his hind feet in the can, chittering and snapping at our faces over the brim. Hub takes the bucket and grins down into it, pretty terrible-toothed himself. Him and the animal chitter back and forth a minute, then he opens his lunchbox and dumps the gopher right in, right with his plaid thermos bottle and his apple and his celery and his Saran-wrapped sandwiches, and snaps it shut.

I'll turn him loose up at the logging show, Hub says, turning his yellow grin toward Joon the Goon.

Be careful, Joon says, grinning herself, that you don't get mixed up and turn loose your cheese sandwich and eat the gopher. Yeah, Sherree says, *ree*-ally – like she can – and goes out to wait for the bus. Caleb says Yeah, *ree*-ally. Mom says
14

Here comes the bus Quiston get your assignment sheet Caleb where's your shoes! Hub says he will be careful, thanks for breakfast, see y'all this evening. . . .

I don't know what I'll say, first period oral assignment – Tell What You Did For Your Mother On Mother's Day.

Tranny Man Over the Border

IN THE PLAZA

— hibiscus blooms fall with heavy plops, lie sprawled on the sunny cobblestones and cement benches like fat Mexican generals, scarlet-and-green parade uniforms, gawdy and limp, too hot and tired to rise back to the rank of their branches. Later, perhaps. Now, siesta. . . .

'Not good!' yells the grey crewcut American from Portland with his fifty-year face running sweat and his new Dodge Polaro sitting behind a tow truck outside the Larga Distancia Oficina. 'Not three thrown in less than five thousand miles!'

Yelling from Puerto Sancto, Mexico, to Tucson, Arizona, where he'd bought his last transmission after buying his second in Oroville, California, where he'd paid without much complaint because it *is* possible to strip the gears with the hard business miles he'd put on it, but a tranny again in Tucson? And now, less than a week later? The third blown?

'Not good at all! So listen up; I'm gonna jerk the thing out and ship it back first train your direction. I expect the same promptness from you garage boys, right? I expect a new transmission down here in time for us to make the festival in Guadalajara one week from tomorrow! There's no excuse for this kinda workmanship I can tell you *that!*'

What he didn't tell the garage boys in Tucson was that he was pulling a twenty-four-foot mobile home.

'I been a Dodge man ten years. We don't want a ten-year-relationship to blow up from one fluke, right?'

He hung up and turned to me. Next in line, I had been his nearest audience.

'That'll get some greasemonkeys' asses smoking in Tucson, won't it, Red?' He leaned close, as if we had known each other for years. 'They aren't a bad bunch. Fact is, I hope I can find me a mechanic down here with a *fraction* the know-how as those Arizona boys.'

Reaffirmation of Yankee superiority left him so flushed with

16

feeling for his countrymen that he chose to overlook the stubbled look of me.

'What's your name, Red? You remind me of my oldest boy a little, behind that brush.'

'Deboree,' I told him, taking his hand. 'Devlin Deboree.'

'What brings you to primitive Puerto Sancto, Dev? Let me guess. You're a nature photographer. I saw you out there after those fallen posies.'

'Way wrong,' I told him. 'It isn't even my camera. My father sent his along. He came to Sancto last year with my brother and me, and nobody took picture one.'

'So Dad sent you to bring back the missed memories. He musta been a lot more impressed than I been.'

'Wrong again. He sent me to bring back jumping beans.'

'Jumping beans?'

'Mexican jumping beans. When we were down here last year he met a mechanic who also grew jumping beans. He bought a hundred bucks' worth of this year's harvest.'

'*Jump*ing beans?'

'Five gallons. Dad's going to give one bean away with each quart of his new ice cream, to publicize the flavour. Not Jumping Bean – Piña Colada. We run a creamery.'

'"Debris", huh?' He gave me a wink to let me know he was kidding. 'Like in "rubbish"?'

I told him it was more like in Polish. He laughed.

'Well, you remind me of my kid, *what*ever. Why don't you join me in the Hotel Sol bar after your call? We'll see if I remind you of your old man.'

He winked again and left, roguishly tipping his fishing cap to the rest of the tourists waiting to contact home.

I found him under a palapa umbrella by the pool. His look of confidence was already a little faded, and he was wondering if maybe he shouldn't've also had a good U.S. mechanic come *with* the transmission – pay the man's way now, fight it out with the Dodge people later. I observed some of these Mexican mechanics were pretty good. He agreed they *had* to be pretty good, to keep these hand-me-downs running, but what did they know about a modern automatic transmission? He pulled down his sunglasses and drew me again into that abrupt intimacy.

'You can take the best carburettor man in the whole country,

17

say, and turn him loose in an area he isn't qualified in, and you're going to have troubles. Believe me, numerous troubles. . . .'

This truth and his drink made him feel better. The grin returned and the ungreased whine of panic was almost oiled out of his voice by his second Seagram's and Seven-Up. By the bottom of his third he was ready to slip 'er into whiskeydrive and lecture me as to all the troubles a man can encounter along the rocky road of life, brought about *mainly* by unqualified incompetents in areas where they didn't belong. *Nu*merous troubles! To steer him away from a tirade I interrupted with what I thought was a perfectly peaceful question: How many did he have with him? One eye narrowed strangely and slid over my backpack and beard. With a voice geared all the way back into suspicion he informed me that his *wife* was along and what about it.

I gaped, amazed. He thinks that I meant how many *troubles* meaning his wife or whoever meaning I'm trying to cast some snide insinuation about his family! Far out, I thought, and to calm him I said I wished *my* wife and kids were along. Still suspicious, he asked how many kids, and how old. I told him. He asked where they were and I said in school –

'But if I have to wait much longer for these jumping beans I'm going to have them all fly down. Sometimes you have to skip a little school to further your education, right?'

'Right!' This brought him close again. 'Don't I wish my woman'd known that when my kids were kids! "After they get their educations" was her motto. Right, Mother, sure. . . .'

I thought he was going to get melancholy again, but he squared his shoulders instead and clinked his glass against mine. 'Decent of you and your brother to take a trip with your old dad, Red.' He was glad I had turned out not to be some hippy rucksack smartass after all, but a decent American boy, considerate of his father. He twisted in his chair and called grandly for the waiter to bring us another round uno mas all around, muy goddamn *pronto*.

'If you aren't a little hardboiled,' he confided, shifting back to wink at me, 'they overcharge.'

He grinned and the wink reopened, but for one tipsy second that eye didn't match up with its mate. '*Over*charge!' he prompted, commanding the orb back into place.

By the time the drinks arrived the twitch was corrected and

his look confident and roguish again. For a moment, though, a crack had been opened. I had seen all the way inside to the look behind the looks and, oh gosh, folks, that look was dreadful afraid. Of what? It's difficult to say, exactly. But it wasn't of me. Nor do I think he was really afraid of the numerous troubles on the rocky road ahead, not even of getting stranded gearless in this primitive anarchy of a nation.

What I think, folks, looking at the developed pictures and remembering back to that momentary glimpse into his private abyss, is that this guy was afraid of the Apocalypse.

HIS WIFE

The Tranny Man's wife is younger than her husband, not much, a freshman in high school when he was a football-hero senior, at his best.

She's never been at her best, although it isn't something she thinks about. She's a thoughtful person who doesn't think about things.

She is walking barefoot along the stony edge of the ocean with her black pumps dangling from a heel strap at the end of each arm. She isn't thinking that she had too many rum-and-Cokes. She isn't thinking about her podiatrist or her feet, spreading pudgy over the sand.

She stops at the bank of the Rio Sancto and watches the water sparkle across the beach, rushing golden to the sea. Upriver a few dozen yards, women are among the big river stones washing laundry and hanging it on the bushes to dry. She watches them bending and stretching in their wet dresses, scampering over the rocks with great bundles balanced on their heads, light little prints spinning off their feet elegant as feathers, but she isn't thinking *We're so misshapen and leprous that we have to drink more than is good for us to just have the courage to walk past.* Not yet. She's only been in town since they were towed in this morning. Nor is she asking herself *When did I forsake my chance at proportion? Was it when I sneaked to the fridge just like Pop, piled on more than a seven-year-old should carry? Was it after graduation when I had those two sound-though-crooked incisors replaced by these troublesome caps? Why did I join the mechanical lepers?*

Her ankles remind her of the distance she has walked. Far

enough for a backache tonight. Looking down, her feet appear to her as dead creatures, drowned things washed in on the tide. She forces her eyes back up and watches the washwomen long enough not to appear coerced, then turns and starts back, thinking, Oh, by now he'll either be finished with the call or ready to call it off if I know him.

But she isn't thinking, as she strides chin-raised and rummy along the golden border. *They saw anyway. They know that we are The Unclean, allowed nowdays to wander among normal people because they have immunized themselves against us.*

'And if he's *not* ready I think I'll take a look around that other hotel.' Meaning the bar. 'See who's there.'

Meaning other Americans.

HIS DOG

The Tranny Man has to climb the hill into the hot steep thick of it, to find the man Wally Blum says will maybe work this weekend and pull the Tucson transmission. He has to take his dog. The dog's name is Chief and he's an ancient Dalmatian with lumbago. There was no way to leave him in the hotel room. Something about Mexico has had the same effect on old Chief's bladder as on the Tranny Man's slow eye. Control has been shaken. In the familiar trailerhouse Chief had been as scrupulous with his habits as back home, but as soon as they'd moved into the hotel it seemed the old dog just couldn't help but be lifting his leg every three steps. Scolding only makes it worse.

'Poor old fella's nervous' – after Chief watered two piñatas his wife had purchased for the grandchildren this morning.

'We never should have brought him,' she said. 'We should have put him in a boarding kennel.'

'I told you,' the Tranny Man had answered. 'The kids wouldn't keep him, I wasn't leaving him with strangers!'

So Chief has to climb along.

THE HOT STEEP THICK

The map that Wally Blum scribbled leads the Tranny Man and his pet up narrow cobblestone thoroughfares where trucks lurch loud between chuckholes . . . up crooked cobblestone streets

20

too narrow for anything but bikes . . . up even crookeder and narrower cobblestone canyons too steep for any wheel.

Burros pick their way with loads of sand and cement for the clutter of construction going on antlike all over the mountainside. Workers sleep head uphill in the clutter; if they slept sideways they'd roll off.

By the time the American and his dog reach the place on the map, the Tranny Man is seeing spots and old Chief is peeing dust. The Tranny Man wipes the sweat from under the sweatband of his fishing cap and enters a shady courtyard; it's shaded by rusty hoods and trunk lids welded haphazardly together and bolted atop palm-tree poles.

EL MECANICO FANTASTICO

In the centre of a twelve-foot sod circle a sow reclines, big as a plaza fountain, giving suck to a litter large as she is. She rolls her head to look at the pair of visitors and gives a snort. Chief growls and stands his ground between the sow and his blinking master.

There is movement behind the low vine-shrouded doorway of a shack so small that it could fit into the Dodge's mobile home and still have room for the sow. A man ducks out of the doorway, fanning himself with a dry tortilla. He is half the Tranny Man's size and half again his age, maybe more. He squints a moment against the glare, then uses the tortilla to shade his eyes.

'Tardes,' he says.

'Buenas tardes,' the Tranny Man answers, mopping his face. 'Hot. Mucho calor.'

'I spik Engliss a little,' says El Mecanico Fantastico.

The Tranny Man recalls reading somewhere how that was where the slur 'Spik' came from. 'Thank heaven for *that*,' he says and launches into a description of his plight. The mechanic listens from beneath the tortilla. The sow watches old Chief with voluptuous scorn. Burros trudge past the yard. Small children drift into sight from El Mecanico Fantastico's shack; they cling to their father's legs as he listens to the Tranny Man's tale of mechanical betrayal.

When the tale finally dribbles to an end, EMF asks, 'What you want for me to do?'

21

'To come down to that big garage where they towed it and take the danged transmission out so I can send it to Tucson. See?'

'I see, si,' says the mechanic. 'Why you don't use the big garage mecanicos?'

'They won't work on it until Monday is why.'

'Are you in such a hurry you cannot wait for Monday?'

'I already called and told Tucson I was shipping the thing back to them by Monday. I like to get on these things while they're hot, you see.'

'Si, I see,' says El Mecanico Fantastico, fanning himself with the tortilla again. 'Hokay. I come down mañana and take it out.'

'Can't we get on it now? I'd like to be sure of getting it on that train.'

'I see,' says the Mexican. 'Hokay. I get my tools and we rent a burro.'

'A burro?'

'From Ernesto Diaz. To carry my tools. The big garage locks their tools in a iron box.'

'I see,' says the Tranny Man, beginning to wonder how to pin down a reasonable estimate for labour, tools and a burro.

Suddenly there is a big brodie of squeals and yelps in the dust. The sow's red-bristled boar friend has dropped in and caught Chief making eyes at his lady. By the time they are pulled apart Chief has one ear slashed and has lost both canines in the boar's brick hide.

But that isn't the worst of it. Giving away all that weight has been too much for the dog's aged hindquarters. Something is dislocated. He has to ride back down strapped atop a second burro. The ride pops the dislocation back in so he can walk again by evening, but he is never able afterward to lift a hind leg without falling over.

HIM AND HIS WIFE AGAIN

They've been there a week now. They are flat-tyring back from the beach to the south in a rented Toyota open-top. The left rear blew out miles back. There is no spare. And a ruptured radiator hose is spewing steam from under the dash so they can barely see the road ahead.

22

Finally the wife asks, 'You're going to just keep *driving* it?'

'I'm going to *drive* the sonofabitch *back* to the sonofabitch that *rented* me the sonofabitch and tell him to shove this piece of broken Jap junk up his overpriced greaser *ass!*'

'Well, drop the dog and me off at the Blums' first, then, if you're going to – if we get close.'

She didn't say If you're going to make a scene. There was steam and furore enough.

HIS FRIENDS

The Tranny Man missed the before-siesta mail out and he's promised himself to get a letter to his sister finished to take down to the post office when it opens after siesta. He's at the Blums' rented villa, alone except for Chief. The dog is stretched on a woven mat, tongue out and eyes open. Wally Blum's at the beach surfcasting. The Tranny Man doesn't know where Betty Blum and his wife have gone.

The Blums' hacienda is not down in Gringo Gulch but up on the town's residential slopes. The yard of a shack across the canyon-of-a-street is level with his window, and three little girls smile at him across the narrow chasm. They keep calling Hay-lo mee-ster, then ducking back out of sight in the foliage of a mango tree and giggling.

That tree is the whole neighbourhood's social centre. Kids play in its shade. Birds fly in and out of its branches. Two pigs and a lot of chickens prowl the leafy rubble at its roots. All kinds of chickens – chickens scrawny and chickens bald, chickens cautious and chickens bold. The only thing the chickens seem to have in common is freedom and worthlessness.

The Tranny Man watches the chickens with a welcome disdain. What good can they be, too sick to lay, too skinny to eat? What possible good? Inspired by the inefficiency, he launches into his letter:

'Dear Sis: Gawd, wot a country! It is too poor to know it's ignorant and too ignorant to know it's poor. If I was Mexico you know what I would do? I would attack the U.S. just to qualify for foreign aid when we whup 'em (ha ha). Seriously, it sure isn't what I had hoped, I can tell you that.'

A green mango bounces off the grill of his window. More giggles. He reads the last line with a sigh and lays down his ballpoint. Wish you were here, Sissy, with all my heart. He drains his Seven-and-Seven and feels a kind of delicious depression sweep over him. A poignancy.

An accordion in one of the shacks begins practising a familiar tune, a song popular back home a couple of years back. What was it? Went *la la la* laa *la la; we'd fight and* neh-*ver win*. . . . That was it! *Those were the days, my friend; those were the days*. . . .

The poignancy becomes melancholy, then runs straight on through sentiment to nostalgia. It stops just short of maudlin. With another sigh he picks his pen up and resumes the letter:

> 'I think of you often on this trip, Old Pal. Do you remember the year Father drove us to Yellowstone Park and how great it was? How wonderful and bright everything looked? How proud we felt? We were the first kids coming out of the Depression whose Father could afford to take his family on such a trip. Well let me tell you, things are not bright anymore and not very likely to get so. Ferinstance, let me tell you about visiting Darold, in "Berserkly." That about says it. You simply cannot believe the condition that nice college town has allowed itself to get into since we were there in '62 for the Russian-American track meet – '

He stops again. He hears a strange clucking voice: 'Qué? Qué?' In the yard across the way he sees a very old woman. She appears to be swaying her way along a clothesline with an odd, weightless motion. Her face is vacant of teeth or expression. She seems unreal, a trick of the heat, swaying along, clucking 'Qué? Qué? Qué?' She sways along until she reaches a frayed white sheet. She gathers it from the line and starts feeling her way back to her shack. 'Qué? Qué? Qué Qué?'

'Blind,' says the Tranny Man, and rises to check Wally's cupboards. He's bound to have *some*thing to pick up where the Seventy-seven left off, something stronger if possible: eighty-eight . . . ninety-*nine!* He bobs this way and that around the strange kitchen, awash with sweat, rendered rudderless by the jagged apparition of the blind crone. He is drifting fast now toward the reefs.

24

THE FIRST CRACK

The Tranny Man's wife arrives half an hour later with Wally Blum's wife, Betty, in Wally's nice little Mexican-built Volkswagen jeep loaded with gifts for the gals back home. She has barely begun telling Betty Blum how grateful she is for the ride not to mention the company when she is pulled about by her elbow and scolded so loudly for going off without taking the mail – so *unfairly* – that the world is suddenly billowing silent about her, all the street sounds ceasing, the hens not clucking, the kids not chattering on the rooftop, the mariachi not pumping his accordion . . . even the river half a mile down the hill, stopping its sparkle around the rocks. The kneeling girls are raised from their wash to listen: how will the gringa señora take it, this machismo browbeating?

'Understand?' the Tranny Man demands in closing. '*Sabe?*'

The evening leans forward from its many seats. Betty Blum begins to take blame and croon apologies in the familiar catty pussyfooting of one browbeaten señora coming to the defence of another. The unseen audience starts to sigh, disappointed. But before the Tranny Man can begin his grumpy forgiving, the Tranny Man's wife hears herself speaking in a voice stiff with care at the delivery of each syllable, telling her husband to let go of her arm, to lower his shouting, and to never treat her as though she were drawing a wage from him – *never again* speak to her like she was one of his broken machines.

'If you do I swear I'll kill you, and if I can get to him I'll kill Donald, and if I can get to them before I'm stopped I'll kill Terry and the grandchildren and then myself, I swear it before *God!*'

Both her husband and Betty stare dumbstruck at this outburst. Then the two of them exchange quick small nods: shoulda seen something like this coming . . . woman this age . . . all those rum-and-Cokes. The Tranny Man's wife is no longer paying attention. She knows she has been effective. For a moment she feels as though the intensity of this effect will set her aflame, that her flesh will melt and run off her bones.

Then the pulse of the street begins to rush again. The kids on the roof whisper excited reviews. The chickens gather in the lobby of shade under the mango branches. The accordionist doesn't resume his practising, but, the Tranny Man's wife feels, this is out of a kind of consideration, as one musician in the twilight to another, not criticism.

THE AFTERMATH

The Tranny Man stalks back into the hacienda; Betty Blum gives his wife a ride back to the Hotel del Sol. When she returns she has a bottle of Seagram's, a pack of cold Seven-Up and a warm smile that hints she can be as sympathetic to misunderstood husbands as to browbeaten wives.

Wally shows up with two yellowtail and the Tranny Man accepts their invitation for supper. After fish and white wine he borrows a pair of trunks from good ol' Wally and a safety pin from bountiful Betty to keep them from falling off his skinny ass, and they all go for a midnight swim. Then they come back and drink some more. He tells Wally it's always the kids that keep a marriage together, but with these kids these days! Is it worth it? Then he confides to Betty – who is still wearing the bikini that looks *damned decent* for a woman her age – how one thing the kids these days *do* have on the ball is getting rid of all those old-fashioned notions about sex being evil. It's natural! Betty could not agree more.

When he figures it is late enough that his wife has been adequately disciplined, he borrows their car to drive back to the hotel with old Chief. 'I bet she's there by now,' he bets.

He wins; she's asleep on the couch. It will be the last time he'd win such a bet.

THE TRANNY MAN'S DREAM

Things can be trusted. Things do not break. Things are not gyps. Pull chains on light switches are not manufactured to snap off inside the fixture just to force a poor sucker to shell out *dinero* for a complete new rig-up that isn't *fair*.

HIS VIRILITY

'Ten pesos for a rum-'n'-Coke? They only cost five pesos two blocks from here!'

They have been drinking at the hotel all afternoon.

26

'This is the beachfront,' his wife reminds him. 'Besides, these have straws.'

The waiter rewards her logic with a grand denture display. Betty and Wally order. The drinks arrive. Betty sips her margarita like a bee choosing a blossom from acres of clover.

'Feh,' she drawls. 'Not great but feh-uh.'

'I love the way you Miami women talk, Betty.' The Tranny Man is drunk. 'In fact I love all women. From the young uns with papaya titties to the old uns with experience!' He spreads his arms. 'I love *all* people, actually; from these – '

He stops short. He has seen something that nips his declaration in the bud. The Tranny Man's wife follows her husband's gaze to see what has stymied this tribute. Across the beach she sees the reason in the shade of a canvas-covered ice-cream pushcart, wearing lime-green barely to the crotch, as provocative as a Popsicle. Busted, her husband leaves it unfinished. He turns his scrutiny to the cover of the Mexican edition of *Time* that Wally has bought from a newsboy. There's a picture of Clifford Irving on the cover. He reads over Wally's shoulder, lips moving.

His wife continues to stare at the young morsel at the ice-cream stand, not out of jealousy, as she knows Betty Blum is silently supposing, but with a sense of sweet wonder, as one stares at a pressed flower discovered in a school annual, wondering, What had it meant when it was fresh? Where did it go? Feeling herself suddenly on the verge of finding some kind of answer she rises from the shaded table, no longer in the mood for oyster cocktail, and walks across the sand toward the surf.

There is a silence as the Tranny Man frowns after her. When he looks back, Betty Blum extends him brown-eyed condolences over the salty rim of her margarita, as if to advise, Don't let her mess with your mind.

'*Time*,' declares Wally Blum, 'is one of those things you can trust because you know just how much to allow for political bias.'

The Tranny Man regains himself with a robust 'Right!' and turns back to the question of nevermind who's Clifford Irving who's Howard *Hughes?*

The three of them walk back to the hotel restaurant and order Lobster Supreme, picking at the shells till nearly ten. Finally the Tranny Man yawns it's his bedtime and excuses himself, letting all present know by the twinkle in his roguish eye that he is far too much a man to let some menopausal bitch mess with his sleep let alone his mind! Over Wally's protests he peels two hundred-peso bills from his wallet and places them beside his plate. To Betty's request that they buy a bottle to drink up on his balcony he graciously explains that ordinarily he would be more than happy to oblige, but tomorrow is the day his new transmission should be coming in from the States, and he likes to get on these things while they're hot. Another time. He squeezes Betty's hand and turns and mounts the stairs, giving them his most erect exit.

PUERTO SANCTO DARKNESS

Here it comes again: the turmoil, the chaos, the hubbub and howls – the nightdogs again – the pre-dawn yapping that starts in the hills south and sweeps across the town, just when you were sure the sonofabitches had, at last, exhausted the shadows and were going to settle down and let you get some rest.

Old Chief whimpers. The Tranny Man burrows under his pillow cursing the night, the dogs, the town, his crazy wife who had suggested in the first place coming to this thorny wilderness, goddamn her! Why *here*, he demands of the darkness, instead of Yosemite or Marineland or even the Shakespeare festival in Ashland? Why *this* goddamn anarchy of thorn and shadows?

A fair question. I had been forced to deal with it there once myself. You see, one day, not long after Betsy had announced we were finally broke, we all finally knew that my father was going to die (of course I am reminded of him by the Tranny Man – not by the person himself but by certain things particular to this type of American: the erect exit, the wink, the John Wayne way he spoke to machinery and mechanics . . . many things). The doctors had been telling us for ages that he only had so much time, but Daddy had continued to stretch that allotted time for so long that Buddy and I secretly believed that our stubborn Texas father was never going to succumb to any enemy except old age. His arms and legs shrivelled and his head wobbled on his 'goddamn noodle of a neck', but we continued to expect some last-minute rescue to come bugling over the horizon.

Daddy thought so too. 'All this research, I figure they'll whip

it pretty soon. They better. Look at these muscles jump around
– '

He'd draw up a pantleg and grin wryly at the flesh jerking and
twitching.

' – like nervous rats on a leaky scow.'

Yeah, pretty soon, we agreed. Then one September day we
were out at the goat pasture sighting in our rifles and talking
about where we were going to take our hunting trip this fall,
when Daddy lowered his 'ought-six and looked at us.

'Boys, this damned gunbarrel is shaking like a dog shitting
peach pits. Let's take some *other* kind of trip. . . .'

– and we all knew it was going to be our last. My brother and
I talked it over that night. I knew where I wanted to go. Buddy
wasn't too sure about the idea, but he conceded I was the big
brother. We presented the plan to Daddy the next day over his
backyard barbecue.

'I don't object to a journey south, but why this Purty Sancto?
Why way the hell-and-gone down there?'

'Dev claims there's something special about it,' Buddy said.

'He wants to show off where he hid out for six months,'
Daddy said. 'Aint that the something special?'

'Partly,' I admitted. Everybody knew I'd been trying to get
the three of us down there for years. 'But there's something
besides that about the place – something primal, prehistoric. . . .'

'Just what a man in his predicament needs,' my mother put in.
'Something prehistoric.'

'Maybe we oughta fly up to that spot on the Yukon again,'
Daddy mused. 'Fish for sockeye.'

'No, damn it!' I said. 'All my life you've been hauling me to
your spots. Now it's my turn.'

'A drive across Mexico would shake him to pieces!' my mother
cried. 'Why, he wasn't even able to handle the drive to the Rose
Parade up in Portland without getting wore to a frazzle.'

'Oh, I can handle the drive,' he told her. 'That aint the
question.'

'Handle my foot! A hundred miles on those Mexican roads in
your sorry condition – '

'I said I can stand it,' he told her, flipping her a burger. He
turned to eye me through the smoke. 'All's I want to know is,
one: why this Puerto Sancto place? and, two: what *else* you got
up your sleeve?'

29

I didn't answer. We all knew what was up my sleeve.

'*Oh* no you don't!' My mother swung her glare at me. 'If you think you're going to get him off somewheres and talk him into taking some of that stuff again – '

'Woman, I been legal age for some time now. I will thank you to leave me do my own deciding as to *where* I go and *what stuff* I take.'

Years before, at the beginning of the sixties, Buddy and I had been trying to grow psilocybin mushrooms in a cottage-cheese vat at the little creamery Daddy staked Buddy to after he got out of Oregon State. Bud made up some research stationery and was getting spore cultures sent to him straight from the Department of Agriculture, along with all the latest information for producing the mycelium hydroponically. Bud and I plumbed an air hose into the vat, mixed the required nutrients, added the cultures and monitored the development through a microscope. Our ultimate fantasy was to produce a psilocybin slurry and ferment it into a wine. We believed we could market the drink under the name Milk of the Gods. All we ever made was huge yeast-contaminated messes.

But in one of those culture kits Buddy ordered they very helpfully included a tiny amount of the extract of the active ingredient itself – I guess so we could have something to compare our yield to, were we ever to get one. Daddy brought this particular package out to the farm from the post office. He was sceptical.

'*That* little dab of nothing?' In the bottom of a bottle smaller than a pencil was maybe a sixteenth inch of white dust. 'All that talk I heard about those experiments and *that's* all you took?'

I dumped the powder in a bottle of Party-Pac club soda. There wasn't so much as a fizz. 'This is probably about the size dose they gave us.' I began pouring it in a set of wineglasses. 'Maybe a little bigger.'

'Well, hell's bells, then,' Daddy said. 'I'll have a glass. I better check this business out.'

There were five of us: Buddy, me, Mickey Write, Betsy's brother Gil – all with some previous experience – and my Lone Star Daddy, who could never even finish the rare bottle of beer he opened on fishing trips. When we'd all emptied our glasses there was still a couple of inches left in the Party-Pac bottle. Daddy refilled his glass.

'I want enough to give me at least some notion . . . I'm tired of *hearing* about it.'

We went into the living room to wait. The women had gone to the shopping centre. It was about sundown. I remember we were watching that last Fullmer-Basilio fight on TV. When the shopping run got back from town my mother came popping in and asked, 'Who's winning?'

Daddy popped right back, 'Who's fighting?' and grinned at her like a goon.

In another hour that grin was gone. He was pacing the floor in freaked distress, shaking his hands as he paced, like they were wet.

'Damn stuff got down in all my *nerve ends!*' Could that have had something to do with getting that disease? We all always wondered, didn't we?

By the merciful end of a terrible hell of a night, Daddy was vowing, 'If you two try to manufacture this stuff . . . I'll crawl all the way to Washington on my bloody hands and *knees* to get it outlawed!'

Not a fair test, he later admitted, but he was damned if he was going to experiment further. 'Never,' he vowed. 'Not till I'm on my deathbed in a blind alley with my back to the wall.'

Which was pretty much the case that September.

The three of us flew to Phoenix and rented a Winnebago and headed into Mexico, usually Buddy at the wheel while Daddy and I argued about our selection of tapes – Ray Charles was all right, but that Bob Dappa and Frank Zylan smelt like just more burning braincells.

The farther south we went the hotter it got. Tempers went up with the temperature. A dozen times we were disinherited. A dozen times he ordered us to drop him at the first airport so he could fly out of this ratworld back to civilized comfort, yet he always cooled down by night when we pulled over. He even got to like the Mexican beer.

'But keep your dope to yourselves,' he warned. 'My muscles may be turning to mush but my head's still hard as a rock.'

By Puerto Sancto Daddy had thrown out all the cassettes and Buddy had picked up some farmacia leapers. We were all feeling pretty good. I wanted to take the wheel to pilot her in on the last leg of our journey, then, the first bounce onto a paved street in hundreds of miles I run over a corner of one of those square

31

Mexican manhole covers and it tilts up catty-corner and pokes a hole in our oilpan. We could've babied it to a hotel but Daddy says no, leave it with him; he'll see to it while we hike into town and get us a couple of rooms.

'Give me one of those pep pills before you go,' he growled, 'so I'll have the juice to deal with these bastards.'

He took a Ritalin. We eased it on to the biggest garage we could find and left him with it. Buddy and I went on foot across the river and into town where we rented a fourth-storey seafront double, then walked down to the beach action and got burned forty bucks trying to buy a kilo of the best dope I ever smoked. From a hippie girl with nothing but a tan and a promise.

We waited three hours before we gave up. On the defeated walk back through the outskirts we passed a bottled gas supply house. I spoke enough Spanish and buddy had enough creamery credentials that we talked them out of an E tank of nitrous. By the time we'd had a hit or two in the stickerbushes and got on back to the garage, the oilpan was off and welded and back on and Daddy knew the first names and ages and family history of every man in the shop, none of whom spoke any more English than he did Spanish. He had even put together the deal for the jumping beans.

'Good people,' he said, collapsing into the back of the Winnebago. 'Not lazy at all. Just easy. What's that in the blue tank?'

'Nitrous oxide,' Bud told him.

'Well I hope it can wait till I get a night in a hotel bed. I'm one shot sonofagun.'

We all slept most of the next day. By the time we were showered and shaved and enjoying room-service breakfast on our breezy terrace, the sun was dipping down into the bay like one of those glazed Mexican cookies. Daddy stretched and yawned.

'Okay . . . what you got?'

I brought out my arsenal. 'Grass, hash, and DMT. All of which are smoked and none of which last too long.'

'Not another fifteen rounds with Carmen Basilio, eh? Well, I aint cared about smoking ever since a White Owl made me puke on my grandpa. What was in that tank, Bud?'

'Laughing gas,' Buddy said.

To a man with thirty-five years' experience in refrigeration, that little tank at least looked familiar. 'Is the valve threaded left or right?'

I held it for him, but he didn't have the strength to turn it. I had to deal it – to my father first, then my brother, then myself. I dealt three times around this way and sat down. Then we flashed, this man and his two fullgrown sons, all together, the way you sometimes do. It wasn't that strong but it was as sweet as dope ever gets . . . at the end of our trip on the edge of our continent, as the sun dipped and the breeze stopped, and a dog a mile down the beach barked a high clear note . . . three wayfaring hearts in Mexico able to touch for an instant in a way denied them by gringo protocol. For a beat. Then Daddy stretched and yawned and allowed as how the skeeters would be starting now the breeze had dropped.

'So I guess I'll go inside and hit the hay. I've had enough. Too much dipsy-doo'll make you goony.'

He stood up and started for bed, his reputation for giving everything a fair shake still secure. It wasn't exactly a blessing he left us with – he was letting us know it wasn't for him, whatever it was we were into, or his hardheaded generation – but he was no longer going to crawl to Washington to put a stop to it.

He went through the latticed door into the dark room. Then his head reappeared.

'You jaspers better be sure of the gear you're trying to hit, though,' he said, in a voice unlike any he'd ever used when speaking to Buddy or me, or to any of the family, but that I could imagine he might have used had he ever addressed, say, Edward Teller. 'Because it's gonna get steep. If you miss the shift it could be The End as we know it.'

And that is what reminds me most of the Tranny Man show. Like Daddy, he knew it was gonna get steep. But he wouldn't make the shift. Or couldn't. He'd been dragging too much weight behind him for too long. He couldn't cut it loose and just go wheeling free across a foreign beach. When you cut it off something equally heavy better be hooked up in its place, some kind of steadying drag, or it'll make you goony.

'Drive you to *distraction* is what!'

This, the Tranny Man tells me at the post office. I stopped by to see if there was any jumping-bean news. There's the Tranny

33

Man, suntanned and perplexed, a slip of paper in each hand. He hands both notes to me when he sees me, like I'm his accountant.

'So I'm glad she took off before we both had some kind of breakdown. It's this crazy jungle pushed her over the edge if you ask me. Serves her right; she was the one insisted on coming. So there it is, Red.' He shrugs philosophically. 'The old woman has run out but the new transmission has come in.'

I see the first note is from the *estacion de camiones*, telling him that a crate has arrived from Arizona. The second is also from the bus station, scrawled on a Hotel de Sancto coaster:

'By the time you get this I will be gone. Our ways have parted. Your loving wife.'

Loving has been crossed out. I tell him I'm sorry. He says don't worry, there's nothing to it.

'She's pulled this kind of stuff before. It'll work out. Come on down to the bus depot and help me with that tranny and I'll buy you breakfast. Chief?'

The old dog creeps from behind the hotel desk and follows us into the cobbled sun.

'Pulled it lots of times before . . . just never in a foreign *coun*try before, is the problem.'

LAST SHOT OF TRANNY MAN'S WIFE

He used to do reckless things – not thoughtless or careless: reckless – like to toss me an open bottle of beer when I was down in the utility room, hot with cleaning. What could it hurt? If I dropped it there was no big loss. But if I caught it? I had more than just a bottle of beer. Why did he stop being reckless and become careless? What was it caught his attention and stiffened him into a doll? What broke all that equipment? – is what the Tranny Man's wife is thinking on her way to the American Consulate in Guadalajara to try to cash a check.

LAST SHOT OF TRANNY MAN

They wouldn't let me on the plane with the ticking five-gallon can of jumping beans. I had to take the bus. At the Pemex station outside Tepic I saw the Tranny Man's Polaro and his

34

trailer. He was letting old Chief squat in the ditch behind the station. Yeah, he was heading back. To the good old U.S. of A.

'You know what I think I'm gonna do, Red? I think I'm gonna cross at Tijuana this time, maybe have a little fun.'

Winking more odd-eyed than ever. How was his car? Purring right along. Heard from his wife? Not a peep. How had he liked his stay in picturesque Puerto Sancto?

'Oh, it was okay I guess, *but* – ' He throws his arm across my shoulders, pulling me close to share his most secret opinion: ' – if *Disney'd* designed it there'd of been monkeys.'

Abdul & Ebenezer

Listen to that bark and beller out there.

Something extraordinary to raise such a brouhaha, to get me walking this far this late into the pasture this damp with dew. . . .

They've quitted, quieted. But it isn't done they're just listening, there's something – *mygod it's Stewart fighting something right here! Yee! Gittum Stewart, gittum! Yee! Get outta here you phantom fucker you whatever you* – I can't tell if it's a fox, a way-out-of-his-woods wolf or a rabid 'possum.

Bark bark bark! Bark and beller and pound my heart while every hair for acres around springs to rigid attention. Stewart? Pant pant pant. Good gittin', Stew Ball. Who was that strange varmint? Your foot okay? Probably a fox, huh, some teenage fox out daring the midnight. Probably the same one that will sometimes slip up outside my cabin window in the hollow squeaking shank of a strung-out night to suddenly squawl me up out of my swivel chair three feet in the air then disappear into the swamp with yips of ornery delight.

Hush, Stewart. Hush. Let things settle down, it's twelve bells and hell's fire! What's that in the moony mist just ahead, that big black clot? It must be Ebenezer, back in that same spot beside the dented irrigation pipe. So, the drama is still running, after all these days. Over a week since that labour in the stickers and longer than that by almost another week since the slaughter, and she's still by the pipe. Well, it's a good drama and deserves a long run. Not that it has a nice tight plot, or a parable I can yet coax a clear meaning from, but it's a drama nevertheless.

It has a valiant hero, and a faithful heroine. Despite the masculine moniker, Ebenezer is a cow. She got her misleading name one communal Christmas before we communers were cognizant of such things as gender in the lesser life forms.

She is one of the original dogies, Ebenezer is, appropriated that first year I was out of jail and California – back in Oregon at old Mt Nebo farm. Betsy had moved there with the kids while I did my time, and all the old gang had followed. That first giddy year the farm was loaded with lots of loaded people trying

36

to take care of lots of land without much more than optimism and dope to go on. One enthusiastic afternoon we drove the bus to the Creswell livestock auction and bid into our possession eight baby 'bummers'. In the cattle game a bummer is a two- or three- or four-day-old calf sold separately because the owner wants to milk the mom instead of raise the calf, and sold cheap because, we found out a few hours after we got our little string home to their strawfilled quarters, they seldom survive.

The first went to the Great Round-up before the first night was over and the second before the second, their skinny shanks a mass of manure and their big eyes dull from dehydration. By the end of the third night the other six were down. They wouldn't have made it through the week but for the introduction of my brother's acidophilus yogurt into their bottles. True to Buddy's claim, the yogurt fortified their defenceless stomachs with friendly antibodies and enzymes and we pulled the remaining six through.

Hush, Stewart; it's Ebenezer. I can't see her in the dark but I can see our brand: a white heart with an X in it, floating ghostly in a black puddle. We use a freeze brand instead of a burn brand, so instead of the traditional bawling of calves and reek of seared hair and flesh, our stock marking is done with whispers and frozen gas. The heavy brass brand soaks at the end of a wooden stick in an insulated bucket bubbling with dry ice and methyl alcohol while we wrestle a calf to the sawdust. We shave a place on the flank, stick the frosted iron to the bald spot, then hope everything holds still for the count of sixty. If it's done right, the hair grows back out white where the metal touched. Why the crossed heart? It used to be the Acid Test symbol, something to do with spiritual honesty, cross thy heart and hope to etc.

It worked on Ebenezer the best; maybe the iron was colder, or the shave closer; perhaps it's simply that she is an Angus and pure black for the white to show against. Her ⊗ has tripled in size since it was frosted on years ago yet still shines sharp and clear. The insignia gives her a look of authority. Indeed, Ebenezer has led the herd with an influence that has continued to grow ever since she first realized that she was the smartest thing in the field, and the bravest, and that if anybody was going to lead a charge of periodic grievances through the fence to protest pasture conditions, it would have to be her. When there is a beef, so to speak, Ebenezer is the spokesman of this whole eighty acres of grazers – cows, calves, steers, bulls, sheep, horses, goats, donkeys, and vegetarian four-footers all.

I refuse to say spokesperson.

The crown of leadership has not been a light one. She's paid for her years of barricade busting and midwinter protest marches. She's been hung with irritating bells, tethered to drags, hobbled, collared with yokes made from Y's of sturdy ash sticking a yard above her neck and a yard below to stop her from squeezing between the strands of barbed wire (stop her until she really got resolute, of course; any of our fencing during those first years was at best a tacit agreement with the half-ton tenants), and she has had bounced off her hide barrages of rocks, clods, bean poles, tools, tin cans and tent stakes and, on one rainy raging night, after hours of mediation over a border dispute, fiery Roman candle balls.

She doesn't do it so much any more. She's learned the price of protest and I've learned how to build stronger fences and feed better hay. Still, we both know we can look forward to future demonstrations. There's a farm doggerel, goes: 'Ya know ol' Ebenezer . . . she *will* do what'll please 'er!'

Hi, Ebenezer. Still here at the dent in the pipe, eh, chewing away cool and calm? I see you haven't let no hot-rod fox mess with your memories in the ruminating night. . . .

She's had other old men. The first was Hamburger, a big Guernsey bull, low-browed and hard-looking and horny enough to one time try to mount an idling Harley, biker and all, because a heifer in heat had rubbed against the rear wheel. During the bidding the auctioneer admitted Hamburger was no good-looker to speak of, but he claimed he knew the beast personally and could *guarantee* he was a hard lover with *bound*less ardour. We knew he had spoken the truth as soon as the bull came down the truck ramp into our clover. He hit the ground with his hard already on. From that time on, almost any hour of any day when you saw Hamburger hanging out, it looked like he could have broke new ground by just walking on his knees.

But ardour that knows no bounds neither knows any boundaries. He wasn't a movement leader like Ebenezer but he was just as hard on my fences. One morning he wasn't in our pasture. I found the twisted gap in the wire, but Hamburger was nowhere to be seen. Butch, my neighbour Olaf's son, finally brought us the news that his dad had Hamburger chained in his barn. When I went over to get him, Olaf says, 'Come on in the house. I'll have the woman make us a pot of fresh coffee. I want to talk to ya.'

I trust Olaf. Like most of my farming neighbours he has to hold down a job to support his right to labour on his own land. He's out working his fields the minute he's home from the woods; he doesn't even change out of his calk boots.

We chatted the first cup away. After the second cup he says, 'That bull's become a breacher – dangerous. Guernsey bulls'll do that, all to once one day *decide* to be hateful. And this'n has decided. From now on he's gonna go through any fence any gate *any* damn thing that happens to stand between him and anything he fancies. Till eventually he's gonna turn on a human being. Maybe not a grown man, but he wouldn't hesitate to turn on a kid or a woman trying to head him. Ya can bet money on it. He's got that look in his eye.'

We went out to his barn and peered through the rails. There was no denying it: what had once been just hard and horny was now a look burning with the first coals of hate for the human oppressor.

'I'll butcher the bastard tomorrow,' I said.

'Now don't do that. Ya don't want to be eatin' hate. He's still young enough so he oughten be too tough, but he'll have all that breachin' and screwin' and sod-pawin' in his blood. The meat'd be rank as a billygoat. What it is ya'll have to do is put him in a fattening pen and top him off with grain for about forty days. Try to get his mind off all the hellin' around after hot heifers.'

We built the pen out of railroad ties and telephone poles, but I had my doubts about changing Hamburger's mind. Not only was he still horny, with those heifers crooning at him every night from miles around – '*Ham*burger . . . *Hammm*-burger, honey' – those coals in his eyes were hotter with each passing penned-up day. When we saw that the weeks of solitary were making him no mellower, were in fact making him rush daily fiercer at the fence when we brought his grain out, and roar and rumble nightly louder and louder like a pent-up volcano of sperm, we finally resorted to putting a potion in his serving of morning mash, hoping to raise his consciousness, if not up to the Knowledge of the Glorious All-Pervading Mercy that Passeth Understanding, at least up out of his scrotum.

39

Our potion produced more agitation, it seemed, than enlightenment. He stood staring into the empty bucket a few minutes, slobbering and twitching. Then he gave a mighty fart and charged. He levelled a railroad tie with his first rush (it must have been a good one; we had estimated his weight as that of six men and medicated him accordingly). When he crashed out we headed for high places, stumbling over each other in our realization of what we had wrought, but his hormones were apparently stronger than his hate; forgetting his scattering tormentors, he stampeded straight for the neglected herd. Far into the night we could hear the debauchery.

Betsy phoned Sam's Slaughtering. The little refrigerated aluminum truck was there at dawn. Sam's son John got out and took the .22 rifle from the rack behind the seat. Sam no longer did the actual knockover. He was content to stay back at the butcher shop and argue with deer hunters while his son took care of the field work. John was only about eighteen at this time. Though not a licensed butcher, years of accompanying his father on these killing runs had taught John something about death and timing. He knew to arrive at dawn, to stroll out to the condemned animal before it was fully awake (a wave of his hand, a call – 'Hey! Here!' – a sharp crack . . .) and to drop it with the first shot.

The resulting quake of terror that runs from one end of the farm to the other after this shot must never enter the mind of the victim, or the meat. Ya don't wanta to be eatin' *fear*, neither. As far as John and I and the cows are concerned, this is what kosher was originally supposed to be about.

After Hamburger we went through several steer misses – chance bulls, spared by our ineptness with the elastrator or weak rubber bands; but these fellows were at best bush-league bulls who kept trying to get into their own mothers, so they lasted no length of time. After a couple seasons of no bull, and fast approaching a time of no beef, I made a deal with my dad and brother and Mickey Write to get new blood on the property. Mickey had a couple of ponies foundering on my far pasture, and my father knew a milk producer with an extra young bull to swap. Mickey hauled the ponies to the producer in his girlfriend's horse trailer and returned a few hours later with our trade. We all stood in the bee-loud field and witnessed the cautious coming-out of a

40

black Aberdeen yearling, as demure and dimensionless in the trailer as midnight itself. This was to be Abdul, the Bull Bull.

Barely a boy bull that afternoon, he backed off the ramp as cowed-looking as a new kid on a strange playground. A cute new kid, too. Almost dainty. He was long-lashed and curly-locked and hornless, it appeared to us, in more ways than one. He took one apprehensive look around at our array of cows watching him in a row, tails twitching and eyes a-glitter from two years of bull-lessness, and struck out south for mellower climes like San Francisco, through our fence, our *neigh*bour's fence, and our neighbour's neighbour's *neigh*bour's fence before we could head him off.

When we finally got him back he took another look at our cows and headed this time for Victoria. It took two days of chasing him with rocks and ropes and coaxing him with alfalfa and oats to get him back and secured and calmed or at least resigned that this was, ready or not, his new home. He stayed, but all the rest of that summer and fall he kept as much field as possible between himself and that herd of hussies stalking his vital bodily essence.

'What kind of Ferdinand have you rung in here on me?' I asked my father.

'A new experimental breed,' Dad assured me. 'I think they call 'em *Fagg*erdeen Anguses, known for docility.'

When hard winter set in, young Abdul finally took to associating openly with the herd, but for warmth and meals only, it appeared. After the daily hay was gone he would stand aside and chew in saintly solitude. With his shy face and his glossy black locks he looked more a pubescent altar boy considering a life of monastic celibacy than the grandsire of steaks.

There comes into the story now a minor cow character, one of Hamburger's heifers named Floozie. A cross-eyed Jersey-Guernsey cross – runty, unassuming, and as unpretty as her father – yet this wallflower was to be the first to clear Abdul of the charge of Flagrant Ferdinandeering. Betsy had told me some of the cows looked pregnant but I was a doubter. I was even more sceptical when she said that it was homely Floozie who was due to drop her calf first.

'Any time now,' Betsy said. 'She's secreting, her hips are distended, and listen to her complain out there.'

'It's only been barely nine months since we bought him,' I

reminded her. 'And the only thing he jumped that *first* two months was fences. She's just bellering because the weather's been so shitty. Everything is complaining.'

That had been the coldest winter in Oregon's short recorded history – 20 degrees below zero in Eugene! – and the bitterest in even the old mossbacks' long recollection. Nor did the freeze let up after a few days, like our usual cold snap. The whole state froze for one solid week. Water went rigid in the plumbing if a faucet was left off for a few minutes; submersible pumps burned out sixty feet down; radiators exploded; trees split; the gasoline even froze in the fuel lines of moving cars. After a week it thawed briefly to let all the cracked water mains squirt gaily for a day; then it froze again. Another new record! And snowed. And blew like a bastard, and kept freezing and snowing and blowing for week after week right through February and March and even into April. By Easter it had warmed up a little. Fairer days were predicted. The snow had stopped but those April showers were a long way from violets.

Sleet is worse than snow with none of the redeeming charm. With nasty slush all day long and black ice all night, every citizen was depressed, the beasts as bad as the folks. Beasts don't have any calendar, any Stonehenge Solstice, any ceremonial boughs of holly to remind them of the light. Cows have a big reservoir of patience, but it isn't bottomless. And when it's finally emptied, when month after miserable month has passed and there is no theology to shore up the weatherbeaten spirit, they can begin to despair. My cows began to stand ass to the wind and stare bleakly into a worsening future, neither mooing nor moving for hours on end. Even alfalfa failed to perk them up.

Then one dim morning Betsy came in to tell me Floozie was in labour down in the swamp and looked like she needed help. By the time I was bundled up and had followed Betsy back down, the calf had been born: a tiny black ditto of daddy Abdul without a doubt, curly-browed and angel-eyed and standing against the sleet as healthy and strong – to coin a phrase – as a bull. Floozie didn't look so good, though. She was panting and straining through sporadic contractions, but she couldn't seem to rally strength enough to pass the afterbirth. We decided to move them up to the field next to the house to keep an eye on them. I carried the calf while Betsy shooed Floozie along behind. We all had to duck our heads into the stinging icy rain. I was cursing

42

and Betsy was grumbling and Floozie was lowing forlornly about the woes of this harsh existence, but the little calf wasn't making a sound in my arms; his head was too high and his eyes too wide with the wonder of it all to think of a complaint.

The sleet got colder. Betsy and I went inside and watched out the window. The calf lay down in the shelter of the pumphouse and waited for whatever new wonder life had in store. Floozie continued to low. The afterbirth dangled from her rump like a cluster of grape Popsicles. Some of it finally broke away and dropped to the icy mud. The remainder started drawing back inside. Betsy said we ought to go out there and dig the rest of it forth. I observed that cows had been surviving calving for thousands of years now without my help. Dig my arm into that mysterious yin dark? I was not – to coin another – into it.

That afternoon Floozie was down. She still hadn't passed the afterbirth, and fever was steaming from her heaving sides. She was making a sighing wheeze every few breaths that sounded like a rusty wind-up replica of a cow running down. The little calf was still standing silent, nuzzling his mother with soft, imploring bumps of his nose, but his mother wasn't answering. Betsy said peritonitis was setting in and we'd need some anti-biotics to save her. I drove into Springfield, where I was able to buy a kit for just this veterinarian problem. It was a pint bottle of oxytetracycline antibiotic hooked by a long rubber tube to a stock hypo with a point big as a twenty-penny nail. Waiting for a freight at the Mt Nebo crossing I had time to read the pamphlet of directions for the inoculation. It showed a drawing of a cow with an arrow indicating the vein in the neck I was to hit. It said nothing about where to tie her off, however.

The rest of the drive home I spent considering various ties. A garden hose, I thought, would be best, with a slip knot . . . but before I was even turned into our drive I saw that I wasn't going to get the chance, not that day. I could see the sides heaved no more. The little calf was still standing beside the steaming mound, but was no longer silent. He was bawling as though his heart would break.

The rest of that sleet-smeared day I spent shivering and shovelling and thinking how if I had just gone ahead and stuck my hand up that cow that morning I wouldn't be digging this huge goddamned hole this afternoon. While I dug and the calf bawled, the cows – one by one – came to the fence to stare in on the scene, not at the dead sister, who was already little more to them than the mud being shovelled back over her, but at the newborn marvel. As the cows stared you could see them straining back through the long dark tunnel of the winter's memory, recalling something. That little calf's cry was tugging on the udders of their memory, drawing down the milky remembrance of brighter times, of longer days and clover again, of sunshine, warmth, birth, of *living* again.

Before that dingy day had muddied to full dark my cows were calving everywhere, not weakened by forlorn despair but strengthened by jubilant certainty. Ebenezer calved so fast she thought there must be more to come. We were able to slip Floozie's little maverick alongside; in her jubilation Ebenezer never doubted for a moment that she had dropped twins. By the next morning I couldn't tell the orphan from its stepbrother or from any of the other curly-browed calves that continued to pop out all that day in a steady black line.

During all this maternity business, the father hadn't come in from the field. After the last cow had calved I walked out, and I could see him in a far corner near my neighbour's fence. I reached him just as the sun pried through a jam of clouds. He listened shyly while I tendered him apologies and congratulations, then turned his back on me to enjoy the bundle of alfalfa I had brought. I noticed further bellering and saw two of my neighbour's Holsteins with fresh black babies and, in my neighbour's *neigh*bour's field of high-rent red Devons, saw more of Abdul's issue hopping about in the sun like a hatch of crickets.

'Abdul, by God you *are* one bull bull!'

He didn't deny it, chomping away with altar-boy innocence; he didn't brag about it, either. It wasn't his style.

The seasons wheeled on. Our herd soon doubled and then some. We banded the baby bulls, ate the fatted steers, and spared the heifers toward the time when even I get it together enough to realize my dairy farm vision. As the herd got bigger, it got blacker. Better than two thirds were now three-quarters black, with fading smatterings of Guernsey, Jersey, and Oregon Mongol. Abdul got broader and less dainty, yet never lost his altar-boy demeanour; he never butted or assaulted a heifer with that typical show of cruel strength that gives origin to the name 'bully'.

No one ever saw him score; taking advantage of his natural camouflage, he chose darkness for his wooing ground. If his midnight nuptials sometimes took him through a fence or two, he usually returned before dawn; when he didn't, there was never any attitude but gentle obedience toward any of us who went to fetch him back. The only anger I ever saw crimp his brow was aimed at no human but at the bull who serviced Tory's herd across the road, an old blowhard Hereford. It was easy to see why. After every broad-daylight hump of some sleepy heifer, this rednecked old whiteface had to parade up and down his fence and bawl his boasting across the road at our young Angus. Abdul never answered; whenever Old Blowhole across the road started, Abdul always headed for the swamp.

At length, Betsy began to worry about the number of our herd and about the size of some of Abdul's daughters. They were getting 'that age', as it were (and as the nasty neighbour bull was quick to make clear whenever one of Abdul's virgin daughters grazed past), and old enough to be capable of inbreeding. I personally didn't think Abdul would stoop to incest, but who wants to take a chance on idiot veal?

'What can we do?' I asked Betsy. We were walking along the fence, checking our charges over. Across the road Tory's bull was following, huffing up some new diatribe.

'Pen Abdul up, or auction him off, or sell him, or – '

She stopped, drowned out by the whiteface. When his harangue bellowed back down I asked, 'Or what?'

'Or eat him.'

'Eat Abdul? I don't want to eat Abdul. That'd be like eating Stewart.'

'Pen him up, then. That's the way you're supposed to keep breeding bulls. . . .'

'I don't want to pen him up, either. I wouldn't give Tory's bull the satisfaction.'

'That leaves sell or trade. I'll put an ad in the paper.'

We found no one wanted to trade anything but deer rifles or motorcycles. And the cash orders came not from kindly cattle breeders but from local beaneries seeking bargain burger.

After a month passed without any results from our ads, and after a night helping Hock, our neighbour to the east, separate Abdul from the half-dozen Charolais Hock'd just bought, I decided to try the pen.

The tie had been replanted, the rails replaced, but not since Hamburger had the little square been occupied. Abdul entered without a squawk. To my surprise, he had to squeeze in the gate that Hamburger used to pass through easily.

'Abdul ol' buddy, you're big enough to know some of the harsh facts of life,' I told him as I fastened the gate. 'It ain't all free love and frolic.'

Abdul stood without comment, munching the bucket of green apples I had used to lure him. Watching from across the road, Tory's bull had a lot to say about his rival's incarceration. He was terrible. All afternoon he kept up his needling of Abdul with bawled innuendos and sexual slurs. By the time I went to bed, the Hereford had worked up to downright racial insults. I promised myself to have a few words with old man Tory about his beast someday soon.

Old man Tory beat me to it. He was there at sun-up, cracking at the windowpane of my front door with a flinty old knuckle.

'Yer bull? Yer gor-gor-gordam black bull?' He was shirtless and shuddering violently, from both the morning chill and the heat of some as-yet-unbottled anger. 'Yer sell him er yer still got him tell me that!'

Tory is a toothless old veteran of some eighty embattled years of farming, with the face of a starved mink, and not much bigger. It is said that he once accosted a pair of California duck hunters trespassing after a flock of mallards they'd seen go down in the slough that gullies through Tory's property, and had proceeded to chew them out with such snapping ferocity that one of the hunters suffered a coronary. Now, as I watched him shuddering and sputtering on my doorstep, toothless and scrawny in his bib overalls and no shirt, I feared that this might be his blood pressure's time to blow. Soothingly I told him, why yes, as a matter of fact, I still had Abdul. 'If you'd like to size him up he's out in my bullpen – '

'The gordam hell if he is! He's been over in my field since afore light, tearin' up fences an' gates an' all sortsa hell. Now he's into it with my bull – t' the death!'

I told him I'd get after the delinquent right away, soon's I got my clothes on and my kids up to help. I apologized for the trouble and old man Tory cooled off a little.

'I'd've broke 'em apart myself,' he growled, as he started hobbling back down the steps, 'but I ain't had my breakfast yet.'

I hollered everybody up and we headed over to our field car, a '64 Merc convertible. We didn't have to drive down to Tory's gate; the hole in his fence looked like a road grader had opened it. I manoeuvred through the fractured wood and wire, then headed us bouncing toward the cloud of dust in the distance. I drove alongside the freshly rutted trail left by the battle's progress. The distance travelled into Tory's land showed who was winning. Bull fashion, the Hereford had planted himself between the black attacker and his whiteface herd, but Abdul had forced him steadily backwards, more than half a mile. When we reached the scene of the conflict the Hereford was nearly to the edge of Tory's gully. His tongue was dripping blood from the corner of his mouth and his eyes were rolling wildly to and fro, from Abdul, standing mountainlike a few feet in front, to the lip of the chasm a few feet behind.

They both turned their heads to regard the car honking and revving its engine at them. I got out. 'Abdul!' I hollered. 'Knock it off! And go home!' He gave me such a look of apology I thought for a moment he might obey, like a dog. But the whiteface tried to take advantage of the distraction with a charge for Abdul's turned neck: *butt!* Abdul staggered. He pawed for his balance, stepping backwards, then dropped his head in time to meet the next attack: ka-*dud!* The two big skulls crunched together with astonishing force. Thousands of pounds of conflicting inertia rippled down their backs to their butts and right on through the earth. You could feel it underfoot: ka-*dud!* Then again: *duddd!* and Abdul regained the turf my shouting had cost him.

What a spectacle! They would collide, and drive, heave, grind until they were exhausted, then stand panting. Sometimes they placed their big foreheads together without a charge, almost affectionately, increasing the force until the huge necks would accordion with the effort; sometimes they would sling their heads from side to side and bring them together with a sharp crack before starting their push. But whatever the tactic, inch by inch Abdul was forcing his weary opponent to what looked like certain defeat; even if the Hereford didn't lose his footing over the edge and expose his underside to Abdul's murderous trampling, he would still be fighting downhill. Downhill from that much weight would put him at a conclusive disadvantage.

I didn't want to be paying Tory purebred prices for a dead

blowhard, so I jumped back behind the wheel of the Merc and gunned it into the fracas. The bumper caught Abdul in the fore shoulder while he was brow to brow and pushing. He didn't budge. I backed off farther and came at them again; again there was no give. But the impact had jammed the radiator back into the fan; the ensuing racket distracted Abdul long enough to let the Hereford escape the precipice. For a second it looked like he was going to turn tail on valour and run for discretion, but his ladies across the chasm raised such an outcry the Hereford had to swing back about. There was nothing to do but fight to the finish or spend the rest of his days hearing them nag.

He spread his feet groggily for his last stand. I tried to manoeuvre the car into position for another side shot, but it was beginning to steam. Abdul hiked a couple of disdainful clods into the air and lowered his head for the kill when a sharp *crack! crack!* startled all of us. Up out of the gulley came old man Tory. A clean white shirt was buttoned over his overalls and his dentures were in; his lips and stubble were flecked with toast crumbs and berry jam. In his hand he carried a little green leather buggy whip, the kind you buy as rodeo souvenirs.

'Good *gord* ain't yer broke these sonsabidges up yet?'

I told him I'd been waiting for them to wear themselves out, they'd be less dangerous.

'Dangerous? Dangerous? Why good gordamighty *damn* stand outter the way. I ain't a-skeered of the sonsabidges!'

And waded into them, whip crackling and dentures snapping. His Hereford received two snaps on the snoot and, to my amazement, took off bleating like a lamb. Abdul spun to give pursuit but there was that little wizard right in his path, green wand cracking like firecrackers. Abdul hesitated. He looked after the panicked whiteface galloping for the barn, then back at the stick conjuring green sparks, and decided if Old Blowhole was *that* scared of it it must be pretty strong medicine. He turned around and started toward home in a shambling walk, his black brow lowered.

'Yer see that?' Tory pointed the whip after his fleeing bull. 'When the sonabidge was a calf my great gran-kids useta tie him to a wagon an' whup him inter pullin' them – with this *shittin' little whup*. Never forget it, did 'e?'

We gave the old farmer a lift back to his farmhouse. I told him I'd fix his fence; he said it was done *past* that; now that my
48

bull had topped his it wouldn't rest till it had topped the *whole herd*. 'Prolly won't even rest then, yer know? There's only one thing to do. And if yer don't I b'gord *will!*'

So that night we called Sam's, and the next morning John came turning in the drive before I'd even had coffee. Riding the running board, I directed him out to where the herd was bedded in the green clover around the main irrigation pipe. Ebenezer commenced bellering a warning, as she has come to do whenever she sees the approach of the silvery little death wagon, but she was too late. John was already out, walking around toward the target I had pointed out. Because of the size, he was carrying a .30–.30 instead of his usual .22. Abdul was just blinking awake when the shot exploded in his brow. He fell over the pipe without a sound.

As the herd bucked and bawled John hooked his winch cable to Abdul's hind feet and dragged the carcass away about fifty yards. I used to insist that he drag them clear from the field out of sight, so the herd wouldn't have to watch the gory peeling and gutting of their fallen relative, but John'd shown me it wasn't necessary. They don't follow the carcass; they stay to circle the spot where the actual death occurred, keening around the taking-off place though the hoisted husk is in full view mere yards away. As time passes, this circle spreads larger. If one were to hang overhead in a balloon and take hourly photos of this outline of mourning, I believe it would describe the diffusing energy field of the dead animal.

Abdul was the biggest animal we'd ever killed, and this mourning lasted the longest. Off and on between grazing, the herd returned to the dented pipe and stood in a lowing circle that was a tight ten feet in diameter the first day, and the next day fifteen feet, and the next day twenty. For a full week they grieved. It was fitting: he'd been their old man and a great one, and it was only right that the funeral last until a great circle had been observed, only natural – with the proper period of respect fading naturally toward forgetting while Nature shuffles her deck for the next deal around.

But at this point up pops a joker.

The bathroom floor rots through. Buddy and cousin Davy drive out in the creamery van with a load of plywood and we work the night away nailing it down. When they leave in the morning

Buddy is attracted by a bellering in the field. It is Ebenezer. Another duty of her office is to let us know when one of the young cows has started to labour. Buddy sees the supine heifer and throws his truck into reverse and comes hollering and honking back. 'Looks like there's a calf about to be borned,' he yells at me. Betsy hops in with him while I open the gate. We head out to where Ebenezer is trumpeting her announcement.

'That's right where Abdul got it last week,' I told Buddy. 'They've been bedding down there every night.'

'Listen to Ebenezer,' Betsy said. 'O, me, I hope she doesn't think – !'

It was too late. Ebenezer had already made the mistaken association: early morning, an approaching truck, a killing still strong in her memory . . . and what had begun as a call for assistance became a shriek of warning. She planted herself between us and her labouring sister and bellowed, 'It's the killer wagon! Head for the woods, honey; I'll try to hold the fiends back.'

We were the rest of the morning trying to find the cow in the swamp. We finally located her hiding place by her ragged breathing. She was on her side under a thicket of blackberries. From the size of the calf's front hooves sticking out, we could see it was a whopper, far too big for so young a heifer. Maybe she could have squeezed it out on her own out in the field when she was still fresh, but Ebenezer's misguided alarm had sent her running and spent her strength. Now she was going to need help.

I tried to get a loop over her head, but she was as skittish as I was unskilled. The rest of the afternoon Betsy and the kids and I chased her from one stickerpatch to the next. There was never really any room for me to get a good toss of my loop. At length, I traded my lasso for my old wrestling headgear and climbed into the low branches of a scrub oak. When Betsy and the kids drove her beneath me I leaped on her and wrestled her down bodily. I held her until Quiston got a loop around a hind leg and Betsy got another around her neck. We got a third tie around her other hind leg and lashed her to three trees. Quis sat on her head to keep her from rearing up. I wrapped the calf's protruding hooves with clothesline and started pulling. Betsy massaged her stomach, and little Caleb talked to her and stroked her neck. When a contraction would start I would brace a foot against each side of her spread flank and tug. When the clothesline broke, I doubled it – and when it broke again, I double doubled it and kept pulling.

The sun went down. Sherree brought the flashlight down from the house and some wet rags to towel some of the stuff from our faces while we laboured. Blood and mud and sweat and shit. Finally, with a mighty tugging and grunting and rending of orifices, out it came: a pretty little bull, all black with one stripe of white in the corner of its mouth, as though he'd been drinking milk already and had drooled. It wasn't breathing. Betsy blew air into its lungs until they started pumping on their own.

We let the cow up but kept the tie around her neck so she wouldn't flee in exhausted craziness before she accepted the calf. Sherree brought her a bucket of water, and while the animal drank we stood back out of sight and shone the flashlight beam on the calf. Calmed by the drink, the cow stepped forward to sniff the wobbly child. I switched off the light.

The moon had come out and was dappling down through the oak leaves. She had begun licking the calf. I wanted to take the rope from around her neck so she wouldn't tangle in the brush, but she wouldn't let me near the loop knot to loosen it. I opened my buck knife and slipped up as close as I could and began sawing very gently at the rope a few feet from her back-straining head, humming as I worked. She looked back and forth from me to her calf in the moonlight. You could see the trust returning.

But apparently both jokers had been left in this deck. As the last strands parted, a car came rattling down the road and screeched to a halt by our mailbox, then backed up and swung in the drive and shut off the ignition. As the engine quit it gave a loud backfire and off the cow stampeded, right over the hapless calf.

Betsy and the kids went after the cow while I went after the car. It was unloading a rowdy-crew and a barking dog. The crew was a bunch of Dairy Manufacturing majors from Oregon State who'd had a few brews after class and decided to drive down from Corvallis, check out how the famous *commune* was doing – and the dog was a goddamned German shepherd barking about how many chickens he could kill given the opportunity. I dispatched them quickly back northward, clattering and backfiring and cursing back at me – 'Grouchy old baldheaded *prick!*' – then I returned to the swamp.

The cow was back with her calf, licking it and lowing. Betsy whispered it looked like she was going to stay. We crept away to the house and washed up. Betsy visited the mother and child once more before we went to bed.

'She's still with it. He hasn't got back up yet, though.'

'He's probably exhausted. Lord knows I am. Let's get under the covers before something else happens.'

In the morning the calf was where we had left him, dead. Lifting his body away from the grieving cow, I could feel some of his little ribs were broken. Who knows? From the rigours of the birth or the backfire that stampeded his mother over him? From Ebenezer's confused warning? Tory's bull's taunting? The position of the stars and the planets, the dice throw of destiny?

I buried him near what was left of his great-aunt Floozie. He made a small new hump next to the big old hump, blooming blue and yellow from the crocus bulbs we had planted there last fall. I haven't decided what we'll plant over his nutrients. Cowslips sounds about right.

Let's go, Stewart; this dew has all my toes froze. Nighty-night, Ebenezer. Lie back down and tell the rest of the gals to cool it. It was just a fox, tell them, just a varmint in the dark.

The Day After Superman Died

Strung out and shaking he was, pacing distractedly about the clutter of his office upstairs in the barn, poking among the books and bottles and cobwebs and dirt-dauber nests, trying to remember what he had done with his coloured glasses.

His special glasses. He needed them. Since before noon he had been putting off the walk to the ditch out in the field because the air was clogged with an evil eye-smiting smoke. Since the first smudge of dawn, long before his eyes had started smarting and his sinuses had begun to throb, and even before the hassle he'd just had with those hitchhikers down in the yard, he had been telling himself that this dreary day was going to be one real bastard without some rose-coloured armour. Those glasses, he had been telling himself, would surely ease the day's sting.

As he paced past his window, he heard the heartbroken bleating of the mother sheep start up again, baffled and insistent, twisted by the hot distance. He pushed the curtain back from the sunlight and looked out over his yard into the field, shading his eyes. He couldn't see the lamb because of the thistle and Queen Anne's lace, but the three ravens still marked the spot. They eddied above the ditch, arguing over the first morsels. Farther away, in the ash grove, he could see the ewe bleating against her rope and, farther still, past the fence, the backs of the two hitchhikers. Little was visible beyond that. Mt Nebo was only a dim line drawn into the hanging smoke. The merest suggestion. It made him think of Japanese wash painting, a solitary mountain form stroked hazily into a grey paper with a slightly greyer ink.

The Oregon farm was uncommonly quiet for this hour. The usual midafternoon sounds seemed held in one of those tense stillnesses that ordinarily prompt the peacock to scream. One New Year's Eve the big bird had called steadily during the half minute of burning fuse before Buddy's cannon went off, and last week it had screamed within seconds of the first lightning that cracked the iron sky into a tumultuous thunderstorm.

A storm would be a relief now, Deboree thought. Even the

53

peacock's horrible squawk would be welcome. But nothing. Only the little clock radio on his desk. He'd left it on for the news, but it was Barbra Streisand singing 'On a Clear Day, etc.'. Terrific, he thought. Then, above the music and the distant grieving of the sheep, he heard another sound: a high, tortured whine. Certainly no relief, whatever it was. At length he was able to make out the source. Squinting down the road toward the highway, he saw a little pink car coming, fast and erratic, one of those new compacts with a name he couldn't remember. Some animal – a Cobra, or a Mink, or a Wildcat – with transmission trouble, whatever the beast was. It squealed around the corner past the Olson farm and the Burch place and came boring on through the smoky afternoon with a whine so piercing and a heading so whimsical and wild that the hitchhikers were forced from the shoulder of the road into the snake-grass. The blond gave it the finger and the blackbeard hurled some curse at its passing. It screamed on past the barn, out of sight and, finally, hearing. Deboree left the window and began again his distracted search.

'I'm certain they're up here someplace,' he said, certain of no such thing.

Deboree's eyes fell on his dog-eared rolling box, and he took it from the shelf. He gazed in at the seeds and stems: maybe enough could be cleaned for one now, but unlikely enough for one now and one later. *Better save it for later. Need it more later. And just as well*, he thought, looking at the box in his hands. The little brown seeds were rattling all over the place. He was still trembling too violently with the surge of adrenalin to have managed the chore of rolling. As he returned the box to its niche in the shelf, he recalled an old phrase of his father's:

'Shakin' like a dog shittin' peach pits.'

He had been up two days, grassing and speeding and ransacking his mental library (or was it three?) for an answer to his agent's call about the fresh material he had promised his editor and to his wife's query about the fresh cash needed by the loan office at the bank. Mainly, since Thursday's mail, for an answer to Larry McMurtry's letter.

Larry was an old literary friend from Texas. They had met at a graduate writing seminar at Stanford and had immediately disagreed about most of the important issues of the day – beatniks, politics, ethics, and, especially, psychedelics – in fact,

54

about everything except for their mutual fondness and respect for writing and each other. It was a friendship that flourished during many midnight debates over bourbon and booklore, with neither the right nor the left side of the issues ever gaining much ground. Over the years since Stanford, they had tried to keep up the argument by correspondence – Larry defending the traditional and Deboree championing the radical – but without the shared bourbon the letters had naturally lessened. The letter from Larry on Thursday was the first in a year. Nevertheless it went straight back at the issue, claiming conservative advances, listing the victories of the righteous right, and pointing out the retreats and mistakes made by certain left-wing luminaries, especially Charles Manson, whom Deboree had known slightly. The letter ended by asking, in the closing paragraph, 'So. What has the Good Old Revolution been doing lately?'

Deboree's research had yielded up no satisfactory answer. After hours of trial and chemistry before the typewriter, he had pecked out one meagre page of print, but the victories he had listed on his side were largely mundane achievements: 'Dobbs and Blanche had another kid. . . . Rampage and I finally got cut loose from our three-year probation. . . .' Certainly no great score for the left-wing of the ledger. But that was all he could think of: one puny page to show for forty hours of prowling around in the lonely library of what he used to call 'The Movement'. Forty hours of thinking, drinking, and peeing in a milk bottle, with no break except that ten-minute trip downstairs to deal with those pilgriming prickheads. And now, back upstairs and still badly shaken, even that feeble page was missing; the typed yellow sheet of paper was as misplaced as his coloured glasses.

'Pox on both houses,' he moaned aloud, rubbing his irritated eyes with his wrists. 'On Oregon field burners poisoning the air for weed-free profit and on California flower children gone to seed and thorn!'

He rubbed until the sockets filled with sparks; then he lowered his fists and held both arms tight against his sides in an attempt to calm himself, standing straight and breathing steady. His chest was still choked with adrenalin. Those California goddamned clowns, both smelling of patchouli oil, and cheap sweet wine, and an angry festering vindictiveness. Of threat, really. They reeked of threat. The older of the two, the blackbeard, had stopped the barking of M'kehla's pair of Great Danes with only a word. 'Shut!' he had hissed, the sound slicing out from the side of his mouth. The dogs had immediately turned tail back to their bus.

Deboree hadn't wanted to interface with the pair from the moment he saw them come sauntering in, all long hair and dust and multipatched Levi's, but Betsy was away with the kids up Fall Creek and it was either go down and meet them in the yard or let them saunter right on into the house. They had called him brother when he came down to greet them – an endearment that always made him watch out for his wallet – and the younger one had lit a stick of incense to wave around while they told their tale. They were brothers of the sun. They were on their way back to the Haight, coming from the big doings in Woodstock, and had decided they'd meet the famous Devlin Deboree before going on south.

'Rest a little, rap a little, maybe riff a little. Y'know what I'm saying, bro?'

As Deboree listened, nodding, Stewart had trotted up carrying the broken bean pole.

'Don't go for Stewart's stick, by the way.' He addressed the younger of the pair, a blond-bearded boy with a gleaming milk-fed smile and new motorcycle boots. 'Stewart's like an old drunk with his stick. The more you throw it, the more lushed out he gets.'

The dog dropped the stick between the new boots and looked eagerly into the boy's face.

'For years I tried to break him of the habit. But he just can't help it when he sees certain strangers. I finally realized it was easier training the stick throwers than the stick chasers. So just ignore it, okay? Tell him no dice. Pretty soon he goes away.'

'Whatever,' the boy had answered, smiling. 'You heard the man, Stewart: no dice.'

The boy had kicked the stick away, but the dog had snagged it from the air and planted himself again before the boots. The boy did try to ignore it. He continued his description of the great scene at Woodstock, telling dreamily what a groove it had been, how high, how happy, how everybody there had been looking for Devlin Deboree.

'You shoulda made it, man. A stone primo groove. . . .'

56

The dog grew impatient and picked up his stick and carried it to the other man, who was squatting in the grass on one lean haunch.

'Just tell him no dice,' Deboree said to the side of the man's head. 'Beat it, Stewart. Don't pester the tourists.'

The other man smiled down at the dog without speaking. His beard was long and black and extremely thick, with the salt of age beginning to sprinkle around the mouth and ears. As his profile smiled, Deboree watched two long incisors grow from the black bramble of his mouth. The teeth were as yellow and broken as the boy's were perfect. This dude, Deboree remembered, had kept his face averted while they were shaking hands. He wondered if this was because he was self-conscious about his breath like a lot of people with bad teeth.

'Well, anyway, what's happening man? What's doing? All this?' Blondboy was beaming about at his surroundings. 'Boss place you got here, this garden and trees and shit. I can see you are into the land. That's good, that's good. We're getting it together to get a little place outside of Petaluma soon as Bob here's old lady dies. Be good for the soul. Lot of work, though, right? Watering and feeding and taking care of all this shit?'

'It keeps you occupied,' Deboree had allowed.

'Just the same,' the boy rambled on, 'you shoulda made it back there to Woodstock. Primo, that's the only word. Acres and acres of bare titty and good weed and outa sight vibes, you get me?'

'So I've heard,' Deboree answered, nodding pleasantly at the boy. But he couldn't take his mind off the other hitchhiker. Blackbeard shifted his weight to the other haunch, the movement deliberate and restrained, careful not to disturb the dust that covered him. His face was deeply tanned and his hair tied back so the leathery cords in his neck could be seen working as he followed the dog's imploring little tosses of the stick. He was without clothes from the waist up but not unadorned. He wore a string of eucalyptus berries around his neck and tooled leather wristbands on each long arm. A jail tattoo – made, Deboree recognized, by two sewing needles lashed parallel at the end of a matchstick and dipped in Indian ink – covered his left hand: it was a blue-black spider with legs extending down all five fingers to their ragged nails. At his hip he carried a bone-handled skinning knife in a beaded sheath, and across his knotted belly a long scar ran diagonally down out of sight into his Levi's. Grinning, the man watched Stewart prance up and down with the three-foot length of broken bean stake dripping in his mouth.

'Back off, Stewart,' Deboree commanded. 'Leave this guy alone!'

'Stewart don't bother me,' the man said, his voice soft from the side of his mouth. 'Everything gotta have its own trip.'

Encouraged by the soft voice, Stewart sank to his rump before the man. This pair of motorcycle boots were old and scuffed. Unlike his partner's, these boots had tromped many a bike to life. Even now, dusty and still, they itched to kick. That itch hung in the air like the peacock's unsounded cry.

Blondboy had become aware of the tenseness of the situation at last. He smiled and broke his incense and threw the smoking half into the quince bush. 'Anyhow, you shoulda dug it,' he said. 'Half a million freaks in the mud and the music.' He was beaming impishly from one participant to the other, from Deboree, to his partner, to the prancing dog, as he picked at his wide grin with the dyed end of the incense stick. 'Half a million *beautiful* people . . .'

They had all sensed it coming. Deboree had tried once more to avert it. 'Don't pay him any mind, man. Just an old stick junkie – ' but it had been a halfhearted try, and Stewart was already dropping the stick. It had barely touched the dusty boot before the squatting man scooped it up and in the same motion side-armed it into the grape arbour. Stewart bounded after it.

'Come on, man,' Deboree had pleaded. 'Don't throw it for him. He goes through wire and thorns and gets all cut up.'

'Whatever you say,' Blackbeard had replied, his face averted as he watched Stewart trotting back with the retrieved stake held high. 'Whatever's right.' Then had thrown it again as soon as Stewart dropped it, catching and slinging it all in one motion so fast and smooth that Deboree wondered if he hadn't been a professional athlete at a younger time, baseball or maybe boxing.

This time the stick landed in the pigpen. Stewart flew between the top two strands of barbed wire and had the stick before it stopped cartwheeling. It was too long for him to jump back through the wire with. He circled the pigs lying in the shade of their shelter and jumped the wooden gate at the far end of the pen.

'But. I mean, everything has got to have its trip, don't you agree?'

Deboree had not responded. He was already feeling the adrenalin burn in his throat. Besides, there was no more to say. Blackbeard stood up. Blondboy stepped close to his companion and whispered something at the hairy ear. All Devlin could make out was 'Be cool, Bob. Remember what happened in Boise, Bob. . . .'

'Everything gotta live,' Blackbeard had answered. 'And everything gotta give.'

Stewart skidded to a halt in the gravel. Blackbeard grabbed one end of the stick before the dog could release it, wrenching it viciously from the animal's teeth. This time Deboree, moving with all the speed the adrenalin could wring from his weary limbs, had stepped in front of the hitchhiker and grabbed the other end of the stick before it could be thrown.

'I *said* don't throw it.'

This time there was no averting the grin; the man looked straight at him. And Deboree had guessed right about the breath; it hissed out of the jagged mouth like a rotten wind.

'I heard what you *said*, fagbutt.'

Then they had looked at each other, over the stick grasped at each end between them. Deboree forced himself to match the other man's grinning glare with his own steady smile, but he knew it was only a temporary steadiness. He wasn't in shape for encounters of this calibre. There was a seething accusation burning from the man's eyes, unspecified, undirected, but so furious that Deboree felt his will withering before it. Through the bean stake he felt that fury assail his very cells. It was like holding a high-voltage terminal.

'Everything gotta try,' the man had said through his ragged grin, shuffling to get a better grip on his end of the stake with both leathery hands. 'And everything gotta – ' He didn't finish. Deboree had brought his free fist down, sudden and hard, and had chopped the stake in twain. Then, before the man could react, Deboree had turned abruptly away from him and swatted Stewart on the rump. The dog had yelped in surprise and run beneath the barn.

It had been a dramatic and successful manoeuvre. Both hitchhikers were impressed. Before they could recover, Deboree had pointed across the yard with the jagged end of his piece and told them, 'There's the trail to the Haight-Ashbury, guys. Vibe central.'

'Come on, Bob,' Blondboy had said, sneering at Deboree. 'Let's hit it. Forget him. He's gangrened. Like Leary and Lennon. All those high-rolling creeps. Gangrened. A power tripper.'

Blackbeard had looked at his end. It had broken off some inches shorter than Deboree's. He finally muttered, 'Whatever's shakin',' and turned on his heel.

As he sauntered back the way he had come into the yard, he drew his knife. The blond boy hurried to take up his saunter beside his partner, already murmuring and giggling up to him. Blackbeard stripped a long curving sliver of wood from his end of the stick with the blade of his knife as he walked. Another sliver followed, fluttering, like a feather.

Devlin had stood, hands on his hips, watching the chips fall from the broken stick. He had glared after them with raw eyes until they were well off the property. That was when he had hurried back up to his office to resume the search for his sunglasses.

He heard the whine again, returning, growing louder. He opened his eyes and walked back to the window and parted the tie-dye curtains. The pink car had turned around and was coming back. Entranced, he watched it pass the driveway again, but this time it squealed to a stop, backed up, and turned in. It came keening and bouncing down the dirt road toward the barn. Finally he blinked, jerked the curtain closed, and sat heavily in his swivel chair.

The car whirred to a stop in the gravel and mercifully cut its engine. He didn't move. Somebody got out, and a voice from the past shouted up at his office: 'Dev?' He'd let the curtain close too late. 'Devlinnnn?' it shouted. 'Hey, you, Devlin Deboreeeee?' A sound half hysterical and half humorous, like the sound that chick who lost her marbles in Mexico used to make, that Sandy Pawku.

'Dev? I've got news. About Houlihan. Bad news. He's dead. Houlihan's dead.'

He tipped back in his chair and closed his eyes. He didn't question the announcement. The loss seemed natural, in keeping with the season and the situation, comfortable even, and then

60

he thought, *That's it! That's what the revolution has been doing lately, to be honest. Losing!*

'Dev, are you up there? It's me, Sandy . . .'

He pushed himself standing and walked to the window and drew back the curtain. He wiped his eyes and stuck his head into the blighted afternoon. Hazy as it was, the sunlight nevertheless seemed to be sharper than usual, harsher. The chrome of the little car gleamed viciously. Like the knife blade.

'Houlihan,' he said, blinking. The dust raised by the car was reaching the barn on its own small breeze. He felt it bring an actual chill. 'Houlihan dead?' he said to the pink face lifted to him.

'Of exposure,' the voice rasped.

'When? Recently?'

'Yesterday. I just heard. I was in the airport in Oakland this morning when I ran into this little hippie chicky who knew me from Mountain View. She came up to the bar and advised me that the great Houlihan is now the late great. Yesterday, I guess. Chicky Little had just got off the plane from Puerto Sancto, where Houlihan had been staying with her and a bunch of her buddies. At a villa right down the road from where we lived. Apparently the poor maniac was drinking and taking downers and walking around at night alone, miles from nowhere. He passed out on a railroad track between Sancto and Manzanillo, where he got fatally chilled from the desert dew. Well, *you* know, Dev, how cold it can get down there after sunset.'

It was Sandy Pawku all right, but what a change! Her once long brown hair had been cropped and chromed, plated with the rusty glint of the car's grill. She had put heavy eye make-up and rouge and lipstick on her face and, over the rest of her had put on, he guessed, at least a hundred pounds.

'Dead, our hero of the sixties is, Devvy, baby. Dead, dead, dead. Of downers and drunk and the foggy, foggy dew. O, Hooly, Hooly, Hooly, you maniac. You goon. What did Kerouac call him in that book? The glorious goon?'

'No. The Holy Goof.'

'I was flying to my aunt's cottage in Seattle for a little R and R, rest and writing, you dig? But that news in Oakland – I thought, Wonder if Dev and the Animal Friends have heard? Probably not. So when the plane stopped in Eugene, I remember about this commune I hear you all got and I decided, Sandy,

61

Old Man Deboree would want to know. So Sandy, she cashes in the rest of her ticket and rents a car and here she is, thanks to Mr Mastercharge, Mr Hughes, and Mr Avis. Say, is one supposed to drive these damn tricks in D1, D2, or L? Isn't L for driving in the light and D for driving in the dark?'

'You drove that thing all the way here from the airport in low gear?'

'Might have.' She laughed, slapping the flimsy hood with a hand full of jewelled fingers. 'Right in amongst those log trucks and eighteen-wheelers, me and my pinkster, roaring with the loudest of them.'

'I'll bet.'

'When it started to smoke, I compromised with D1. Goddamn it, I mean them damn manufacturers – but listen to me rationalizing. I probably wrecked it, didn't I? To tell the truth? Be honest, Sandy. Christ knows you could use a little honesty. . . .' She rubbed the back of her neck and looked away from him, back the way she had come. 'Eee God, what is happening? Houlihan kacked. Pigpen killed by a chicken-shit liver; Terry the Tramp snuffed by spades. Ol' Sandy herself nearly down for the count a dozen times.' She began walking to and fro in the gravel. 'Man, I have been going in circles, in bummer nowhere circles, you know what I mean? Weird shit. I mean, hey listen: I just wasted a *dog* on the road back there!'

He knew he must have responded, said, 'Oh?' or 'Is that right?' or something, because she had kept talking.

'Old bitch it was, with a yardful of pups. Whammed her good.'

Sandy came around the front of the car and opened the right door. She tipped the pink seat forward and began hauling matching luggage out of the back and arranging it on the gravel, all the while relating vividly how she had come around a bend and run over a dog sleeping in the road. *Right* in the *road*. A farmwife had come out of her house at the commotion and had dragged the broken animal out of the culvert where it had crawled howling. The farmwife had felt its spine then sentenced it to be put out of its misery. At her repeated commands, her teenage son had finally fetched the shotgun from the house.

'The kid was carrying on such a weeping and wailing, he missed twice. The third time, he let go with both barrels and blew bitch bits all over the lawn. The only thing they wanted from me was six bits apiece for the bullets. I asked if they took credit cards.' She laughed. 'When I left, goddamn me if the pups weren't playing with the pieces.'

She laughed again. He remembered hearing the shots. He knew the family and the dog, a deaf spaniel, but he didn't say anything. Shading his eyes, he watched this swollen new version of the skinny Sandy of his past bustle around the luggage below him, laughing. Even her breath seemed to have gained weight, husking out of her throat with an effort. Swollen. Her neck where she had rubbed it, her wrists, her back, all swollen. But her weight actually rode lightly, defiantly, like a chip on her shoulder. *In her coloured shoes and stretch pants and a silk Hawaiian shirt pulled over her paunch, she looks like a Laguna Beach roller derby queen*, he thought, *just arriving at the rink. She looks primed*, he thought. Like the hitchhiker; an argument rigged to get off at the slightest touch. The thought of another confrontation left him weak and nauseous.

M'kehla's Great Danes discovered her in the yard and came barking. Sandy sliced at them with her pink plastic handbag. 'Get away from me, you big fuckers. You smell that other mutt on my wheels? You want the same treatment? Damn, they are big, aren't they? Get them back, can't you?'

'Their big is worse than their bite,' he told her and shouted at the dogs to go home to their bus. They paid no attention.

'What the shit, Deboree?' She sliced and swung. 'Can't you get your animals to mind?'

'They aren't mine,' he explained over the din. 'M'kehla left them here while he went gallivantin' to Woodstock with everybody else.'

'Goddamn you fuckers, *back off!*' Sandy roared. The dogs hesitated, and she roared louder. '*Off! Off!* Clear *off!*' They shrunk back. Sandy hooted gleefully and kicked gravel after them until they broke into a terrified dash. Sandy gave chase, hooting their retreat all the way to the bus, out of his view.

The ravens were flying again. The sun was still slicing a way through the impacted smoke. The radio was playing 'Good Vibrations' by The Beach Boys. Back in the yard below, at her luggage, Sandy was humming along, her hysteria calmed by her victory over the dogs. She found the bag she had been searching for, the smallest in a six-piece set that looked brand-new. She opened it and took out a bottle of pills. Deboree watched as she shook out at least a dozen. She threw the whole handful into her

63

mouth and began digging again into the case for something to wash them down with.

'Ol' Thandy'th been platheth and theen thingth thinth Mexico,' she told him, trying to keep all the pills in her mouth and bring him up to date at the same time. Seen lots of water under the bridges, she let him know, sometimes too much. Bridges washed out. Washed out herself a time or two, she told him. Got pretty mucked up. Even locked up. But with the help of some ritzy doctors and her rich daddy, she'd finally got bailed out and got set up being half owner of a bar in San Juan Capistrano; then become a drunk, then a junkie, then a blues singer *non*-professional; found Jesus, and Love, and Another Husband – 'Minithter of the Univerthal Church of Latterday Thontha-bitcheth!' – then got p.g., got an abortion, got disowned by her family, and got divorced; then got depressed, as he could well understand, and put on a little weight, as he could see; then – Sunday, *now* – was looking for a place where a gal might lay back for a while.

'A plathe to read and write and take a few barbth to mellow out,' she said through the pills.

'A few!' he said, remembering her old barbiturate habit. 'That's no "few".' The thought of having more than one carcass to dispose of alarmed him finally into protest. 'Damn you, Sandy, if you up and O.D. on me now, so help me – '

She held up her hand. 'Vitamin theeth. Croth my heart.' Pawing through a boil of lingerie, she at last had found the silver flask she had been seeking. She unscrewed the lid and threw back her head. He watched her neck heave as the pills washed down. She wiped her mouth with her forearm and laughed up at him.

'Don't worry, Granny,' she said. 'Just some innocent little vitamins. Even the dandy little Sandy of old never took *that* many downers at once. She might someday, though. Never can tell. Who the hell knows what anybody's gonna do this year? It's the year of the downer, you know, so who knows? Just let it roll by. . . .' She returned the flask to the suitcase and snapped it shut. Rayon and Orlon scalloped out all around like a piecrust to be trimmed. 'Now. Where does Sandy take a wee-wee and wash out her Kotex?'

He pointed, and she went humming off to the corner of the barn. The big dogs came to the door of their bus and growled

64

after her. Deboree watched as she ducked under the clothesline and turned the corner. He heard the door slam behind her.

He stayed at the window, feeling there was more to be revealed. Everything was so tense and restrained. The wash hung tense in the smoky air, like strips of jerky. The peacock, his fan moulted to a dingy remnant of its springtime elegance, stepped out of the quince bush where he had been visiting his mate and flew to the top of one of the clothesline poles. Deboree thought the bird would make his cry when he reached the top, but he didn't. He perched atop the pole and bobbed his head this way and that at the end of his long neck, as though gauging the tension. After watching the peacock for a while, he let the curtain close and moved from the window back to his desk; he too found he could be content to let it roll by without resolution.

Over the radio The Doors were demanding that it be brought on through to the other side. Wasn't Morrison dead? He couldn't remember. All he could be sure of was that it was 1969 and the valley was filled to the foothills with smoke as 300,000 acres of stubble were burned so lawn-seed buyers in subdivision in California wouldn't have to weed a single interloper from their yards.

Tremendous.

The bathroom door slammed again. He heard the plastic heels crunch past below; one of M'kehla's dogs followed, barking tentatively. The dog followed the steps around the other corner, barking in a subdued and civilized voice. The bitch Great Dane, he recognized. Pedigreed. She had barked last night, too. Out in the field. Betsy had got out of bed and shouted up the stairs at him to go check what was the matter out there. He hadn't gone. Was that what offed the lamb? One of M'kehla's Great Danes? He liked to think so. It made him pleasantly angry to think so. Just like a Marin County spade to own two blond Great Danes and go off and leave them marooned. Too many strays. Somebody should go down to that bus and boot some pedigreed ass. But he remained seated, seeking fortification behind his desk, and turned up the music against the noise. Once he heard a yelping as Sandy ran the bitch back to the bus. Sometimes a little breeze would open the curtain and he could see the peacock still sitting on the clothesline pole, silently bobbing his head. Eventually he heard the steps return, enter the barn below, and find the wooden stairs. They mounted briskly and crossed the floor of the loft. Sandy came through his door without knocking.

'Some great place, Dev,' she said. 'Funky but great. Sandy gave herself the tour. You got places for everything, don't you? For pigs and chickens and everything. Places to wee-wee, places to eat, places to write letters.'

Deboree saw the pitch coming but couldn't stop her chatter.

'Look, I blew the last of my airline ticket to Seattle renting that pink panther because I knew you'd want Sandy to bring you the sad news in person. No, that's all right, save the thanksies. No need. She *does* need, though, a little place to write some letters. Seriously, Dev, I saw a cabin down by the pond with paper and envelopes and everything. How about Sandy uses that cabin a day or so? To write a letter to her dear mother and her dear probation officer and her dear ex et cetera. Also maybe catch up on her journal. Hey, I'm writing up our Mexico campaign for a rock'n'roll rag. Are you ready for *that*?'

He tried to explain to her that the pond cabin was a meditation chapel, not some Camp David for old campaigners to compile their memoirs. Besides, he had planned to use it tonight. She laughed, told him not to worry.

'I'll find me a harbour for tonight. Then we'll see.'

He stayed at his desk. Chattering away, Sandy prowled his office until she found the shoe box and proceeded to clean and roll the last of his grass. He still didn't want to smoke, not until he was finished with that dead lamb. When he shook his head at the offered joint, she shrugged and smoked it all, explaining in detail how she would refill his box to overflowing with the scams she had cooking in town this afternoon, meeting so-and-so at such and such to barter this and that. He couldn't follow it. He felt flattened before her steamrolling energy. Even when she dropped the still-lit roach from the window to the dry grass below, he was only able to make the feeblest protest.

'Careful of fire around barn?' She whooped, bending over him. 'Why, Mistah Deboree, if you ain't getting to be the fussy little farmer.' She clomped to the door and opened it. 'So. Sandy's making a run. Anything you need from town? A new typewriter? A better radio – how can you listen to good music on that Jap junk? A super Swiss Army? Ho ho. Just tell Sandy Claus. Anything?'

She stood in the opened door, waiting. He swivelled in his

chair, but he didn't get up. He looked at her fat grin. He knew what she was waiting for. The question. He also knew better than to ask it. Better to let it slide than encourage any relationship by seeming curious. But he was curious, and she was waiting, grinning at him, and he finally had to ask it:

'Did he, uh, *say* anything, Sandy?' His voice was thick in his throat.

The black eyes glistened at him from the doorway. 'You mean, don'cha, were there any, uh, *last words?* Any *sentences commuted*, any *parting wisdoms?* Why, as a matter of fact, in the hospital, it seems, before he went into a coma, he did rally a moment and now wait, let me see. . . .'

She was gloating. His asking had laid his desperation naked. She grinned. There he sat, Deboree, the Guru Gung Ho with his eyes raw, begging for some banner to carry on with, some comforter of last-minute truth quilted by Old Holy Goof Houlihan, a wrap against the chilly chaos to come.

'Well, yep, our little hippie chick did mention that he said a few words before he died on that Mexican mattress,' she said. 'And isn't that irony for you? It's that *same ratty Puerto Sancto* clinic where Behema had her kid and Mickey had his broken leg wherein our dear Hooly died, of pneumonia and exposure and downers. Come on! Don'cha think that is pretty stinking ironic?'

'What were they?'

The eyes glistened. The grin wriggled in its nest of fat. 'He said – if Sandy's memory serves – said, I think it was, "Sixty-four thousand nine hundred and twenty-eight." Quite a legacy, don'cha think? A number, a stinking number!' She hooted, slapping her hips. 'Sixty-four thousand nine hundred and twenty-eight! Sixty-four thousand nine hundred and twenty-eight! The complete cooked-down essence of the absolute burned-out speed freak: sixty-four thousand nine hundred and twenty-eight! *Huh-woow woow wow!*'

She left without closing the door, laughing, clacking down the steps and across the gravel. The injured machine whined pitifully as she forced it back out the drive.

So now observe him, after the lengthy preparation just documented (it had been actually three days and was going on four nights), finally confronting his task in the field: Old Man Deboree, desperate and dreary, with his eyes naked to the smoky sun, striding across the unbroken ground behind a red wheelbarrow. Face bent earthward, he watches the field pass beneath his shoes and nothing else, trusting the one-wheeled machine to lead him to his destination.

Like Sandy's neck, he fancies himself swollen with an unspecified anger, a great smouldering of unlaid blame that longed to bloom to a great blaze. Could he but fix it on a suitable culprit. Searching for some target large enough to take his fiery blame, he fixes again on California. *That's* where it comes from, he decides. Like those two weirdo prickhikers, and Sandy Pawku, and the Oakland hippie chick who must have been one of that Oakland bunch of pillheads who lured Houlihan back down to Mexico last month . . . all from California! It all started in California, went haywire in California, and now spreads out from California like a crazy tumour under the hide of the whole continent. Woodstock. Big time. Craziness waxing fat. Craziness surviving and prospering and gaining momentum while the Fastestmanalive downs himself dead without any legacy left behind but a psycho's cipher. Even those Great Danes – from California!

The wheelbarrow reaches the ditch. He raises his head. He still cannot see the carcass. Turning down into the ditch, he pushes on toward the place where the three ravens whirl cursing in and out of the tall weeds.

'Afternoon, gents. Sorry about the interruption.'

The birds circle, railing at his approach. The wheel of the barrow is almost on top of the lamb before Deboree sees it. He is amazed at the elegance of the thing lying before him: a rich garment, not black at all, not nearly, more the reddish brown of devil's food cake. A little chocolate lambie cake, served for some little prince's birthday on a tray of purple vetch, garlanded with clover blossoms, decorated with elegant swirls and loops of red ant trails and twinkling all over with yellow jackets, like little candles. He blows them out with a wave of his hat. The three ravens swoop away to take up positions on the three nearest fence posts. Black wings outspread, they watch in imperious silence as Deboree flaps the ants away and bends to inspect the carcass.

'What got him, gents? Any ideas?' Betsy was right; not a tooth mark to be found. Maybe the dogs were running him and he tripped in the ditch and broke his neck. 'He looks too healthy to just up and die, don't you birds think?'

68

The ravens rock from foot to foot and advance no theories. They are so righteously disgruntled that Deboree has to smile at them. He considers leaving the carcass where it is on the ground, to be attended to by the ravens and bees and ants and the rest of Nature's undertakers. Then he hears the mother bleating again from the ash grove where Betsy tethered her.

'I guess not. No sense in agony for ecology's sake. I'm gonna have to bury him, boys, to get him off his mom's mind. You can sympathize. . . .'

Not in the slightest, the ravens make it clear as soon as they see their rightful spoils being lifted into the wheelbarrow. They rise from their separate posts, beating the air with their wings and calling. They flap into a circling formation above the wheel-barrow, calling together in perfect cadence as they follow all the way through the pasture to the swamp at the other end of the seventy acres. Sometimes the circle rises higher than the cottonwood tops so their continual rain of abuse sounds almost musical in the distance. Other times they circle close enough that Deboree could have swatted them with the spade.

He picks a shady spot under an overhanging oak and sticks the spade into the dirt. It's clay: mud in winter, baked concrete in summer. It would be easier digging up by the pond, but he likes it here. It's hidden and cool. The arms of the old scrub oak are ceremoniously draped with long grey-green shrouds of Spanish moss. The pinched, dry oak leaves are motionless. Even the ravens have abandoned their raucous tirade and are watching in silence from a branch in the tallest of the cottonwoods.

He hangs his hat on an oak stob and sets to digging, furiously now that he has chosen the site, hacking and stamping and chopping at the mat of clay and roots until his lungs wheeze and the dust runs off his face in gullies of sweat. He finally wipes his eyes with the hem of his shirt and stands back from the simple black basin. 'Ought to be deeper if we want to keep the foxes from smelling it and digging it up.' He looks down into the hole, panting and shaking so violently that he has to support himself with the shovel. 'But then, on the other hand,' he decides, 'it's deep enough for folk music, as they say,' and tips the corpse into the hole. To make it fit he has to bend the front legs back against the chest and force the hind legs together. It looks actually cute this way, he concedes, a kid's woolly doll. Hardly used. Just have to sew on a couple of bright new buttons for eyes, be good as new.

Then the trembling starts to get worse. *This must be how they begin*, he thinks. Freak-outs. Breakdowns. Crack-ups. Eventually shut-ins and finally cross-offs. But first the cover-up . . .

He spoons the earth back into the hole over the little animal much slower than he had dug it out. He can feel that he has blistered both hands. He wishes he'd remembered to bring his gloves. He wishes Sandy hadn't smoked his last joint. He wishes he had his glasses. Most of all, he wishes he'd thought to bring some liquid relief. His throat is on fire. There is water back up at the stock tub, a short walk away, but water isn't enough. There are fires in more than the throat that need attention. And no hope in the house. Why hadn't he driven to the liquor store in Creswell before he started this flight? Always good to have a parachute. Never know when some unexpected downdraft might pop up, throw the best flier into a tailspin. He closes his eyes and frowns, examining the possibilities. No downers, no tranquillizers, no prescription painkillers even. All went with the main troops on the Woodstock campaign. Not even any wine left at the house, and Betsy still off with the only working vehicle.

In short, no parachutes nowhere.

He begins to shudder uncontrollably, his teeth chattering. He's afraid he is having a stroke or a seizure. They run in the family, fits. Uncle Nathan Whittier had a seizure slopping the hogs in Arkansas, fell into the sty, and the hogs ate him. No hogs here, just those ravens up there and these still oaks and, over there, in another little glade only a dozen yards deeper into the swamp, atop a stump in a beam of smoky sunlight, by the grace of God, a gallon of red wine? Burgundy? From the heavens a bottle of burgundy?

He drops the spade and reels through the branches and banners of moss until he has the bottle in his hands. It *is* a wine bottle, cheap Gallo to be sure but still half full and cool in the shady bottom air. He unscrews the top and upends the bottle and drinks in long swallows until he loses his equilibrium and has to lower his head. He turns around and sits on the stump until he catches his balance, then tips his head back for the bottle again. He doesn't stop swallowing until his lungs demand it. There is less than a fourth remaining after his unbroken

70

guzzle, and he can feel the liquid already spreading through his body's knotted thoroughfares, already bringing relief.

It's only then that he notices that it is not a light, dry 12-per cent burgundy after all but a syrupy sweet 18-per cent wino port with a bouquet just like he'd smelled out of Blackbeard's mouth a couple of hours back. He looks around and sees two raggedy bedrolls, a World War I shoulder pack, and the remains of a small fire. There is a dog-eared pile of underground comics beside one bedroll and a paperback *On the Road*. In the other bedroll's area lies a pile of shavings, idly whittled slivers, some as thin as the fallen cottonwood leaves.

'So this is why they were up the road from this direction, not down from the highway direction like every other pilgrim. Asshole bums . . .'

But there is no heat in the curse. He tips up the bottle again, more thoughtfully now, and somewhat curious. Maybe they're more than bums.

'Team,' he says to the ravens, 'I think we ought to put a stakeout on these assholes.'

The birds don't disagree. They seem to have already begun the vigil, hunching their heads deep into their black breasts and settling down on their limbs in the smoky air. Deboree picks up the paperback and the stack of comics and retreats to the wheelbarrow, his finger still hooked in the gallon's glass handle. He selects a blackberry patch about twenty steps from the camp and bores into the brambles from behind, using the wheelbarrow as a plough and the spade like a machete until he has cleared a comfortable observation post in the centre of the thorny vines. He tilts the wheelbarrow up and packs it with the Spanish moss from an overhanging oak limb until the rusty old bucket is as comfortable as any easy chair. He settles into his nest, arranging the leaves in front of his face so he can easily see out without having to touch the vines, and takes another long drink of the sweet wine.

The shadows climb slowly up the tree trunks. The ravens desert, squawking off to their respective roosts after a disappointing day. The air turns a deeper red as the sun, dropping to the horizon, has even more smoke to penetrate. The wine goes down as the Checkered Demon and Mr Natural and the Furry Freak Brothers flip past his eyes. At last there is only an inch left, and the paperback. He's read it three times before. Years ago. Before heading off to California. Hoping to sign on in some way, to join that joyous voyage, like thousands of other volunteers inspired by the same book, and its vision, and, of course, its incomparable hero.

Like all the other young candidates for beatitude, he had prowled North Beach's famous hangouts – City Lights, The Place, The Coffee Gallery, The Bagel Shop – hoping to catch a glimpse of that lightning-mouthed character that Kerouac had called Dean Moriarty in *On the Road* and that John Clellon Holmes had named Hart Kennedy in *Go*, maybe eavesdrop on one of his high-octane hipalogues, perhaps even get a chance to be a big-eyed passenger on one of his wild rapping runs around the high spots of magic San Francisco. But he had never imagined much more, certainly not the jackpot of associations that followed, the trips, the adventures, the near disasters – and, worse danger, the near successes that almost put Houlihan on stage. Houlihan was Lenny Bruce, Jonathan Winters, and Lord Buckley all together just for starters. He couldn't have helped but been a hit. But a nightclub format would have pinched his free-flying mind, and no stage in the world could have really accommodated his art – his hurtling, careening, corner-squealing commentary on the cosmos – except the stage he built about himself the moment he slid all quick and sinewy under the steering wheel of a good car: the bigger, the boatier, the more American, the better. The glow of the dash was his footlights, the slash of oncoming sealed beams was his spots. And now, and now, and now the act is over. No more would that rolling theatre ever come bouncing and steaming and blaring rhythm and blues and Houlihan hoopla up the drive all full of speed and plans and hammering hearts.

For now, now, now, the son of a bitch is dead.

And, with the last inch of wine lifted in a salute before finishing it, Deboree begins to weep. It is not a sweet grief, but bitter and bleak. He tries to stop it. He opens the familiar Kerouac paperback, looking for some passages that will wash out that bitter burn, but the tears won't let him focus. It's getting dark. He closes the book and his eyes both, and enters again the library of his memory, looking under H. Looking for Houlihan, Hero, High Priest of the Highway, Hammer-tosser, Head-twister, Hoper Springing Eternally. Or maybe not so. Now it is the disciple, looking and hoping, hoping to ward off the circling

72

heralds of desolation with some kind of gallant scarecrow, stuffed with some strawhead records showing just who this wondrous Houlihan was, what his frenetic life had meant, stood for, died for. Hoping to stave off the mockery of his hero's senseless death and to buttress himself against those bleak digits by checking out a collection of inspirational Houlihan aphorisms (Six four nine two eight: the complete works of another one of those Best Minds of Their Generation!), anecdotes, anything!

But the section is empty. The H shelf has been stripped, the works all recalled, out of print, confiscated as invalid in the light of Latest Findings. Deboree laughs aloud at his library metaphor and finds his throat dried almost hard. He drinks the last of the wine as though he is fighting a brush fire. 'Year of the downer,' he says, speaking up through the little arch of berry vines, watching the last rays of the rusty sun fade from the tops of the cottonwoods, staring until the last smoulder has drifted away and the wine has carried him back into the forlorn stacks and shelves of his memory. This time he finds a slim volume – not under H at all but under L – about the time Houlihan the famous Fastestmanalive met the renowned Stanford Strongman, Lars Dolf, and lost to Dolf in man-to-man charismatic warfare. Under L, for losing. . . .

During the late fifties and early sixties, these two giants had towered over the budding Bay Area revolutionaries. Both men were titans of their own special and singular philosophies. Owing to his appearance as a hero in a number of nationally distributed novels, Houlihan's rep was the greater, the more widespread. But in his own area, Lars Dolf was Houlihan's equal. Everybody that had any touch with the hip life on the peninsula had heard of Lars. And because of his Bay Area proselytizing for a Buddhist seminary, many had met him personally and were all in awe of his soft-spoken power.

One spring partying evening, Lars Dolf had dropped into the Deboree house, across the street from the Stanford golf course. Dolf claimed he had heard of Devlin, and he wanted to meet him, and he was open to invitations, especially concerning wine. Deboree saw immediately that they were due to argue – it was in the way the man placed his feet – and passed him the bottle.

It was first over art. Lars was an unknown painter, and Deboree could match him that in the field of writing. Then over philosophy. Lars was a greying, wine-torn Zen beatnik champ,

73

and young Devlin was a psychedelic challenger with a higher-than-wine insinuation. And, eventually, naturally, over the much more ancient and basic issue: physical prowess. This category happened to be Devlin's strong point during that time. He was driving three times a week to the Olympic Club in San Francisco hoping to represent the United States in freestyle wrestling in the upcoming Rome Olympics. Lars was also the bearer of such laurels: the All-American Stanford linebacker dropout Kraut. Tales about him were many. The most memorable and oft repeated described him taking on a truckful of Mexican artichoke pickers at a Columbus Day picnic in Pescadero and fighting them to their own national stand-off; when local deputies stopped the battle and an ambulance driver examined Lars, the broken points of three Tijuana switchblades were found sticking out of his great round shoulders.

Deboree can't remember who started the contests that day on the Lane. Probably he himself, with one of the trick feats he had learned from his father, probably going through the broom so supple that Lars Dolf didn't even uncross his legs to try. Then, as he recalls it, the spotlight was wrested from Devlin by his brother Bud, who was down from Oregon for some culture. Buddy went through the broom both forward and backward, which Devlin never had been able to do. It was Buddy who started the Indian wrestling.

Standing palm to palm and instep to instep, Buddy flipped through one after the other of the gang of awkward grad students, besting them each so easily that he became embarrassed with his one-sided victories and was about to turn the centre ring back to Deboree (who hadn't challenged him; the Indian-wrestling issue had long before and many times been decided between the brothers; Devlin was heavier and older and longer reached) when Lars Dolf spoke from his lotus position near the wine:

'Ex-cuse me. May . . . I . . . try?'

He remembers the way Lars spoke, deliberately slow and simple. He always addressed a listener in odd, singsong phrases that might have seemed retarded but for the twinkle behind his tiny eyes. That and the fact that he had been an honour student in mathematics before he left the Leland Stanford Jr Farm for North Beach.

Now, observe Buddy and Buddha standing there in the middle
74

of a 1962 beer-and-bongos council ring. Observe Buddy, blushing and grinning, enjoying his prowess at the game not out of any sense of competitiveness but out of playfulness, playing only, as all their family had been raised to play, for fun; win, lose, or chicken out. And now see standing opposite Buddy this opponent of entirely different breed, hardly seeming part of the same species, in fact seeming more mechanical than animal, with legs like pistons, chest like a boiler, close-cropped head like a pink cannonball set with two twinkling bluesteel bearings, planting a bare foot beside Buddy's and offering a chubby doll-pink hand:

'Shall . . . *we* . . . try?'

Buddy took the hand. They braced, waited the unspoken length of decorum, then Buddy heaved. The squat form didn't budge. Buddy heaved the opposite direction. Still no movement. Buddy drew a quick breath for another heave but instead found himself sailing across the room, into the wall, leaving the impression of his shoulder and head in the particle board.

Lars Dolf had not seemed to move. He stood, grinning, as inert and immobile and, despite the expression on his round face, as humourless as a fireplug. Buddy stood up, shaking his head.

'Dang,' he marvelled. 'That was something.'

'Care to try . . . again?'

And again his brother was sent flying to the wall, and again and again, each time getting up and coming back to take the pink hand without any kind of anger or chagrin or hurt pride but with Buddy's usual curiosity. Any marvel of the physical world interested Buddy, and this squat mystery tossing him to and fro absolutely fascinated him.

'Dang. Something else. Let me try that again. . . .'

What the mystery was Deboree couldn't see. Squat or not, Dolf still probably outweighed Buddy by close to a hundred pounds.

'He's just got too much meat and muscle on you, Bud,' Deboree had said, his voice testy. He didn't like the way his little brother was being tossed around.

'It isn't the weight,' Buddy answered, panting a little as he got up to take his stance before Dolf again. 'And it isn't the muscle, exactly. . . .'

'It's where a man . . . thinks from,' Dolf explained, grinning back at Buddy. There didn't seem to be any hostility coming from him, or any cruelty, but Deboree wished they would stop. 'When a man thinks from . . . *here*' – incredibly sudden, the pink hand shot out, one bullet-blunt finger extended. It stopped less than a quarter inch from poking a hole between Buddy's eyes – 'instead of *here*' – his other hand came forward from the hip in a hard fist, right at Buddy's belt buckle, this time stopping even nearer and opening, like a gentle flower, to spread over Buddy's solar plexus – 'he is of course . . . unbalanced. Like a Coca-Cola bottle . . . balanced mouth-to-mouth with another Coke bottle: too much weight *above* . . . and *below* . . . and no connection in the middle. See . . . what I mean? A man must have balance, like a haiku.'

It had been too pompous for Deboree to let pass. 'What I see is less like poetry and more like ninety pounds Buddy is giving away.'

'Then you try him,' Buddy had challenged. 'I'm curious to see how you do, hotshot, giving away only maybe a third of that.'

The moment he took Lars Dolf's hand he had understood Buddy's curiosity. Though he knew the round little form still had the advantage by perhaps two dozen pounds, he could feel immediately that the difference was not one of weight. Nor was it speed; during his last three seasons on the Oregon team Deboree had been able to tell within the first few seconds of the opening round whether his opponent had the jump on him. And this man's reactions were almost slothlike compared to those of a collegiate wrestler. The difference was in a kind of ungodly strength. He remembers thinking, as Dolf snatched him from the floor with a flick of his forearm and hurled him through the air into a crowd of awestruck undergraduates watching from the daybed, bongos mute in their laps, that this would be what it was like to Indian-wrestle a 250-pound ant.

Like his brother, Deboree had risen and returned to battle without any sense of shame or defeat. To take the hand, to be thrown again and again and return again and again, more out of amazement and curiosity than any sense of masculine combativeness.

'It's where you think from, do you begin to see? The eye that seeks the lotus . . . never sees the lotus. Only the search can it see. The eye that searches for nothing . . . finds . . . the garden in full bloom. Desire in the head . . . makes a hollow in the centre . . . makes a man . . . *ahm!*' – as he threw Deboree into

76

the particleboard wall, with its growing array of dents and craters – 'unbalanced.'

When Lars Dolf left after that evening, he took three of the undergraduates back to the city with him – two psychology majors and a frat boy who had not yet settled on a field – to enrol them in the Buddhist seminary on Jackson Street, never mind that spring term at Stanford was only two weeks short of over. Deboree himself was so impressed that he was half considering such a transfer until Lars informed him that the sutra classes began at four in the morning six days a week. He decided to stick it out at the writing seminar instead, which only met three times a week, and at three in the afternoon, and over coffee and cookies. But, like his brother and everyone else, he had been awestruck. And Lars Dolf had reigned as the undisputed phenomenon of the peninsula until the next fall, when a Willys jeep with a transmission blown from driving it too far too fierce too fast had brought Houlihan into his yard and his life.

The famous Houlihan. With his bony Irish face dancing continually and simultaneously through a dozen expressions, his sky-blue eyes flirting up from under long lashes, and with his reputation and his unstoppable rap, Houlihan became a sensation around the Stanford bongo circuit before the tortured jeep had hardly stopped steaming. He was a curiosity easily equal to Lars Dolf in charisma and character and, without the heavy-handed oriental dogma, a lot more fun to be around.

There were, in fact, no real similarities between the two men. But comparisons could not be avoided. As fast as Dolf was phlegmatic, as sinewy and animated as Dolf was thick and solid, poor Houlihan was matched with the Buddhist Bull before he was even aware of an opponent's existence. By mid-fall term, all the talk in the hip Palo Alto coffeehouses was about the latest Houlihan blitz – how he had climbed on stage during Allen Ginsberg's reading in Dinkelspiel Auditorium, without a shirt or shoes, carrying a flashlight in one hand and a flyswatter in the other, to stalk invisible scurriers about the podium: 'Maybe so, Ginsy, but I saw the best mice of *my* generation destroyed by good 'ol American grit – *there's* one take that you rodent you oop only winged 'em there he goes anyhow – you were saying? Don't let *me* interrupt'; how he had talked the San Mateo deputy sheriff into giving his stalled sedan a jump start instead of a speeding ticket after being pulled over on Bayshore, and, so

77

persuasive and brain-boggling was Houlihan's rap, got away with the cop's cables in the bargain; how he had seduced the lady psychiatrist who had been sent by a distraught and wealthy Atherton mother to save a daughter deranged by five days' living in the back of the family's station wagon with this maniac, *and* the mother who had sent her when they all got back to Atherton, *and* the nurse the family had hired to protect the daughter from further derangement. Usually, eventually, these coffeehouse tales of Houlihan's heroics were followed by conjecture about future feats and finally, inevitably, about the meeting of the two heroes.

'Wonder if Houlihan'll be able to mess with Lars Dolf's mind like that? Should they ever lock horns, I mean. . . .'

Deboree saw the historic encounter. It took place in the driveway of a tall, dark-browed, spectral law student named Felix Rommel, who claimed to be the grandson of the famous German general. No one had given much credence to the claim until a huge crate arrived from Frankfurt containing – Felix had announced – his grandfather's Mercedes. Lars Dolf had been phoned to find out if he would like to see this classic relic from his fatherland. He arrived on a bicycle. There was a champagne party on Felix's wide San Mateo lawn while the car was ceremoniously uncrated and rolled backward into the garage under the lights, grey and gleaming. Lars looked it over carefully, smiling at the double-headed eagle still perched on the radiator cap and some of the Desert Fox's maps and scrawled messages Felix showed him in the glove compartment. 'It is a beaut,' he told everybody.

The car had been carefully preserved, unscratched except for the right side of the front bumper, which had been bent in shipping and was crimped against the tyre. Felix even started the engine with a jump from Deboree's panel. Everybody drank champagne in the yard while the big engine idled in the garage. Felix asked Dolf if he would like to drive it when the bumper got straightened, that there might be a chauffeur's job open as soon as the California bar exams allowed Felix to practise. Felix said he couldn't legally drive it himself for another nine months because of a DUIL, and his wife wouldn't drive it because she was Jewish, 'So I need somebody.'

Dolf was politely thanking the couple for the offer but was saying he would probably stick with his old Schwinn – 'For *my*

78

German vehicle' – when into the drive came a steaming, lurching '53 Chevy with a noisy rod about to blow under the hood and noisier driver already blowing wild behind the wheel. Houlihan was out the door and into the startled yard before the signal from the ignition had reached the poor motor, shirtless and sweating and jabbering, zooming around to open the other doors for his usual entourage of shell-shocked passengers, introducing each to everybody, digressing between introductions about the day's events, the trip down from the city, the bad rod, the good tyres, the lack of gas, and grass, and ass, and of course the need for speed – 'Anybody? Anybody? With the well-known leapers? Bennies? Dexies? Uh? Preludins even? Oops? I say something wrong?' – admonishing himself for his manners and his hectic habits, complimenting Felix on his idling heirloom, kicking the tyres, clicking his heels and saluting the two-headed hood ornament, starting all over again, introducing his bedraggled crew again only with the names all different . . . a typical Houlihan entrance that might have gone on uninterrupted until his departure minutes or hours later, if Felix hadn't distracted him with a huge joint that he drew out of his vest pocket as though he'd been saving it for this very occasion. And while Houlihan was holding the first vein-popping lungful of smoke, Felix led him by the elbow to the little cement bench in the shadow of the acacia where Lars Dolf had retreated to sit in full lotus and watch. Without speaking, Dolf had slowly untwined his legs and stood to take Houlihan's hand. Houlihan had resumed his chatter, the words spilling out as irrepressible as the smoke:

'Dolf? Dolf? Didn't I, yass I did hear tell of a fella supposed to have confiscated all the switchblades in Ensenada – or was it Juárez? – went by that name Lars Dolf, also by the nick of "Snub", Snub Dolf the sportswriters called him, used to be a footballer, all-something, all-defensive something of the something, forsook future with the Forty-niners for meditation, which, the way I see it, correct me if I'm wrong, is mainly the exchange of one coach and his philosophy for another coach and another game plan – same game – single wing 'stead of double – this meditation practice probably just as beneficial as tackling practice – rather beat off, myself personally, if it's for spiritual purposes we are considering. . . .'

And on and on, in a fashion best left inimitable, until the

round, grinning face and the ominously unblinking eyes began to affect Houlihan in a manner none of the fans had ever witnessed before. In the face of Dolf's deliberate silence, Houlihan began to stammer. His rap began to rattle and run down. Finally, with his brow creased over the same mystery that Buddy and Deboree had encountered Indian wrestling, Houlihan stuttered to a rare stop. Dolf continued to smile, holding on to Houlihan's hand, watching him fidget in his unaccustomed silence and humiliation. Nobody broke the silence as the moment of victory and defeat was wordlessly accepted and formalized.

When the victor felt that his power had been sufficiently acknowledged by this silence, Dolf let go the hand and said, softly, 'That is the way . . . *you* see it, Mr Houlihan.'

Houlihan could not retort. He was buffaloed. The dozen or so spectators smiled inside and congratulated themselves on being present during the decisive settling of this historic duel. They had all known it all along. When it comes right down to it, the mouth is no match for the muscle. Houlihan turned away from the grinning puzzle, seeking some route of escape. His eyes fell again on the idling Mercedes.

'Well on the other hand hey, what say, Felix, that we take 'er for a little turn?' He was already opening the right side door to climb behind the steering wheel. 'Just round the block . . .'

''Fraid it would have to be one way around,' Felix said casually, hands in his pockets as he followed around the front of the car after Houlihan. He took him by a naked arm and drew him back out of the car. He pointed at the bent bumper with his long chin. 'Until we get that straightened, the best you could do is keep going in circles.'

'Ah, cocksuck,' Houlihan grunted, looking down at the wedged tyre in disappointment. It was the first time Deboree had ever heard him use the word. On the contrary, Houlihan was often heard correcting others for cursing; he claimed it was spiritual sloth to allow oneself to stoop to obscenity. But this didn't sound like sloth to Deboree. It sounded more like desperation.

'Cock *suck*,' he said again and started to walk away. But Dolf wasn't finished rubbing it in.

'You don't have to . . . keep going in . . . circles.' Dolf was coming into the garage, walking around the grill, smiling his merciless little Zen smile. 'You just have to be . . . strong enough . . . to straighten the problem out.'

And while everybody's eyes popped, the little chubby hands reached down and hooked on each side of the bumper, and the back bulged in a ragged turtleneck and, as smoothly and inexorably as some kind of powerful hydraulic device intended for this very work, pulled the heavy metal away from the tyre and back into proper place. Gawking, jawhanging, Houlihan couldn't even curse. He left, muttering something about needing to crash, maybe at an ex-wife's digs in Santa Clara, someplace alone, his crew abandoned on the lawn.

In the years of association that followed, as they became close comrades in adventure and escapade and revolution (yes, damn it, revolution! as surely as Fidel and Che had been comrades, against the same tyranny of inertia, in the guerrilla war that was being fought, as Burroughs put it, in 'the space between our cells'), Deboree often saw Houlihan at a loss for words, or, more specifically, at an emptiness of words after days of speeding and driving and talking nonstop had left the dancing Irish voice raw and blistered and the enormous assets of cocky self-made intellect momentarily overdrawn, but never again so completely stymied. At least not so blatantly stymied. For Houlihan had a trick of filling the lapses with meaningless numbers – 'Hey, you dig just then that lovely little loop-the-loop cutie doin' the ol' four five seventy-seven jive back thar on the corner Grant and Green, or was it eighty-seven?' – until his stream of consciousness commenced to trickle again and he got back on the track. Nonsense numbers to fill the gaps. An obvious trick, but none of his audience ever saw it as something to cover a failure. It was just noise to keep the rhythm going, just rebop until he found the groove again. And he always seemed to. 'Keep rollin' and you'll always eventually cross your line again.' And that faith that saw him through his lapses had become a faith for everybody that knew him, a mighty bridge, to see them across their own chasms. Now the bridge was washed out. Now, at long last, it did seem that he had lost it for good, in terminal nonsense and purposeless, meaningless numbers of nothing. Forever.

Worse! That it had *all* been a trick, that he had never known purpose, that for all the sound and fury, those grand flights, those tootings, had all, always, at bottom, been only rebop, only the rattle of insects in the dry places of Eliot, signifying nothing.

81

Forever and ever amen.

So. Strung out and distracted and drunk in the dark, Deboree starts awake in his nest of moss in the wheelbarrow in the blackberry bush. Through the darkness he hears again the twang made when fence wire is strained, its barbs plunking through the staples as the barrier is breached by a head of stock forcing its way through, where no breach is intended, or by a foot climbing over. The twang is followed by a curse and a chorus of giggles and the crashing of sticks. He leans forward in his nest far enough to see a battery-powered lantern wheeling through the shadows of the cottonwoods that line the border of his swamp and his neighbour Hock's pasture. Followed by more crashings and cursing, the light comes toward him, erratically, until it breaks into the clearing around the stump and is hung from a branch. It is the two hitchhikers loaded with packages and sacks, followed by Sandy Pawku. Sandy is carrying an enormous stuffed teddy bear. So loudly is she cursing and staggering about with the bear that the blond puts down his load and turns back to hush her.

'Cool it, huh? You want that old fart and his dogs down here?'

'I don't want that old fart and his dogs at *all*,' Sandy answers. 'You two farts will do, to share . . . for Sandy and her bear.'

Fascinated, Deboree watches from the brambles as Sandy waltzes in a slow circle, then leans the huge doll against the stump and sits in its lap. 'Give us a hand,' she says, picking at the button of the collar taut across her throat, 'an' a drink.' Blackbeard draws a half gallon of wine from one of the grocery sacks. He uncorks it and drinks beneath the gently swinging light, his eyes on the fat woman and the doll. He lowers the bottle and takes a big summer sausage from the other sack and begins to chew the plastic wrapping away. Blondboy kneels beside Sandy, giggling, to help with the buttons of her blouse. Blackbeard watches, and Deboree. The 10:10 toots past at the Nebo junction. The shadows rock. The fumbling fingers have the garment off one shoulder when, abruptly, Sandy's head falls back to the bear's shoulder and she begins to snore. The giggle bubbles louder over the healthy teeth as Blondboy hefts the bra strap up and down.

'What kinda credit card got you these, mama?'

Sandy sags and snores louder. The boy tries to reach behind

82

her sleeping back to find the clasp. Blackbeard is going through her shopping bag. He takes out a little transistor radio and turns it on. He leans against the oak tree, gnawing the sausage and tuning the radio as he watches his partner wrestle with the sleeping woman's brassiere. At last, Deboree has to close his eyes to the spectacle, and the dark swirls over him. His head is ringing. He hears the radio dial travel on until it finds The Beach Boys' hit. The harmony softens Sandy's snores and grunts and covers the crunch of twigs. Deboree can barely hear any of it. It comes from a long way off, through a twining, leafy tunnel. The tunnel has almost twined shut when he hears Blackbeard speak.

'What did she say he was doing out there on the railroad tracks? Counting?'

'The ties,' Blondboy answers. 'Counting the ties between Puerto Sancto and the next village. Thirty miles away. Counting the railroad ties. They got him doped up and dared him and he did it, didn't he, hee hee?'

'Houlihan,' says Blackbeard's voice, gentler. 'The great Houlihan. Done in by downers and a dare.' Blackbeard sounded honestly grieved, and Deboree found himself suddenly liking him. 'I can't believe it. . . .'

'Don't let it bother you, bro. He was fried, you know? Gangrened. But c'mere and check this. I bet this makes you take that wienie outta your mouth. . . .'

Deboree tries to lift his eyes open, but the tunnel is twining too fast. Let it close, he tells himself. Who's afraid of the dark now? Houlihan wasn't merely making noise; he was *counting*. We were all counting.

The dark space about him is suddenly filled with faces, winking off and on. Deboree watches them twinkle, feeling warm and befriended, equally fond of all the countenances, those close, those far, those known, those never met, those dead, those never dead. Hello faces. Come back. Come on back all of you even LBJ with your Texas cheeks eroded by compromises come back. Khrushchev, fearless beyond peasant ignorance, healthy beside Eisenhower, come back both of you. James Dean all picked apart and Tab Hunter all put together. Michael Rennie in your silver suit the day the earth stood still for peace, come back all of you.

Now go away and leave me.

Now come back.

Come back Vaughn Monroe, Ethel Waters, Krazy Kat, Lou Costello, Harpo Marx, Adlai Stevenson, Ernest Hemingway, Herbert Hoover, Harry Belafonte, Timothy Leary, Ron Boise, Jerry Lee Lewis, Lee Harvey Oswald, Chou En-lai, Ludwig Erhard, Sir Alec Douglas-Home and Mandy Rice-Davies, General Curtis LeMay and Gordon Cooper, John O'Hara and Liz Taylor, Estes Kefauver and Governor Scranton, the Invisible Man and the Lonely Crowd, the True Believer and the Emerging Nations, the Hungarian Freedom Fighters, Elsa Maxwell, Dinah Washington, Jean Cocteau, William Edward Burghardt Du Bois, Jimmy Hatlo, Aldous Huxley, Edith Piaf, Zasu Pitts, Seymour Glass, Big Daddy Nord, Grandma Whittier, Grandpa Deboree, Pretty Boy Floyd, Big Boy Williams, Boyo Behan, Mickey Rooney, Mickey Mantle, Mickey McGee, Mickey Mouse, come back, go away, come on back.

That summer-sweet Frisco with flowers in your hair come back. Now go away.

Cleaver, come back. Abbie, come back. And you that never left come back anew, Joan Baez, Bob Kaufmann, Lawrence Ferlinghetti, Gordon Lish, Gordon Fraser, Gregory Corso, Ira Sandperl, Fritz Perls, swine pearls, even you black bus Charlie Manson asshole. And you better get back to Tennessee Jed come back, get back, now come back afresh.

We are being summoned. We get a reprieve, not just a rebop. He wasn't just riffing; he was counting. Appear and testify.

Young Cassius Clay.

Young Mailer.

Young Miller.

Young Jack Kerouac before you fractured your football career at Columbia and popped your hernia in *Esquire*. Young Sandy without your credit card bare. Young Devlin. Young Dylan. Young Lennon. Young lovers wherever you are. Come back and remember and go away and come back.

Attendance mandatory but not required.

The Search for the Secret Pyramid

1: SAFARI SO GOOD

September 26, 1974. Yom Kippur, the Day of Atonement. At-One-Ment. To be observed, God makes it plain, this one-day fast from sundown to sundown once a year, forever and ever. An auspicious day to embark on a pilgrimage to the pyramids.

September 28, Saturday. Paul Krassner's in S.F. I ask Krassner if he observed the Yom Kippur fast. He said he would have but he was too busy eating.

September 29, Sunday. Seventeenth Sunday after Pentecost. Krassner's packed and ready. He plans to visit the pyramid with me as part of his conspiracy research, something about using the angle of the Grand Gallery to prove conclusively that the bullet that killed Kennedy could not possibly have come from Jack Ruby's gun.

September 30, Monday. Jack Cherry from *Rolling Stone* drives Krassner and me to the airport where we are going to fly to Dayton, Ohio, to talk with the great underground pyramid expert, Enoch of Ohio, about the Great Underground Pyramid. Cherry is to fly to New York later to rendezvous with the safari. He speaks Egyptian.

October 1, Tuesday. Succoth, the First Day of Tabernacles. Enoch of Ohio runs a tattoo parlour where he specializes in tattooing women and pierces nipples on the side. The walls of his shop are filled with colour Polaroids of his satisfied customers. When we arrive he is buzzing a rendition of Adam and Eve Being Driven from The Garden into the flaccid flank of a forty-year-old housewife from Columbus, wiping aside the ooze of ink and blood every few seconds. Krassner stares as I question the artist.

Enoch tells us, over the whir of the needle and the whine of the housewife, what he knows about the secret underground temple. Enoch of Ohio is a famous Astral Traveller and has visited the Valley of the Kings often in his less corporeal form. He is full of information and predictions. His eyes burn brighter as he talks, and his needle produces more flourishes and blood. The housewife continues to groan and grimace until we can barely hear his prophecies.

'Okay, Sweetmeats, that's enough for today. You look a little pale.'

I follow him to the back of his shop where he washes his hands clean of the stain of his trade, still expounding on ancient and future Egypt. A gasp and a crash from the other room rushes us back. But the housewife is fine. Krassner has fainted.

October 2, Wednesday. I throw Lu, The Wanderer, and am ready to move on. But Krassner has had enough of the arcane. 'They'd probably search me and find out that I am circumcised,' he says and flies back to San Fran.

I buy a creamo '66 Pontiac convertible from a furniture designer and head out to Wendell Berry's in Port Royal, Kentucky, hoping to enlist him in the cause. I hear over the car radio that the earliest frost in fifty years has smitten the Kentucky tobacco crop. Fields on both sides of the road are full of limp leaves and dour farmers. Much as I dislike cigarettes I can't help but be touched by these forlorn figures in overalls and baseball caps. There is a quality timeless and universal about a farmer standing in the aftermath of a killer frost. It could be a hieroglyph, a symbol scratched on a sheet of papyrus depicting that immortal phrase of fruitless frustration: 'Stung!'

October 3, Thursday. Birthday of St Theresa. Another record-breaking cold night. After biscuits and eggs Wendell and I hitch up his two huge-haunched Belgian work mares and gee and haw out into the cold Kentucky morn to see if his sorghum survived. The leaves are dark and drooping but the stalks are still firm. We cut a few samples and head on up to the ridge for the opinion of two old brothers he is acquainted with.

'The Tidwell twins'll know,' Wendell allows. 'They been farming this area since the year 'ought-one.'

The wagon rumbles along the winding, rocky ruts, through thorn thickets and groves of sugar maple and osage and dogwood. We find the brothers working a lofty meadow high above the neighbouring spreads. No woe is frosted on the faces of this pair; their tobacco crop is hanging neatly in the barn since well before the cold snap, and they are already discing under the stalks. Erect, alert, and nearing eighty, the picture presented by these two identical Good Old Boys might describe another hieroglyph: Them as *Didn't* Get Stung.

They examine Wendell's stalk of sorghum and assure him how it ain't hurt in the joint, which is what roorins the crop.

'Don't let no cows into it, though,' they warn. 'Freeze like that makes prussic acid sorghum. Mought make a animal sickly. . . .'

Listening to these two old American alchemists one can better understand why Wendell Berry, an M.A. from Stanford and a full professor with tenure two days a week at the U of Kentucky, busts his butt the rest of the time farming with the same antiquated methods the land of his forefathers; there is a wisdom in our past that cannot be approached but with the past's appurtenances. Think of Schliemann finding ancient Troy by way of Homer.

On the way back down from the ridge I tell Wendell of the team of scientists from Berkeley who tried probing the pyramids with a newfangled cosmic ray device in search of hidden chambers. 'What they found was that there was something about pyramids that thwarted our most advanced gadgetry. The only thing their ten tons of equipment accomplished was to electrocute a rat that tried to nest in the wiring.'

'Killed a rat, did they?' says Wendell, tromping the brake to keep the wagon from overrunning the mares down the steep slope. 'For Berkeley scientists, that's a start.'

October 4, Friday. Dateline Paris (Kentucky, that is).

Looking for the Bible in the drawer of my ancient hotel room, I find a phone number pencilled onto the unfinished wood of the drawer bottom, a dark number, etched deep and certain, after which is pencilled even darker this rave review:

EPIK FUCK!

The phone is on the nightstand right next to the drawer and I must admit I'm housed upstairs alone with the classic travelling-salesman horniness. I look at the number again, but farther back in the drawer there's the Bible, after all. Besides, I have hired out to do an article, not an epic.

The passage I am seeking is Isaiah, chapter 19, verses 19 and 20. It is a pivotal quote in the first volume of a four-volume set on pyramidology that I bought in S.F. for sixty bucks, but the author has written the passage in its original Hebrew, fully aware that your usual reader will have to refer to the Bible to find out what is said. The only thing else he lets you know about the passage is that it contains 30 words and 124 Hebrew letters, and that when the numerical value of these ancient words and letters is added up by a process known as gematria the sum total of the passage equals 5,449, which is the height of the Great Pyramid in pyramid inches.

The pyramid inch is a unit so close to our own inch (25 pyramid inches = 25.0265 of our inches) that I will henceforth refer to these units simply as inches: 5,449 is also the weight of the pyramid in tons times 100. Comparisons continue ad infinitum. Compressed within the scope and accuracy of the Great Pyramid's angles and proportions seem to be all the formulas and distances pertinent to our solar system. This is one of the reasons we don't want to switch to the metric system. It'd be like cutting off our feet so we can get Birkenstock transplants.

The book falls open to Psalm 91 – 'He that dwelleth in the secret place of the most High shall abide under the shadow of the Almighty' – which is one of the Egyptian verses written, according to the *Urantia Book*, by that first great teacher of monotheism, King Akhnoten, who, according to Enoch, was schooled personally by Melchizedec himself, who, according to Cayce blah blah, you see what I mean? The path to this pyramid can lead you down endless alleys of rumination. On to Isaiah.

Here it is, chapter 19, and underlined in the *same dark pencil* as was used to record the phone number on the drawer bottom:

> 19 In that day shall there be an altar to the LORD in the midst of the land of Egypt, and a pillar at the border thereof to the LORD.
>
> 20 And it shall be for a sign and for a witness unto the LORD of hosts in the land of Egypt; for they shall cry unto the LORD because of the oppressors, and he shall send them a saviour, and a great one, and he shall deliver them –

Wait a minute. That way lies the musclebound madness one sees caged behind the isometric eyes of the Jesus freaks – not the way I wish to wander in this quest. I don't need a course in spiritual dynamic tension. I return the gift of the Gideons to its drawer and shut it away along with the secret gematria of the Epik Fuck. All very interesting but I don't need it. Being raised a hard-shell Baptist jock I consider myself still fairly fit faithwise. Besides, going to the Great Pyramid to find God strikes me as something of an insult to all the other temples I have visited over the years, an affront to the words of spiritual teachers like St Houlihan and St Lao-tzu and St Dorothy who, perhaps best of all, sums it up: 'If you can't find God in your backyard in Kansas you probably can't find him in the Great Pyramid in Egypt, either.'

In fact (I may as well tell it now) this expedition is not aimed at the Great Pyramid of Giza at all, nor any of the other dozens of already-studied and profusely interpreted temples lining the west bank of the mighty Nile, but another marvel, as yet undisclosed and said to contain in its magnificent halls all the mysteries of the past – *explained!*

Like *just how did* they cut those stones so hard and move them so far and fit them so tight? And what was the device that once crowned the summit of Cheops with such power that it echoes all the way down to the back of our Yankee dollar? Where did those builders come from? Where do *we* come from and, more important, as our nation's worth leaks away and the gears of this cycle's trip grind from Pisces to Aquarius in approach of the promised shifting of the poles, where are we *bound?*

This expedition is going to try to find the edifice called by John the Apostle the New Jerusalem and by Enoch of Ohio the Secret Temple of Secrets and by Edgar Cayce, in countless readings that prophesy the discovery of this hidden wonder sometime between 1958 and 1998, the Hall of Records.

Next stop: The A.R.E. Library, the Association for Research and Enlightenment, in Virginia Beach, Virginia.

October 5, 6, 7, 8. Research at Cayce's A.R.E. Library.

As the great accusing aftermath that followed the French Revolution dragged on and the lines of heads scheduled to be lopped off grew too long to be serviced by Dr Guillotine's nifty machine, the overflow of minor-league aristocrats was relegated to a more cut-rate end. When their time came they were grasped by the arms and hustled indecorously from their cells to an open field where a burly nonunion executioner held aloft a simple sword.

To alleviate the boredoms of these day-in day-out head-offs, the head hostlers developed this simple sport: just before the sword came down they would hiss in the ear of the trembling wretch they were holding bent forward, 'You are free, *mon ami: run!*' and release his arms. Then the spectators would bet on how many steps the headless body would run before toppling. Seven steps was not unusual; twelve was par for a particularly spirited specimen. The record was set by a woman – twenty-four strides and no sign of falter before the sightless body encountered a parked manure wagon.

Some things keep going farther than others. 'A *spirited* lass, that one. . . .'

This same ongoing spirit surrounds the big white A.R.E. building that houses the 49,135 pages of verbatim psychic readings given by the unassuming little man known as the Sleeping Prophet.

What I learn after four days' research is that hundreds have preceded me in this search for Cayce's Secret Pyramid. The most noteworthy is a certain Muldoon Greggor. Scholar Greggor has written a book on the subject, called *The Hidden Records*, and is in fact at present in Cairo, according to his brother, continuing his research. Has he unearthed anything new?

'He can be found at the university,' the brother advises me without looking up from *his* research. 'Why don't you wait until you get to Cairo and ask *him?* Myself, I'm into almonds.'

October 9, Wednesday. New York City. I'm in this raging Babylon not half an hour and my car gets towed away. It takes me the rest of the day and 75 bucks to get it back. A little girl waiting with her daddy in the angry line at the redeeming pier tells me their car was stolen, too, and is probably crying after the abduction.

'They drag them away by their hind foot, you know.'

October 10, 11. More museums and libraries. I think I've got the information to piece the history together. I had planned to write

90

my assimilation of all this material during these few days before Jacky Cherry arrives for our departure, but this city is too overpowering. Awful and awesome. It is here that the leak is most evident, a constant hiss of escaping economy. When you stand near the New Jersey Turnpike you can feel a great protein wind blowing from all over the nation into Long Island and right on out into the ocean to the ten-mile square of floating garbage.

Jack is here and we fly to Cairo tomorrow. My next filing will be from the other side of the globe.

II: RAMADAN: 'THEY TEEM BY NIGHT!'

October 13. Nineteenth Sunday after Pentecost. Our 747 comes wallowing down out of the clouds into the Amsterdam airport like a flying pig, bellying in to the trough.

Three big trucks swarm out to service her, to see carefully to her comfort. In turn, this pampered porker spares no expense when it comes to the comfort of her clientele. We are lavished with it. Refreshments are served constantly by an ample staff of smiling nubilians. For entertainment you have stereo music, in-flight movies, and a *free magazine*. Passengers are invited to take this free piece of worthless printed crap home. Of course, there is the very latest in sanitation: everything that comes in human contact is incinerated afterwards.

What a difference when we deplane in Ankara, Turkey, and board the dowdy old DC-8 that will carry us on to Cairo. The plane is smelly as a subway, jammed to the gunwales with every sort of heavy-lidded heathen.

'No wonder the terminal search took so long,' Jacky whispers. '*Every*body looks like a terrorist.'

He says he recognizes the tongues of Turks, Serbs, Kurds, Arabs, Berbers, and, he thinks, some Nurds – all flying to the climax of their month-long religious observance, all sweating and singing and noisily spattering each other with their various dialects and languages that sound, as Jack the language gourmet puts it, 'like popcorn popping.'

We unload a bunch at Istanbul, more than half. Oddly enough, the plane gets even noisier, swarthier. The remaining passengers look Jack and me over with new respect. 'You? You go to *Cairo?*' We tell them yes, we are going to Cairo. They roll their eyes.

'*Ya latif! Ya latif!*'

In the air again, I ask Jack what it means.

'*Ya latif* is the Arab equivalent for Far Out. To the devout it means, "Nice Allah, making for me more surprises."'

As we cross the Suez we break from the clouds into open night. Out the window thunderheads stand like bored sentries, the shoulders of their rumpled uniforms laced round with rusty stars. They are rolling little balls of heat lightning back and forth, just to keep awake. They wave us on through. . . .

Sunday midnight. Cairo. The turmoil at the airport is unbelievable, tumultuous, teeming – that's the word: teeming – with pilgrims coming and going and relatives, waiting for pilgrims, coming and going. Porters wait on passengers; ragged runners wait on the porters. Customs officials bustle and soldiers in old earth-coloured uniforms stroll and yawn. Hustlers of every age and ilk hit you up from every angle known to man. Jacky takes the action in suave stride.

'My year in the Near East,' he tells me, 'I saw *all* the gimmicks.'

We work our way through, filling forms and getting stamped, moving our bags through a circle of hands – this guy hands the stuff to this next guy who wheels it to this next guy who unloads it by the desk of this next guy – all expecting tips – until we finally make it outside into the welcome desert wind.

The hustler's runner's porter who has attached himself to us runs down a taxi and hustles us in. He tells us, Do not worry, is *great* driver, and sends us careening terrifically down an unlit four-lane boulevard teeming from curb to curb with bicycles, tricycles, motorcycles, sidehackers, motorscooters, motorbikes, buses dribbling passengers from every hole and handhold, rigs, gigs, wheelchairs, biers, wheelbarrows, wagons, pushcarts, army troop trucks where smooth-chopped soldier boys giggle and goose each other with machine guns . . . rickshaws, buckboards, hacks both horse- and camel- and human-drawn, donkey-riders and -pullers and -drivers, oxcarts, fruitcarts, legless beggars in thighcarts, laundry ladies with balanced bundles, a brightblack farm lad in a patched nightshirt prodding a greatballed Holstein bull (into town at midnight to what? to butcher? to trade for beans?) plus a huge honking multitude of other taxis, all careening, all without head- or taillights ever showing except for the occasional *blink-blink-honk-blink* signal to let the dim mass rolling ahead know that, by the Eight Cylinders of Allah, this Great Driver is coming through!

Miraculously, we make it through the clotted city centre and across the Nile to the steps of our hotel, the Omar Khayyam. The Omar Khayyam is now somewhat faded in splendour from its heyday, when its statues still had all their noses and nipples and the lords and colonels and territorial governors still raised their lime squashes in terse toasts to the Empire that the bloody sun would *never* set on!

We are shown to our room and unpack. It's after two in the morning but the incredible hubbub from across the river calls us back out into the night. As we walk through that obsolete colonial lobby, Jack fills me in on some of the other wonderful things the British did for the Egyptians.

'They introduced the rulers of Egypt to the idea of buying things on credit. Egypt as a result immediately went into stupendous debt, so the British were honourably obliged to come in and clear up their finances for them. This task took seventy years.

'The British plan was to convert Egypt to a single-export economy – cotton. To encourage this they started building dams on the Nile. It bothered the British that the country got so flippin' *flooded* every year.

'Without the yearly flood that had always brought new soil to replenish the land, the Egyptians were soon dependent on wonderful fertilizers. Also, now that they didn't have to worry about those nasty floods, the British didn't see any reason why they shouldn't get two crops a year instead of one. Perhaps even *three!* The rulers, none of whom were Egyptian-born or even spoke Arabic, thought it was *all* wonderful. Albanians, I believe, and they were throwing incredible sums of money around, building Victorian-style mosques, importing things, and paying European creditors absurd rates of interest. . . .

'What happened when there were three crops a year instead of one was that the farmers spent a lot more time standing around in the irrigation ditches. So there was a tremendous increase of bilharzia, a parasite that's spread by a little water worm that starts at the foot, so to speak, of the ladder, and climbs to the eyes. It gave Egypt the highest rate of blindness in the world. Over seventy per cent of the population had it at one point.

'Peculiarly enough, for all the modernization they were introducing to the Egyptians, the British never quite got around to building any hospitals. The mortality rate from birth to age five was about fifty per cent. They have a proverb here, "Endurance is the best thing." The British helped emphasize this.'

We have reached the other side of the Nile, where Jacky's history of recent Cairo is drowned out by the city's stertorous present. Nowhere else have you heard or imagined anything like it! It has a flavour all its own. Mix in your mind the deep surging roar of a petroleum riptide with the strident squealing of a teenage basketball playoff; fold in air conditioners and sprinkle with vendors' bells and police whistles; pour this into narrow streets greased liberally with people noisily eating sesame cakes fried in olive oil, bubbling huge hookahs, slurping Turkish coffees, playing backgammon as loud as the little markers can be slapped down without breaking them – thousands of people, coughing, spitting, muttering in the shadowy debris next to the buildings, singing, standing, sweeping along in dirty damask gellabias, arguing in the traffic – *millions!* and all jacked up loud on caffeine. Simmer this recipe at 80 degrees at two in the morning and you have a taste of the Cairo Cacophony.

After blocks with no sign of a letup we turn around. We're tired. Ten thousand miles. On the bridge back, Jack is accosted by a pockmarked man with a tambourine and a purple-assed baboon on a rope.

'Money!' the man cries, holding the tambourine out and the baboon back with a cord ringed into the animal's lower lip. 'Money! For momkey pardon me sir, for mom-key!'

Jacky shakes his head. 'No. *Ana mish awez. Don't want* to see monkey dance.'

'Momkey not dance, pardon me sir. *Not dance!*' He has to shout against the traffic; the baboon responds to the shout by rearing hysterically and snarling out his long golden fangs. The man whacks the shrieking beast sharply across the ear with the edge of the tambourine. 'Momkey get sick! Rabies! Money' – he whacks him again, jerking his leash – 'to get momkey *fixed*.'

The baboon acts like his torment is all our fault. He is backing towards us, stretching the pierced lip as he tries to reach us with
94

a hind hand. His claws are painted crimson. His ass looks like a brain tumour on the wrong end.

'Money for *mom*-key! *Hurr*-ee!'

Walking away, 50 piastres poorer, Jack admits that Cairo has come up with some new gimmicks since he was here ten years ago.

As we round the end of the bridge we surprise a young sentry pissing off the abutment of his command. Fumbling with embarrassment, he folds a big black overcoat over his uniform, still hanging open-flied.

'Wel-come,' he says, shouldering his carbine. 'Wel-come to Cairo. . . . Hokay?'

October 14, Monday morning. Jack and I are out early to look up a Dr Ragar that Enoch of Ohio sent me to see. We find him at last, set like a smoky stone in the wicker chair of his jewellery shop, a rheumy-eyed Egyptian businessman in a sincere serge suit and black tie. We try to explain our project but he doesn't seem as interested in digging up an undiscovered temple as in putting down his assortment of already discovered stuff. He slams a door to a glass display case.

'Junk! I, Dr Ragar, not lie to you. Most of it, junk! For the tourist who *knows* nothing, *respects* nothing, is this junk. But for those I see *respect* Egypt, I show for them the *Egypt I respect*. So. From what part of America you come from, my friend?'

I tell him I'm from Oregon. Near California.

'Yes, I know Oregon. So. From what part Oregon?'

I tell him I live in a town called Mt Nebo.

'Yes. Mt Nebo I know. I visit your state this summer. With the Rotary. See, is flag?'

It's true; hanging on his wall among many others is a fringed flag from the 1974 Rotary International meeting in Portland, Oregon.

'I know your *whole state*. I am a doctor, archae*ologist!* I travel all over your beautiful state. So. What part the town you are living? East Mt Nebo or West Mt Nebo?'

'Kind of in the middle,' I tell him. Mt Nebo is your usual wide spot in a two-lane blacktop off a main interstate. 'And off a little to the north.'

'Yes. North Mt Nebo. I know very well that section your city, North Mt Nebo. So. Let me show you something more. . . .'

He checks both ways, then draws his wallet from a secret inner-serge pocket. He opens it to a card embossed with an ancient and arcane symbol.

'You see? Also I am Shriner, thirty-two degrees. You know Masons?'

I tell him I already knew he was a Mason – that was how Enoch knew of him, through a fraternal newspaper – and add that my father is also a Mason of the same degree, now kind of inactive.

'Brother!' He claps his palm tight to mine and looks deep into my soul. He's got a gaze like visual bad breath. 'Son of a brother *is* brother! Come. For you I not show this junk. Come down street next door to my home for some hot tea where it is *more quiet*. You like Egyptian tea, my brothers? Egyptian essences? Not drugstore perfumes, but the *true essences*, you know? Of the lotus flower? The jasmine? Come. Because your father, I do you a favour; I *give* you that scarab you favoured.'

He clasps my hand again, pressing the gift into my palm. I tell him that's not necessary, but he shakes his head.

'Not a word, Brother. Some day, you do something for me. As Masons say, "One stone at a time."'

He holds my hand, boring closer with sincerity. I wonder if there is some kind of eye gargle for cases like this. I try to steer us back to archaeology.

'Speaking of stones, doctor, you know the legend of the missing Giza top stone? Where the Temple of Records is supposed to be hidden?'

He laughs darkly. 'Who could *better* know?' he asks, pulling me after him along the sidewalk. 'But first, come, both of you; for refreshment.'

Jacky follows but he isn't to be so easily distracted. 'Then you've heard of this place, doctor? This hidden temple?'

'Dr Ragar? – Archaeologist, *Shriner?* – hear of the Hidden Temple of Records?' He laughs again. Like that flag from Portland, there is in his laugh a dark insinuation that keeps you guessing. '*Every*body hear of the Hidden Temple. Hear this, hear that . . . but The Truth? Who knows The Truth?'

He stops and holds his Masonic ring out for me to see, not Jacky.

'We of the Brotherhood know The Truth, which we cannot by

oath tell the uninitiated. But *you*, my brother son-of-a-brother, to you I can maybe show a little light not allowed others, eh?'

I nod, and he nods back, tugging me on a few steps more to a narrow doorfront.

'First here we are at my factory with excellent spice tea . . . white sugar – none for me, I must apologize; this holy fast – then we talk. Ibrahim!' he shouts, unlocking the heavy door. 'Tea for my friends from America!'

We enter a smaller, fancier version of the other shop. It is hung clear to the ceiling fan with old rugs and tapestry. This muffles the noise of downtown Cairo to a medium squawl. But good Christ, is it stuffy. Doctor turns on the fan but it can barely budge the swaddled air.

'So. While we wait my cousin bring the tea you will smell the *true essence* of the *Nile lotus* which *no woman* can *resist*.'

Jacky ends up buying $50 worth of perfume for the girls back at *Rolling Stone*. All I get from the wise doctor, besides my free scarab, is the use of his telephone to call the American University of Cairo. I leave a message for Mr Muldoon Greggor to please contact me at the Hotel Omar Khayyam. After an afternoon in the essence factory I can tell that if you want some straight information here in Cairo, you're going to have to see an American.

Walking back to our hotel we pass a street display of the '73 war, the campaign when Egypt crossed the Suez and kicked Jew ass and got away with it. In the centre of the display is a two-storey cement foot about to crunch down on a Star of David. I want to shoot a picture of it, but everybody watching makes me nervous about this damn big negative-print Polaroid.

An intense young vet of that war leads us personally through the exhibit, pointing out strategic battle zones and fortifications in the big sand model he has built. He is passionately patriotic. He points to a bazooka shell propped against the sand that depicts the Bar-Lev, the Israeli version of the Maginot line.

'That missile? Made in America. These captured guns? Also American.'

His eyes are hard when he says these things to me, but there is no animosity. Even when he speaks of the Jews (pointing out their faces in the photographs so I can tell the bedraggled Israeli captives from the dust-ridden Egyptian captors), his voice holds no blame. He talks of the Israeli soldiers the way a player from

97

one team speaks of his rivals across the river, with respect. And such close rivals, I realize, looking at the way Fate and the United Nations have placed Cairo and Jerusalem within a jet's moment from each other. No wonder the military show on every street.

Returning over the bridge I see again our little soldier standing shabbily at guard beside his tent and his haphazard pile of sandbags. We salute and I march toward the hotel, feeling a new familiarity with the political situation.

October 15, Tuesday. Still unable to begin my article. Lots of walking in town. There are some hard sights, putting my put-down of our pampered lifestyle to the test: childworn wives leading patched families past the fruit stands to the mildewed piles of cheaper foods in the rear; a dog peeled to the bone with terminal mange, gnawing on a Kotex; a cryptic black lump in the middle of the sidewalk, about the size of a seven-year-old, all balled up with a black blanket pulled tight over everything except the upturned palm stuck on the end of a withered stick; whole families living in gutted shells of Packards and Buicks and Cadillacs biodegrading against the curbs. . . .

'Jacky, what this town needs is some New York tow-away cops. Keep the riffraff on the run.'

And always the smell of urine, and the unhealthy stools half-hidden everywhere. As Cairo has a distinctive and subtle recipe of sound all its own, so it has its odour.

All in all, it's awful to behold. I carry the special Polaroid I bought in New York with me everywhere, but as yet I'm too squeamish to point it at this hard privation. I remember an argument I had with Annie Liebovitz: 'Listen, Annie. I don't want any pictures of me shaving, shitting, or strung out!' Neither would I want any shots of my teeth rotted away, or my eyes gummed over with yellow growths, or my limbs twisted and tortured.

Tuesday night or Wednesday morn. Today is the last day of the Ramadan fast. Christmas in Cairo. Like New York, the power of this city is overwhelming, a presence too frightful to face. Unlike New York, though, the power of Cairo is generated by more than the daily flow of liquid assets through economic

98

turbines. Cairo's main current streams from its past, out of a wealth that flows toward something yet-to-be – a power of *impending* power. This is a city of influence since before New York was a land mass, a place of ancient records since before the Old Testament was in rough draft. Somewhere between the brittle no-magic nationalism of the young patriot in the park and the shopworn mysticism of the Illuminoid in serge, this larval account is swelling.

Even now the cannon fires – the signal for the last day of Ramadan. The caterwaul of traffic politely drops so the amplified chants can be heard from the minarets on this night of nights.

It gets quiet. You can hear the responses of the faithful in the scattered Moslem night, the prayers rising from the mosques and sidewalks. This afternoon I saw a streetsweeper prostrate himself alongside the pile of dirt he was herding, answering the call from Mecca with cabs swerving all around him.

Ye gods, listen! It spirals louder yet. Let me out of this mouldering room! I'll take my pen and camera and face this thing while it's still damp with dawn.

I hurry past third-rate Theseus and his plaster legions, through the lofty lobby where chandeliers hang from ceilings infested with gilt cupids, around the praying gateman outside up the sidewalk to the belly-high cement wall that runs along the steep bank of the Nile.

I put my notebook on the wall. The prayer is still going on but the city's business has stopped holding still for it. Engines sing; brakes cry; horns tootle; head- and taillights blink off and on. Long strings of coloured lights go looping along the streets, past elaborate cafe neons and simple firepots cooking kebabs on the curb. In the minarets the chant leaders are vying with the city and each other in amplified earnest, as thousands upon thousands of lesser voices try their best to keep up.

It's windy, the historic wind that blows against the current so the Nile boatmen of eons can sail south upstream and then drift back downstream north. A dog in the back of a passing pickup barks. The soldier comes out of his tent and sees me at the wall writing in my notebook. He turns up the collar of his long overcoat and comes toward me with a flashlight. He carries it with his hand over the lighted end so it is like a little lamp glow between us. We smile and nod at each other. This close I notice the bayonet on his shouldered carbine is rusty and bent.

The din across the river jumps even higher in response to the chanting dawn. We turn back toward the city just in time to see first the fluorescent tubes across the bridge, then the landing lamps on the opposite bank, then every light in Cairo blow out – *zam!* Allah be praised! We turn to each other again, eyebrows uplifted. He whistles a low note of applause to the occasion: '*Ya latif!*' I nod agreement.

The amplifiers have been silenced by the power overload, but the chanting in the streets hasn't stopped. In fact, it is rising to the challenge of the phenomenon. Wireless worship. A voice spun from fibres strong as the fabled Egyptian cotton – longest staples in the world! – spindling out of millions of throats, into threads, cords, twining east toward that dark meteorite that draws all stands of this faith together like the eye of a needle, or a black hole.

The soldier watches me write, kindly leaking a little light onto my notebook. '*Tisma, ya khawaga,*' he says. 'Een-glees?'

I tell him no, not English. 'American.'

'Good.' He nods. 'Merican.'

My throat is dry from the wind and the moment. I take my canteen from my shoulder and drink. I offer it to the soldier. After a polite sip he whistles a comment on the quality of such a canteen.

'Merican army, yes?'

'Yeah. Army surplus.' Ex-marine friend Frank Dobbs had helped me pick it out, along with my desert boots and pith helmet. 'United States Army surplus.'

He hands back the canteen and salutes. I salute him back. He gestures toward my notebooks, questioning. I point to the sound from across the river, cup my ear. I lift my nose and smell the Nile wind, then scribble some words. Finally I make a circle with my hand, taking in the river, the sky, the holy night. He nods, excited, and lays his closed fist on his heart.

'Egypt?' he asks.

'Yes,' I affirm, duplicating his gesture with my fist. 'Egypt.'

And all the lights of Cairo come back on.

We lift our eyebrows to each other again, as the amplifiers skirl back up, and the lights and the traffic join again in noisy battle. When the soldier and I unclench our fists there's maybe even tears. I fancy that I see the face of Egypt's rebirth, charged both with a new pride and the old magic, silhouetted innocent and wise against that skyline of historic minarets and modern highrises – the whole puzzle. I must get a picture! I'm trying to dig the Polaroid out of the bag when I notice the light in my face.

'No.' He is wagging the light from side to side. 'No photo.'

I figure it must be some religious taboo, like certain natives guarding their souls, like me with Annie Liebovitz.

'I can dig it. I'll just snap a shot of that skyline dawn across the Nile.'

'No photo!'

'Hey, I wasn't aiming anywhere near you.' I start to stomp away, down the wall. 'I'll shoot from somewhere else if you're so – '

'*No photo!*'

Slowly I take my eye from the viewfinder. The flashlight has been put aside on the wall to leave both hands available for the carbine. Too late I realize that it is the bridge he is guarding, not his soul.

I put the camera away, apologizing. He stands looking at me, suspicious and insulted. There is nothing more for us to say, even if we could understand each other. Finally, to regain a more customary relationship, he puts two fingers to his lips and asks, 'Seegrat?'

I tell him I don't smoke. He thinks I'm lying, sore about the picture. There is nothing to say. I sigh. The puzzle of Cairo shuffles off to stand in token attention on the abutment, his collar up and his back turned stiffly toward me.

The light is coming fast through the mist. The wind dies away for a moment and a sharp reek fogs up around me. Looking down I see I have stomped into a puddle of piss.

October 16. The Ramadan holiday. Erstwhile Egyptologist Muldoon Greggor calls, tells us to come over to his place; he'll go with us to the pyramid tonight after his classes.

'Check out of that morgue right now!' he shouts through the phone static. 'I've reserved rooms at the Mena House!'

So it's outta that rundown Rudyard Kipling pipedream through the surging holiday streets up seven floors to the address Greggor gives us. A shy girl lets us in a ghetto penthouse. Jacky and I spend the rest of the afternoon drinking the old man's cold

Stella beers, watching the multitudes below parade past in their gayest Ramadan gladrags. The shadows have stretched out long before Muldoon Greggor comes rushing in with a load of books. We barely shake hands before he hustles us down to catch a cab.

'Mena House, Pyramid Road! We want to get there before dark.'

So it is at dusty sundown that I see it at last: first from the window of the cab; then closer, from the hotel turnaround; then through the date palms walking up the hill; then – Great God in Heaven Whatever Your Name or Names! – here it is before me: mankind's mightiest wedge, sliced perfect from a starblue sky – the Great Pyramid of Giza.

III: INSIDE THE THRONE

Imagine the usual tourist approaching for his first hit: relieved to be finally off the plane and out of that airport, a bit anxious on the tour bus through that crazy Cairo traffic but still adequately protected by the reinforced steel of the modern machine, laughing and pointing with his fellow tour members at the incongruous panorama of the Giza outskirts – donkeys drawing broken-down Fiats, mud huts stuck like dirt-dauber nests to the sides of the most modern condominiums – 'Pathetic, but you gotta admit, Cynthia: very picturesque' – fiddling with his camera, tilting back in his seat a little sleepy from the sun; when, suddenly, the air brakes grab and the door hisses open and he is ejected from his climatized shell into the merciless maw of the parking lot at the bottom of Pyramid Hill.

A hungry swarm of his first real Egyptians comes clamouring after him: buggy drivers and camel hasselers and purveyors of the finest Arabian saddle steeds. And guides? Lord, the guides! of every conceit and canon:

'Wel-come, mister, wel-come; you are fine, yes?'

The handshake, the twinkle, the ravenous cumin-winded come-on:

'You like Cairo, yes? You like Egypt? You like Egyptian people? You like to see authentic hidden mummy the late King *Koo*-Foo? I am a *guide!*'

Or, even worse, the *Not-Guides:*

'Oh, pardon sir if I cannot help but notice you are being bothered by these phoney fellaheen. Understand please; I am

102

not a guide, being official watchman, in employ the Department of Antiquities in Cairo. You come with *me*. I keep these nuisances *away* from your holiday. I am *Not-Guide!*'

Our poor pilgrim fights his way through the swarm up the curving walk to the *aouda* (a big limestone lot in front of the northern base of the pyramid, swarming with more of the same), presses on to the monstrous stack of stone blocks which are perched all over with *more* damned guides and Not-Guides grinning like gargoyles . . . pays his piastres for the tickets that allow him and his nose-wrinkled wife to crawl up a cramped and airless torture chamber to a stone room about the size of the men's room of the bus terminal back home – and smellier! – then hightails it back to the relief of the bus:

'But tell me the truth, Cyn, wasn't that thing unbelievable big like nothing you ever saw in your life? I can't wait to see these shots projected on the screen at the lodge.'

Unbelievable big doesn't come close. It is inconceivably big, incomprehensibly big, brutal against the very heavens it's so big. If you come after the rush hour and are allowed to stroll unsolicited to it, you witness a phenomenon as striking as its size. As you cross the limestone lot the huge triangle begins to elongate into your peripheries – to *flatten*. The base line stretches, the sloping sides lengthen, and those sharpening corners – the northwest corner in the corner of your right eye; the northeast corner in your left – begin to *wrap* around you!

Consequently the vertex is getting shorter, the summit angle flatter; when you finally reach the bottom course of base stones and raise your eyes up its fifty-degree face even the two-dimensional triangle has disappeared! The plane of it diminishes away with such perfection that it is difficult to conceive of it as a plane. When it was still dressed smooth in its original casing stones the effect must have been beyond the senses' ability to resist; it must have turned into a seamless white line – a phenomenon of the first dimension.

Even in its present peeled condition, the illusion still disorients you. You tell your senses, 'Look maybe I ain't seen the other sides but I did see this one so it's gotta be at least a *plane*.' But planes are something we know, like airfields and shopping centre parking lots, hence horizontal. This makes it seem that you could walk right out on it if you just lean back enough to get on the perpendicular. Ooog. It makes you stumble and reel. . . .

To calm my stomach I leaned against one of the casing stones. It was smooth to my cheek; it made me feel cool, and a little melancholy.

'It's sad, isn't it?' Muldoon said. 'Seeing the old place so rundown and stripped.'

Muldoon Greggor wasn't the tweedy old Egyptologist we had expected. He was a little past twenty, wearing patched Levi's and a T-shirt, and a look in his eyes that still smouldered from some psychedelic scorcher that had made him swear off forever.

'It's eroded more in the six centuries since the Arabs stripped it than it did in the forty centuries before – if you accept the view of the accepted Egyptologists – or in the hundred and seventy centuries – if you go for the Cayce readings.'

'Sad,' I agreed. 'How could they do it?'

'They figured they needed it.' Jacky came to the defence of those long-gone Arabs. 'For *Allah*.'

'More than just sad,' I kept on. 'It's *insulting* . . . to whoever composed this postcard in stone, and took the trouble to send it to us.'

'The Arabs needed the stones to rebuild Cairo. Remember Nasser's construction of the High Dam?'

Jacky was talking about Nasser's flooding of architectural treasures with the construction of a hydroelectric dam. For the sake of the power-poor millions I had seen in Cairo, I was forced to admit that I would have done the same.

'Removing the casing stones is different,' Muldoon said. 'It's like a goal-tending foul committed before the rule was enacted. Now we don't know; was the shot going to go through or not? Those whoevers that built this thing were trying to transmit information important to everybody, for all time. Like how to square the circle or find the Golden Rectangle. None of the other pyramids convey any of this. Their message is pretty ego-involved, saying essentially: "Attention, Future: Just a line to remind you that King Whatnuton was the Alltime Greatest Leader, Warrior, Thinker, and Effecter of Stupendous Accomplishments, a few of which are depicted on the surrounding walls. His wife wasn't half bad either." There's none of that around the Great Pyramid. No bragging hieroglyphs. A much more universal message is suggested.'

'Maybe,' Jacky said, 'it isn't obliterated at all. Maybe in the intervening eons since they sent it we have simply forgotten how to read.'

'Or maybe this was just a decoy,' I said, 'for the Arabs. Maybe the message was never in there in the first place.'

I can maybe with anybody.

A patter of gravel drew our attention up the face. A small figure had come out of the entrance tunnel and was working his way down to importune us.

'Come on,' Muldoon said. 'There's a place back behind the southern face where they don't find you.'

Jacky and I followed around the northeastern corner and along the western base to the rear. It was darker, the lights of Cairo being blocked now by the huge structure. Carefully Muldoon led us into the excavated ruins of a minor funerary temple located between the rear of the Great Pyramid and the eastern face of its companion giant, the Pyramid of Chephren.

'See that black ball down there?'

Muldoon pointed off down the hill in the direction of the Giza village. I could make out a spheroid shape a quarter mile away.

'That's the back of the Sphinx's head.' He found a seat facing the ominous silhouette.

Jacky located a spot where he could look longingly east toward the twinkle of Cairo After Hours. I picked a rock with a backrest aimed so I could see the whole dim trio of pyramids, called in tour booklets 'The Giza Group'. Check the picture on a pack of Camels.

Far to the west is little Mykerinos. Much nearer is Chephren. With a crown of casing stones still in place on its summit, Chephren is almost the size of its famous brother. It is in fact some few feet farther above sea level, having been built on a slightly higher plateau than the Great Pyramid. It looks every bit as massive. But – as Muldoon mentioned about the other ruins and edifices – Chephren just doesn't have the *chutzpah*. The little crown of casing stones that eluded the Arabs actually gives it a quality slightly comic, like a cartoon peak sculpted by a Disneyland architect. Oh, it's also unbelievably big, Chephren is; and you are amazed by the manipulation of all that masonry, and gratified that its top is still there and cased; but it does not hold you. Your eye keeps being drawn back to the topless headliner, the star. . . .

'What's that dark slot?' I ask Muldoon. 'Is there a back door in the Great Pyramid?'

'That's what Colonel Howard-Vyse thought, about 1840. He was the guy that blasted open the chambers above the King's Chamber, you know, and disclosed that damned cartouche of Khufu.'

It's this name 'Khufu' found scratched in an upper attic that goes hardest against the Cayce readings.

'The Colonel was big on blasting, and he had this Arab working for him named Dued who apparently lived on blasting powder and hashish. Years of working with these two combustibles had made Dued deaf but had given him some fine theories about excavation. Like Vyse, he had a theory that there was another entrance, and he believed that, with the proper combination of his favourite ingredients, he could find it.'

The wind had dropped and it had grown very still. For a moment I thought I saw something coming around the southwestern corner toward us, but it vanished in that fathomless shadow.

'One of those blasts in the upper chambers short-fused and the Colonel thought he had lost a prize powder monkey. But after a couple days Dued woke up, with a *vision* – that there was a *back* door, situated exactly opposite the *front* door. The simplicity of the vision interested the good Colonel.'

I noticed all the dogs in the village below had stopped barking.

'Not that there are any other southern entrances in any of the other shitload of pyramids, of course, but old Howard-Vyse thought that, just to be on the safe side, they'd go around back and *check* . . . knock a couple of kegs' worth.'

'Did he find anything?' Jacky wanted to know.

'Just more rock. It is called "Vyse's Resultless Hole".'

'Wouldn't ya know it,' Jacky said.

'He fired Dued and moved his operations to Mykerinos, where he found a sarcophagus that he claimed held the pharaoh's mummy, but as luck or fate would have it the boat sank on the way back to England and Howard-Vyse lost his trophy. All he had to show for five years of digging and blasting is that resultless hole there and those damned upper chambers. One of which was filled with a mysterious black dust.'

'Yeah? What was it?'

'When science progressed enough to analyse it, it was found to be the bodies of millions of dead bugs.'

106

'Terrific.' Jacky stood up and straightened his necktie. 'I'm inspired to walk back to the hotel and kill mosquitoes. Let me know if you turn up anything resultful.'

After Jacky moped off, Muldoon painted in some of his past for me. Raised by parents both ecclesiastical and into the Edgar Cayce readings, Muldoon had grown up pretty blasé concerning theories arcane. Enoch of Ohio was his first real turn-on.

'He came to town and set up his tent. During the day he did horoscopes and tattoos, then at night he'd have these *meetings*. He'd go into a trance and answer questions, as "Rey-Torl". Rey-Torl used to be a cobbler in Mu, made Mu shoes, then his business went under so he moved on to Atlantis and became an unlicensed genetic surgeon. He eventually got run out of town and ended up in Egypt, helping Ra-ta build the pyramid.'

'Sounds hot. Did Rey tell you any good dirt?'

'Not really. The same thing that Cayce and all the other prophecy brokers say: that the Piscean Age is flopping toward the end of its two-thousand-year run and the Grand Finale is coming up soon, and that it's going to happen in this last quarter of this century. Rey-Torl called it Apodosis. Enoch called it the Shit Storm.'

'The last quarter?'

'Give or take a couple of decades. But soon. That's why the Cayce people place so much importance on locating that secret hall. It's supposed to contain records of previous shit storms plus some helpful hints on how to survive them. How*ever* – '

I had the feeling this wasn't the sort of stuff Muldoon talked about with fellow Egyptology students at the university.

' – everything has to be exactly right before you can find it: you, the time, the position of the earth, that damned Cat's Paw.'

Looking off toward the black lump of the Sphinx's head he quoted by heart the most famous of the Cayce predictions:

' *"This in position lies, as the sun rises from the waters, the line of the shadow (or light) falls between the paws of the Sphinx, that was later set as the sentinel or guard, which may not be entered from the connecting chambers from the Sphinx's paw (right paw) until the* time *has been fulfilled when the changes must be active in this sphere of man's experience. Between, then, the Sphinx and the river."* '

It was the same prophecy that had drawn me to the pyramid by way of Virginia Beach. Everybody at the Cayce library was familiar with it. Whenever I mentioned that I was on my way to Egypt the usual response from blue-haired old ladies and long-haired ex-hippies alike was, 'Gonna look for the Hall of Records, huh?'

'And the Sphinx isn't the only guard,' Muldoon went on. 'The readings mentioned whole squadrons of "sentries" or "keepers" or "watchmen" picketed around the hidden hall. *All* around here, actually. This whole plateau is a geodetic phenomenon protected by a corps of special spooks.'

I shivered from the wind. Muldoon stood up.

'I've got to head back to Cairo if I'm going to make my eight o'clock tomorrow.' He snapped his Levi's jacket closed, still looking off at the Sphinx. 'A woman from the A.R.E. *did* come over and try, you know? After a lot of rigamarole and red tape they actually let her drill a hole in the front of the right paw. . . .'

'Did she find anything?'

'Nothing. How she chose that one spot out of the mile or so between the paw and the river she never disclosed, but it was solid rock as far down as she drilled. She was very disappointed.'

'What about those ghostly guards, did they smite her?'

'That was not disclosed either. She did, however, end up marrying the Czechoslovakian ambassador.'

Hands in his pockets, Muldoon headed off into the shadows, saying he'd see me '*bukra fi'l mish-mish.*' It was a phrase you hear a lot in Cairo. 'It's the Arabic version of *mañana*,' I remembered Jacky had said, 'only less definite. It means "Tomorrow, when it's the season of the apricot."'

Left alone, I tried to recall what I knew about geodetic phenomena. I remembered my trip to Stonehenge, watching the winter solstice sun rise up the slot between those two rocks directly in front of me, knowing that exactly half a year later it would slide up between those other two rocks exactly to my right, and how the phenomenon forced you to strain your concept of where you are to include the tilt of our axis, the swing of our orbit around the sun, the singular position on our globe of this circle of prehistoric rocks – how it made you appreciate being in the only place on earth where those two solstice suns would rise thus.

I know that the pyramid was built in such a place – one of the acupuncture points of the physical planet – but no matter how I tried I couldn't get that planetary orientation that Stonehenge gives you.

For one thing I was still disoriented by that feeling of dimensions dropping away – everything still seemed flat, even the back of the Sphinx's head – and for another, I couldn't quite convince myself that I was alone. There seemed to be someone still close, and coming closer! The two hundred Egyptian pound notes in my pocket were suddenly bleeping like a beacon and I was beginning to glance about for a weapon when, down the hill, the Sphinx's whole head lit up and proclaimed in a voice like Orson Welles to the tenth power:

'I . . . am . . . the . . . Sphinx. I am . . . very old.'

It boomed this out over the accompanying strains of Verdi's *Aïda*, as Chephren lit up a glorious green, and little Mykerinos glowed blue, and the Great Pyramid blazed an appropriate gold.

It was the Sound and Light show, put on for the benefit of an outdoor audience at the bottom of the hill. From the tombs and mastabas everywhere banks of concealed floodlights illuminated the pyramids in slowly shifting hues while the Sphinx ran it all down in grandly amplified English. I just happened to hit it English night. The other performances rotate through French, German, Russian, and Arabic.

In this golden glow I suddenly saw the little figure I had sensed, hunkered on a limestone block about thirty yards away, watching me. Taking advantage of the light, I got up and headed immediately back around the Great Pyramid in long strides. I didn't turn until I had reached the road.

He was right behind me.

'Good evening, my friend. A very nice evening, yes?'

He hurried the last few steps to fall in beside me. He wore a blue gellabia and scuffed black oxfords without socks.

'My name is Marag.'

I came to know that it was spelled that way but it was pronounced with a soft 'g' so it rhymed with collage, only with the accent on the first syllable: *Mah*-razhhh.

'Excuse me but I hear you wish to buy some hashish? Five pounds, *this* much.'

He made a little circle with his thumb and finger and smiled through it. His face was polished teak, alert and angled, with a neat black moustache over tiny white teeth. His eyes flashed from their webwork of amused wrinkles. An old amusement. I judged him to be at least forty, as easily seventy, and not quite as tall as my thirteen-year-old son. Hurrying along beside me he seemed to barely touch the ground. When at last I relinquished the five-pound note and shook his hand to seal our deal, his fingers sifted through my grip like so much sand.

There's a little outdoor restaurant at the edge of the *aouda* where I sipped Turkish coffee and watched the pyramid change colours until the lights went out and the Sphinx shut up, then I paid my tab and left. I had waited nearly an hour. He had said twenty minutes. But I knew the rules, they're international: whether you're in Tangiers or Tijuana, North Beach or Novato, you don't get up off the bread till you see the score. Twenty minutes . . . in the season of the apricots.

But just as I came out of the restaurant I saw a little blue figure come whisking around up the shadowy trail from the village. Panting and sweating, he slipped five little packages into my hand, each about the size of a .45 cartridge and wrapped in paper tape. I started digging at one with my thumbnail.

'I had to go more far than I think,' he apologized. 'Eh? Is good? Five pieces, five pounds?'

I realized he was telling me that the score had cost him exactly what I had put out, none left over for his efforts. His face sparkled up at me. Reaching again for my wallet, I also realized that he could have packaged five goat turds.

He saw my hesitation. 'As you wish.' He shrugged.

I gave him two American bucks, worth about a pound and a half on the black market. After examining the two greenbacks he grinned to let me know he appreciated my logic if not my generosity.

'Any night, this corner. Ask for Marag. Everybody know where to find Marag.' Reaching out, he sifted his hand again through mine, his eyes glittering. 'And your name?'

I told him, somewhat suspicious still: was he going to burn me, bust me, or both, as the dealers were known to do in Tijuana?

'*D*'bree? D'*bree*?' Trying the accent at each end amused him. 'Good night to you, Mr D'bree.'

Then was whisked back into the shadows.

Back in the hotel room I found the little packets were bound so tight I had to use my Buck knife. I finally shelled out a tiny brown cartridge ball of the softest, smoothest, sweetest hash I had ever tasted, or maybe ever will, the way Lebanon's going crazy.

It is at this point my journal resumes:

October 17, Thursday. First day at the Mena House. Great place. After a huge breakfast and lots of strong coffee we head up the hill. The holiday crowd has arrived and are mounting the great hill from all sides like a gaudy herd of homecoming ants. But not all the way to the top. They climb a few courses and sit among the stones and eat pickled fish and fruit, or mill around the *aouda* below, eyes eager for action. They are drawn to Jacky and me as though we were sweating honey.

Impossible to take a photo and damn near as hard to write. They love to watch me with my notebook, watch my hand drag the pen across the page whereas their hands push the script, gouging the calligraphy from right to left as into a tablet of clay.

Jacky and I climb to a niche about twenty-five courses high and watch the multitudes throng kaleidoscopic up the hill.

'I was here after Ramadan ten years ago,' Jacky marvels, 'and it was nothing like this. It's the victory last year against the Israelis. They feel proud enough to come face this thing.'

A cop in a white uniform comes clambering up the stones, belt in his hand. He lays into the kids who had been climbing up to observe us. They flee screeching with delight. He stops, breathing hard. Jacky asks him why such a fuss about the kids. He explains in Arabic, then heads off after another batch of climbing kids, leather belt twirling.

'He says a kid fell yesterday and died. Today they got ten cops patrolling each face.'

'I can't see that it's that dangerous. Some kid just horsing around, probably.'

'No. He said there has been a kid killed on the pyramid on Ramadan feast every year for thirty years. That last year there were *nine* killed. He respectfully requests that we move down or go inside before we lure any others to their doom.'

At the hole the tickets are 50 piastres apiece. This is the tunnel known as El-Mamoun's. We move in as far as the granite plugs and wait while the stairs empty of sweat-soaked pilgrims streaming down wild-eyed. You must remember: these are all Egyptians, not tourists, and it is probably 90° outside compared

111

to the famous constant 68° you know it to be inside. Nobody outside was sweating.

You also know from your research that the ascending passage is 26° 17', up a tunnel about four foot square. But you have no notion how steep this is, or how small, until halfway up another stream coming down has to push past you. No wonder the sweat and wild eyes. It's too small a place for this many people! Not enough oxygen and nobody in charge and everybody knows it, just like those early rock shows – *nobody in control*.

Pushing hysteria upward, you break at last into the lofty relief of the Grand Gallery. The crowd behind goes gasping on up. You know, though, that you only have to continue on horizontally through the spur tunnel to the Queen's Chamber to find fresh air. None of the natives seem so researched.

'Ahhh,' breathes Jacky. 'Unbelievable. And none of the other pyramids have ventilation like this?'

'Nope. That's why this one is considered to be maybe something other than a tomb!'

'Right. The dead don't need ventilation.'

'I think it was another Howard-Vyse breakthrough. He figured because there were vents at these points in the King's Chamber above, maybe there was something similar here in the Queen's Chamber. So he calculated where they ought to be, gave a good knock, and there they were, within inches of coming all the way through.'

'Weird.'

'Not the weirdest, though. Look here. . . .' I run my hand over the wall, like I'm showing a classmate around the family attic. 'This stuff on the walls and ceiling? It's salt, and only in the Queen's Chamber and passages – crystallized sea salt.'

'How do the Egyptologists explain that?'

'They don't. There's no way to explain it except that this whole chamber was once filled with seawater . . . by some ancient plumber for some unknown reason, or by a tidal wave.'

'Let's go.' Jacky has had enough. 'Let's get outta here back to the hotel for a sensible beer.'

'One more stop,' I reassure him, ducking back into the passage out of the Queen's Chamber.

We reach the Grand Gallery and resume our climb, still as steep, but there is nothing oppressive in this vaulted room. More than ever I am assured that these were initiatory walkways;

112

when lit by torches instead of these fluorescent tubes, the Grand Gallery would appear to lift eternally above one's head.

Before we enter the King's Chamber I have Jacky stand and feel the protruding Boss Stone right where I know it to be in the pitch-dark little phonebooth-sized foyer. 'In case the Bureau of Standards ever goes belly up, here is the true inch.'

We duck on into the King's Chamber. The crowd of pilgrims are laughing and boo-boo-booming like frogs in a barbershop quartet contest. We walk past them to the coffer.

'It's carved from a solid piece of red granite. In angles so accurate and dimensions so universal that if every other structure were swept from the earth it would still be possible for some smart-ass cave kid with a mathematical bent to arrive at damn near all we know about plane and solid geometry, just by studying this granite box.'

We lean and look into its depths as the crowd goes boom *boom* BOOM boom ahee *hee!* – mixing laughter and rhythm and Arabic discord until the room rings like the midnight streets.

'They've captured the essence of Cairo,' Jacky admits, 'right down to the smell.'

When our eyes became accustomed to the gloom of that empty stone sepulchre we both realize that the bottom is about an inch deep in piss. Boom *boom* BOOM ahee aheeee. . . . To stave off delirium I take out my Hohner. Startled by German harmonics, the crowd becomes silent. Jacky plucks at my sleeve but I keep blowing. They all stand staring as I blow myself dizzy, filling the stone vault with good ol' G chords, and C's and F's. I'll show you ignorant pissants how a Yankee pilgrim can play and boom-boom both! I'm clear into the chorus before I realize what I'm singing:

'*Shall* we gather by the rih-ver, the beautiful the beautiful the rih-hih-verrr. . . .'

Stare away! What beautiful river did you think it was, you Moslems, you Methodists, you Bible-belters – the Mississippi? The Congo? The Ohio?

'*Yes* we'll gather by the rih-ver – '

The Amazon? The Volga? The Yangtze? With that ancient picture on the back of your dilapidated dollar and that newborn profit in your bullrushes, what the hell river did you think it was?

' – that flo-o-ohs by the throw-own . . . of God.'

Jacky hauls me out before I start preaching. By the time we're back through the Grand Gallery my head has stopped spinning but my insides are churning like a creekful of backslid Baptists.

'You look bad,' Jacky says.

'I feel bad.'

We just make it into the open. To the applause of the whole *aouda* I toss my great Mena House breakfast all over the face of the Great Pyramid.

October 18. Sick unto death. The Curse of the Pharaohs pins me sweating to the bed. I read some awful holocaust theories, have horrible dreams of humanity backsliding forever.

October 19. I try to climb back up to the thing and am again wiped out with a high fever. More reading and dreams. Extrapolating. Okay, let's say it's coming: the Shit Storm. Let's say the scientists have definitely spotted it, like in *When Worlds Collide*. People everywhere are soiling their laundry, rushing around in circles, demanding somebody do something. Do what? Send an elite sperm bank into space, as Dr Leary proposes in *Terra II*, thus giving the strain at least a shot in the dark?

Accept it as the Will of Allah and let it wash over us?

Try to outswim it?

But wait. There isn't any real evidence for the need of a lifeboat to preserve the species. The Shit Storm has happened many times and *Homo sapiens* has hung in there. What is really in jeopardy is not our asses, or our souls. It's our civilization.

Imagine, after some sudden absolute-near-annihilation (they've found mastodons frozen with fresh flowers in their mouths – *that* sudden) – that there are little clots of survivors clinging to remote existences. Imagine how they struggle to preserve certain basic tricks. How would we hang on to let's say for example *pasteurization?* It's hard to explain bacteriology to a caveful of second-generation survivors, even with the aid of some surviving libraries. Rituals would have to come first.

'Remember, *boil*-um that milk! *Boil*-um that milk!'

'Will do, Wise Old Grandsir. Boil milk!' They break into the milk song: '*Boil*-um that milk an' *kill*-um that bug that nobody see but *make*-um sick.'

The libraries exist! Old rituals hold clues to their whereabouts. Old chants! Chambers! Charts – !

114

At this point Jacky Cherry breaks into my fever in a fervour. 'Muldoon's here! He's found somebody who says he knows where it is! He's going to lead us out there tonight.'

'Knows what?' I rally a bit from my stupour. 'Who?'

'A local visionary. He had a vision three Americans were looking for a secret hall so he drew a map to it!'

'A map?'

'To an underground hall! The guy must have something on the ball to know we were looking for one, sounds to me like.'

Sounds to me like Jacky is getting a little desperate over the flak from the home office about the resultless state of our expedition, but I dress and totter out to the street. Muldoon is negotiating with a little man in a blue gellabia.

It is Marag.

IV: DOWN THE TOMBS OF TAURUS

'A drought is *upon her waters; and they shall be dried up: for it is the land of graven images, and they are mad upon their images!'*
—Jer. 50:38

Still October 19, Saturday afternoon, only a few tense seconds having elapsed.

'Good morning, my friend,' says Marag, sifting his hand from the sleeve of his blue gellabia; 'It *is* a good morning?'

I tell him it isn't a bad morning for two in the afternoon and shake his hand. We look each other over for the first time in daylight. He's older than I thought, greying, but his eyes are as youthfully bright and black as his teeth are white. He's smiling at me to see what I'll do. There's protocol at stake here on this sunny sidewalk: an acknowledgement that this is my main hash man could be a *faux pas* costing me a good connection; on the other hand discretion might be taken as a snub, etc.

Muldoon ends my dilemma by introducing him to me as Marvin instead of Marag. I tell him my name is Devlin. Muldoon says Marvin has this *map*, and quick little hands produce a roll of paper. Something is dimly pencilled second-hand over a kid's math assignment still showing through. We lean to look and it rolls back up like a windowshade.

'Marvin says it's a map, to a Secret Hall of Holy History – '

115

'Secret *Tunnel*,' Marag corrects, 'of Angel History. Not far. I have car and driver will take you there *very reliable*. Hut! Nephew! My friends from America. Hut hut hut!'

He waves at a guy slouched against the fender of his cab at the curb, a surly sort about twenty years old, wearing polyester-knit slacks and a polo shirt, sleeves rolled up to emphasize the arms-folded biceps. He looks us over, the set of his jaw and the beetle of his brow letting us know *here*, by Allah, is a customer cool yet dangerous. He answers Marag's hail with a curt nod, the very image of rawboned threat were the effect not flawed by the driver's actual squat-legged big-butted round-shouldered shape.

'Not so much education,' Marag confides, 'but a fine driver.'

'Say, Marvin, just where'd you get that map?' I can't remember mentioning anything to him the other night about the Hall of Records.

'I hear talk the American doctors one with baldness are searching for the Secret Tunnels. I draw this last night this map.'

'You drew it?'

'And have my son write in the words. Very reliable secret map. My family is live at Nazlet el-Samman many hundreds of years, pass down *all* is know.'

Muldoon says all he is know is Marvin wants ten pounds for it. Ten pounds! Jacky and I say at once.

'Only five for me,' Marag hastens to add. 'Other five for car and my nephew driver.' He notes our hesitation and shrugs good-naturedly. 'As you wish, my friends. I don't blame you being cautious. We take only five now – for car, gasoline – and *my five* for map when you are return satisfied. Is good? Only five now?'

Five seems to be the going front figure. Marag keeps grinning at me.

'Let's go for it,' I decide. I take a five-pound note out of my wallet. The hand comes out and the note vanishes into the folds of the blue gellabia; not as quick as the nephew's eye, though; he comes fuming over and he and Marag have a splendid argument in screaming Egyptian.

As squat as the nephew is, he still is some inches taller than his bantyweight uncle, and you can tell he's pushed a little iron down at the YMMA. Still, it's an obvious no-contest. That

116

bright-eyed little mink of a man would swarm all over Cool Yet Dangerous, leaving nothing but a pear core.

'My nephew is a *fool with money*,' he confides, showing us all toward the battered Fiat. 'But a most reliable driver you can be insured.'

As he bustles around the car closing us in, I realize he isn't coming along.

'Also most *furthersome*. His name is T'udd.'

'Thud?' we all ask in mutual dawning apprehension. '*Thud?*' – as a thick brown thumb punches the starter into a victorious roar. Pumping the foot feed, Thud turns and gives us a thick-lipped leer of triumph. The map is crumpled in his hand.

'I haven't seen a grin like that,' Jacky concedes, 'since Sal Mineo won the Oscar for *Young Mussolini*.'

Thud adjusts the mirror so he can see his reflection, brushes back an oily lock, then 'peels out' is, I believe, the term: lays rubber in a squealing fishtailing brodie away from the Mena House turnaround off down Pyramid Boulevard, the pedal to whatever metal there is in a Fiat floorboard.

Too late we realize we are in the sainted presence of Brainless Purity; as Las Vegas has distilled Western Materialism down to its purest abstract, so Thud is the assimilated essence of motor-mad Egypt. Blinking his headlights and blaring his terrible warhonk, he charges the afternoon traffic ahead, fearless as the Bedouin! wild as the Dervish! He reaches the creeping tail end of the traffic pack at full fifty. Never touching the brake he goes rocking shockless over the shoulder to the right of a poky VW, cuts back sharply between two motorcycles, and guns into the left lane to pass a tour bus, the passengers gawking horrified as we cut back just in time, then to the other lane around one of those big six-wheeled UAR machines the two soldiers on top with a cannon – passing left or right, again and again, just making it each time by the skin of our grill, finally getting in front of the pack to what looks like a promising clear stretch a chance to really un*wind* – except for one minor nuisance, a little accident jam ahead, about thirty cars, coming up fast –

'Thud!'

There is the sickening metal-to-metal cry of brakes screaming for new shoes; then the shudder of the emergency against more scored metal; finally the last-minute cramping skid. My door is inches from the rear of a flatbed full of caged turkeys.

'Jacky for the love of God, tell him no more! I've got a wife and kids! Tell him, Muldoon!'

It's no use; both interpreters are in tongue-tied shock. Thud can't hear anyway, has his horn full down and his head out the window, demanding to know the *meaning* of all this mangled machinery impeding us. He eases ahead so we can see. It's two flimsy Fiat taxis just like ours, amalgamated head on, like two foil gum wrappers wadded together. No cops; no ambulances; no crowd of rubberneckers; just the first of those skinny street jackals sniffing the drippings, and what apparently is the surviving cab driver groggily standing on the centre stripe with a green print handkerchief pressed to his bloody ear with one hand, waving the oncoming traffic around with the other.

Thud keeps shouting until he provokes a response. He pulls his head back in and passes the information on to us, so matter-of-factly that Jacky is brought from his trance to translate.

'He says that's a relative, mother's side. The dead cabby is also a relative. Was a good relative but not a very good driver – not *amin*, not reliable.'

'Tell him about my unreliable heart!'

Too late – Thud has spotted what looks to him like a remote possibility, is peeling around the rival driver – the green paisley handkerchief hanging unheld to the injured ear as the man shakes both fists after us in outrage – Thud paying no heed – all under control – situating the rumpled map on the dash so he can study it as he simultaneously scans the road checks his face in the rearview honks his horn drives down the wrong side of the centre line straight at a big fucking yellow Dodge panel oncoming with furniture all inside packed clear to the windshield a brass bedstead lashed to the grill in front springs on top while *Thud* – [Here, the page of the journal is smeared]

October 20. Twentieth Sunday after Pentecost, just after dawn and before breakfast . . . out in back of my cabana in chaise lounge without the chaise.

Jacky went to the desk last night and raised a *dausha* about them not putting his call through to Jann Wenner and us not getting separate rooms yet. He was so effective they moved us right out of our nice room into two poolside cabanas, tiny cement cells intended for bathing-suit changers, not residents: a

118

hard cot, no windows, no hot water, costing as much apiece as our other room. But Jacky was going nuts with me prowling weird in the wee wired hours from all that Turkish coffee and Pakistani hash. . . .

I've wheeled the lounge chair from the pool to where I can sit looking at the Great Pyramid over the hotel ledge. The morning sky is spectacular, piled with thunderheads. The air is so still I can hear the pyramid ravens jiving around the summit, a dozen black specks jostling for the king perch on the long wooden pole that is planted atop the pyramid to indicate where the peak would be if the capstone was in place. They are having a great time, swooping and skawking. Must be better than Turkish coffee. Kirlian photographs of small pyramid models show force fields streaming straight up out of the peaks, like volcanoes erupting pure energy.

There are all sorts of tales of mysterious machinations manifesting on top of the Great Pyramid: compasses going crazy, wine *botas* shooting sparks, radium paint crumbling off the wristwatch dials to rattle around inside the crystals like green sand. I should check it out before going home. . . .

Yesterday was the first time away from the pyramid since coming out from Cairo a week ago. I had resolved that I would concentrate my time only on the Giza area and resist the tourist's mistake of trying to 'see it all'.

But yesterday we were driven to see one of those *alls*, for all of my resolve, and damn near to our doom as well. Thud turned out to be about as reliable and furthersome as Marag's map, and a much dirtier burn.

As soon as we were a good skid away from the Mena House he forsook the ability to comprehend any English whatsoever, and when he finally realized that Jacky and Muldoon weren't shouting Arabic phrases for his hairbreadth triumph through that amazing pile-up he went into such a cloudy sulk that even *they* couldn't reach him. Every request for slower speeds was answered with a '*Mish fahim abadan.*'

'It means?'

'It means "I don't understand,"' Jacky screamed. 'But what it really means is we have insulted the sonofabitch! He's kidnapping us is what it amounts to.'

Thud wrenched the car full right, off the crowded Pyramid Boulevard onto a narrow blacktop running between a high shady row of Australian gum on the right side and a wide irrigation canal full of half-sunken cows and car carcasses on our left. Free at last of the sticky traffic, Thud could cruise full out with nothing in the way but insignificant items – chickens, children, donkeys, and the like.

'Thud' – I tried to make contact over a more universal frequency – 'you trite pile of outdated camel shit, *you're driving too fast!*'

'Also too far,' Muldoon added, scratching his head. 'I think he's taking us out to Sakkara, to the Step Pyramid.'

'That damned Marag set me up.'

'You mean Marvin?' In the front seat Jacky has captured the wad of paper from the dash. 'Maybe not. See, this map isn't actually to Zoser but to some area a ways past it, to a place called the Tunnels of Serapeum. See? He might have thought it meant *seraphim*, as in angels.'

We gave up trying to get through to Thud. Jacky said all our shouting was just making it worse, and Muldoon added that it was probably a good idea for us to see Sakkara anyway. For perspective. 'The Step Pyramid is the old-age champion grandaddy in all camps, except Cayce's. It's worth seeing, got a lot of soul.'

'Have you seen this Tunnel of Angel thing?'

'Serapeum? I went through it with a class. It's got a lot of – of I guess you might say *balls*.'

After about twenty miles along that canal road we took another right, west up out of the narrow Nile Valley onto another limestone plateau. When you crest the rise you can see the Giza group shining across miles of sand, like channel markers in the sun. Then, the other direction and much nearer, the step structure of King Zoser.

'Very badly gnawed by the tooth of time,' said Muldoon. 'One of the guys at the university has an act called Tennessee Egypt. He sings a song about this tomb called "The Old Rugged Pyramid".'

Thud was so placated by his magnificent drive that his comprehension returned and Muldoon talked him into detouring for a look. We followed Muldoon through the reconstructed temple gates toward the dilapidated old structure. 'Built for King Zoser, they say, by an architectural genius named Imhotep. About fifty years before the Great Pyramid, the Egyptologists say.'

120

It was hard to think of this primitive pile as being only fifty years older than the masterwork of Giza, but it was even harder to think of it as being 5,000 years younger than Cayce's construction date.

Muldoon took us to a tipped stone box at the rear of the pyramid where you climb up and look through a two-inch peephole. A stone effigy is sitting at the rear of the module, tipped back in the same incline as the box, like an astronaut ready to fire himself into space.

Muldoon told us how they think the pyramid was built by a continual adding of new wings to the basic block tomb, finally stacking them up in diminishing steps. 'Some of Khufu's contractors saw it later, the theory goes, and said, "Hey! if you just filled in those steps you'd have a *great* pyramid; let's build one for the Chief."'

He escorted us down into beautiful chambers of alabaster, tattooed ceiling-to-floor with comic strips of daily Egyptian life 5,000 years ago. There were farmers ploughing, planting, harvesting; a thief was traced from crime to capture to trial; fishermen cast nets from boats over underwater reliefs depicting finny denizens in meticulous zoological detail, some familiar, some long since disappeared.

Thud followed behind, getting more and more impatient with all this interest in things immobile. Finally he would follow no farther; he stood with his arms folded, calling out threats.

'His dander is up again,' Jacky translated. 'He says if we don't get back to his taxi he's going to go on without us.'

Even fixed again behind the wheel Thud's dander didn't go back down. All the rest of the desert drive to the Serapeum location he bitched at us for taking so long, and just to look at a lot of *dirty graves!* We tried to humour him, offering him gum, asking him to join us down the Serapeum tombs. *Phhht!* Crawl down in a big hole like a lizard? Not on *all* our lives!

We left him revving his motor and walked out into the sand. We had no problem following the trail of torn tickets to the underground temple's entrance, a wide, sloping slot cut through the limestone down to a high square door. It looked like a steep driveway down to a sub-level garage for desert trucks.

At the bottom the armed Arab took our piastres and handed us three half tickets from the pile of already torn halves. We entered the high door and turned left down a spacious passage,

121

roughly hewn through the earth. Another guard asked us for another payment and took the scraps from us and halved them again. He solemnly returned our halved halves to us and placed his on his dusty pile (which was only half the size of the other guy's halves, being only quarters) and waved us on. It grew dimmer. There was another turn, left or right (I'm lost now), and another high door and we were in the main tunnel.

It's a simple, solitary passageway cut through solid stone, rough-walled, high-ceilinged, level-floored, big enough to handle a complete subway system; two trains could come and go side by side and still have ample room along the walls for gum machines and muggers. But it's completely empty. It runs on vacantly ahead of you, until out of sight in the dim distance.

It is lit indirectly, the light coming, you realize, from large rooms chiselled alternately into each side of the tunnel about every twenty paces. These rooms are rugged, regular cubicles and similar in size, about forty feet on a side, a little higher than the roof of the tunnel and sunk a man's height deeper than the tunnel floor so when you stand at each crypt, leaning on a safety rail, you are looking down on the top of the room's sole furnishing.

It is the same in every room: one enormous granite coffer with corresponding lid pushed slightly aside allowing a peek into the empty insides. Except for different chiselled inscriptions the coffers are all identical, each carved from a single solid block of dark red granite, each stark and sombre and huge. You could have put Thud's taxi inside and closed the lid.

As far down this eerie subway as you care to walk, it is the same, room after room; one to the left; then, a few dozen paces on, the next to your right, each with its arched entrance, each with its grim granite vault identical almost to the angle of the ten-ton lid pushed askew to allow the contents to be long ago pilfered.

'They were for dead bulls,' Muldoon told us. 'Sacrificial bulls. One a year, every year for thousands of years, evidently.'

We walked down steel steps into one of the sepulchres and stood next to the giant coffer. I could reach to the top of the lid. Muldoon searched over the inscribed granite sides until he found a picture of the tomb's sacrifice.

'The bull had to look like this; had to have exactly this pattern on his rump, plus had to have two white hairs in his tail and a

122

birthmark under his tongue shaped like a scarab. Here, sight down these sides.'

The granite sides of the huge hollowed block were as flat as still water.

'Yet the archaeologists won't give them anything better than copper! That's all the tools there is evidence of from this period. Our modern high-speed diamond drill takes a *week* to poke a little hole through, but the archaelogists won't give these poor carvers anything but *copper*.'

The whole effect was macabre, disconcerting; such modern precision, for something so stone-aged. Jack stamped around the giant enigma in dismay. 'What the hell was their trip? I mean forget about the goddamned tools; even if they were equipped with Goldfinger's laser and Solomon's worm, it's *still* a hard way to carve your roast.'

'Nobody knows why they did it. Maybe it was initially intended as some kind of symbolic burial of the Age of Taurus, and they got so deep into it they kept going. But nobody knows.'

Jacky Cherry couldn't get over it. 'There's something down-right perverse about it, you know? Something – '

'Bullheaded,' Muldoon filled in. 'Which reminds me: we better see if our driver is still reliably waiting.'

We found Thud in such a thunderous peeve he wasn't going to look at us, let alone drive us home. He stared in the direction of Cairo and claimed we had robbed him of a whole afternoon's livelihood, tips and everything. He diatribed he was going to sit there and listen to the radio until some tourists arrived on one of those camel caravans from Giza. After their voyage aboard one of those smelly ships of the desert, plenty tourists would be ready to jump camel for a berth on his luxury liner, hopefully pay him enough extra to make up for what our dawdling had cost.

It was a bare-faced bluff. There might not be another caravan until tomorrow and he knew it, but he was going to milk every possible piastre out of the predicament. Worse yet, I realized, when the bastard finally consents he has it in his four-cylinder mind to scare the shit out of us!

It was getting downright depressing all around. While Thud argued with Jack and Muldoon I remembered my Polaroid; I would while away this bullshit time practising my photography.

I got the bag and bucket of negative developer out of the rear

123

seat and carried it to a little stone bench at the edge of the parking lot. When I took the camera from the bag I heard Thud's diatribe stumble slightly. And every time I snapped a button or turned a dial his concentration was further distracted. As an experiment I swung the lens toward him and he hushed entirely so he could suck in his gut. I swung on past to take a shot of the Step Pyramid. He tried to resume his tirade, but he was faltering fast. Then he saw it *produced pictures immediately!* He was a lost man.

He left Jack and Muldoon in mid-squabble and came bargaining humbly to me: all our insults, all our dawdling and delays would be forgotten and forgiven, but for only one picture of himself *produced immediately*.

I squeezed off another prizewinning shot of the sand and sky, pretending not to *fahim*. When he saw that precious film being wasted on wasteland he began to beg shamelessly.

'Snap,' he wheedled. 'Snap me; snap T'udd!'

I told him I had only one more snap in this packet and wanted to save it to get a shot of those farmers I had seen back down in the valley, so picturesque working that deep dark Nile soil. 'But I'll tell you what, Thud. You drive us nice and slow back to the Mena House and I'll get another pack.'

We were away at once. When I tried to photograph the farmers he jumped out and ran around the front of the taxi to try to find a place in the frame. I cropped out all but his bicep, but even that meagre sliver was enough to make his breath come thick and his hands grasp uncontrollably.

It was the worst attack of covetousness I have ever had the displeasure of witnessing. It was degrading and embarrassing, and a little frightening. Thud knew he was losing all cool but he couldn't help himself. He climbed under the wheel like a whipped spaniel. He readjusted the mirror, this time so he could watch me. He watched me like Dog Watches Man With Meatball. He didn't even turn on his transistor.

All the strained ride home he kept helplessly clearing his throat into the silence. When we turned up Pyramid Boulevard he forced himself to drive so slowly that it was almost as unpleasant as his speeding. By the time we reached the hotel all of us were trembling, and Thud's hands were shaking so he could hardly turn off the key. His stomach was growling. His brown face had actually gone ashen with the agony of that stretch of unnatural driving forced on him by his terrible yen.

'Snapping now?' he begged pitifully.

'Going to get film,' I told him. 'At the cabana.' I didn't dare take the camera along. He would have driven right across the pool after me.

'Hurry back and snap him soon,' Jacky Cherry called. 'Before he snaps himself.'

When Thud saw me returning he almost broke into tears. I loaded the camera and noticed my hands were shaking under the scrutiny. Jacky positioned him with sideshadow, the pyramid at his back: 'For dramatic effect.'

He stood on the curb. It took him nearly a minute to pull himself together and pump up to the right pose before nodding he was ready.

'Now! Snap *me!*'

He snatched the Polaroid print away before I could coat it. Its impact on him was incredible. As he studied his developing image on the little square of paper, we could actually see his face begin to change and shift. He set his jaw, then his shoulders. He worked his features until they presented once again the countenance of a very cool cat, watch out. His breathing slowed. His colour returned. When he had it all together, as they say, be damned if the fucker didn't demand an extra five pounds!

Another huge hassle. Thud laughed scornfully at our deal with Uncle Marag. Who is Marag? Where is he, this Marag, with the so-called car's five pounds promised, eh? Why isn't this Marag here to complete the transaction? Okay, okay, Jack sighs and hands over the five. No no, that was just the usual *fare!* (Thud glanced again at his photograph for reassurance; yep, he was still there.) *Another* five was what he was talking about, for all the time we made him wait.

I was getting tired of it. I said okay, here's the extra five. But I get the picture back.'

He gasped.

Hadn't that been the deal? I gave you picture; you gave us nice ride and no extra? He blinked, looking around. He wasn't alone. Some of the other cabbies and hustlers had ambled over to see what was happening. They were all grinning. It was very *clear* what was happening. Thud was cornered.

To save face, he had to give face up.

He snatched the bill from me and slapped the photo down on the street (face up) and roared off in his taxi, shoulders back, stomach sucked in, head held high. Almost made you proud of him.

Later that night, however, the power of the picture must have run down. He came knocking on my cabana door with one of those little metal outfits you throw away when your pack of Polaroids is empty. A little flimsy black box. He'd found it under the seat where I'd kicked it, my bag already full to the brim with the print peelings and all that other Polaroid waste.

He grinned triumphantly, holding the little box high in the air.

He would trade, he carefully explained, this obviously valuable photographic attachment for the picture, which could be of no possible value to me. He stood, grinning and waiting. How could I explain to him that I had never coated his picture and that the prints from these special positive-negative Polaroid films fade blank in minutes without that coating goop? Besides, that other deal had gone down. So I told him no dice; he could keep the valuable photographic attachment, I'd keep the picture, albeit nonexistent.

'No dice?' he cried. 'No dice is no trade?'

'No trade is what no dice is. No picture. No deal.'

He was dumbfounded. He stared at me with a new respect; here was someone as bullheaded as he was. He cursed and threatened me for a while, in Arabic and English and three or four other fractional languages, brandishing a black metal box that was as empty as his threats.

When he finally stalked off, bewildered and pissed, I made a mental note to henceforth check both ways very carefully before crossing any busy Egyptian thoroughfares.

Back from supper I finish washing my negatives in the little gallon bucket of chemicals you have to carry with this kind of Polaroid film. A hassle and a nuisance.

I bought this complicated process because of all the photogs over the years who have sought to snare my likeness – affronting my view, plaguing my pose, making me stumble where I had walked sure before, always promising, 'I *know* it's a bit of a bother but I'll send you *prints!*' – only to disappear into their darkrooms never to be seen again.

126

I thought this process would be more equitable; the subjects could have their print, I'd have the negative. But piss on it. It's just too much hassle.

V: WITHIN THE STONE HEART

For there is nothing covered, that shall not be revealed; and hid, that shall not be known.   *—Jesus*

When you got nothin' to say, my Great-uncle Dicker advised me once in a kind of Arkie ode to optimism, go ahead and say it.

'Because it's like having nothin' to serve for supper but say a pot of water and some salt; could be after you get the water boiling and salted, some coloured cook on a potato wagon might aimlessly run over one o' yer prize hens . . . *ob*-ligate herself to you.'

Advice I have followed, as a potboiler of aimless words, to many a last-minute successful stew.

'How-and-*ever*,' Uncle Dicker must have amended, 'don't invite a bunch over to take supper on the basis of this could-be. Help is just too blessed unree-*lie*-abul!'

An amendment I must have forgotten, because here I am trying to write in Egypt, with a table full of invited readers, bellies growling, salty pots steaming, but no sign of any last-minute Jemima *or* her potatoes.

To tell the truth, when Marag and his map didn't come through, I pretty much gave up watching the road past the henhouse. I wish I could duck out of the kitchen entirely. Let Jann Wenner make a change in his menu: 'Scratch the chicken stew special, Jacky, and open some windows; the whole diner is steamed up.'

The vaunted Secret Sanctorum? I was closer to opening it in Dayton, Ohio, than moping here in Giza watching my linen maid suck a persimmon – I can't even open a conversation. 'Hot today,' is all the talk I can come up with, though I know her name to be Kafoozalum and the juices of the fruit are dripping. Her eyes are on me like the top two buttons of her Mena House uniform, talk about open.

I know she speaks English. I've had many an opportunity to watch her prattle around the cabanas, cart full of fresh white

127

linen and uniform full of ripe brown hide, but never had occasion to make conversation more than Hello or Thanks, even when she gave me her most treasured smile, 14-carat incisors, conversation pieces both of them . . . until this noon.

I'd been hurrying back to the hotel with an exciting find. Buttoned in my khaki shirt pocket was the best thing I'd found since the '66 Pontiac convertible: a fantastic old Roman coin, I think, or Greek, with a noble profile still clearly raised from its time-battered bronze.

In my enthusiasm to show Jacky Cherry that I could find *something* of ancient value, I had headed back as the crow flies. Instead of circling the grounds to the front gates I had managed a running vault over the rear wall of the compound. I lit, feet first, right between the spread brown knees of Kafoozalum on a little square tablecloth.

I thought she was having lunch. Staggering to keep from stepping in her beans or on her knees, I managed quite a dance before I could catch my balance and hop off. I saw then that instead of food the cloth had been spread with what looked like some kind of Egyptian tarot. She gathered the cards prudently out of my way, glaring up at me in an expression both enticing and curious.

I apologized and explained about my coin, and that I meant nothing disrespectful, jumping on her.

'I mean on your cards. Can I see them?'

'You bet!' The grin flashed and the two golden incisors winked out at me. 'Sure!'

When I was comfortable on a sack of cement, she smoothed the linen back out and began spreading the cards in rows for me to see. They weren't tarot after all. They were her personal collection of those saccharoidal 'posecards' that you see sold at all the knick-knack stands. Only these are for the natives, not the tourists. They display Egyptian fashion models, male and female, in stiffly tailored romantic poses. Mostly of marriage and courtship. Instead of a major arcanum like *The Lovers*, for instance, you have *Handsome Young Couple at the Girl's Door Saying Goodnight with Soulful Looks* or *Fiancée Alone, Beaming Wet-Eyed at Her Mailbox by the Flowery Gate with a Letter from Him* – all always in Cairo's latest hair and haberdashery, all always beautiful, loving, beaming. In short, sickening. But I was impressed by the way she presented her presentation.

128

She reverently dealt the last one, her favourite (*Beautiful Young Couple Still in Wedding Finery Alone for the First Time at Last or So They Think for We See in the Windowpanes Behind Them the Wedding Party Watching, as He Lifts Her Veil, Tenderly, and as She Touches His Moustache, Provocatively*), then lifted her lashes to me with a look asking, in any language, What are you waiting for, fool? I responded by inviting her to drop into my cabana when she got her next break, I'd show her my Polaroid negatives –

Now she's accepted, traipsed into my cell with an armload of fresh folded damask and let the door blow closed behind her. Preliminary rites have been observed; we've exchanged pictures and she's taken the persimmon from the dish. Nothing remains but for me to incant some key words, unlock the doors of our delight. And all I can say is Hot today.

'What is you write?' Dripping on my notebooks, here.

'Nothing. Notes. To remember what happened. . . .'

All for lack of simple courage, for fear of international faux pas. I sit gnawing my tongue until she mercifully takes us off the hook.

'*Ya Salam!*'

Photos traded, fruit gone, there is nothing left for a maid to do but check the time on her wrist *how* it flies! She thanks me in a rush and scoops up her unrumpled linen, peeks a quick check both ways out my door, and is off to her cart, sucking on the seed.

When she has traded all the clean laundry on her cart for soiled she comes wheeling back past my open door and inquires in at me, 'Is yet hot to you, the day?' I tell her yes, yes hot. She encourages me to brace up; the winds change any day now.

'All will pass.' She smiles. 'Even the diarrhoeas.'

And wheels on, leaving me tongue-tied like a hick fool indeed. What a low blow from a linen maid! Nevertheless, better toss the little filly a nice tip when you check out. How nice? Real nice. This is why the help in foreign realms always like us Americans best: we can always be expected to tip more, because we are always so inadequate of what is expected.

October 23, Wednesday. The mosquitoes and scarabs have pinned Jacky Cherry up against his cabana wall. Also Yasir Arafat is taking a side trip from the Moslem convention in Cairo to visit the historic pyramids. He was allegedly seen lunching in a private portico off the main dining room. A sinister-looking coterie of bodyguards and lieutenants is spotted darkly around to make sure the Holy Land tour members don't start anything. This doesn't make Jacky any more comfortable. He catches the 900 bus into Cairo to see if he can't get lodging with fewer pests.

I walk up the hill, stopping at the shop nearest the pyramid to buy a miniature hookah I've had my eye on. The shop is an orderly little side cranny of a building labelled Poor Children's Hospital. I ask the proprietor how he happens to have a place so close to the pyramid. He says because the profits help the hospital cure the Poor Children. I ask him what it is exactly that these Poor Children are sent out here, to the base of the Great Pyramid, to be cured of. After struggling to find a name for the disease he finally points back toward the city.

'Of the pray-sure – eh? – of the city Cairo, they come to be cure. You understanding?'

I take the hookah, nodding, and go out to seek my own cure. I had thought to find a private place somewhere on the pyramid's outskirts, but there is a big crowd of tourists. I climb up to the third course and sit on the casing stones and watch the hustlers descend on each new shipment of live ones. They are merciless. One poor woman actually breaks into tears.

'Seven years I saved for this, damn you! *Leave me alone!*'

The dapper camel-panderer, backing away for fear of perpetrating a coronary, gets tangled in his animal's rope and falls into a heap of fresh camel manure. He stares at the stain on his fresh white gellabia with such dejection I think he might cry himself.

I wonder if they have a similar hospital in Cairo to take care of pyramid pressure casualties. . . .

October 24, Thursday late. Just wobbled down from a bizarre bar scene where I finally made contact with my resident pyramid colleagues, the cosmic ray scientists. All of them (except for the Egyptian students) proved to be very learned and equally drunk.

The new Mena Lounge is a terrible bar, pretentious and expensive. I stalked in wearing my British walking shorts and pith helmet (a dusty day at the digs) and splurged on one of

130

their overpriced gin-and-tonics – for tradition's sake – just as a real Englishman complete with muttonchops and ascot came reeling over from one of the tables behind the plastic arabesque.

'*Be-ah*, please,' he enunciated, 'And some *pea*-nuts.'

In a voice so high-handed it's no mystery why the British were kicked out of all their colonies.

The dour Egyptian behind the bar bit his tongue and obeyed. I told the Englishman he hadn't better use that tone on a bartender in Oregon.

'Unlikely one would bloody ever *be* in Oregon,' he said, finally focusing on me. 'But see our *out*fit! Monty's Dynasty, what? That Rommel campaign? By God's wound one has to agree with the professor – this great grimy crude pot of a place *does* serve up specimens from every period.'

He'd been pointed out to me previously as one of the ray experts here with the new spark chamber specially constructed for another try at probing the pyramid. I told him I'd also come to this great pot of possibilities in search of hidden chambers.

'This is what I thought one was supposed to wear.'

'Great pot of nonsense, you want my inebriated expert's opinion. On the other hand, if you demand sober-er-er experts, come. . . .'

He picked up his beer and peanuts, then hooked my arm to tow me back to his table, introducing me as the renowned fellow pyramidiot, Sir Hidden Chambers-Pott. 'On with our pith helmet, Sir Hidden; give these loutish clods an eyeful of the real archaeological élan!'

They were five in all: the Real Englishman, a burly black-bearded American about my age, a suave old German wearing tinted glasses and a white linen suit, and two apprentice experts from the University of Cairo. The loutish clods barely noticed me, for all my élan. They went right back to their interrupted conversation concerning the deeply significant sociopolitical, teleological, and religious ramifications of the upcoming heavy-weight title fight in Zaire.

'I don't care if Ali takes up Tibetan Yoga and learns to levitate,' the American proclaimed. 'Foreman is still going to waste him. Kayo-*pow!* Guar-an-teed.'

He had a virile delivery and build, burly arms and neck squeezed into a T-shirt. A stencil across the chest declared him a

131

member of the *Stanford Linear Accelerator Computer Spacewar Team*, their motto: *Never Say Hyper!*

'Sure, Ali *was* great, a goddamned saint of a fighter. But what made him great wasn't his faith. It was number one his speed – which has slowed considerably – and number two his needle. If *any*thing esoteric gave him special powers it was his goddamn needle, right?'

'Just so,' said the Real Englishman. 'His bloody needling blacky's mouth – '

'But he tries to pull his needle on *this* man – "Yo' gonna fall in nine, you honky-lovin shine!" – it simply is not going to work. Not on Big George. This ain't no Uncle Liston! This ain't no paranoid cub scout Floyd Patterson! This is a bona fide bright-eyed one-track-minded *Jeezus* freak and could give less a shit about what the black crowd thinks of him.'

He was speaking toward the two students, but I had the impression that it was really for the benefit of the older man.

'So if Ali can't psyche him then what's it come back to? Physical ability. Speed, size, and strength. And Foreman is faster bigger younger. I don't care *what* country he's fighting in.'

'Just so,' agreed the Englishman. 'Modern tactics over heathen superstition. Guaranteed kayo.'

This stirred the German professor to rebuttal. 'So?' He chuckled softly and shook his head at the Englishman. 'Just so like your modern British tactics kayoed the heathen Nasser?'

'Not fair!' the Englishman flared back, stung. 'But for that bloody Eisenhower we *would* have – '

'I must again remind you young gentlemen: this battle will be taking place in the middle of the African continent at three in the morning under the full Scorpio moon.'

The American told the old man he'd been reading too much Joseph Conrad. 'Maybe a few years ago Ali could've put the whammy on Foreman, but this is 1974. Things've changed, as old Ali's gonna find out. Just because the guy he's fighting is black ain't no guarantee any more the African whammy's gonna work on him.'

'Neither is being Christian a guarantee of the certain kayo,' the professor reminded them, smiling. 'As we in Germany found out.'

'Been a mystery to me ever since, now you bring it up,' the

Real Englishman said, pouting over his peanuts. 'Damned unlike him, meddling in over here.'

'Unlike Ali? Not really, not if you followed Ali's career. Ali's style – '

'Not Ali, you Yankee dimwit,' the Englishman snapped. '*Eisenhower!*'

This provoked such a fit of mirth that the American tipped over his drink, laughing. Then, scooting back to avoid the spill, he fell out of his chair. The students helped him back up and set him in his chair, still laughing. This time he drew the German's sting; the moment the tinted glasses fixed him the giggle hushed. The German took off his coat and folded it in his lap deliberately. A tense quiet fell over our table – over the entire room, in fact. The drinkers at the other table sipped in thoughtful silence while the Moslems moved their lips, thanking Allah for forbidding them the evil of alcohol.

True, all three scientists were soused to their Ph.D.s, but that didn't explain the tension. After a minute I asked how the cosmic ray probe was coming. 'Very satisfactory,' the American told me. 'On Chephren and Mykerinos, damned satisfactory!' He took a drink of my gin-and-tonic and hulked again over the table, attempting to rally from the old German's strange sting. He admitted they'd found nothing earthshaking in these two, but for the Great Pyramid they had great expectations.

'Going to scan from the *outside*, this time, goddammit! Set the receiver up *inside* the Queen's Chamber. The holiday crowds should have dwindled enough to install it by tomorrow afternoon, the next day for certain!'

The Real Englishman disagreed. 'Device worth upwards a million pounds sterling? Want some camel driver micturating in it? These people are wild! Unpredictable!'

I asked them what they hoped to find, their best hope? The American said what he wanted was a chamber of filthy hieroglyphs. The German said he also hoped to find a chamber, but one containing that dream of every Egyptologist: an unrobbed coffin. The students said the same. The Englishman, regaining some of his puff, said that what *he* hoped to find was an *end* to all this bloody tommyrot and twaddle, once and for all.

'Likely all we'll grub out of that sanctified hill of beans will be a couple of carved geegaws worth about three and six on the geegaw market. But at least that'll be an *end* to it.'

'So why risk it?' I had to ask. 'A device worth a million pounds sterling? What justifies such an investment?'

'Careful.' The German laid his kindly smile on me like the tip of a whip. 'This is not the kind of question to ask in the field.'

'True enough,' the American agreed. 'That's the kind of question that'll be asked a-plenty back at the home office. For what it's costing to send me over here Stanford could *build* a pyramid.'

'Exactly! What's the home office's best hope? Why do – '

I didn't finish. The German's linen jacket had slid from his lap, disclosing the explanation for the table's mysterious vibes: he was holding not only the American's beefy paw in one of his long-nailed hands, he was also holding the hand of the Egyptian student seated next to him in the other. All eyes averted diplomatically from the little hand show, to drinks, peanuts, etc. The Englishman chose to turn his attention to me and my question.

'You mean what's it worth, don't you, duck? What's in the pot? Right-o, then; let's put our pyramid stakes on the table.'

He swept a space clear of shells.

'First, let me list some of the Known Negotiable Assets: It's a multidimensional bureau of standards, omni-lingual and universal, constructed to both incorporate and communicate such absolutes as the bloody *inch* (a convenient ten million of which equals our polar axis) *plus* our bloody damned circumference, our weight, the bloody length not only of our solar year and our sidereal year but also our catch-up or *leap* year . . . not to mention the bloody distance of our swing around our sun, or the error in our spin that produces the wobble at our polar point that gives us the 26,920-year Procession of the bloody Equinoxes. This *is* the dawning of the age of Aquarius, you see.

'Digging deeper in our stone safe we find deposited such bluechip securities as the rudiments of plane geometry, solid geometry, the beginnings of trigonometry, and – probably more valuable than all these mundane directions and distances and weights put together – the three mightiest mathematical tricks of them all: first being of course pi, that constant though apparently inconclusive key to the circle. Second, phi, the Golden Rectangle

134

transmission box of our aesthetics enabling us to shift harmoniously and endlessly without stripping gears so long as 2 is to 3 as 3 is to 5 as 5 is to 8 as 8 is to 13. Get it? And, third, the Pythagorean theorem, which is really just an astute amalgam of the first two short cuts and about as attributable to Pythagoras as soul is to Eric Clapton.'

'Bravo,' the German applauded, but the Englishman's blood was up and he was not to be distracted.

'In Accounts Probable, the dividends look equally inviting. Based on the admission that so far we have been able to comprehend and appreciate the pyramid's info in terms of and thus only up to *our own*, then how much must be contained in this bloody five-sided box that we *cannot yet see?* Wouldn't a folk who knew enough about the sun to utilize its rays and reflections – even its periodic sunspots and their effects – be likely to have a suggestion or so for us about solar power? Hut! Call the Minister of Energy! And mightn't an astronomy so accurate as to aim a stone tunnel in *pure parallel* with our axis at a starless space in space, or point a radius from the centre of the earth through the summit of this stone pointer at the star in Pleiades – that is indicated by drawings gleaned from centuries as the *centre* star about which the *other six* of the constellation are orbiting and *perhaps our sun as well!* – have some helpful hints for NASA? Call them, I say – hut hut – the Home Office, the UN, the Pentagon. What's a few billion in research to the Pentagon if they can get their hands on a ray so precise as to cut granite to watchwork accuracy yet so powerful as to sink a whole bloody continent from the face of the waters to the mud and mire of mythology?'

'It's as viable as research on the fusion bomb,' the American encouraged.

'But let us speak frankly, mates. The aforementioned is all just collateral, just bloody pignoration compiled to get us bonded by the bureaucrats. The *real* treasure, as all Pyramidiots passionately know in their secretmost chamber of hearts, whether they mention it in their prospectus or not, lies in Accounts Receivable.'

The vision of this priceless prize brought him unsteadily to his feet. He stood weaving a moment, his chin trembling, then spread his arms as though he addressed all creation.

'Something is *owed* us. The debt is clearly implied by the scar

135

of its erasure. We've been short-changed and the books have been brazenly juggled. It's obvious to even the densest bleeding auditor: they are trying to cover up our fall! A whole long column has been rubbed out and written over and the embezzlement assiduously concealed by fraudulent bookkeepers from Herodotus to Arnold Toynbee! But for all their artfulness the debt still shows, a bloody eighteen-and-a-half-minute buzzing gap marking the removal of something important – no, of something imperative! – to this court's search for our dues. How much has been pilfered from us, mates? How much of our minds, our *souls?* How is it that the same species responsible for that great temple out there is now administering this bloody bushwah tourist trap featuring flat beer and unpredictable hoodlums strolling the grounds outside my window wearing dark glasses and revolvers?'

He had found his focus again. His voice rang through the lobby like Olivier in a Shakespearean tirade.

'I demand an explanation! As a human being I am *owed* an accurate accounting, by the heavens, *owed* an honest audit!'

It was a cry for the benefit of all the short-changed everywhere, spoken out of a cauldron of social outrage and cosmic inspiration and flat beer. He did not let his eyes drop back to us. He turned on his heel and strode from the lobby in his stateliest stagger. There was actual clapping.

When the reviews of the Englishman's speech subsided I hoped to find out more about their ray results, but the mention of the Mena House's new gun-toting tenants had led instead to the topic of Arafat. Not a man much loved, I gathered; even the Moslem students had bad things to say about the Palestinian guerrilla leader. The German was scathing.

'Storm trooper at heart, a filthy terrorist with a limousine.' He took off his glasses and massaged the bridge of his nose. 'I was at the Munich games when they murdered those fine young Israeli athletes. Wrestlers, as I remember. Filthy! I will confess to you all: If given the opportunity I would sprinkle ground glass in his Turkish coffee when they wheel the cart past in the hall.'

The American said he would use LSD instead. 'It'd be a gasser watching Yasir on a bummer. Clean up his Karma, too, heh heh. If we just knew where to get a hit . . .'

I excused myself and bought a beer and carried it back here to my cabana. I suppose I could have given them my Murine bottle;

I'm sure not using it. But I'm against dosing. We just don't have the right to launder other people's Karmas, no matter how filthy. Besides, those desert gunsels? Who knows what they might do with the jams kicked out. Watching them prowl around with their revolver butts showing, I too find myself thankful their prophet forbade them booze: they're wild enough sober. As the Englishman said, unpredictable.

October 27, Sunday. It's all looking less and less resultful to Jacky. This morning we found a fence had been put up around the Sphinx.

'Little like closing the barn door,' Jacky observed, 'after the Turks have already shot off the Sphinx's nose.'

Ignoring the mixed metaphor, the big cat-thing kept on glowering, over our heads past the squalor of Nazlet el-Samman, toward the Nile.

This afternoon things look a bit better to Jack. He's struck up an acquaintance with Kefoozalum, even had room service bring them two rum Cokes.

'She's not a Moslem, she's a Copt. The Copts are a sect of Egyptian Christians, tolerated because of their tiny size and their seniority. In fact they claim to be the *first* Christians, the people who cared for Joseph, Mary, and the Kid while they were in Egypt escaping Herod. Some even say they are the last remnants of the Essenes, thus actually *preceding* Christ as Christians by dint of second sight and signs and visions supposedly indigenous to their faith.'

'That could explain her stare,' I mused; the traditional Moslem woman is never supposed to look into any man's eyes but her father's, brother's, or husband's. 'So frank and forward.'

'Could be,' Jacky said. 'She buses into Cairo every Sunday morning to attend church, the very church, she told me, that housed the holy family twenty centuries ago. A place most miraculous. Just a few years ago, she said, a workman saw a woman on the roof. He went inside and got the Coptic minister, who came out and ordered her down. Then he noticed a *light* emitting from her: "Holy Mary Mother of God," he exclaims, "it's the Virgin!" Or something to that effect.

'Anyway, the whole congregation came out and saw her, and next Sunday *saw her again*. The next Sunday the churchyard was

137

packed – Moslems, Christians, agnostics – everybody saw her! It went on for two months. Thousands witnessed her weekly appearance.'

Jacky smiled and raised his brows.

'The crowds finally got so big the Egyptian government put a wall around the place and charged twenty-five piastres at the turnstile. The apparition immediately stopped appearing.'

'Far out,' I say. 'I wouldn't have stood for it either. Not when they're getting fifty piastres a head to look at those empty bull coffins.'

October 28, Monday. Jacky finally lands a room in Cairo. I go in with him and check at the KLM office. I can get a plane out this coming Thursday morning, or Monday night November 4. I tell the coiffed Dutchess to book me on the Thursday morn flight.

Now that he's been accepted back into metropolitan civilization, Jacky wants to stay another week. 'Why not take a room with me in Cairo? Wait and catch the November fourth flight? See some belly boogie? That way you could spend Halloween night at the tombs.'

I tell him I'd rather spend the eve with the kids in Oregon, passing out popcorn balls to mummies in rubber masks. He shrugs. 'Whatever. But do you think Thursday gives you enough time to find – to finish your pieces?'

I appreciated his mid-sentence alteration. I would have been forced to concede it was highly unlikely that I will be able to 'find it' by Thursday, or by Monday for that matter. The closer I've looked the less I've seen. The pyramid disappears within itself as you approach it. The longer you look the more your theories become dwarfed by the blunt actuality of the puzzle.

I walk the ruins around the Giza plateau largely unaccosted now. I have learned a trick of bending down to pick up a rock as soon as I detect an approaching hustle. I then examine it through the little sighting lens on my engineer's compass, and the hustlers back off respectfully. 'Shh. Observe. The Yankee doctor has found a clue. Observe the manner he thoughtfully scratch his great bald puzzle piece.'

Little do they know. I'm just drifting. Peter O'Toole crossing the desert on his camel, watching his shadow ripple hypnotically over the sand. Omar Sharif rides up from behind and swats him with his camel crop. What?

138

You were drifting.

Oh, no! I was thinking. I was –

You were drifting.

After a solitary supper I shuffle back to my cabana. I can't rest or write. Rest from what? Write what? I have less an idea of what I'm looking for than when I left Oregon a month ago. My poke's about played out and the cards have been cold or crooked, like that Marag and his five-pound fake map.

And my ace in the hole? The Murine bottle that I had promised myself to use should all else fail? Out of the question. As Muldoon Greggor expressed it, 'I wouldn't want to try to divine its secret with acid. Soon as your armour was blasted away, these watchmen and hustlers would crawl all over you. They wouldn't leave anything but a dry husk.'

I do have one of those five hash fingers left. That's safer. Perhaps, if I could get a place on the bad side in one of those tombs, under the stars in sight of the Sphinx . . . bound to afford more inspiration than this cinderblock cell. So I gather my paraphernalia and strike out into the night.

It's late. The road is empty of cabs. The sentries nod me past. The searchlights and speakers of the evening's Sound and Light are shut away in their tombs and bolt-locked, but there's plenty of illumination: the moon heralded new by that Ramadan cannon two weeks ago is now nearing full; the Great Pyramid shines mournfully under it for lack of anything better to do.

On the moony slope I find the seat where we were brought by Muldoon that first night. There's more wind than I thought. I roll a page from my notebook and light it with my last match. I didn't twist it tight enough and it flares up but I'm determined to get one hit, sucking so frantically at the hookah mouth tube that I'm unaware I have company.

'Good evening, Mr D'bree.'

I see his little face glittering so close that I think at first it's the flame itself. Hash sparks fly everywhere.

'You have trouble with hubble-bubble this good evening?'

I tell him not any more, no. With the last flicker we both can see the bowl is empty. I toss the ash into darkness. He tells me he is most sorry, but to come, follow him, for a *more nicer smoke* than hubble-bubble. Does he mean a joint? This hash and hookah business is very ritzy but a joint would be nice. . . .

Marag takes me to one of the tombs down the slope where the

limestone plateau just begins to drop away toward the village. There is a faint rectangle of light hissing from the tomb's door; Marag stops me with a feathery hand on my arm before we get too close.

'This is my friend,' he whispers. 'A young desert boy but already guard this corner. Very good position! Still, he is not at ease, it is not his home. You got hashish?'

'You're not gonna mix it with tobacco? I don't smoke, and cigarettes hit me harsh.'

'No. No harsh cigarette. Good stuff, from Finland. You'll see.'

He reaches the door of the tomb just as a faceless form is coming out with a carbine to check on the noise. The light hisses brighter and they stand talking in it. Our desert boy wears a mask of shadows. I can see the rifle is an ancient American Springfield .30–.06 left over from the battle of Bordeaux, and I can see the way his hands fondle it, but his face I can't see.

Marag brings him over. He tells him my name but not me his; nor do we shake hands. He doesn't speak. The turban he has cowling his face is patched and frayed with age, though I judge him some years short of twenty. But not a boy; probably never a boy.

I get some kind of pass from this phantom because he lowers the .30–.06 and trades it for a carpet. He unrolls the carpet on the sand and nods us to sit. From his gellabia pocket he takes a tin box and opens it. Marag reaches again for my hashish and I relinquish it reluctantly.

The phantom carefully heats and crumbles the hash into the box. Nobody says anything. He's very meticulous and takes a very long time to roll three big sticks. We would have been smoking the first one while he practised but nobody says anything. He finally lights and passes it to me.

'It is tobacco all right!'

'But not cigarette,' Marag hastens to add. 'It's pipe tobacco. And Finnish!'

The guy's wife steps from the door of the tomb into the moonlight, carrying a copper tray and three glasses. She is traditionally barefooted and pregnant and the fact embarrasses her. When she leans to place the tray on the sand you can feel the blush. Marag makes some crack in Arabic about her girth and she skitters back into the tomb.

140

The tea is wickedly strong and sweet but the Finnish tobacco, I'm forced to admit by the time we're done with the first round, isn't all that bad. The wife appears with a kettle as the husband is lighting the second joint – spliff, rather – refills our glasses, and disappears again, all in a moment. This round of tea is milder and they are running low on sugar, but right on cue with the third joint she appears to replenish us. Hardly more than hot water. She remains outside, indicating that the goodies are gone; if more is wanted it will require her trotting barefooted to the village. She stands as though weightless for all her swollen condition, the globe of her belly buoying her up. The husband finishes the weak drink and returns the glass to the tray before he shakes his head no; we've had enough.

She leans to take up the tray. This time the young husband reaches to her foot and affectionately squeezes her bare instep. Marag gasps at this most un-Moslemlike display.

'It *is* as they say.' He clucks. 'These kids smoke dope and our old ways of behave are forget.'

I guess it must be Marag's version of irony, but it's hard to say. That last one did it. The gas light from the tomb hisses back down and the moon moons. We sit for a long time, looking at the stars and listening to the dogs keep each other abreast of the neighbourhood night. When it's time to leave, we all three stand at once. The young guard puts the tin box in his pocket and rolls up his carpet. The shadow head on the shadow body nods goodbye and disappears after its mate.

Never a word. Never a chin or cheekbone let stray out in the prying moonlight. But that faceless presence has furnished a circle in the dirt with the grandeur of Araby.

We are scrabbling down into the village, where Marag is going to make another score for me. I'm high like a motherfucker. The Sphinx looks like a big old mouser purring by the path, fat on camels and Fiats.

'My young friend is far from his Bedouin home.' Marag feels he must explain, looking back up the dim trail at me. 'I get him this position. He is family. I leave that village too, when I am very little, very young. *His* relative get *me* position.'

He was turned around walking backwards down the steep rut now.

'This young fellow, I think he will not stay long. He will go back to the desert for the birth. When he comes back I will get him another position. It is good, is it not? Having a person like family at the pyramid?'

I can't help wondering what he's trying to promote me into. Maybe I should make it clear that a wealthy globetrotter I am not. It could be years before I can afford to return, decades. He should save his pitch for a better prospect.

I can't go with him to score, he explains. I will wait at his home. I follow him down sandstone paths that get wider and leveller until they become miniature streets crisscrossing between a maze of tiny block dwellings. The streets are too narrow for cars but there's plenty of traffic – nocturnal strollers and striders, men and women, goats and kids. Cronies squatting against the wall grin and wink at Marag whisking past with a big live one in tow.

In the square of light before one of the doorless doorways a knot of kids are playing with homemade clay marbles. A little boy jumps up from the game and scampers after us. He looks about seven, which means he's probably close to eleven if you allow for the protein lag. Marag pretends not to notice him, then gruffly makes as if to swat him away. The kid ducks, laughing, and Marag takes him by the hand.

'This is Mister Sami,' he explains, still gruff. 'My oldest son. Sami, say hello to my friend Mister Deb-*ree*.'

'Good evening, Mister Deb-ree,' the boy says. 'Is nice evening?' His handshake is as light as his father's.

We cross a shared yard jammed between four mud huts and enter Marag's home. From the ceiling a single dim bulb gradually coaxes the room from the night. It is only slightly bigger than the guard's tomb. There are two big trunks; one carpet and one grass mat; one big bed and two bunks; no chairs or cupboards; no tables. For decoration there is a hanging tapestry with kids' art pinned to it and a long bundle of sugarcane in the corner, bound with a gay red ribbon.

Marag introduces me to his wife, a tiny woman with one of the milked-over eyes so frequently seen in the Egyptian poor. Also to Mister Ahmed, Missy Shera, Mister Foo-Foo, all younger than Sami.

Marag takes a pillow from the bed and places it on the floor next to the wall and bids me sit. The kids squat in a semicircle and stare at me while Marag helps his wife pump a little white

142

gas burner to hissing flame. I blow my harmonica for the kids and let them play with my compass. The wife begins to prepare tea for us in a little copper kettle.

I ask Sami how he got a crescent scar on his forehead. Grinning, he points toward the pyramid and pantomimes a tumble with his hands.

'It was a bad fall,' Marag says. 'But maybe it convince him the spirit want him to be an *educated*, not a pyramid goat. He can read and count and draw pictures now, Mister Sami can.' He beams at the boy in unabashed wonder. 'He can *write*.'

From the foot of the top bunk he takes down a notebook to show me, the very one that donated a page for that map. He proudly points out the pictures and words.

'Mr Deb-ree is an *artist* and *doctor*, Sami. Maybe he draw for you a picture while I go on an errand.'

After Marag leaves with my five-pound note, Sami and I exchange drawings. I do a Mickey Mouse and Sami does the pyramid. I tell him it looks too steep and he turns to the back page. Taped to the inside cover with electrician's tape is a dollar bill. It's taped Great Seal side up, and written beneath it, first in Arabic, then English, in the careful and patient hand of any good gradeschool teacher in any language, is the translation of the two Latin slogans: NEW ORDER OF AGES and ALLAH HAS PROSPERED OUR BEGINNINGS.

'Did your daddy give you this the other night?'

Yes, he nods, frowning at the page to remember what else his teacher has told him. 'It is Roman lira pound?'

'No,' I tell him; 'it is Yankee dollar, American simoleon buck.'

Marag is gone a long time. The wife puts Missy Shera and Mister Ahmed to bed. It must be past midnight but they're still wide-eyed and excited, staring at me from their bunks.

She takes up little Mister Foo-Foo and sits on the edge of the bed and drops one shoulder of her smock. In the dim light she looks withered way beyond her years. But all the kids are healthy, plumper than most of the pyramid pack I've seen. Maybe that's why she's withered.

Foo-Foo roots in. Mom closes her one good eye and rocks gently to and fro on the edge of the bed, humming a monotonous nasal lullaby. Foo-Foo watches me unblinking as he sucks and rocks.

A scrawny turkey chick wanders in the open door and Sami shoos it back outside. In a corner of the yard I see a very old woman milking a goat. She grins at Sami shooing the chick and calls something in Arabic.

'Mother-my-father,' he explains. 'Is right?'

'Grandmother, we say. Sami's grandmother.'

After she finishes she rubs the goat's bag with oil from a jar and brings the bucket of milk in. She doesn't acknowledge me at all. She pours half the milk into the copper kettle on the cold gas burner and covers the rest with a cloth over the top of the bucket. She unties a long stalk of sugarcane from the bundle in the corner. She takes up her half bucket and shuffles out. The stalk brushes the bulb and the shadows rock back and forth. The humming never stops and all the little eyes are still wide in the dreamy light swinging, watching me, even the goat's square pupils in the yard outside, flowing yellow at me as she chomps the cane. . . .

Back at the cabana. I fell asleep on Marag's floor and had a hell of a dream, that the village had been struck by a sandstorm. I couldn't see. In despair I tried to call but sand filled my throat. All I could make out was the rising din of thousands of impatient horns.

When Marag returned and woke me I was sweating and panting. So was he, after his run. But this time he had only one little taped cartridge to show for his hours of effort. He handed it to me, apologizing. It lay in my hand in the dim light and both of us felt very sad.

As he guided me from his house through the tiny thoroughfares to Sphinx Street, he continued to apologize and promise to make things good. I told him the deal was cool and not to *worry* over it! It was just a little burn.

'The deal is *not* cool!' he insisted. 'Is a bad burn. I bring the rest of the deal tonight, eight o'clock at Mena House – guaranteed!'

He kept on and on about it in a distracted tirade. I finally got him off the subject by telling him what a nice family he had.

'You are kind saying so. What about Sami, you like Sami? Is smart boy, my Mister Sami?'

I told him yeah, I liked Sami, he was plenty smart.

'Smart enough to catch up in one of your modern schools?'

144

'Sure. He's a bright kid. Personable and alert and bright, like his daddy. I bet he would be up with the other kids in a matter of weeks.'

'I bet, too,' he said, pleased.

I told him good night at the Sphinx. I was over the hill and nearing the hotel before I finally put it together. Marag hadn't been promoting himself – it was Sami. Like any father he has his dream: the son is taken back to the Land of Opportunity by some gentleman, raised in a modern home, sent to a modern United States school. The kids get a chance to break into the twentieth century; the gentleman gets a permanent liaison with the past. . . . 'A friend always at the pyramid.' Not a bad scam. No wonder you were so upset about that hash; you had bigger deals wheeling. For all your light touch and soft sell, Marag, you're a stone hustler. . . .

October 29. Twenty-first Sunday after Pentecost, 300th day. Slept till Muldoon and Jacky wake me just in time to see the sun going down. They push me into the shower and send a pool boy to bring a pot of coffee. Jacky has reservations at the Auberge to see Zizi Mustafa, the most famous dancer of them all, and Muldoon has news of a hot archaeological find in Ethiopia.

'An abdomen that ought to be put in the Louvre!' Jacky promises.

'A *human* skull that pushes us millions of years back further than Leakey's find!' says Muldoon. 'And no monkey business about it; this cranium is *human!* Darwin was full of crap!'

'Maybe,' says Jacky, always a little reluctant to reorient his thinking or his anatomical focus. 'On the other hand, maybe his evolutionary theory was right but his time scale was slightly off. That we still come from monkeys only it took us longer.'

'That's not the question, Jacky.' I'm out of the cold shower and hot into the discussion. 'The question is did we or did we not *fall!'* As we are walking through the lobby I suddenly remember Marag's resolve to meet me at eight with the rest of my purchase.

'Eight in Egyptian means somewhere between nine and mid-night,' Jacky translates. 'That's if he shows up at all.'

I leave word at the desk to have Marag go on down to my cabana if he shows up before I return. I go back and unlock the door just in case and leave the hookah on the nightstand.

After we eat the elaborate Auberge supper we find that the dancer doesn't come on until nine. At ten they say midnight. Muldoon says he's in the middle of exams and can't wait any longer. I talk Jacky into coming back out to the Mena House with me; we can check out Marag and still make it back for the dancer. We get a cab, drop Muldoon at his place, and head back to Giza. By the time we get to the Mena House it is after eleven and no sign of Marag. The door to my cabana is ajar but nothing is waiting for me on the nightstand. We walk out to the street while Jacky regales me with some Arabic wisdom regarding gullibility. The doorman signals for a cab, then asks in a hazy afterthought, 'By the way, sir, are you not Mister Deb-ree?'

I tell him I am called so by some.

'Ah, then, there was waiting for you a person. But he has left.'

When? Ah, sir, minutes ago, sir; he waited a long time. Where? In utility room, sir, out of sight. Didn't you tell this person to go on down to my cabana as I instructed? Oh, no, sir; that we cannot do! They would be bothering our guests, these persons. . . . They! Who the hell do you think *you* are? Official doorman, sir. How long did this person wait for me? Oh, that we could not say; the person was sitting waiting when we came on duty at seven thirty.

'But when he left,' he says, finally dragging his fist free of his gaudy pocket, 'he gave for you me this package.'

And he holds out my red handkerchief. Inside are the other four taped cardboard cartridges and my Uni pen.

October 30, Wednesday. My last day in Egypt.

I feel shitty about Marag. No luck at all trying to locate his house in the labyrinth of that village. Nor with the tomb where the young Bedouin couple were living. They left in the night, a new watchman tells me. Does he know Marag? *Every*one knows Marag. Held the World Record Up-and-down Pyramid, Marag. Where does he live? Somewhere in village. When does he come on duty? Sometimes late night, sometimes early morning, sometimes not for days. . . . Oh, a man of unpredictable moods, Marag, many of them dark.

In Cairo I smoke a cartridge with Jacky and Muldoon and give one to each. I have to be clean on the plane back. I give

Muldoon my four-volume PYRAMIDOLOGY by Rutherford. We mumble goodbyes and I hurry back out to Giza. Still no Marag on the dark *aouda*. My plane isn't until 10 A.M. but I leave word at the desk to wake me at 6.

VI

October 31, Halloween morn. Up before the sun. I recheck my packing (three girls from Oregon are right now serving a life sentence for dope in Turkey, where my plane lands after Cairo); nothing but the last ball of hash. And the Murine bottle. The hash I can swallow at the airport, but what about this stuff? Just flush it down the toilet? That's like carrying the key all the long battle to the castle and up the wall to the maiden locked behind the massive tower door, then chickening out for fear she'll be a bitch and tossing it in the moat.

I've got to try. Never get another chance. There's not enough time left to swallow it – it would be flight time before I took off – but if I *bang* it . . .

So I'm headed again up the hill for one last desperate attempt, the Murine bottle in my shoulder bag, the insulin outfit in my pocket. By the time I reach the *aouda* I'm shaking all over with trepidation. I lean against the casing stones to reinforce my resolve but I keep shivering. It's chilly and grey. A whirlwind comes winding across the empty *aouda*, gathering a fanatical congregation of scraps. The wind spins, like the spirit of a new messiah, inspiring corn husks, cigarette packs, the shells of yesterday's pumpkin seeds . . . lifting newspapers, gum papers, toilet papers high and higher. What a following! Then the spirit evaporates and the wind unwinds. The Zealots drift back to the limestone.

'Good morning, Mr Deb-ree . . . is a nice morning?'

'Good morning, Marag.' I had planned to apologize for the fuck-up at the hotel; now I realize again there is nothing to say. 'It's not a bad morning. A little chilly.'

'A new season comes. The winds will now blow from the desert, more cooler and full of sand.'

'No more tourists for a season?'

He shrugs. 'As long as great Khufu stands there will be tourists.' His bright little eyes are already chipping away at my chill. 'Maybe my friend Mister Deb-ree want a guide take him to the top? Guide most reliable? You know how much?'

'Five pounds,' I say, reaching for my wallet. 'Let's go.'

Marag tucks his gellabia in the top of his shorts and leads the way like a lizard. It's like climbing up 200 big kitchen ranges, one after another. I have to call a stop to him three times. His tiny eyes needle merrily at me gasping for breath.

'Mister Deb-ree, are you not healthy? Do you not get good nourishment in your country?'

'Just admiring the view, Marag; go on.'

We finally reach the top and flush the ravens off. They circle darkly, calling us all kinds of names before they sail off through the brightening morn toward the rich fields below. What a valley. What a river to carve it so!

'Come, friend.' Marag beckons me to the wooden pole in the centre of the square of limestone blocks. 'Marag show you little pyramid trick.'

He has me reach as high as I can up the pole with a chip of rock and scratch a mark. I notice a number of similar scratches at various heights. 'Now have a seat and breathe awhile this air. Is magic, this air on top pyramid. You will see.'

I sit at the base of the pole, glad for a breather. 'How does it affect you, this magic pyramid air?'

'It affect you to shrink,' he says, grinning. 'Breathe deep. You'll see.'

Now that he calls it to mind I remember noticing that most of the pyramid scalers are indeed men of unusually slight stature. I breathe deep, watching the sun trying to push through the clouded horizon. After a minute he tells me to stand with my stone and scratch again. It's hard to tell, with all the marks of previous experiments, but it looks to me like I'm scratching exactly next to my first mark. I'm about to tell him his pyramid air is just more of his bull when I find myself flashing.

It's an old trick. I used to use it myself as a way to get an audience off. I tell them to take fifteen deep breaths, hold the last lungful and stand, then everybody *om* together as the flash comes on. Hyperventilation. Every junior-high weirdo knows it. But the business with the scratch and the magic air was so slick I didn't make the connection, even when I felt the familiar faint coming on.

I grab the pole for support, impressed. Marag has positioned himself in front of me, hands on his hips, grinning skyward. He's done this before. He flaps a moment, then the breeze stills. I follow his gaze up into the milky sky and see what he has been waiting for: the thumb of God. I see it come down out of the haze and settle on top of Marag's head, bowing him like a deck of cards until his face snaps, revealing another behind it, and another, and another, face after face snapping and fanning upward in an accelerating riffle – some familiar, from the village, the *aouda*, some famous (I remember distinctly two widely known musicians who I will not name in case it might bring them hamper), but mostly faces I've never seen. Women and men, black, brown, red, and whatever, most of them looking at least past the half-century mark in earthly years. The expressions completely individual and various – bemused, patient, mischievous, stern – but there is a singular quality uniting them all: each face is kind, entirely, profoundly, unshakingly benevolent. The fan spreads up and up, like the deck at the climax of Disney's *Alice in Wonderland*, clear to the clouds. From a distance these two vast triangles would resemble an hour-glass, the bottom filled with grains of limestone, the top with face cards.

At the last there are a number of blanks, positions available for those willing and qualified. When the last blank is snapped away there is a hole left in the shape of Marag's slight body. Through this hole I can see the Sphinx, and beyond his paws those lanes of huts housing these faithful sentries who have for thousands of years guarded the treasury of all our climbs and all our falls. It is not buried. It is hidden on the very surface, in the cramped comings and goings, the sharing of goat's milk and sugarcane, in the everlasting hustle by the grace of which this ancient society has managed to survive. For thousands of years this people has defended this irreplaceable treasury and its temple with little more than their hustle and bustle and their bladders.

As long as there's piss in the King's Coffin there isn't going to be a pair of McDonald's arches on the *aouda*.

'What you think, Mister Deb-ree?' Marag snaps back into the space before me. 'Is a good trick?'

'Is a good trick, Marag. Is a great trick.'

Back on the *aouda* I give him gifts for his family. Handkerchiefs, shoulder-bag stuff. My harmonica for Sami, and I will talk to my wife about the boy coming to Oregon for a year of school. To Marag I give my canteen, my compass, and a page from my notebook inscribed *This man Marag is a servant who can be relied upon.* Signed with my name and gooped over with my Polaroid fixative to preserve it. We shake hands a last time and I hurry down to check out.

My cabana door is open. Sitting on my bed is Dr Ragar.

'Brother! I have brought for you the map of the Hidden Hall, known only to Masons of many degrees.'

I begin to laugh. I'm delighted to see him. I wonder, was he one of the faces? I can't remember.

'Sorry, Doctor, I've already seen the Secret Hall. What else have you got?'

He misunderstands my exuberance. He thinks I am ridiculing him. His eyes take on a wronged look, whimpering from beneath his dark brow like two whipped dogs.

'I Dr Ragar do have,' he says in a hurt voice, 'a formula for a blend of healing oils. Used by the Essenes, it is said for the feet of your Jesus. The usual price of this formula is five pounds, but, my brother, for you – '

'Five pounds is perfect! I'll take it.'

He helps me carry my bags and shares the taxi as far as Cairo. He is reluctant to leave me. He knows something more than money is up for grabs, but not what. He keeps running that rancid glim over me sidelong. When he gets out we shake hands and I press the Murine bottle into his palm.

'In return for all you've done for me, Brother Ragar, please to accept this rare American elixir. One drop in each eye will clear away the cobwebs; two in each will open the third; three if you wish to see God as he appeared in San Francisco in 1965. I would not divulge this powerful stuff but for the fact that my father, you recall, was a Mason. I think he would want it so. Please, be so kind. . . .'

He studies me, wondering if I'm drunk at nine in the morning, then takes the bottle. 'Thank you,' he says uncertainly, blinking thickly at the gift.

'One stone at a time,' I tell him.

Epilogue. Nine forty-four by the cabbie's watch. He's finding holes no Fiat ever fit through before but I'll never make it. They said to allow at least one hour for getting through Cairo customs. Look at that mob of tourists! Like rats panicked at a sinking porthole. Nine fifty. *No*body's going to make it.

But the plane is delayed because an old pilgrim had a heart attack and they had to unload him. The guy I strap in next to tells me about it.

'Right there trying to put his camera bag in the overhead and the Lord took 'im. Happens all the time on these Holy Land hops.'

The guy is a preacher from Pennsylvania and a tour host himself: very, very tired.

'Wasn't part of my group thank the Lord. But I'm due. Y'see there's so many of them that are Senior Citizens, old folks that have saved enough to take a gander at the Holy Land even if it's the last thing they do.'

The engines are finally running and we taxi to the end of our runway. The spirit on board lightens. Nervous chatter is heard. Just before we take off somebody yells, Hey, who won the fight last night?

What fight? somebody calls back.

Between the Heathen and the Infidel.

Everybody laughs, even the Turks and Nurds, but nobody knows who won. The stewardess says she'll ask the captain and report back. We blast off. When we level out the Pennsylvania preacher says, 'It wasn't Foreman. I don't care what she reports back.' I thought he was sound asleep. I say what? and he repeats the statement without opening his eyes: 'I said Foreman didn't win, no matter *what* the outcome.' When he doesn't elaborate I turn back to my window.

We're banking right over Cairo. There's the bridge crossing the Nile to the Omar Khayyam. There's the Statue of Isis Awakening, lifting her veil to watch us leave. There's Pyramid Boulevard. . . . The Mena House. . . . Giza village . . . but I don't see . . . could I have overlooked it in this haze? There! No wonder; even from up here you don't see it because you're looking for something smaller. But you don't overlook it. You can't. You underlook it.

'And you wanna know why?' the preacher has rolled his head to ask. 'Because he's got a *discrepancy* is why! How can he be the good Christian he claims to be and still be hitting people for money?'

He fixes me with eyes worn red and raw from two weeks' keeping track of his rattled flock.

'*That's* what does it, the thing really gets these Holy Landers. It's not age, not the heart. It's the *discrepancy!*'

His eyes close. His mouth falls open. I turn back to the window. The airplane's shadow flits across the golden ripples of the Sahara. We level out. The speaker pops on and the pilot addresses us in sophisticated Amsterdam English.

'This is your captain, Simon Vinkenoog. It appears we have to take a little detour in our routing to Istanbul, west of the Nile delta, because of . . . political reasons. We do not estimate much time loss. Lean back relax. The weather in Istanbul is clear and cool. The report from Zaire last night – before a crowd of ten thousand Muhammad Ali knocked out George Foreman in the eighth round, regaining the World Heavyweight Championship. Have a pleasant flight home.'

Killer

I wander thru each charter'd street
Near where the charter'd Thames does flow
And mark in every face I meet
Marks of weakness, marks of woe.

William Blake

Killer, the one-eyed one-horned billygoat – rearing fully erect on his hind legs, tall as a man, tucking his cloven hooves beneath his flying Uncle Sam beard, bowing his neck, slanting his one horn, and bulging his ghastly square-lensed eye at M'kehla's back – came piledriving down.

'M'kehla, watch out!'

M'kehla didn't even turn to check. Using the fence post like a pommel horse he vaulted instantly sideways. Amazing nimble for a man his size, I marvelled, not to mention been up driving all night.

The goat's horn grazed his thigh, then struck the post so hard that the newly stretched wire sang all the way to the post anchored at the corner of the chicken house. The hens squawked and the pigeons flushed up from the roof, hooting angrily. They didn't like the goat any better than M'kehla did.

'Choose *me* off, will you, you smelly motherfucker!' M'kehla pistoned a furious kick against the blind side of Killer's shaking head – 'I'll kick your mother *skull* in!' – then two more to the jaw before the dazed animal could back away from the post.

'Hey, c'mon, man. This isn't anything' – I had to think a moment to come up with an alternative word – '*per*sonal. Honest, he does it with everybody.'

This was only partly honest. True, Killer had tagged just about everybody on the farm at one time or another – me, Betsy, the kids when they tried crossing his field instead of going around – but the goat *had* seemed to choose M'kehla off special, from the moment the man had arrived.

It had been early that morning, before anybody was up. I half heard the machine pull in but I figured it was probably my

153

brother in his creamery van, out to get an early start on the day's roundup. I rolled back over, determined to get as much sleep as possible for the festivities ahead. A few seconds later I was jarred bolt upright by a bellow of outrage and pain, then another, then a machine-gun blast of curses so dark they sounded like they were being fired all the way from a ghetto of hell.

Betsy and I were instantly on our feet.

'Who in the world?'

'Not Buddy,' I said, dancing into my pants. 'That's for sure.'

Still unzipped I reached the front door. Through the open window I saw a shiny black bus parked on the gravel of our drive, still smoking. I heard another shout and another string of curses, then I saw a big brown man in a skimpy white loincloth come hopping out of the exhaust fumes at the rear end of the bus. He had a Mexican huarachi on one foot and was trying to put the mate on as he hopped. After a wild-eyed look behind him he paused at the bus door and started banging with the sandal.

'Open the door, God damn your bastard ass – *open this door!*'

'It's M'kehla,' I called back toward our bedroom. 'M'kehla, and here comes Killer after him.'

The goat rounded the rear of the bus and skidded to a spread-legged stop in the gravel, looking this way and that. His lone eye was so inflamed with hate that he was having trouble seeing. His ribs pumped and his lips foamed. He looked more like an animation than a live animal; you could almost hear him muttering in his cartoon chin whiskers as he swung his gaze back and forth in search of his quarry.

M'kehla kept banging and cursing at somebody inside the bus. I glimpsed a face at a side window but the door did not open. Suddenly, the banging was cut short by a bleat of triumph. Killer had found his mark. The horn lowered and the hooves scratched for ramming speed. M'kehla threw the sandal hard at the onrushing animal, then sprinted away around the front fender, cursing. You could hear him all the way down the back stretch, heaping curses on the bearded demon at his heels, on the bastard ass behind the bus door, on the very stones underfoot. When he appeared again at the rear of the bus I swung open our door.

'In here!'

He covered the twenty yards across our drive in a tenderfooted stumble, Killer gaining with every leap. I slammed the door

154

behind him just as the goat clattered onto the porch and piled against the doorframe. The whole house shook. M'kehla rolled his eyes in relief.

'Lubba mussy, Cap'n,' he finally gasped in a high Stepin Fetchit voice, 'where you git a watchdog so mean? Selma Alibama?'

'Little Rock. Orville been developing this strain to guard melon fields.'

'Orville Faubus?' he wheezed, rolling his eyes again, bobbing in a foolish stoop. 'Orville allus did have a *knaick!*'

I grinned at him and waited. Betsy called from the bedroom – Everything all right? – and he instantly dropped the fieldhand facade and straightened up to his full six-foot-plus.

'Hello, Home,' he said in his natural voice, holding out his hand. 'Good to see you.'

'You too, man. Been a while.' I put my palm to his, hooking thumbs. 'How've you been?'

'Still keepin ahead,' he said, holding the grip while we studied each other's faces.

Since we last saw each other I had wasted ten foolish months playing the fugitive in Mexico, then another six behind bars. He had lost one younger brother in Laos and another in a 7-Eleven shootout with the Oakland police, and an ailing mother as a result of the first two losses. Enough to mark any man. Yet his features were still as unmarred as a polished idol's, his eyes as unwavering.

'. . . still movin still groovin and still keepin at least one step ahead.'

There had always been a hint of powers recondite behind that diamond-eyed gaze, I remembered. Then, as if he had read my thoughts, the expression changed. The eyes dialled back to gentle, the lips loosened into a grin and, before I could duck free, he hauled me close and kissed me full on the mouth. He was slick all over from his scrimmage with the goat.

'Not to mention still sweatin and stinkin.' I wriggled free. 'No wonder Charity wouldn't let you back on the bus.'

'Isn't Charity, Dev; she kicked me out last month. I can't *imagine* why . . .'

He gave me a glance of wicked innocence and went on.

'All's I said was "Get up and get me some breakfast, bitch, I don't care if you are pregnant." For that she tells me "No, *you*

155

get up, get up and get out and get *gone*." Just like that. So I been going.'

He nodded toward the bus.

'That's Heliotrope's pup, Percy,' he said. 'My complete crew this trip – cabin boy, navigator, and shotgun.' Then he leaned down to holler out the open window: 'And he better quit *dickin* with me, he ever expect to see his *mama* again!'

The face at the bus window paid no attention; there were closer things to worry about. Killer had returned to the bus door and was working the hinges with his single horn. The whole bus was rocking. M'kehla straightened up from the window and chuckled fondly.

'Stuck out there, that billygoat between him and his breakfast cereal heh heh heh.'

Heliotrope was a paraplegic pharmacologist from Berkeley, beautiful and brilliant, and a bathtub chemist of underground renown. M'kehla always liked to pal around with Heliotrope when he was on the outs with his wife or when he was out of chemicals. Percy was her ten-year-old, known to some around San Francisco as the Psychedelic Brat. He had boarded with us occasionally, staying a week, a month, until one of his parents came to round him back up. He was redheaded, intelligent, and practically illiterate, and he had a way of referring to himself in the third person that could be simultaneously amusing and infuriating.

'Percy Without Mercy he calls himself nowadays; likes to keep the pedal to the metal.'

'Hello, Montgomery.' Betsy came out of the bedroom, belting on her robe. 'I'm glad to see you.'

Not sounding all that glad. She'd seen the two of us go weirding off together too many times to be too glad. But she allowed him a quick hug.

'What did I hear you telling Dev about Charity? That she got you gone instead of getting you breakfast? Good on her. And she's pregnant? She ought to get you neutered if you ask me.'

'Why, Betsy, Charity don't want nothing *that* permanent. But speakin of breakfast' – he edged around her toward the kitchen, the one huarachi flapping on the linoleum – 'is you nice folks fetched in yet the aigs?'

'The henhouse is that way.' Betsy pointed. 'Past the billygoat.'

156

'Mm, I see. Well then, in *that* case . . . where y'all keep the *cawn*flakes?'

While Betsy ground the coffee, M'kehla and I went out to contain the goat so we could gather the eggs. Percy was delighted with the action. His freckled face followed from bus window to window as we manhandled the animal back into the field he'd butted out of. While we were swinging the gate closed he caught M'kehla a sharp hind-hoof kick on the shin. I had to laugh as M'kehla danced and cursed, and Percy hooted and jeered from the bus. Even the peacocks and chickens joined in.

Out in the henhouse M'kehla told me his story.

'I don't know whether it was my Black Panther dealings or my white powder dealings. Charity just says get the hell gone and give her some respite. I say Gone it is, Baby! Naturally I called Heliotrope. Long distance. She's been the last year up in Canada with Percy's older brother, Vance, who's dodging the draft. And a bunch of Vance's buddies of like persuasion. Heliotrope persuaded me to sneak Percy off from his old man in Marin and bring him up . . . help her start a mission.'

We had the chickens fed and quieted and all the eggs that the rats and skunks had left us piled nicely in the feed bucket. We stood in the henhouse door, watching the morning sun pull hard for a Fourth of July noon, circa 1970.

'A mission? In Canada?'

'Yeah.' He was looking across the chickenyard at his bus. The black door had cracked open and Percy was peeping out to see if the coast was clear. 'A sort of modern underground railway.'

'You mean leave the States?'

'Heliotrope was very persuasive,' he answered. 'And who can say how thick this Vietnam shit is gonna get?'

'M'kehla, you're way past getting drafted.'

'But I'm not past knowing bum shit when I see it border to border. Hang around shit long enough you're gonna get some on you I also know *that*.'

'Listen. When I was on the run I came across a lot of American expatriots. You know what they all had in common, especially the men?'

He didn't answer. He picked an egg out of the bucket and rolled it around his long magician's fingers.

'They were all very damn hangdog apologetic, that's what they all had in common.'

'Apologetic about what?'

'About running away from home with all this bum shit needing cleaned up is what! Besides, what about Percy? He isn't draft age either.'

'In a way he is. His square daddy keeps trying to force him to shape up. His teachers are always on his case – pledge allegiance, cut his hair, mind his tongue.'

He paused. Percy's red head had ducked out of the bus and he was sneaking across our yard.

'There are some pegs that'll never fit a square hole. No matter how much force is used.'

'We can change the hole,' I reminded him.

'Can we?' M'kehla carefully put the egg back in the bucket and looked at me. 'Can we really?'

This time it was me didn't answer. The issue was too long between us for short answering. During the decade of our friendship we had shared a vision, a cause if you will. We were comrades in that elite though somewhat nebulous campaign dedicated to the overthrow of thought control. We dreamed of actually changing the human mind to make way for a loftier consciousness. Only from this unclouded vantage, we maintained, could humanity finally rise out of its repetitive history of turds and turmoil and realize that mighty goal of One World. One World Well Fed, Treated Fair, At Peace, Turned On, and In Tune with the Universal Harmony of the Spheres and the Eternal Everchanging Dharma of . . . of. . . . Anyway, One Wonderful World.

We never claimed to know precisely when the birth of this New Consciousness would take place, or what assortment of potions might be required to initiate contractions, but as to the birthplace we had always taken it for granted that this shining nativity would happen *here*, out of the ache of an American labour.

Europe was too stiff to bring it off, Africa too primitive, China too poor. And the Russians thought they had already accomplished it. But Canada? Canada had never even been considered, except recently, by deserters of the dream. I didn't like seeing them leave, these dreamers like brilliant and broken

158

Heliotrope and old comrade M'kehla. These freckle-faced Huck Finns.

After his second helping of eggs Percy began to yawn and Betsy packed him away to share Quiston's bunk. M'kehla looked wider awake than ever. He finished his coffee and announced he was ready for action. I explained the day's plan. We had a new string of calves that needed branding and an old string of friends coming out to help. We would herd, corral, brand, barbecue, swim, and drink beer and end up at the fireworks display in Eugene at dusk.

'What we have to do now is prepare. We need to spread sawdust, buy beer, reinforce the corral to be sure it'll keep the calves in – '

'And the goat out,' Betsy added.

M'kehla was already heading for the door. 'Then let us so embark.'

We got the tractor started and the auger hooked up and holes for new posts drilled. I set the posts while M'kehla tamped them fast with stones and gathered more stones from the ditches. I had to hustle to keep up. I was glad when the first visitor showed up to give me an excuse for a break.

It was my cousin Davy, the ex-boxer. His nose was red and his eyes even redder. I asked Davy what he was doing out this early. He said it was as a matter of fact this *late*; he had come because in the course of a long night's ramble he had acquired an item that he thought might interest me:

'For your Independence Day doo-dah.'

He brought it from the back seat of his banged-up Falcon station wagon, a beautiful American flag trimmed with gold braid. It was a good twenty feet long. Davy claimed to have won it in a contest during the night. He didn't remember what kind of contest, but he recalled that the victory was decisive and glorious. I told him it was a great item; too bad I didn't have a pole. Davy turned slowly around until he spotted a small redwood that the frost had killed the winter after I planted it.

'How about yon pole?' he drawled, then pointed at the last unposted hole where M'kehla and I were working, 'in hither hole.'

So the three of us felled and bucked the dead limbs off the redwood. Davy made a try at barking it with the draw knife but gave up after ten minutes. M'kehla and I deepened the augered hole by hand until it would support the height of our spar, and drug it over. We attached the hooks and pulleys and tilted the pole into the hole just as Frank Collin Dobbs and crew were arriving in his cutaway bus. In our hurry to get the flag aloft for their arrival we just tossed in dirt, promising to tamp it later. Dobbs got out just as I pulled the brilliant banner aloft. He and Davy snapped to a rigid salute. They launched into the *Marine Hymn* so far off key I was moved to join them.

M'kehla had chosen not to honour the ceremonies. He turned his back on the foolishness and was finishing our fencing task, reaching around the flagpole and hammering in the last section of wire.

This is when Killer made that piledriving sneak attack that started this story about verve and nerve, and the loss of it, and old friends, and strange beasts.

How came I with this awful goat? Much the same way the farm came by a lot of its animal population: the animals were donated by animal fanciers who had run out of space or patience. Our original peacocks had been abandoned by Krishnas whose ashram had been repossessed; the horses were from rock stars' girlfriends, adrift without permanent pastures. Donkeys without gold mines, sheep without shearers, parrots without perches – they had all found their various ways to the seeming stability of our farm.

Stewart, for instance, had simply come trotting in one day, a halfgrown pup eager to enlist. Varmint-Boy was living in our swamp in an old U.S. Army tent so he decided he would act as the induction officer. He whistled the pup into his tent and shot him up with a boot-camp dose of methadrine. For hours the new recruit drilled chasing birds and fetching sticks, until the shadow grew long and the drill instructor bored. The exhausted pup lay down to sleep but of course could only stare and ponder. Pondering is hard for a dog and not necessarily healthy, but Stewart survived (though he never lost that strung-out stare) to become the top dog. The Varmint was finally drummed off the place for this and other such crimes against innocence.

Killer came from much more conventional sectors. He was the mascot for our high school team, the Nebo Hill Billies. Our symbol is the charging goat. For ten seasons Killer was tied to the bench of the football team, where visiting teams tried to run over him. He was paraded across basketball courts where opposing symbols reared and teased at him. Terry-cloth bears and papier-mâché eagles. Enough to sour any animal.

The meaner he turned the more they came at him. The eye was put out by a baseball spike in a close play at home. The horn he lost during a Creswell homecoming game. A Creswell scatback was down after a hard hit on the punt return and the ambulance had driven across to get him. Killer had tugged at his tether when the flashing contraption drove onto the field. The fallen hero was lifted into the machine and the siren was started. This was more than Killer could endure. To the applause of the stands he snapped his dog chain and charged head-on into the ambulance. Fans that witnessed this famous charge spoke afterward of it with wonder and affection. 'Not only knocked the headlight and turn signal clean off he *then* got tangled underneath in the front suspension; it was *another half hour* before they could get it all unloosed and towed off the field.'

The wonder lasted but the affection fled with the goat's aromatic recovery. The vet said the roll beneath the ambulance had ruptured the little musk sacks on each side of the goat's anus – he could no longer turn the sacks on and off. Only leave them on. The vet said the only solution was neutering, cutting of the testosterone that stimulated the musk. The Nebo Hill Boosters thought it over and concluded that rather than have a ballless billy for a mascot they would build one out of papier-mâché, and Killer was out of a job.

When they asked over the school announcements who had a place capable of adopting a poor retiring mascot, my oldest boy, Quiston, an Aries, had volunteered our farm.

It took three of us to separate the man and the goat, Dobbs and I holding the animal, Davy wrestling with M'kehla. This was a mistake. It very nearly got M'kehla and my cousin into it. Something was said in the scuffle and Davy and M'kehla sprang apart, glaring; they were already into their karate and boxing stances before we could step between them.

Dobbs mollified Davy with a cold Oly and I convinced M'kehla to come down to the pond with me to cool down and scrub off. After his first dip he was laughing about the flare-up, said it wouldn't happen again. Maybe, however, he should drive his bus down here out of goat territory. He could park it in the shade of the ash trees on the swamp side of the pond.

I stood in the open stairwell and directed him down. The sound of the engine brought Percy straight from his nap and running from the house.

'Look at him hop.' M'kehla laughed. 'He thought I was leaving without him.'

He parked where he could get some of the overhanging shade and still see the water. He swivelled out of the driver's seat and strolled to the rear of his living room on wheels.

'Come on back. Let's get high and analyse the world situation.' He sprawled across his zebra skin waterbed like an Ethiopian nabob.

The day mellowed. A soft breeze started strumming the bus roof with the hanging Spanish moss. My kids and Percy were splashing in the pond with their tubes; their shouts and laughter drifted to us through the swaying daisies and Queen Anne's lace. M'kehla and I sipped Dos Equis and argued. We had just started on the Third World and our fourth beer when someone came banging at the bus door.

M'kehla opened it and my nine-year-old son Quiston leaned in, wet and wide-eyed.

'Dad!' Quiston yelled up the stairwell. 'Percy's found a *monster* in the pond!'

'What kind of monster, Quis?'

'A *big* one . . . crouched on the bottom by the pumphouse!'

'Tell him I'll come out after while and get it,' I told Quiston.

'All *right*,' he said and headed back toward the pond with the news, his white hair waving in the weeds. 'Dad's gonna get him, Percy! My Dad's gonna get him!'

I watched him go, feeling very fatherly. M'kehla came up and stood beside me.

'It doesn't worry you, Dad? All this faith?'

I told him, Nope, not me, and I meant it. I was feeling good. I could see my friends and my relatives arriving up by the barn. I could hear the squawk of the sound system as Dobbs got it wired up to announce the branding, rodeo style. I could see the new honey-coloured cedar posts in the corral and the pigeons strutting on the bright new wire. And Old Glory was fluttering over all.

'I got faith in all this faith,' I told him.

'Do you?' he asked. 'Do you really?' And this time I answered right back: Yep, I really did.

162

We drank beer and enjoyed our old arguments and watched the crowd gather. Rampage and his kids, Buddy and his. The Mikkelsens, the Butkovitches. The women carried dishes to the kitchen; the kids went for the pond; the men came down to the bus. Bucko brought a case of Bohemian stubbies. After about an hour of tepid beer and politics Dobbs tossed away his half-empty bottle out the window.

'All right e-*nuff* of this foam and foofarah,' he declared, right at M'kehla. 'Break out the heavy stuff!'

As a man of the trade, M'kehla always had a formidable stash. He uncoiled from his zebra lounge and walked to the front of the bus. With a flourish he produced a little metal box from somewhere behind the driver's seat. It was a fishing tackle case with trays that accordioned out when he opened it, making an impressive display: the trays in neat little stairsteps, all divided into partitions and each section filled and labelled. From a tiny stall labelled ROYAL COACHMAN he picked up a gummy black lump the size of a golf ball.

'Afghany,' he said, rolling it along his fingertips like the egg in the henhouse.

He pinched off a generous chunk and heated it with a butane lighter. When it was properly softened he crumbled it into the bowl of his stone-bowled Indian peacepipe and fired it up. At the first fragrant wisp of smoke Percy came baying up the stairwell like a hound. He had smelled it all the way to the pond.

'Hah!' he said, coming down the aisle rubbing his hands. 'In the nick of time.'

He was wearing Quiston's big cowboy hat to keep from further sunburning his nose and neck, and he had a bright yellow bandanna secured around his throat with a longhorn tie slide. He looked like a Munchkin cowpoke.

He plumped down in the pillows and leaned back with his fingers laced behind his neck, just one of the fellas. When the peacepipe came back around to M'kehla he passed to Percy. The little boy puffed up a terrific cloud.

Davy wouldn't join us, though. 'Makes a man too peaceful,' he explained, opening another beer. 'These are not peaceful times.'

'That's why Perce and me are pullin stakes and rollin on.'

'Up to Canada did I hear?' Dobbs asked.

'Up it is,' M'kehla answered, reloading the pipe. 'To start a sanctuary.'

'A sanctuary for shirkers,' Davy muttered.

'Well, Dave,' Dobbs said, lifting his shoulders in a diplomatic shrug, 'patriots and zealots don't generally need a sanctuary, you got to admit that.'

F. C. Dobbs had served in the early days of our inglorious 'police action' as a marine pilot, flying the big Huey helicopters in and out of the rice-paddy hornet's nests of the Cong. After four years he had been discharged with medals and citations and the rank of captain, and a footlocker full of Burmese green. He was the only vet among us and not the least upset by M'kehla's planned defection, especially under the pacifying spell of M'kehla's hash. Davy, on the other hand, was growing less and less happy with M'kehla and his plan. You could see it in the way he brooded over his beer. And when M'kehla's Indian pipe came around to him again, he slapped it away with the back of a balled fist.

'I'll stick to good old firewater from the Great White Father,' he grunted. 'That flower power paraphernalia just makes a man sleepy.'

'I been driving since noon yesterday,' M'kehla said softly, retrieving his pipe. 'Do I look sleepy?'

'Probably popping pills or sniffing snow all the way,' Davy grumbled. 'I seen the type on the gym circuit.'

'Not a pill. Not a sniff. Well, just a puff of some new flower power stuff. One little hit. But I'll bet there isn't *one* of you big white fathers with the balls to try *half* what I am gonna do.'

'Me!' Percy chirped.

'Leave that shit alone,' Davy ordered, pushing the boy back and tilting the hat down over his eyes. 'You half-baked buckeroo.'

I stepped up to get between Davy and M'kehla. 'I might try a taste. What is it, like smoking speed?'

M'kehla turned without answering. He reached a clay samovar down from his staples cupboard and opened it. He pinched out a wad of dried green leaves.

'Not much,' he answered, smiling. 'Just a little ordinary mint tea – '

He thumbed the wad down into the bowl of the pipe, then

164

took a tiny bottle out of his tackle box, from a partition marked SNELLED HOOKS. Carefully, he unscrewed the lid.

' – and a little S.T.P.'

'Eek,' said Buddy.

Dobbs agreed. 'Eek indeed.'

We had never tried the drug but we all had heard of it – a designated bummer, developed by the military for the stated purpose of confusing and discouraging enemy troops. The experiment had reportedly been dropped after a few of the hapless guinea pigs claimed that the chemical had promoted concentration instead of confusion. These lucky few said it seemed to not only sharpen their wits but double their energy and dissolve their illusions as well.

Nothing the army wanted to chance, even for our own soldiers.

The sight of the little bottle had produced a twisted silence on the bus. The wind-stirred brushing on the metal roof stopped. Everybody watched as M'kehla drew from his hair a long ivory knife and a very thin curved blade. He dipped the point into the bottle and put a tiny heap of white powder on the bowlful of green mint, three times.

'Observe,' he said, and raised the pipe to his lips.

With the lighter boring a long blue flame into the stone bowl, M'kehla drew one deep breath and held it, eyes almost closed. Within seconds we all saw his eyes snap wide, then narrow, glittering afresh with that dark, sharp humour. He breathed out an inviting sigh and lifted the pipe toward my cousin. Davy dropped his eyes and shook his head.

'Not this father,' he muttered.

'I guess I might try one blade tip,' I ventured, feeling like somebody should defend the family honour. 'For the sake of science.'

We all watched as M'kehla repacked the pipe. He swayed as he worked, singing in a sweet, incomprehensible whisper. His hands danced and mimed. When he picked up the tiny vial a dusty sunbeam streamed through the window and illuminated the green glass. The hair on my arms stood up. I cleared my throat and looked at my brother.

'You want to join me, try some of this superstuff?'

'I never even tried it in my car. I'll get the dry ice ready for the brand. Come on, Percy. Learn something.'

Buddy stood up and started for the door, pushing Percy ahead of him. I looked at Dobbs. He stood up too.

'I guess I gots to finish the sound, boss.'

Rampage was supposed to be picking up the keg at Lucky's and Bucko had to take a leak. One by one they ambled to the front and out the door, leaving only M'kehla and me.

And the pipe. I finished my beer and set the bottle back under my stool. 'Well, as you say . . . let us so embark.'

M'kehla hands me the pipe and fires it up with his little blue flame. Green smoke wriggles out of the stone hole. The mint mild in my throat . . . cool, mentholated, throat raw smoke Kools throat raw smoke Koo –

Everything stops. The green wriggle, the dust motes in the sunbeam. Only M'kehla is moving. He glides into my vision, his eyes merry. He asks how it goes. I tell him it goes. He tells me ride loose sing with it never let it spook you. Riding loose here. Good, and don't move until you feel compelled. Nothing moving, boss. Good, and what is the terrain this time? The terrain, boss? Yeh, Home, the terrain. . . . What does it look like this time? It looks, this time it looks, it looks to me like you're right it looks like the *future!*

M'kehla smiled and nodded. I shot to my feet.

'Let's go get them cows!' I yelled.

'Yaa-*hoo!*' M'kehla whooped.

We stepped out into the Fourth of July noon just as Dobbs cued up James Brown and the Famous Flames blaring 'Out of the Blue' over the airwaves, and the breezes blew, and the leaves danced, and the white pigeons bloomed above us like electric lilies.

I was a new man, for a new season.

In the pasture we moved with the smooth certainty of a well-trained army. M'kehla commanding the right flank, me the left, Betsy at the rear calling out calm instructions, and the fleet-footed kids filling in the gaps. The herd would try to escape to the right and M'kehla's force would advance. They would try to plunge left and I would press my platoon forward. We corralled the whole herd without one renegade breaking through our lines.

The branding was even more efficient. The kids would cut out a little maverick and haze him into a corner of the corral and

166

M'kehla and I would rush in and throw him on his side and hold him. While Buddy stirred the big metal brand in a tub of dry ice and methyl alcohol, Betsy would shave the animal's side with the sheep shears. Then everyone would hold everything while Buddy stuck the icy iron against the shaved spot for the required sixty seconds. If the spot was shaved close enough, and the brand was cold enough, and the animal held still long enough, the hair would grow back out in the shape of the brand – snow white. Nothing moved, yelled, or bellered during this holy minute. Just Buddy's counting and the calf's heavy breathing. Even the mother in the adjoining corral would hold her worried lowing.

Then Buddy would say ' – sixty!' and we'd turn loose with a cheer. The branded dogie would scramble to his feet and scamper away through the escape chute, and the army would be advancing on the next wild recruit.

If I had been impressed earlier by M'kehla's strength and agility, I was now astounded at my own. We were catching and throwing animals with ease, some topping two hundred pounds, one after the other. From just the tiniest pinch of powder! It dawned on me why it had been nicknamed after the superslick race-car additive; I was not only newly powdered but freshly lubricated as well, functioning without friction, without liberation. No debates over right or wrong good or bad to impede the flow and delay decisions. In fact, no decisions. It was like skiing too steep or surfing too far out on the curl of a breaker too big: full go.

And the women couldn't even tell we were high.

Davy stood near the keg, sipping beer and watching from under a defeated scowl. He made no move to help, and the only time I saw him smile was when Percy drawled a suggestion how we could *avoid* all this unnecessary toil.

'Say, you know? What *Ah* say we ought to do . . . is cross these calves with all these damn pigeons.' He hitched at his belt like a Hollywood cattle baron. 'And get you a herd of *homing* cows.'

Everybody laughed in spite of the count. Percy whooped and slapped his leg and elbowed Quiston. 'What do you say to that, Quizzer? Homing cows?'

'Good idea!' Quiston agreed. 'Homing cows!' Always an admirer of the older boy's style, Quiston hitched at his britches and drawled, 'But what *Ah* say we ought to do . . . is we ought to go down to the pond and get that *thing* out, like Dad said he would.'

'What thing?'

'That monster thing.'

'Hey, damn straight, Quiz,' Percy remembered. 'Before it gets too shady. Haul him out an' brand him!'

'At the pumphouse, you say? That's a deep dive.'

'*I* dove it.'

'Yeah, Dad. Percy dove it.'

I stood up and looked around me, tall as a tower. Everything seemed under control. Pastoral. Bucolic. The fresh cedar shavings like soft golden coins under the sun. The calves all cowed and calm. The huge flag not so much waved by the breeze as waving it, like a great gaudy hand stirring the air to keep the flies away.

Buddy plunged the frosted brand back into the fogging tub, watching me.

'How many more?' I asked.

'Just three,' he told me. 'Those two easy little Angus and that ornery spotted Mongol over there.'

I took off one of my gloves and wiped my stinging head. I realized I was rushing like a sweaty river. Buddy was focusing hard on my face.

'We got more than enough hands to finish up here. Why don't you go on down and cool off. Capture their dragon. Get them out from underfoot.'

Everybody was watching. I took off my other glove and handed them to Buddy along with my lariat.

'All right, I will. We'll geld this Gorgon ere he spawns.'

'Yaahoo, Uncle Dev!' yelled Percy.

And Quiston echoed, 'Yaahoooo, Dad!'

I followed the boys past the shade maple where Dobbs was fussing in his sound scene. He had a cold beer in one hand and a live microphone in the other, happy as a duck in Disneyland.

'How-dee!' he greeted us through the mike. 'Here's some of our gladiators now, rodeo fans. Maybe we can get a word. Say, podnah, how's it going out there in the arena? From up here it looks like you're drubbing those little dogies pretty decisively.'

'We got 'em on ice!' Percy answered for me, pulling the

microphone to his mouth. 'We're letting the second string finish 'em off.'

'Yeah, Dobbs,' Quiston added proudly. 'And now we're going after that thing at the bottom of the pond!'

'Hear that, fans? Straight from the barnyard to the black lagoon without a break. Let's give these plucky wranglers a big hand.'

The women making potato salad across the lawn managed a cheer. Dobbs settled the needle on a fresh record.

'In their honour, friends and neighbours, here's Bob Nolan and the Sons of the Pioneers doing their immortal "Cool Water." Take it away Bob!'

He thumbed off the mike and leaned close. 'You okay, Old Timer?'

I told him Sure, better than okay. Super. Just going along with these, get this, rinse the grit off before dinner it smells great I better catch those kids.

The smell of the meat sizzling on the barbecue was, in fact, making my throat constrict. But I didn't feel like I needed sustenance. Every cell in my body seemed bursting with enough fuel to keep me cooking for a decade.

The pond trembled in the sun. The boys were already shucking clothes into the daisies. From up the slope behind us I heard a cheer rise as the wranglers caught the spotted Mongol, and Dobbs's boozy voice joined the Sons of the Pioneers on the chorus, declaring he's a devil not a man, and he spreads the burnin' sand with water –

' – cooool, cleeeer wah-ter.'

I knew it would be cool all right, but none too clear. Even when it wasn't glinting at you, spirogyra and pondweed made it difficult to see more than a few feet beneath the surface. I sat down and started unlacing my boots.

'Okay, lads; where is this mooncalf a-murking?'

'I can show you exactly,' Percy promised and scooted up the ladder to the top of the pumphouse. 'I'll dive down and locate it. Then I'll blow a bunch of bubbles so you can bring it up.'

'When you locate it why don't *you* bring it up?'

'Because it's too big for a kid, Uncle Dev. It's way too big for anybody but a *man.*'

He pulled his goggles over his eyes and grinned at me like some kind of mischievous kelpie. He sucked in a deep breath and jumped out into the air, hollering 'Yaaahoo' all the way to the water. His splash shattered the glint and for a moment we saw him froglegging down. Then the surface closed over him. Quiston came and stood beside me. I finished pulling off my boots and Levi's and tossed them inside the pumphouse. I shaded my eyes against the bounce of the sun and stared hard at the water. There wasn't so much as a freckled flicker.

After nearly a minute Percy came spewing up through the surface. He paddled to the shore where I could give him a hand out.

'Didn't find him,' he panted, his hands on his knees. Finally he looked up. 'But I will!'

He clambered back up the ladder and dived right back in. No yell. Again the water snatched him from our sight. Quiston reached up to slip his hand into mine.

'Percy said it had teeth like a shark and a hide like a rhinoceros,' Quiston recalled. 'But he's probably just fooling.'

'Percy's never had a reputation for reliability.'

We squinted at the water for his signal. Nothing but the chromium undulation. Quiston squeezed my hand. At length Percy spurted to the surface.

'Must be deeper . . . than I thought,' he puffed, crawling ashore.

'It's a deep pond, Percy.'

'I *knew* you were fooling,' Quiston claimed, relieved.

Percy flushed red and thrust a fist under Quiston's nose.

'Listen you, you see *this*? Mess with the *Perce*, go home in a hearse!'

'Take it easy, Perce. Forget it. Why don't you kids go down to the shallow end hunt some tadpoles?'

'Yeah, that's it!' Quiston had never been greatly fond of this dark water by the pumphouse anyway, even without monsters. 'Tadpoles in the cattails!'

'I'm not after *tad*poles,' Percy said and fumed back up the ladder. He snatched off his goggles and flung them away as though they had been the trouble. He drew a great breath and dived.

The water pitched, oscillated, slowed, and stilled. I began to worry. I climbed up the ladder, hoping to decrease the angle. Impervious as rolled steel. Quiston called up at me: 'Dad . . . ?'

I watched the water. Percy didn't come up. I was just about to dive in after him when I saw his face part the surface.

He lay back treading water for a long while before he paddled for shore.

'Never mind, Percy,' Quiston called. 'I believe you. We believe you, don't we, Dad?'

'Sure. It could have been anything – a sunken branch, that deck chair Caleb threw in last fall. . . .'

Percy refused Quiston's offered hand and pulled himself up the muddy bank to the grass. 'It wasn't any branch. Wasn't any chair. Maybe it wasn't any monster but it wasn't any goddamn furniture either so *fuck you!*'

He wrapped his arms around his knees and shivered. Quiston looked up at me on the pumphouse roof.

'Okay, okay, I'll take a look,' I said and both boys cheered.

I removed my watch. I tossed it to Quiston and stepped to the high edge of the pumphouse roof. I hooked my toes over the tarpapered plywood and started breathing. I could feel my blood gorging with oxygen. Old skindiver trick the kid didn't know. Also he'd been jumping too far out, hitting too flat. I would go straighter down . . . breathe three more, crouch low, spring as high as possible, and jackknife.

But in the middle of the leap I changed my dive.

Now I'm no diver. My only period near a diving board was the year we spent in Boyes Hot Springs while my father was stationed at Mare Island. Buddy and I were about Quiston and Percy's ages. A retired bosun friend of my dad's devoted many after-school afternoons teaching us to go off the high board. Buddy learned to do a respectable one-and-a-half. The best I could accomplish was a backward cutaway swan, where you spring up, throw your feet forward and lie backward in the air, coming past the board close with your belly. It looks more dangerous than it is.

All you have to do is get far out enough.

And when I took off from the pumphouse I knew I was getting plenty far out. I was so pumped by the distance and height my wonder muscles had achieved that I couldn't help but think the future *is* now, and I went into my cutaway.

For the first time in more than twenty years. Yet everything was happening so helpfully slow that I had plenty of time to remember all the moves and get them correct. I lay back with a languid grace, arms spreading into the swan, chest and belly bowed to the astonished sky. It was wonderful. I could see the pigeons circling above me, cooing their admiration. I could hear the Sons of the Pioneers lope into their next ballad: 'An old cowpoke went riding out . . .' I could feel the breeze against my neck and armpit, the sun on my thighs, smell the sizzle of the barbecue – all with a leisurely indulgence, just hanging there. Then, somewhere beneath all these earthly sensations, or beyond them, remote and at the same time disturbingly intimate, I heard the first of those other sounds that were to continue in increase all the rest of that awful afternoon and evening. It wasn't the familiar howling of decapitated *brujos* that you hear on peyote comedowns, nor the choiring arguments of angels and devils that LSD can provoke. Those noises are merely unearthly. These sounds were un-*any*thingly – the chilly hiss of decaying energy, the bleak creaking of one empty space scraping against another, the way balloons creak. Don't let it spook you, he said, ride loose and sing, so I sung to myself O listen to this entropy hiss . . .

And I came loose from the sky.

I tilted on backward and down, shooting past the pumphouse roof and through the seamless water. My body had become flawless, almost fictional in its perfection, like Tarzan in the old Sunday funnies with every muscle and sinew inked clean, or Doc Savage after forty years of ferocious physical training. The water sang past me, turning cold and dark. I was not alarmed. I wasn't surprised that I didn't have to swim to perpetuate my deepening plunge – the dive had been that frictionless – and I wasn't startled when my outstretched hands finally struck the jagged mystery at the pond bottom. It seemed perfectly natural that I had arrowed to the thing, like a compass needle to the pole –

'Hello, Awfulness. Sorry I can't leave you lurking here in peace, but some lesser being could get bit.'

– as I grasped it by its lower jaw and turned for the surface.

I knew what it was. It was the fifty-gallon oil drum M'kehla and I had lost some half-dozen psychedelic summers before. We had been using it to cook ammonium nitrate fertilizer, piping the gas out the threaded bung through a hose down under the water so we could catch the bubbles in plastic bags. Trying to manufacture nitrous oxide. It had been an enormous hassle but had worked well enough that the whole operation – me, M'kehla,

172

hose, barrel, and Coleman stove – had all tumbled into the water, flashing and splashing.

We saved the stove but the lid came off and the barrel went down before we could catch it. It must have landed at a slant, mouth down, because a pocket of air still remained in the corner so that it rocked there on the blind bottom, supporting itself at an angle, as if on its haunches. What I grabbed was the rusted-out rim below that corner with the air pocket.

I kicked hard, stroking one-handed for the dim green far above. I felt the thing give up its hold in the mire as brute inertia was overcome by my powerful strokes. I felt its dumb outrage at being dragged from its lair, its monstering future thwarted by a stout Tarzan heart and a Savage right hand. I felt it tug suddenly heavier as it tilted and belched out its throatful of air in protest. A lot heavier. But my inspired muscles despaired not. Stroke after stroke, I pulled the accursed thing toward the light. Upward and upward. And upward.

Until that stout heart was pounding the walls in panic, and that Savage right hand no longer held the thing; the thing held the hand.

That discharge of its buoyant bubble had jerked the rusty teeth deep into my palm. To turn it loose without first setting it down would mean letting those teeth rake their way out. All I could do was stroke and kick and hold my own, and listen to that alarm pound louder and louder.

Everything was suddenly on the edge of its seat. The ears could hear the panic thumping through the water. The eyes could see the blessed surface only a few feet away – only a few more feet! – but the burning limbs consulted the heart, the heart checked with the head, and the head computed the distance as already impossible and getting more impossible by the instant!

When the lungs got all this news, the sirens really went off. The nerves passed the signal on to the glands. The glands wrung their reserves into the bloodstream, rushing the last of the adrenalin to the rescue, giving the right hand the desperate courage it needed to uncurl and release its grip on the damned thing. I felt it rip all the way to the fingertips and away, swirling the cold water in derision as it escaped back to its lair.

I squirted gasping into the air, pop-eyed and choking and smearing the silver surface with my lacerated palm. I splashed to the bank. Quiston looked as terrified as I felt. He took my arm to help me out.

'Oh, Dad, we thought we saw your *breath!* It was all yellow and stinky. Percy ran to get help. I thought something *got* you. . . .'

His face was as white as his hair, and his eyes were wild, going from me to the pond and back to me. The tears didn't begin in earnest until he saw my hand.

'Dad! You're hurt!'

I watched him cry and he watched me bleed and we couldn't do a thing for each other. The water shined, the Sons of the Pioneers chased Ghost Riders in the Sky overhead, and in the distance, beyond M'kehla and Dobbs and Buddy sprinting toward us from the corral I saw the flag, dipping foolishly lower and lower, though the noon sun had not budged an inch.

As Betsy cleaned and wrapped the wound I forced myself back to a presentable calm. I had my place and my plans to see to, not to mention my reputation. I can put up a front as well as the next fool; I just didn't know how long I could keep it up.

I tried to assuage Quiston's fears by reassuring him that it was just a rusty old barrel, at the same time trying to amuse Buddy and Dobbs and the rest of the gang by adding, 'and it's a good thing it wasn't a rusty *young* barrel.' Quiston said he had known all along it wasn't any real monster. Percy said so had he. The guys laughed at my joke. But there was no real amusement in the loud laughter. They were all humouring me, I discerned; even my kid.

So I didn't participate much in the remaining events of that day. I put on my darkest shades and wired on a grin and stayed out of the way. I was stricken by a fear so deep and all-pervading that finally I was not even afraid. I was resigned, and this resignation was at last the only solid thing left to hold on to. Harder than fear, than faith, harder than God was this rock of resignation. It gleamed before me like a great gem, and everything that happened the rest of that shattered holiday was lensed through its cut-diamond facets. Since it was our national birthday this lens was focused chiefly on our nation, obliging me to view its decay and diseases like a pathologist bent to his microscope.

Flaws previously shrouded now lay naked as knife wounds. I saw the marks of weakness, and woe everywhere I turned, within

174

and without. I saw it in the spoiled, macho grins of the men and in the calculating green eyes of the women. I saw it in the half-grown greed at the barbecue, with kids fighting for the choicest pieces only to leave them half eaten in the sawdust. It was in the worn-out banter at the beer keg and the insincere singing of old favourites around the guitar.

I saw it in the irritable bumper-to-bumper push of traffic fighting its way to the fireworks display at the football stadium – each honk and lurch of modern machinery sounding as doomed as barbaric Rome – but I saw it most in an event that happened as we were driving back from the fireworks late that evening.

The display was a drag for everyone. Too many people, not enough parking space, plus the entrance to the stadium had been manned by a get-out-of-Vietnam garrison complete with pacifist posters and a belligerent bullhorn. A college football stadium on the Fourth of July in 1970 is not the smartest place to carry anti-American signs and shout Maoist slogans, and this noisy group had naturally attracted an adversary force of right-wing counterparts.

These hecklers were as rednecked and thickheaded as the protestors were longhaired and featherbrained. An argument over the bullhorn turned into a tussle, the tussle into a fight, and the cops swooped down. Our group from the farm turned in our tracks and headed back to Dobbs's bus to watch from there.

The women and kids sat out on the cut-open back porch of the bus so they could see the sky; the men stayed inside, sampling M'kehla's tackle box and continuing the day's discussion. M'kehla kept his eyes off me. All I could do was sit there with my hand throbbing, my brain like a blown fuse.

The cop cars kept coming and going during the show, stifling drunks and hauling off demonstrators. Davy said the whole business was a black eye for America. M'kehla maintained that this little fuss was the merest straw in the wind, a precursor of worse woes on the way for the U.S. of A. Dobbs disagreed with both of them, grandly claiming that this demonstration demonstrated just how free and open our society really was, that woven into the fabric of our collective consciousness was a corrective process proving that the American dream was still working. M'kehla laughed – Working? Working *where*? – and demanded evidence of one area, *just one area*, where this wonderful dream was working.

'Why right here before your eyes, Bro,' Dobbs answered amiably. 'In the area of Equality.'

'Are you shitting me?' M'kehla whooped. 'E-*quality?*'

'Just look.' Dobbs spread his long arms. 'We're all at the front of the bus, aren't we?'

Everybody laughed, even M'kehla. However pointless, it had scotched the dispute just in time. The band in the distance was finishing up 'Yankee Doodle' and the sky was surging and heaving with the firework finale. Pleased with his diplomacy and timing, Dobbs swung back around in his driver seat and started the bus and headed for the exit to get a jump on the crowd. M'kehla leaned back in his seat, shaking his head, willing to shine it on for friendship's sake.

But on the way out of the lot, as if that dark diamond was set on having the last severe laugh, Dobbs sideswiped a guy's new white Malibu. Nothing bad. Dobbs stepped out to examine the car and apologize to the driver, and we all followed. The damage was slight and the guy amiable, but his wife was somehow panicked by the sudden sight of all these strange men piling out. She shrank from us as though we were a pack of Hell's Baddest Bikers.

Dobbs wasn't carrying a licence or any kind of liability so M'kehla offered his, along with a hundred-dollar bill. The guy looked at the tiny nick on his fender's chrome strip, then at M'kehla's big shoulders and bare chest, and said, Ah, forget it. No big deal. These things happen. Prudential will take care of it. Even shook hands with M'kehla instead of taking the money.

The last glorious volley of rockets spidered across the sky above; a multitudinous sigh lifted from the stadium. We were all bidding each other good night and hurrying back to our vehicles when the woman suddenly said 'Oh' and stiffened. Before anyone could reach her she fell to the pavement, convulsing.

'Dear God no!' the husband cried, rushing to her. 'She's having a seizure!'

She was bowed backwards almost double in the man's arms, shuddering like a sapling bent beneath a gale. The man was shaking her hysterically.

'She hasn't done it in years. It's all these explosions and these damn police lights! Help! Help!'

The wife had thrashed her way out of his arms and her head
176

was sideways on the asphalt, growling and gnashing as if to bite the earth itself. M'kehla knelt to help.

'We got to stop her chewin' her tongue, man,' he said. I recalled that Heliotrope was also an epileptic; he had tended to convulsions before. He scooped up the woman's jerking head and forced the knuckle of his middle finger between her teeth. 'Got to gag a little, then – '

But he couldn't get in deep enough. She gnashed hard on the knuckle. M'kehla jerked it back with an involuntary hiss:

'Bitch!'

The guy went immediately nuts, worse than his wife. With a bellow he shoved the woman from his lap and sprang instantly to his feet to confront M'kehla.

'You watch your dirty mouth, *nigger!*'

It rang across the parking lot, louder than any starshell or horn. Everybody around the bus was absolutely stunned. Hurrying strangers stopped and turned for fifty yards in every direction, transfixed beneath the reverberation. The woman on the pavement ceased her convulsions and moaned with relief, as though she had passed some demon from her.

The demon had lodged in her husband. He raged on, prodding M'kehla in the breastbone with a stiffened hand.

'The fuckin hell is *with* you anyway, asshole? Huh? Sticking your fuckin finger in my *wife's mouth!* Who do you think you *are?*'

M'kehla didn't answer. He turned to the crowd of us with a What-else-can-I-tell-you? shrug. His eyes hooked on mine. I had to look away. I saw Quiston and Percy watching over the rear rail of the bus porch. Quiston was looking scared again, uncertain. Percy's eyes were shining like M'kehla's, with the same dark, igneous amusement.

It was after midnight before we chugged up the farm driveway. The men were sullen, the kids were crying, the women were disgusted with the whole silly affair. It was nearly one before all the guests had gathered up their scenes and headed home. Betsy and the kids went to bed. M'kehla and I sat in his bus and listened to his Bessie Smith tapes until almost dawn. Percy snored on the zebra skin. The crickets and the spheres creaked and hissed like dry bearings.

When the first light began to sift through the ash leaves, M'kehla stood up and stretched. We hadn't talked for some time. There had been nothing to say. He turned off his amplifier and said he guessed it was time to once again embark.

I mentioned that he hadn't had a wink in forty-eight hours. Shouldn't he sleep? I knew he would not. I was wondering if either of us would ever again enjoy that blessed respite knitting up the ravelled sleeve of care.

"Fraid not, Home. Me and Percy better get out before it closes up on us. Want to come?"

Avoiding his eyes I told him I wasn't ready to pull stakes quite yet, but keep in touch. I walked up the slope and opened the gate for him and he drove through. He got out and we embraced and he got back in. I stood in the road and watched his rig ease out our drive. Once I thought I saw Percy's face appear in the rear window, and I waved.

I didn't see any waving back.

The farm lay still in the aftermath, damp with dew. It looked debauched. Paper plates and cups were scattered everywhere. The barbecue pit had been tipped over and the charcoal had burned a big black spot on the lawn. Betsy's pole beans were demolished; someone or something had stampeded through the strings in the heat of the celebration.

The sorriest sight was the flag. The pole had leaned lower and lower until the gold braid of the hem was trailing in the wood chips and manure. Walking to it I noticed Cousin Davy passed out in the back of his station wagon. I tried to rouse him to help me go bring it down and fold it away, but he only rooted deeper into his sleeping bag. I gave up and climbed over the fence and shuffled through the wood chips to do it myself, and this is the last scene in my story:

I was on my knees and my elbows at the base of the pole, cursing the knot at the bottom pulley – 'God bless this goddamned knot!' – because my fingers were too thick to manage the thin cord, musing about M'kehla's invitation, about Percy, when all at once the sky erupted in a dazzling display of brand-new stars.

The curse had been a prayer, I realized. These stars herald heaven's answer! The knot was blessed even as it was damned! Trumpets celebrated. Bells rang and harps twanged. I sank to the sawdust, certain that my number had been up yonder called.

In this attitude of obeisance I felt the lightning of the Lord lash me again. Ow! I recanted my recanting. Crawl off to
178

Canada? Never! Never never and service forevermore bright with foam only for-give *me* all right? I heard an answering roll of thunder and turned just in time to see Him launch His final chastising charge, His brow terrible, His famous beard flying like amber waves of grain, His eye blazing like cannonfire across the Potomac.

Davy finally managed to drive him from me with a broken bean stake. He took me under the arm and helped me over to the watering trough. It was empty. We had forgotten to turn it back on. The cows were all gathered, thirsty. Davy found the valve and turned it on. I watched the crimson sparkle in the rush of water on the tub's rusty bottom.

The cows were edged near, impatient. Behind them the calves, cautious, each with one side freshly clipped. The peacocks hollered. The pigeons banked over in a curious flock and lit in the chips.

My cousin sat down on the battered brim of the trough. He handed me his wet handkerchief and I held it to the oozing lump where I had been driven into the flagpole. Salt was stinging the scrapes on my cheek and chin. Davy turned away and watched the milling array of beasts and birds.

'Homing cows,' he reflected aloud. 'Not a half-bad idea for a half-baked buckeroo.'

Oleo
Demon Briefs & Dopey Ditties

CALEB DREAMS

Wild wolves and panthers and bears roamed the Wisconsin woods in those days. Sometimes Laura was afraid. But Pa Ingalls preferred to live miles from his nearest neighbours. He built a snug little house on the prairie for Ma and his daughters Mary and Baby Carrie and Laura. And his son Caleb.

Pa kept a fire going all winter to keep out the cold. He taught Laura and Cal how to get things done in the wild frontier.

Laura Ingalls . . . Laura Ingalls Wilder.

Pa hunted and trapped and farmed. Ma knew how to make her own cheese and sugar. At night the wind moaned lonesomely but Pa just stoked the fireplace and played his fiddle and sang to his children, Laura and Mary and Baby Carrie. And young Caleb. Young Cal was much wilder than any of his sisters. He was wilder than the wolves and the panthers. Caleb Ingalls Wilder was wilder than all get out.

Yet, once you really get to know Caleb you will see that he is not really a firebug. You will understand how disappointed he is when, instead of being cast as Clean Air in the Mt Nebo school play, he is chosen to be Litter. You'll understand how ashamed he is when he finds he is too scared to ride the Ferris Wheel at the Lane County Fair and why he almost cries when almost no one votes for him as home room president.

Cal begins to feel he is not much good at anything and he begins to daydream during Social Studies. But what good is Social Studies? Social Studies doesn't get things done. Social Studies doesn't keep out the cold.

You are sure to understand that's why he dropped the book of matches in the wastepaper basket.

CHILLY SHERREE

>When the chill is on the ankles
>And the ice is in the pipes,

Then it's time to get out blankets
And put away the gripes.

So let's bake a lot of goodies
And fill the house with scent,
Till the temperature comes up again
And all the chill has went.

BE KIND TO YOUR WEBFOOTED FRIENDS

– for a mother may be ducking somebody.

Upstairs June Sunday Summer Solstice as my sweet Swallow of the Wire sails up to watch me type and the mud wasp in the wall whirs busily.

Had a fine day fishing. Colonel Weinstein showed up on the train last night with a surprise son from his first wife just Caleb's age; this morning early the four of us drive up the Willamette, then up little Salmon Creek, where I was able to sniff my way back to one of Daddy's favourite fishing holes – stop atop a rise, hike down through the brush and stickers to a spot where the Salmon banks off a sheer mossy cliff. Cool blue-green pool the swirling potential of an expensive billiard table deepest felt. Any shot is possible.

Caleb and Weinstein's boy pull out a dozen cutthroats apiece while the Colonel and I share a bottle of cabernet and talk about Hemingway. I tell him about the Sex & Television fast I've vowed to maintain for six months.

'By Winter Solstice I expect to have my top and bottom chakras both scoured clean.'

'What about the middle?'

'That's too submerged for me. Look! Your Sam has hooked into another one. He's doing real well for his first time.'

'Your Caleb's teaching him well. Speaking of submerged, you know what it takes to circumcise a whale?'

'Nope.'

'It takes four skin divers.'

Almost thirty trout. We got back in time to ice them good so the Colonel and his son could take them back south on the train this afternoon. Returned from the train station to find Dorothy James, known as Micro Dotty for the painted VW bus she drives. She has driven up with some white snow and her red-haired overbudded fourteen-year-old ooh mercy daughter in gym shorts and man's short-sleeved dress shirt, collar turned up. The girl leans against their VW bus while her mom comes up to my office, chewing gum.

Dotty shares a couple doobies with me upstairs, and then I tell her Come on, I'll show you around. On the way down to the pond the daughter joins us. She has changed out of the shirt into a blue tubetop. She oozes along on my other side as I tell her mother about the farm. From the corner of my eye I can see the girl squeezing out of her tubetop like freckled toothpaste.

I introduce them both to Quiston down at the pond. He's casting after the bass, still griped that he missed out on the trip to Salmon Creek. The sight of all that red hair and squeezed skin wipes that gripe out of his mind immediately. He asks if she'd like to try a cast, that there's a Big One by the reeds if she's into it. Instead of answering Redbud oozes away to console the half dozen horny mallard hens, making it clear with a toss of hair that she wasn't into boys her own age or fish of any size.

'She's rather advanced,' Micro Dotty whispers by way of explanation. 'In fact she's been on the pill nearly a year.'

Quis goes back after the bass, Dotty goes off to bother Betsy in the garden, I come back upstairs. The swallow watches from the wire. Quiston and Caleb head off across the field with Stewart to meet Olaf's kid, Butch. The sun edges toward the end of its longest workday of the year.

The girl returns to the Microbus and gets a sleeping bag and a paperback by Anaïs Nin. Under my window she smiles up at me.

'Okay with you if I nest down by your pond? I like to sleep under the stars and I might like a little sunset swim in the open. Know what I mean?'

'I do indeed,' I tell her. Nest anywhere you choose; swim open as you please mercy yes. 'Okay with me.'

The swallow swoops. The wasp takes a break from his mud daubing to buzz out for a better look. Betsy and Dot go inside to cook sugar peas. The sun makes it to Mt Nebo. I decide I better make the rounds, feed the ducks, check on the pond; don't want any sunset calamities.

She is sitting on the bank with her dripping arms wrapped around her knees, watching the ducks and being by them
182

watched. She smiles. I hunker and toss the food into the water's
edge. The ducks come gabbling after it.

'Wheat?' she asks.

'Brown rice,' I say. 'We got two gunny sacks of it, left by
some macrobiotics that lived with us. It was all they would eat.'

'Ugh. Did they like it?'

'I don't think so. There used to be a dozen. Ducks, I mean,
not macrobiotics. Something got the six drakes. A fox, we think.'

'That's too bad.'

'Nature,' I say. 'Red in tooth and claw.'

'Still, it is sad. The poor lonely sweethearts . . .'

'Yeah.'

The sky got gold and we watched the ducks for a long
time without saying anything else. I felt good, virtuous, almost
righteous, as that first day ended and I enjoyed the dawning
realization that my dual fast was actually working: I hadn't gone
near the TV and I didn't want to screw any of those ducks.

BLACKBERRY VINES

> Blackberry vines and barelegged wimmin
> They led me astray, they took me in
>   swimmin
> I reached for a cherry but I got me a
>   lemon
> 'Midst blackberry vines and barelegged
>   wimmin.

DEATH VALLEY DOLLY

> On a barstool in Barstow I met her
> In Kingman I quelled all her qualms
> In Phoenix I fought to forget her
> To the clapping of 29 Palms
>   Oh, Molly, my Death Valley dolly,
>   You're gone, by golly, you're gone.
>   Where the roadrunners run from the coyote sun
>   My fierce little falcon is flown.

> Eating noodles in Needles she caught me
> With a Nogales gal on my knee,

So while brawling in Brawley she shot me
Then jumped in the sour Salton Sea
 Oh, Molly, my Death Valley dolly
 You're gone, by golly you're dead
 Where the scorpions hide
 and the sidewinders slide
 You lie in your alkali bed.

RAGWEED RUTH

Ragweed Ruth was unmowed maze
She was nightshade in the morning
Her ragged flag was often raised
But she raised it like a warning.

No mate had she but emptiness
No family filled her time
She sipped instead on bitterness
Just like it was sweet wine
 like it was sweet wine
She soothed her throat with emptiness
Just like it was sweet wine.

The best spread once found anywhere
Was left by her old man's leaving
But she farmed those fields like a fool at prayer
And watered them with dreaming.

Her hay was wind and wanderings
Shocked up by her forked rakes
Her grain was threshed by thunderings
Her trees were tangled snakes.
 trees were tangled snakes
Her grain was threshed by thunderings
Her trees were tangled snakes.

Each spring the farmers from around
Brought axes and advices
But Ruth would firmly glare them down
To forge her own devices.

For she was plenty to herself
She survived the seasons through
She was dark bread dipped in health
She was her own strong brew
    was her own strong brew
She was dark bread dipped in salty health
She was her own strong brew.

Then came the dry when the farming men
Failed and cracked and fled
Ruth invited all the families in
And somehow all were fed.

Plough never cleft her bottomland
Nor harrow stroked her sod
Still, golden ears and marzipan
Up sprung from where she trod
    sprung from where she trod
Golden ears and marzipan
Sprung up from where she trod.

The passing of her wandering walk
Could fill a tree with fruit
At her glare the shrivelled stalk
Would straighten, stand and root.

The dry time passed as all times will.
Back to the crippled county
Returned the rain, the sprouts to till,
And seeming endless bounty.

The guests all gathered up and left
With their advice and axes . . .
Old Ruth ragdanced on to death
Her land was sold for taxes
    land was sold for taxes
Ragweed Ruth danced on to death
Her land was sold for taxes.

PACK OF WALNETTOS

Sister Lou had a shop on the corner
Four kids and a veteran in bed
All day to the old she sold dresses
    made over
And dressed soldiers all night in her head . . .

    God grant me a pack of Walnettos
    And the Good Book to sermon upon
    Let me shine like a flash through the trash
      in the ghettos
    And I'll light those darkies' way home.

At the keyboard they found the professor
Done in by downers and wine
The bottle still cold on the old
    walnut dresser
The metronome still keeping time . . .

    God give me a pack of Walnettos
    And the Good Book to sermon upon
    Let me burn like a beacon for the weak
      in the ghettos
    And I'll light those darkies' way home.

Annie Greengums ate nuthin but veggies
Rubbed organic oils on her skin
Wore leg hair and a pair of corrective
    wedgies
She had found in the recycling bin . . .

    God send me a pack of Walnettos
    And the Good Book to sermon upon
    Let me loom like a lamp in the damp
      and dark ghettos
    And I'll draw those darkies back home.

Little Lupe learned feminist lingo
With a lesbian accent to boot
But she married a ring and a grape-growing
    gringo
With weekdays to match every suit.

Please God just a pack of Walnettos
And the Good Book to sermon upon
Like a torch send me forth to scorch
    out the ghettos
And I'll hotfoot those darkies on home.

Brother Memphis hit a St Louis deli
For a pig's foot and a handful of change
Got away on a train with a pain
    in his belly
Died next day in Des Moines of ptomaine.

Dear God a pack of Walnettos
And the Bible to sermon upon
Shine like a flash through the trash
    of the ghettos
Light all us poor darkies back home.

Finding Doctor Fung

'Oh, by the way,' is how the question was usually broached, whenever I encountered anybody able to understand enough English, 'have you any information regarding the fate or whereabouts of your nation's renowned philosopher, Dr Fung Yu-lan?' This usually received pretty much the same response – 'Fung Yu Who?' – and usually prompted some wordplay from one of my three American companions, such as 'Yoo-*hoo*, Yu-lan?' when they saw me drop back to quiz some citizen.

This trio – our magazine editor, the sports photographer, and Bling, the Beijing-born Pittsburgh-raised student of Chinese law – had all concurred days ago that the object of my inquiry was, at his earthly most, a mist from China's bygone glories. At his least, just another hoked-up curiosity in Dr Time's seamy side-show – like the Cardiff Giant or D. B. Cooper. The quest did lend a kind of Stanley-looking-for-Livingstone class to our tour, however, so they weren't impatient with my inquiring sidetrips.

Nor was I discouraged by all the blank stares the name produced. I had learned of the missing doctor only a couple weeks earlier myself, on the trip down from Oregon. Instead of flying down to San Francisco to catch our China Clipper, I decided to drive. I had some back issues of our little literary magazine, *Spit in the Ocean*, that I hoped I could maybe unload in the Bay Area. A whole packed trunk and backseat full of back issues, to be honest. My swaybacked Mustang whined and hunkered beneath the weight so I left Mt Nebo a good two days before our plane's departure in case the big load or the long haul should delay her. But the old rag-topped nag covered the 600 miles of dark freeway nearly nonstop, like a filly in her prime. When the dim swoop of the Bay Bridge came into view I still had more than a day and a half before our flight, so I swung off at Berkeley to visit an old minister pal of mine that I hadn't seen since Altamont.

I had a tougher time locating his church than I expected. I found what I thought was the right backstreet and corner but with the wrong building; that, or the defunct woollen mill which

188

had always seemed so suited to the shaggy flock that my friend shepherded had been completely changed. Instead of a drab cement block there was a cute little church fronted with bright red brick. Wire-mesh factory windows had been replaced with beautiful stained glass, and where a grimy smokestack once angled up from the roof there was now a copper-spired steeple shining in the morning sun. I wasn't sure it was the same place at all until I walked around back: the tin-roofed garage that served as the minister's rectory was the same ratty run-down trash pile from five years ago.

The vine-framed door was ajar and I went in. When my tired eyes adjusted to the messy grey gloom I saw the man sound asleep and completely naked on a raised waterbed. The huge plastic bladder was as much a mess as the rest of the room, a Sargasso Sea of clutter, with my friend floating peacefully amid the rest of the flotsam. I gave a bare patch of the grey plastic a slap that sent a shimmying swell coast to coast. I saw consciousness slowly rising to the surface of the bearded face. Finally he raised up on a wobbly elbow, causing books and bottles and beer cans and pizza boxes and tarot cards to undulate around him while he squinted at my face. His hard night had left his eyes redder than my long haul had mine. At length he grunted hello, then flopped right back down and drew a turtleneck sweater sleeve across his brow. I pulled up the nearest orange crate and set down to fill him in on all the Oregon gossip. None of my news got more than an occasional grunt out of him, not until I mentioned the reason I happened to be passing through. This heaved him sitting full up like a seismic wave. 'You're going where to cover *what?*'

'To Peking. To cover the Chinese Invitational Marathon.'

'To Beijing *China?* Why Godalmighty, mate, you can find out what has become of Fung Yu-lan!'

'Who?'

'Dr Fung Yu-lan!' the minister cried. '*Master* Fung Yu-lan! Merely one of the most influential philosophers in the modern mother world! Or was . . .'

He waited a moment for that shock wave to subside, then began Australian crawling his way toward the shoreline.

'I'm not exaggerating. Twenty-five years or so ago Fung was considered the brightest star in the East's philosophical firmament, a beacon for panphenomenalistic voyagers for fifty years! Then, one day, suddenly – *foof!* nothing. Not the dimmest glimmer. All trace of him blotted out, buried beneath that black cloud known as the Cultural Revolution.'

I told him that it was supposed to be my primary task to cover a live race, not uncover some buried fossil. 'At least this is the opinion of the shoe manufacturers who own the sports mag that's sending me to China. I better stick to their schedule. They *are* footing the bill, so to speak.'

'That doesn't mean you have to toe their line every step of the way, does it?' he demanded. 'You can work it into your story. A little extracurricular shouldn't give them any gripe. If it does, tell the capitalistic shoemongers to go bite their tongues. Tell them to look to their soles. Tracking down Fung is more important than some bourgeois bunion derby. And this isn't just any old fossil, this is a rare old fossil! He, he's a – wait! I'll show you what he is.'

The minister released my hand and stepped back up into his waterbed . He waded through the swell to the bedside wall of orange crates he had nailed up for shelves and bookcases. He began pawing among the books, hundreds of books, checking titles, tossing them aside, all the while keeping up a running rap over his shoulder as he searched.

'Sixty-some years ago the youthful scholar Fung observed that all of his philosophical peers seemed to be either stubbornly stuck in the Eastern camp or obstinately in the Western. The twain of which are never to meet, right? The Transcendental versus the Existential? The bodhisatva digging his belly button under the bo tree as opposed to the bolshevik building bombs in his basement? These opposing camps have been at each other for centuries, like two hardheaded old stags with horns locked, draining each other's energy toward an eventual, and mutual, starvation. Our hero decided that this was *not* his cup of orange pekoe. Or oolong, either. Yet what other alternatives were being served? It was either go West, young Fung, or go East. Then, one bright day, he caught a fleeting flash of a third possibility, a radically *new* possibility, perhaps, for the mental mariner to try. Radical enough that even back then Fung knew better than to go blabbing it around established academia, East or West. He would continue to honour those two classic ways of thought, but he resolved that he would never join either camp. Instead, he would dedicate himself to what I term "The Way of the Bridge".

He would construct an empirical concept that would *span* those opposite shores of outlook! Some complicated job of construction, right? This dude was Frank Lloyd Wright, Dag Hammarskjöld, and Marco Polo all in *one* – get the picture?'

Not very well but I nodded, always impressed by the extent of my friend's rambling expertise.

'From that day on he has laboured at this colossal bridgework. And get this: Fung's *family* name means "power to cross a wild stream" – a mythical river of the barbarian tribes of Manchu, to be precise – and his *given* names mean "elite friend". So this bridge-builder's complete monicker means "Stream-crossing Elite Friend". Get it? He lived up to the name, too. For nearly half a century this stream-crosser travelled around our globe, lecturing and publishing and teaching. And learning. In the late thirties he guest-chaired a year at Harvard without pay, claiming all he wanted was the chance to learn about our modern Yankee music. The only reward he took back to China was a footlocker full of swing band seventy-eight his students gave him. Ah! Here he is . . .'

He had found the volume he was seeking. He waded out of the waterbed's welter, blowing dust from a black leather cover. Back on the floor he opened the book and bent over a random page in reverent silence for a few moments, as oblivious of the ludicrous picture he presented as one of those nude bronze statues of Rodin's. Then he closed the book with a sigh and raised his eyes to mine.

'It is *so* goddamn important to me, old buddy, to enlist you wholeheartedly in this cause, that I am going to break one of my most cardinal rules – I am going to loan a hardbound.'

He let his fingers trail across the worn cover a final time, then handed me the book. I carried it to the orange crate nearest a dirty window so I could make out what was left of the gold letters on the spine: *The Spirit of Chinese Philosophy*. Inside the musty cover I read that the work had been translated by E. R. Hughes of Oxford University and published by Routledge & Kegan Paul, Ltd., of London, England, in 1947. The front flyleaf had an embossing that said the book was the Property of the University of California Library Rare Book Room and the date slip at the back indicated it was nearly sixteen years overdue. While I leafed through the yellowing pages, my friend searched the room for his scattered clothes, talking all the while.

'You're holding volume three of his four-volume *History of Chinese Philosophy*, a work that is still considered out there in the forefront of the field. Way out. Revolutionary. Because instead of couching the prose in the customary Mandarin idiom of the elite, Fung wrote in common street vernacular, thereby availing the loftiest thinking in China's incredibly long history of cerebral pursuit to *the common coolie!* An impertinence that continually had him in Dutch with the Manchu feudalist powers-that-were. But, with what must have been some pretty foxy footwork, Fung was able to keep a step ahead of the axe and maintain his position at the university, and to keep on writing his opus.

'Then, right in the middle of volume four, the Japs take over Beijing. Naturally a wise old fox teaching Mencius and listening to Glenn Miller is soon seen as a potential thorn in the rump of the Rising Sun. One night after class Fung gets wind that he's in Dutch again, this time with the Japanese. He hurries out of his office. Bootsteps approaching down the front hall. Sentries posted at the rear. Trapped! So, thinking faster than Mr Moto, Fung borrows a charwoman's babushka and broom and sweeps right past the Nip dragnet sent to snare him. He sweeps on off the campus and right on up the hills, where he joins Chiang Kai-shek and his band of Chinese resistance fighters.

'By the end of World War Two he is so highly esteemed by Generalissimo Chiang and the Nationalists that he is made chairman of the Philosophy Department at the U of Beijing – permanent. At last, he thinks, he is in harmony with the mighty song of state! Then, out of nowhere, up to the conductor's podium comes Mao Tse-tung and down goes Chiang's band, and Fung realizes he's out of step again and marching right back toward that old doghouse. Not only has he been tight with the Nationalists, he's also published essays that seem to praise China's feudalistic past. In the eyes of the new regime this is a big strike against him. Worse, he hails from a "landlord background" and has an "elitist Mandarin education". Strikes two and probably three. He's already seen a lot of his colleagues sent to the Shensi cabbage collectives for less. So, thinking fast again, Fung decides to make a move before he's cornered. He writes to Mao personally. He confesses his bourgeois background, sops on the self-criticism, and begs the Honourable Chairman to accept his resignation – "I feel it is in the best

192

interests of our great country and your mighty revolution et cetera that I resign my chair here at the university and go to work on a rural commune, to better acquaint myself with the glorious roots of socialism." Didn't I tell you he was – oops, watch it – *foxy?*'

I looked up from the book almost in time to catch the card table he had knocked over trying to hop into his too-tight Levi's. Pens and pencils and paper clips scattered among the peanut shells and paper cups on the floor. He kept right on hopping and rapping.

'As you might imagine, with that kind of hat-in-hand approach, it wasn't long before Fung was back at his position at the university – simultaneously teaching his new works and at the same time denouncing his older efforts as mere maunderings of a misled mind. Mainly trying to keep his profile low and that doghouse distant, if you get the picture.'

I nodded again. I actually was beginning to get a picture of the man behind all this fancy scrimshaw of history, an image faint but fascinating.

'Then the old maestro, Papa Mao, begins to lose *his* grip on the podium, not all at once but enough that Mama Mao and her quartet can grab the baton. And, merciful God, the tune that *they* strike up! It's so erratic and discordant and downright heartlessly juggernaut *cruel* that even old Fung the Fox can't figure how to stay out of its way. It's like a thundercloud of noise and confusion blasting out in all directions, a poisonous black cloud, boiling with terrible bolts of power and gouts of gore and shrieks of agony, rolling bigger and blacker until it closes over all China, over art and music and the modern sciences, over the poor nation's history as well as its future, and over Dr Fung Yu-lan.'

The preacher had delivered this diatribe while balancing on one foot and trying to buckle a Uniroyal-soled sandal on the other; now he seemed to give up. He stood barefoot, the sandal dangling and his face downcast, strangely weary.

'Anyway, nobody has heard from the old teacher in more than fifteen years. Nary publication nor postcard. Foof. Not even an obituary. Foof and nada. Intriguing, huh?'

'Does anybody suppose he's still alive?'

'Nobody in the philosophy department of Cal, I can assure you! They've already got him comfortably catalogued and shelved away in the minor-league stacks along with all the other nearly-made-it-bigs. He was probably offed ages ago, everybody supposes, and even if he wasn't rubbed out by that first big purge of intellectuals – I mean big like *millions*, we're just now finding out; maybe not more than Hitler but right up there with the likes of old Joe Stalin – they maintain that the chances of a man his age surviving that time of turmoil are slim and nil.'

'How old would he be?'

'I don't know.' He raised his foot and slipped on the sandal. 'Old. There must be a bio in the book.'

I found it in the introduction. 'Born in Canton, during the Chino-Japanese war, in 1894. That would make him . . . eighty-seven! Slim, nil, and *none* my supposition, in a country with the shortest life expectancy in the world.'

'Oh, no, not any more! For whatever misery he caused, Papa Mao's reforms have practically doubled the lifetime of the Chinese citizen. So Doc Fung could still be around somewhere, still waffling, still trying to reconcile the undeniable logic of Marxist dialecticables with the un-pin-able-downness of the free spirit.'

'Still in Dutch in China?'

'Almost certainly still in Dutch in China. By now he'd probably be branded a booklicking toady by the *new* gang, see?'

'I see,' I said, beginning to get yet a clearer picture of this old oriental fox. 'Yeah, it is intriguing, but I don't see how I could work it into my sportswriting trip. Where's the pertinence? What's the meaning? The moral?'

'Hey, I don't know,' the minister answered from inside the black turtleneck he was pulling over his head. His face emerged from the frayed collar shadowed by that look of weariness and defeat again. He heaved a heavy sigh. 'Maybe it means that He Who Waffles East and West Waffles Best. Maybe that's the moral. But, shit, shipmate, *I* don't know what it all means. That's why I want you to find old Fung. Then you can ask *him*. Answering questions like that is what he's trained for.'

He headed for the door, his face down.

'C'mon, let's hit the streets. I need a beer. And I know a couple bibliophiles around the Telegraph scene that might have information more recent than mine.'

Trying to cheer him out of his downcast mood, I complimented his pretty new church as we passed. He wouldn't even turn to look at it.

'I hate the prissy pile of shit,' he said. 'It looks like some kind of chapel boutique. No spirit, no spirit at all. The woollen mill maybe didn't have a fancy fucking *spire* but it did have some spirit. Remember? We used to get some fierce stuff spinning in that old mill. Marches. Sit-ins. But no more. No more.' He shoved his hands in his pockets and walked faster. 'I liked it the way it was – funky but fierce.'

'Why'd you get it refurbished then?'

'I didn't! It was my bosses, the California Ecumenical Council and so forth! Did you happen to see a couple years ago when I got awarded the Presidential Commendation? For our Runaway Ranger Programme? That's what started it. The AP ran a shot of our kids on the back porch. When the diocese daddies saw what an eyesore they had representing their faith in Berkeley, they all shit bricks. I think they used some of those very bricks on that facade back there. If my backhouse hadn't been hid by all those morning glories they'd have shit another pile and bricked it over too. It's all part of the city council's integrated policy for the beautification of Berkeley – brick those eyesores over. It might not heal the sore but at least it hides the pus, is the policy. You'll see what I mean.'

I did, as soon as we reached Telegraph district. There were as many patch-pantsed street people as ever, but the pants were cleaner, and the patches seemed more a product of fashion than necessity. Coffeehouses that once seethed with protest songs as black and bitter as their espresso now offered sweet herbal teas and classical guitar. I saw panhandlers buying Perrier water and Hari Krishnas wearing pantsuits and wigs to aid them in their pitch for donations. Nondescript doorways where spectral dealers with hooded eyes once hissed secret questions – 'Assid? Sspeed? Hashisssh?' – now were openly decorated with displays of every kind of absurd apparatus, and the dealers sung out their wares like carny barkers: 'Bongs bongs bongs! Freebase without fuss when you buy from us! Our paraphernalia will never fail ya!'

Even those pitchy clots of young bloods you used to see playing bongos back in alleyways had been cleared up. Now the clots coursed right along with everybody else in the mainstream, carrying big chrome-trimmed ghetto blasters that played *tapes* of bongos. I had to shake my head.

'I see what you mean, yep.'

The minister gave me a wry grin. 'Fruits and berries, brutes and fairies,' he sang in a sad voice. 'Hot and hysterical and hopin' for a miracle. Did you hear that Cleaver is Born Again? Did you hear that they are trying to change the name of Earth People's Park to Gay People's Gardens? Oh, *what* has become of our Brave New Berserkeley of Yesterday, comrade?'

I couldn't even guess; and the Telegraph bibliophiles had no more information about what had become of Fung the Philosopher than I had about Berkeley the Brave. And these citizens here in Beijing have been just as little help. Since landing in China more than a week ago I have hit on every English speaker I could collar, but the name hasn't struck the slightest spark. Our smiling guide, the very faithful and conscientious and ominous Mr Mude, even denied having ever heard of *any* Chinese citizen with such a ridiculous name.

Then, ironically, this same Mr Mude furnished the first ray of hope that the old man still lived. Exasperated by my continued inquiries after the missing teacher, Mude had stood in the door of our little tour bus before allowing us to get off at the main gate of the University of Beijing, where we were going to check out their athletic department. Frowning darkly, he had advised that it would be better if such questioning were curtailed during the remainder of our sojourn through the People's Republic. Better for all concerned. Then, smiling again, had added –

'Because Dr Fung Yu-lan is not for anyone *beneficent* to meet with – ah? – even if such a personage *is*.'

– indicating that such a personage must still be in disfavour somewhere. But in what doghouse, in what province? Mude probably knew, for all the good that did; he had driven off to other inscrutable duties before I could pursue the point. Yet if he knew, others must. Who else? It was after we had left the shabby little gymnasium and were following Bling back across the campus that an obvious possibility suddenly occurred to me.

'Hey, Bling. What say you we swing by the philosophy department?'

'To ask after your fossilized egghead?' Bling laughed at me. 'Man, I've spent weeks trying to track down profs I *know* live on this crazy campus, asking everybody. These Beijing bureaucrats don't know, don't want to know, and wouldn't tell you if they *did*.'

196

Yet the first woman behind the first desk we came upon in the stark old building had lit up with delight at Bling's translation of my question. After listening to her chatter a moment, Bling turned to the rest of us, his eyes unslanted by surprise.

'She says *yes*, by golly, that he's very much alive, still on the faculty, lives about two blocks away, practically next door to the gym we just left! Furthermore, she wants to know if we'd like her to phone and see if he is amenable to a visit from some foreign pilgrims?'

So, at last, I was standing with my three companions before a small cottage hunched back under a grove of looming gum trees, waiting for a little girl in pigtails to go tell her great-grandfather that his visitors had arrived. We all stood in a foolish row, our Yankee banter hushed by the small swept yard and the nearness of a man we had barely believed in and were yet to see. Beijing's afternoon pollution was still. The only sound coming through this undersea murk was a scratchy tune being played on a phonograph somewhere, faint and vaguely familiar.

'Say, isn't that a Goodman solo?' the photographer wondered in a whisper. 'Benny Goodman and the Dorsey orchestra?'

Before anyone could wonder further, the screen swung wide and was held back by the girl. For a long moment there was nothing; then the old man was standing there in the grey Sun Yat-sen Maoutfit and grey felt bedroom slippers, as spectral and dim as last month's mildew.

Except for the eyes and the smile. The eyes came slicing out of a pair of wire-rimmed lenses, sharp as two chips of jade. And there was a gleam in the smile both mysterious and madcap – something between Mona Lisa and Mork from Ork. The old man let this expression play across the four of us from an amused pause without speaking, then held a liver-spotted hand toward me, standing nearest. One might have expected to see a pebble in the palm and hear him say, 'So, Grasshopper . . . you have come at last.'

Instead he said, in English as musty and precise as the pages of that old book back in my hotel room, 'Gentlemen, please . . . won't you come in?'

I took the hand. One might have hoped I'd have the wit to reply, 'Dr Fung, I presume?' Instead I stammered, 'Yeah yes we'd be happy to, Mister You Lawn . . . proud.'

The child held wide the door and bowed slightly to each of us

197

as we followed her great-grandfather into his home. We passed through a small foyer and into the room that was obviously his study and parlour. The windows were nearly covered by the drooping grey-green foliage of the gum trees, yet the room was by no means dim. The air in fact seemed brighter than it had outside. Light appeared to glow out of the ancient furnishings like foxfire from humus. It shimmered along the old trowelled plasterwork and glistened between the tiny network of cracks on the leather upholstery. Even the dark wood of the kitchen door and the bookcases shined, rubbed to a rich lustre by years of dusting.

No decorations adorned the walls save for a long calendar, hand-penned, and a framed photograph of students posing in a black-and-white past. Nothing obstructed the polished floor except one floor lamp, one empty urn, and three pieces of furniture – a leather divan, a two-person loveseat, and a stuffed chair that would have looked at home in any living room in middle America in the twenties. This was clearly the Doctor's chair. He stood beside it, smiling, nodding the editor and little Bling onto the divan and the beefy photographer into the wide loveseat. To me, as to a student called to his professor's office for a little tête-à-tête, he assigned the ceramic urn.

When we were finally situated to his satisfaction, Fung Yu-lan lowered himself into the stuffed chair, folded his hands in his lap, and waited, smiling at me. I could feel the blood rush to my cheeks and my head go empty. I began gibbering awkward introductions and explanations and stuff. Babble. I don't think I would have recalled a word of what was said in that room if I hadn't happened to nervously thrust my hands into the pockets of my bulky safari jacket and come upon Bling's cassette machine. I still had enough journalistic presence of mind to surreptitiously fidget it on.

And now, weeks later and thousands of miles away, as I try to type up a transcript of a taped encounter in the privacy of my own study – to have *some* little sample of the wisdom of the Orient to send down to my minister friend in backsliding Berkeley – I still find the exchange almost too embarrassing to abide:

FUNG MEETING – BEIJING CAMPUS –
DAY BEFORE MARATHON

DR FUNG: May I request you gentlemen some tea?
AMERICANS: Oh yeah. Yes. Of course. Please.

FUNG: I shall do so. Pardon me.

An order is given in Chinese. There is the sound of the little girl's clog sandals on the floor, and the kitchen door spring creaking. For a moment, as the door swings, a big band can clearly be heard swinging through the jazz classic Sing Sing Sing.

FUNG: So please tell me: what brings you all to China?

BLING: Sir, me, I live here . . . a student at this very institution.

F: Ah? Studying what, may I ask?

B: Chinese Law and Track and Field.

F: Very good. And the rest of you?

DEBOREE: Sir, the rest of us are journalists.

F: Please. The years have made me somewhat deaf.

D: The rest of us are journalists! Here covering the big race! The Beijing Invitational Marathon? It happens tomorrow. Paul there is the editor of our periodical; Brian is the photographer. I am the writer.

F: Ah. A sportswriter . . .

D: Not really. Fiction, usually. Stories, novels. Actually, back home, I'm quite a big-time writer.

This evokes muffled Yankee snorts: Oh boy, will ya listen to that? Big-time Writer back home.

D: Also, I am a very big fan of the *I Ching*, the Chinese Book of Changes. I have been consulting the *Ching* oracle religiously for more than ten years, throwing it every day.

More snorts, low and inside: My, my, him also Big-time Ching Thrower, too.

D: But what I *essentially* came to China for, actually, was to find out what has become of *you*, Doctor. Perhaps you are not aware of it but for many years in our country, scholars of philosophy have been wondering, 'What has become of Dr Fung Yu-lan? What is Dr Fung Yu-lan doing now?' I mean, those of us who have been seriously influenced by your work . . . have been wondering –

This is mercifully interrupted by the sound of the door swinging back open and the tinkle of the tea service.

AMERICANS: Thank you. This is very nice. You bet. Just what we needed. . . .

F: You are all welcome.

Fidgeting. Sipping. Clink of china on china. And a kind of patient, silent amusement.

199

D: So, ah, here we are. How are you then, Doctor? I mean, what have you been doing all this time?

F: I have been working.

D: Teaching?

F: No. I have been working on my book.

D: Very good. And what book have you been working on?

Again, that subtle moment of amused silence.

F: I have been working on my *History of Chinese Philosophy*. As always. On what else would I be working?

D: Oh. Of course. I guess what I meant was on what *aspect*. A revision? For a new edition?

F: No. Not a revision, a continuation. Volume five. It is an attempt to examine the Cultural Revolution, a task for which I fear I am woefully inadequate. But I feel that these last fifteen years must be examined and understood.

D: These last fifteen years? I should say! Boy, we will all be very interested in reading *that*. That's terrific. Isn't that terrific, you guys?

Much agreement, and more slurping of tea and rattling of cups on saucers. Then more silence.

D: This tea is very good. What kind of tea is it, anyway?

F: Chinese.

See? Embarrassing. Disquieting, even before this chance to review the tape. Back at the hotel that very evening the Big-time Writer couldn't get the humiliating encounter off his mind. Unable to sleep, he dug the borrowed book from the bottom of his luggage. He opened it beneath a bed lamp and found himself immediately captured by the clarity of the prose; it had been swept as clean as that bald yard. . . .

Two hours later, the Big-time Writer lays the book down and bows his head, finally beginning to get some inkling of the stature of the mind he had found in this far-off keep.

He discerned that Philosopher Fung had arbitrarily fashioned four views of man, as a means of observing the gradations of evolving ethical human awareness. These four views, or 'realms' as Fung calls them, are (1) The unselfconscious or 'natural' realm, (2) The self-conscious or 'utilitarian' realm, (3) The other-conscious or 'moral' realm, and (4) The all-conscious or 'universal' realm.

The first two realms, according to Dr Fung's canon, are 'gifts of nature', while the second two are realized only as 'creations of the spirit'. That these two conditions must sometimes necessarily be in conflict was taken for granted by the old Doctor; that either side should ever completely triumph over the other was considered the most dangerous of folly.

The writer looked up from the closed book, recalling the walk through blighted Berkeley and the question to the minister concerning the old man's pertinence. Here was how he pertained, this teak-jawed Chinaman, to the Telegraph of today as well as to last season's idealism. Wasn't he trying to light up the very dilemma the sixties had stumbled over? the problem of how to go with the holy flow and at the same time take care of basic biz? Sure, you can to thine own cells be true and liberate parking lots from the pigs, but how do you keep them free of future swine without turning into something of a cop yourself? There was the block that had stumbled a mighty movement, and Fung Yu-lan pertained because he had tried to light it with his intellect, without bias, from all sides. And is still trying, bright as ever. How does he manage it, in this dim corner? How does he keep the faith and keep ahead of the axe at the same time? And for so many years?

The Sharp Old Fox would have had answers to such pertinent questions, had the subjects ever been touched on, but all our Big-time Writer could think to ask were things like 'What kind of tea?' Embarrassing . . .

It is only at the end of the tape, after the visitors have slurped their way to the meeting's end and are once again outside in the shifting Chinese twilight, that he asked a question that was remotely close:

D: One more thing, Doctor. There are some pretty grisly – I mean we've heard a lot of accounts, stories, about how quite a lot of teachers and intellectuals were . . . I mean how *did* you get through that dreadful time of turmoil?

F (*shrugging*): I have been a student of Chinese philosophy for more than three quarters of a century. Thus – (*he shrugs again, flashing such a jaunty, devil-may-care grin that one might almost expect him to say, It was a piece of cake. Except for a sharpness that one senses beneath that jaunty flash, a carnivorous quality that suggests the toothy old smiler is not only capable of biting off and swallowing* any *time of turmoil* – any *period of upheaval or downfall brought about by any single dictator or by any Gang of*

201

Force with their rinky-dink revolution whether cultural or dreadful – but that he can thrive on it! As though the turmoil had not only been a piece of cake, easily downed and digested, it had been savoured as well) – I have become very broad-minded.

Run Into Great Wall

Verses appearing here are from the Tao Te Ching *by Lao-tzu. An older contemporary of Confucius (551–479 B.C.), Lao-tzu was the Chinese historian in charge of archives at the royal court of the Chou dynasty. He wrote nothing of his own but taught by example and parable. When the famous sage was at last departing his homeland for the mountains of his end, the keeper of the mountain pass detained him.*

'Master, my duties as sentry of this remote outpost have made it impossible for me to visit your teachings. As you are about to leave the world behind, could you not also leave behind a few words for my sake?'

Whereupon Lao-tzu sat down and filled two small books with 81 short verses, less than some 5,000 characters, and then departed. No one ever heard where he went.

> *There is a thing confusedly*
> *   formed,*
> *Born before heaven and earth.*
> *Silent and void,*
> *It stands alone and does not*
> *   change,*
> *Goes round and does not weary.*
> *It is capable of giving birth*
> *   to the world.*
> *I know not its name*
> *So I style it 'the way . . .'*
> *Man models himself on earth,*
> *Earth on heaven,*
> *Heaven on the way,*
> *And the way on that which is*
> *   naturally so.*

The dark was already pressing down out of the eastern sky when Yang at last swung off the main road from the village and opened up for his finishing sprint down the canal path. A

203

hundred and thirty metres away, at the end of the row of mud-and-brick houses crouching along both sides of the dirt lane, his uncle's dwelling was tucked back beneath two huge acacias. A large estate compared to the other 10-by-10 yard-with-huts, the building housed his uncle's dentist shop and cycle-repair service, as well as his uncle's wife and their four children, his uncle's ancient father, who was Yang's grandfather and an inveterate pipe-smoker, windbreaker, and giggler . . . also Yang's mother and her bird and Yang's three sisters, and usually a client or two staying over on one of the thin woven mats to await the repair of their transportation or recuperate from the repair of their molars.

Yang could not see the house as he ran toward the looming acacias, but he could easily picture the scene within. The light would already have been moved from above the evening meal to the dishwashing, and the family would be moving to the television in the shop room, trying to find places among the packing crates of dental moulds. The only light there would be the flutter of the tiny screen beating at the dark like the wings of a black-and-white moth.

Yang knew just how they would look. His uncle would be cranked back in the dentist chair, a cigarette cupped in his stubby hand, his shirt open. His wife would be perched beside him on her nurse's stool. On the floor, in half lotus, Grandfather would be leaned forward, giggling, his long pipe only inches from the screen. Farther back his four cousins and his two youngest sisters would be positioned among the paraphernalia on the floor, trying to appear interested in the reports of how the flood along the Yangtze might affect rice quotas. Along the rear wall his oldest sister would be preparing the infants for the night, wrapping their bottoms and sliding them, one after the other, onto the pad beneath the raised cot. The bird would be hung near the door, covered against evening draughts.

In the other room his mother would be cleaning the dishes as quietly as possible.

His uncle would be angry that Yang was late again, but nothing would be said. A quick scowl turned from the television. No questions. They all knew where he had been. The only dalliance he could afford was the public library. For one-half fen a reader could rent two hours on a wooden bench and enjoy the kind of privacy a library creates, even when the benches were packed, reader to reader.

Yang had hoped to borrow one of the newly allowed classics of Confucius. He'd heard that their library had received the very first shipment to honour at last the birthplace of the great philosopher. But the books were all already on loan. Yang instead had to choose a more familiar work, Wang Shih-fu's *Romance of the Western Chamber*. It was a novel his father had continued to teach even during the harshest criticism of the 'slave-ridden classics'.

The last loan date on *Western Chamber* was almost five years ago. The last borrower was his father.

Without slackening his stride, Yang pushed the book into his trouser tops and buttoned his jacket over it. Not that his uncle would not know a book was there, of course. He almost certainly would. Therefore it was not that he was concealing it, Yang told himself. He carried it in his belt to have both hands free, for his balance.

For his sprint.

Fists clenched, he pumped hard against the descending gloom, trusting his feet to avoid the rocks and ruts in the dark path. He could have run it blindfolded, navigating by sound and smell – Gao Jian's machine, sewing there to the left; Xiong-and-son's excrement wagons parked in reeking rows, ready for the next day's collections; half-wit Wi snoring with his sows. He ran harder.

He was small for his nineteen years, with narrow shoulders and thin ankles. But his thighs were thick and his upper arms very strong from the weight work of wrestling. Beneath the book his belly was like carved oak. He was in good shape. He had been running home from school every night for almost four years.

With a final burst of speed he ducked beneath the curtain of acacia and into the yard of his uncle's shop. He nearly stumbled in wonderment. Everything was lit, the whole house! Even the bulb above the false teeth – still lit. Something had happened to his mother! Or one of his sisters!

He didn't go to the gate but hurdled the mud hedge and rattled across the brickpile. He charged through the door and the empty front room to the curtain across the kitchen and stopped. Shaking, he pulled aside the dingy batik and peered inside. Everyone was still at the dinner table, the bone chopsticks waiting beside the best plates, the vegetables and rice steaming in the platters. Every head was already turned to him, smiling.

His uncle stood, a tiny glass of clear liquid in each hand. He handed one to Yang and lifted the other in toast.

'To our little Yang,' his uncle declared, the big mouth beaming porcelain. '*Ganbei!*'

'To Yang!' The aunt and sisters and cousins all stood, lifting their glasses. '*Ganbei!*'

Everyone tossed the swallow of liquid into their mouths except Yang. He could only blink and pant. His mother came around the table, her eyes shining.

'Yang, son, forgive us. We have opened your letter.'

She handed him an elaborately inscribed paper. He saw the official seal of the People's Republic embossed at the bottom.

'You have been invited to go to Beijing and race. Against runners from all over the world!'

Before Yang could look at his letter, his uncle was touching the rim of his refilled glass to Yang's.

'It is going to be televised all over the world. *Ganbei*, Yang. Drink.'

Yang started to drink, then asked, 'What kind of race?'

'The greatest kind. The *longest* kind – '

That must be a marathon, Yang realized. Now he swallowed the mao tai in a gulp. He felt the strong rice liquor blaze its way to his stomach. A marathon? He had never run a marathon, not even half a marathon. Why had they picked him? Yang didn't understand.

'We are all so proud,' his mother said.

'All over the world,' his uncle was saying. 'It will be seen by millions. *Millions!*'

'Your father would have also been proud,' his mother added.

Then Yang understood. The provincial chairman of sports had been a friend and colleague of his father: an old friend, and a man of honour and loyalty, if not too much courage. It was surely he who had recommended young Yang. A grand gesture of cleaning up. For things that had happened.

'He would have gone to the square and played his violin and *sung*, son. He would have been that proud.'

Yang didn't say so, but he thought that it would take more

than a grand gesture or a televised footrace to clean up that much.

> When the best student hears about
> 　the way
> He practises it assiduously;
> When the average student hears
> 　about the way
> It seems to him one moment there
> 　and gone the next;
> When the worst student hears about
> 　the way
> He laughs out loud.
> If he did not laugh
> It would not be worthy of being the way.

The American journalists sipped their free drinks in the deep divans of the Pan American Clipper Club room, an exclusive lounge located above the lesser travellers of the San Francisco International Airport terminal.

Exclusive indeed. Not only did one need to know of its esteemed existence and whereabouts, one needed as well to produce evidence of acceptable prestige before gaining entry. While the journalists were not exactly first class, they were in the company of those who where. This was enough to get them to the secret door, past the doorman, and into the free booze.

'How do you *visualize*,' a fellow club sipper insisted on knowing, 'hanging this gig on a *hook*? So it is not just another dumb road race? I mean what are you hoping to *hang* it on?'

The sipper was a ranking executive in the business that owned the magazine paying for this journalistic jaunt to China, so everyone acknowledged his right to be a trifle insistent.

'The hook I have in mind,' answered the first of the journalists, a big bearded boy who was the editor of said mag as well as originator of the jaunt, 'is sport as *détente*. Remember it wasn't really Nixon or Kissinger that initially broke through the bamboo curtain; it was the Ping-Pong ball. This race is the first international sporting event in China since before World War Two. To me, that has *meaning*.'

Meaning he really had no idea at all what to hang it on.

The second journalist, bald, unbearded, bigger and older than the first, muscled his brow in a Brandoesque attitude of heavy consideration.

'Let me think on that a minute,' he begged. He turned to the third journalist, absolutely enormous, with big blue eyes and a monstrous camera hanging over his belly. 'What about you, Brian? What do you plan to aim at?'

'I can't take any point pictures until my writer comes up with something to make a *point* with, can I?' was the way the third journalist avoided the question.

The eyes turned back to the second journalist; his knotted brow indicated he nearly had his answer tied down.

'One of the *main* characteristics,' he began, 'about a bamboo curtain . . . is it's so damn thick. The only thing it lets show through is politics. For years no idiosyncrasies, no quirks, no *personality* has been allowed to show through.'

'Until now?' asked the editor, proud of the way his man had wiggled off this hook business.

'Right. Until now. Now they are sponsoring this big marathon with top runners from all over the globe, even though the *best* Chinese marathoner is slower than the mediocre from the rest of the racing world. This may be the crack in the curtain for us to go angling through.'

'Gotcha!' the ranking exec said. 'Like ice fishing back in Minnesota: hafta hook something before the hole freezes back.' He raised his martini to the trio. 'Well, fishermen: here's to a successful trip. Bring us back a biggie – '

''Tenshun, Clipper Club membahs,' the speaker over the bar drawled, 'Pan Am's Clipper flight for Beijing is now available for boarding. Y'all have a nice trip.'

> *In his every movement a man of*
> *   great virtue*
> *Follows the way and the way only.*
> *As a thing the way is*
> *Shadowy, indistinct.*
> *Indistinct and shadowy,*
> *Yet within it is an image;*
> *Shadowy and indistinct,*
> *Yet within it is a substance,*
> *Dim and dark,*
> *Yet within it is an essence,*

And this is something that can be tested.
From the present back to antiquity
Its name never deserted it.
It serves as a means for inspecting the
fathers of the multitude.
How do I know what the fathers of the
multitude are like?
By means of this.

In the dew-heavy dawn outside one of Tanzania's 8,000 *ujamaa* villages, tall handsome Magapius Dasong (best time: 2:20:46) sat beside the road on his wicker suitcase. He was waiting for the local bus that would take him to the central station in Dar-es-Salaam, where he was to meet his coach for the ride to the airport. The Dawn Express Local was already tardy by nearly forty minutes of daylight and Magapius would not be surprised if it became later by twice that time before the bus arrived. By then, his two coaches and three trainers would have proceeded on to China without their athlete.

How like the Tanzania of recent years, he thought; everybody gets in on the race but the runner. Such inefficiency. Such bureaucracy. Poor topheavy Tanzania, swaying and teetering. Even the most avid supporters of President Nyerere's socialist progress were beginning to admit that the nation's economic strife was caused by more than increased oil prices or the recent droughts and floods. Oil prices had increased for all nations; droughts and floods had always been. And if sweeping socialist reform had increased life expectancy by 20 per cent in a decade, it had probably increased the social woes by 30 per cent! More thefts and less to steal. More schedules set and less of them met.

This decline of care for time was what most troubled Magapius. His countrymen once were proud of their timing. If a bird was to be netted, the netman would be tossing the net as the bird flew by. It was an appointment to be kept, a pact between netman and bird. A courtesy. What was the joy in a longer life when that tribal respect for time was becoming as rare as the old stylized dream dances?

As much as the race itself, Magapius was looking forward to visiting the People's Republic of revolutionary China. If the dream were to live, reaffirmation must be found there, in that mightiest stronghold of the experiment. Everybody knew there

209

was no juice in Russia any more, no *Kunda* as the Bantu put it. No *baraka*, as the Arabs said. And the boatloads hysterical to escape Cuba and Haiti for the capitalistic coasts of Florida did not speak well of Castro's collective. But China . . . ah, China . . . surviving Mao's madness as well as Brezhnev's belligerence. Great China. If China could not accomplish it, perhaps it could not be accomplished.

He heard a motor and stood to wave at the approaching headlights. It was not the bus. It was a loaded sisal truck that had encountered the bus miles back, stuck crossways in the middle of the tiny road, front wheels in one ditch, back wheels in the other. The bus had been turning around to return to pick up last week's mail that the driver had again forgotten.

One of the sisal truck's three drivers boosted Magapius's luggage to the top of the load of fibre and invited him to join them for the ride on to the city. He couldn't join them in the cab, however. There was no room. In the nation's battle against rampant unemployment, there were now three drivers required in every vehicle of transport, whether they could drive or not.

Magapius thanked them and climbed the heap of fibres. How particularly Tanzanian – three men in a clean cab in filthy work aprons; one on top in the blowing white fluff in the only suit the family owned, black . . .

In the cramped kitchen of his uncle's house, Yang was studying mathematics. He had less than a week before the trip to Beijing, and his instructors at school had decided he could best prepare for his absence by staying home and studying on his own. From the adjoining room came the whir of the motorcycle motor as his uncle drilled away at the day's collection of cavities. It was a clever setup. Raised on its kickstand, the rear wheel turned freely against a simple wooden spool that in turn drove the gears that powered the drill cables. The drill speed could be adjusted by the bike's throttle, and the whir of the little two-cycle engine helped blanket the occasional groans his patients made in spite of the bristle of anaesthetic needles in their necks and arms.

Yang was seated near the window. If the sun had been out it would have fallen across his high-boned face and bare shoulders, but it was overcast. It had been overcast for weeks. Since before the floods.

His sister came in from the backyard carrying a pan of green leaves and dumped them in a large kettle of cold water, singing as she did. Yang recalled the stanza. It was from a skit his sister's class had performed for National Day a year ago. The girls had learned the song from a play that was mailed out to all the primaries, a short musical dramatization emphasizing the value of early warning and treatment of stomach cancer, China's number-one killer. His sister had stopped attending school after that, speaking of plans to join the People's Liberation Army. Now she washed cabbage leaves and stacked them beside her aunt's wok – delicately, as though arranging expensive silks – while she sang:

> Oesophageal cancer must be thoroughly
> conquered.
> The pernicious influence of the Gang of Four
> must be wiped out.
> Prevention first, prevention always
> prevention first!
> Thus we prevent and treat cancer of the revolution.

How very fine, Yang agreed without raising his head from the work text; how commendable. But please explain if possible how one uses the principles of Prevention First when dealing with the diseases of the revolution itself? Wouldn't the very cure be dangerously counterrevolutionary?

He closed the big paperback on his finger and turned to watch his sister. She was long past fifteen and rounding out rapidly. In a few months someone would accompany the girl to their communal market for her first binding undergarment. In a few years Yang would not be able to pick her from dozens her same age – the same white shirt, the same black pants, the same pigtails. Perhaps that was why she wanted to join the PLA; if the uniforms were always ill-fitting and baggy they at least were less uniform than what all the other girls her age would be wearing.

Now his sister sang and swayed in unfettered innocence, still flushing with young patriotism. Yang could recall the sensation – a *thrill* to be part of something vast and exciting. He could remember feeling that his blood was tolling in cadence with every heart in the village, to a great shared rhythm. When he was nine, he remembered, there had come a dreadful plague of flies throughout all the land. To deal with the problem their

211

Great Chairman had done a mighty and yet simple thing. Mao had launched an edict proclaiming that while it was not required it would be a very good thing if all the schoolchildren in the land should bring to their schoolteachers every morning *dead flies*. Yang had dedicated himself to the chore with all the fervour of a warrior of old serving his emperor.

He spent hours each afternoon stalking the pestiferous foe with a rolled newspaper, slaying scores past ten. Hundreds and hundreds were poured each morning from his paper cone into the teacher's waiting tray. Throughout the land other children were turning in comparable kills. In less than a month the flies were gone, all across China. Each schoolroom was sent an official pennant to hang in the window. The red silk had filled Yang with the sort of pride that made national songs rise to the throat.

Then he learned from his biology teacher that the year *preceding* the Great Fly Kill had been the year of the Great Sparrow Kill. That year Mao had been advised that there were such-and-so-many wild birds in China and, during its little life, each bird could be calculated to eat at least this-and-that-much grain. Which came to a whole lot. So Mao had edicted that all the kids should go out beneath all the trees where all the birds roosted, and beat clappers all night every night until they roosted no more. After three nights the birds were all dead from exhaustion and irritation. *All across China!* How very impressive and commendable. Except that, in the season after the birdless year, there were *all those flies* . . .

No, the slogan songs no longer brought the old tolling to Yang's blood. He still enjoyed hearing it in his sister's voice but he feared it was gone from him forever, that ring, cold and gone.

But not the wonder, he was glad to say. Not that. For instance, what had all those schoolteachers in all those classrooms all across China *done* with all those dead flies?

> *Is not the way of heaven like the*
> *pulling of a bow?*
> *The high it presses down.*
> *The low it lifts up.*
> *The excessive it takes from*
> *The deficient it gives to.*

The approach of the Beijing Marathon and its international coverage brought about a relaxation of many edicts and a return to some neglected ceremonies. In the *go* parlours, waitresses were allowed to dress in traditional servant's gowns and pour tea for the players engrossed over their click-clicking *go* boards with the elaborated obeisance of old. In the food markets, children could sell cones of nuts and keep their profits, as long as they had personally gathered the nuts.

In Qufu, the small town near Yang's village in Shangong province, a group filed out of the old cemetery. In spite of the solemnity of the occasion, there was about the group an air of victory, of lost grounds regained. Many of the mourners carried unveiled birdcages, a sight forbidden until recently, and some of the women wore heirloom brocade, still musty from so many years secreted away. Yes, victory! For the loved one they had just left behind committed to the keep of the ancestors had not been reduced to the usual wad of yellow-grey ashes and smoke in the wind; he lay in a real grave, and the fresh mound of earth above him glowed like a monument.

Especially in Qufu was this burial sweet. Qufu was the birthplace of Confucius. For centuries the townspeople pointed with pride to inscriptions on family headstones that proved they were direct descendants of the famous philosopher. Then, in 1970 a regiment of Red Guards marched through the town to the ancient cemetery and toppled all those headstones. When they retreated from the cemetery they hung a huge red-and-white banner across the high stone entrance. The words on the banner left little doubt about the Chairman's attitude toward the ancestors:

WASTE NO MORE GOOD EARTH ON THE USELESS DEAD. CREMATE!

Confucius himself was exiled to the purgatory of fallen stars, along with countless poets and essayists who had expounded on his work over the centuries. Teachers like Yang's father who continued to mention the philosopher were stripped of their positions and their clothes and pilloried in town squares as 'enemies of the collective consciousness'. Many were sentenced to correction farms and the cultivation of cabbages and leeks instead of young minds.

Confucius's contemporary, Lao-tzu, was never officially excommunicated, oddly enough. Perhaps because his work is so scant and so obscure; perhaps because historians have never

213

agreed on his identity, or if he was actually a living person at all. He may have been too much a myth to comfortably condemn.

The procession stopped on the slope outside the cemetery and gathered to admire the birds and speak with old acquaintances and colleagues. One of the professors pointed down the hill. A string of runners were angling off the highway onto the dirt road.

'It's our young warriors!' he cried. 'For Beijing. Those two. I have them in class. The two in front!'

He continued to shout and point, though it was obvious to all which pair of athletes he meant; their new uniforms shone like chips of clear blue sky against the dingy grey outfits of their team-mates.

When the two front-runners passed the bottom of the hill the excited teacher yelled, '*Chi oh*, boys; *chi oh!*' – a slang expression the professor heard around school for 'pour on the gas'.

Other men applauded and repeated the call, until the sudden display of local pride made the women hold their ears and the birds fly in panic against the bamboo bars of their cages.

> *He who is fearless in being bold*
> *   will meet with his death;*
> *He who is fearless in being timid will*
> *   stay alive.*
> *Of the two, one leads to good, the*
> *   other to harm.*
> *Heaven hates what it hates,*
> *Who knows the reason why?*

It would be Yang's last workout. The trainer had advised him to keep his customary fervour in check. But as always, when he reached this feeble cotton field with its nine grassy pyramids, Yang veered off the packed ruts and went hurdling through the rows. He headed for the tallest of the mounds. He didn't know the name of the huge escarpment, only that it was a *feng*, one of a multitude of false tombs built centuries ago by sly emperors hoping to thwart desecration by thieves.

He did not look behind him. He knew the rest of the team was far back, some probably still on the avenue, jogging in and out of the swaying buses and bicycles.

The only runner out ahead of him was his friend Zhoa Cheng-chun. Zhoa and Yang had pulled quickly away from the others

214

passing the cemetery. But when he heard the cheering and saw the waving crowd up the hill, Yang had slackened his stride to allow Zhoa to run on ahead.

'*Chi oh!*' he had urged his friend, pretending to pant with exhaustion. 'Pour on the gas.'

To have kept up would not have been respectful. Zhoa was nearly four years his senior and already a member of the academy. Zhoa was the hometown hero and the provincial marathon champion. His time of 2:19 was second only to the 2:13 of the Chinese record-holder, Xu Liang. Yang felt he could have matched Zhoa's pace for many more kilometres, but he did not wish to show a discourtesy. He let him run on.

Besides, Yang liked to have this part of his workout to himself. As he left the road he could hear the people at the cemetery cheering for the rest of their school's team, far behind.

His sprint took him past the field girls working to salvage some of the season's rain-ravaged cotton, then along the dirt dike of the irrigation ditch. Without slowing he long-jumped across the shallow coffee-brown stream, his feet churning the air. His landing startled a small hare from the brush along the bank. Yang called after the zigzagging animal, 'You too, long ears! *Chi oh!*' He heard the girls laugh behind him.

He slowed when he reached the steep path at the corner of the *feng*. It had drizzled again that morning and the worn dirt would be slick. The last thing he wanted to do before tomorrow's trip was slip on the red mud. To soil the beautiful blue warm-ups sent him from Beijing would have been close to traitorous.

The climb made his heart quicken in his ears and brought a light beadwork of sweat to his lower lip. That was good. He did not perspire easily, even in this French-made suit of artificial fibres, and he needed a sweat to flush the poisons and rinse his head. He ran harder.

When he at last achieved the flattened square at the peak of the dirt pyramid he was sweating hard and his panting was no longer feigned. His father had first brought him here, just a babe, carried piggyback. He had played with the milkweed pods at the edge of the little flat square while his father and his grandfather went through the complicated sparring dances with wooden swords or bamboo pikes festooned on each end with coloured ribbons to better describe the swing and swirl of the manoeuvre. His grandfather still came, though rarely, and without the mock weapons. The routines the old man did were simple sequences and might be seen in any park or yard.

Yang went immediately into his tai chi quan routine. He did all the basic manoeuvres plus some his father had created – Stand By to Kick Monkey Nuts, and Feed the Dog That Bites You. Then he moved on to the new National Routine that had been instituted since the fall of the Gang of Four. Much like football warm-ups – jumping jacks, toe touches, neck twists. After these exercises he commenced scurrying around the little earth square in a crouch, shadow wrestling.

He was a good wrestler. The summer before he had placed third in the Torch Festival in his age/weight, and for a time his instructors at middle school wished him to concentrate on that sport, leave distance running to those with longer legs. He demurred but kept in wrestling shape. When there was a wedding in the village he was the one called on by the bride's family for the traditional bout with the bridegroom's supporters. The families knew he could make a good showing against the surrogate suitors and, more important, when pitted against the groom himself, Yang could be counted on to lose.

Spreading his towel, he finished off his workout with forty pushups from his fingertips, then forty fast sit-ups, hammering his stomach muscles as he finished.

He forced his mind to calm as he pounded the familiar knots from his abdomen. Forget those cheering townspeople. What was there to worry about? No one expected victory. Only continuity: run from here to there and back, however long it took.

His fists drove out the embolism and at last he fell back, the clean clothes forgotten, and sent his breathing up into the sky. It was all one colour. There had been no sun all day. There would be no stars that night. For months now the heavy sky had shut them out, like a pewter lid on a shallow pot.

He rolled over and gazed past the checkerboard grid of cotton and cabbage in the direction Zhoa had informed him that they would fly tomorrow to reach Beijing, thousands of miles away. Yang could not conceive of such distance, nor of the towering mountains and terrible gorges where, Zhoa had claimed, *no one lived*. No green fields crawling with work units like aphids on a leaf; no jam of smoky huts; no roads, no bicycles, no people. Just lifeless space, clear, the way it was on the rare winter
216

evenings when the clouds were driven south by the cold, and the long flank of the night between his bed and the stars was laid naked.

He heard the girls laugh again and stretched to see over the milkweeds. The other runners were approaching at last along the road, meeting Zhoa on his way back from the turnaround. The girls were laughing at the way the team grabbed Zhoa's belly to make him smile. Everyone liked to tease Zhoa so they could see his smile. It was spectacular. He had been blessed with an extra tooth, diamond shaped, right between his two regular front teeth. Bright and healthy too, his uncle had said of the phenomenon. Yang could see it flash even from his distant seat.

The giggling suddenly ceased and Zhoa's smile fled. Looking back up the road Yang saw three young men, carrying shotguns and examining the road ruts, pretending that they were on the trail of the runners. A joke, certainly, but no one except the three with guns laughed.

These were not ordinary hunters. Their unkempt hair and loud swagger revealed that they were labour toughs, a growing cadre of semidelinquents who had eschewed education for the factories and the fantan cellars. Their attitude toward the pampered students was well known. Especially sport students. There had been frequent skirmishes, and the toughs had promised more. Pampered people loping nowhere was contrary to the Spirit of the True Revolution, was their claim; just another sign of Western decadence, jogging into China instead of creeping. Let comrades seeking exercise take up the shovel! That is what the Chairman would have said.

Only in the last few years had competition become acceptable enough to come out into the open. It was like the pet birds singing uncovered in the parks again. And just this morning his sister had told Yang that she had seen a woman at the Friendship Hotel carrying a cat. It was still unacceptable to purchase a pet, but the animal had been shipped as a gift to the hotel by a recent guest from London.

'Can you imagine?' his sister had wondered. 'From a foreign land, a cat?'

Only with difficulty, Yang thought, trying to reconcile in his mind such ironies as rude reactionaries and free cats and false tombs. For example, it had always been an irony to him that these *fengs*, the forced effort of thousands of slaves thousands of years ago, afforded him the loftiest feelings of freedom he had ever known. Except for running. If you ran far enough you could get free for a while. Truly free. Another irony. It seemed that freedom came as a result of forced effort, as though the brain needed the minions of the legs and lungs and heart to build for it the solitude of separation.

Suddenly his reverie was shattered by an explosion, then two more, then a final blast. He was on his feet, scanning the rows and ditches below. Early Nation Day firecrackers? The backfire of a tractor working late?

He saw the three hunters, running along the base of his *feng*, laughing and shouting and waving their guns. The leader, the oldest, with the longest hair and the biggest gun, bent to the cotton rows and lifted his prize high by the ears. The hindquarters were blown entirely away but the animal still lived, uttering long thin whistles and pawing the air to the delight of the younger hunters. The girls turned away in horror and Yang sat back to wait for the men to leave. He wrapped his arms around his stomach, shivering.

It was all extremely difficult to reconcile.

In the customs terminal of the Beijing Airport, the American journalists fidgeted nervously through the forms and waited for their bags to be examined, feeling that sudden gulp of realization that Yanks always get along with their first breaths of communist atmosphere – that 'They-can-getcha-and-*keep*-ya!' gulp – wondering and worrying about the copy of *Oriental Hustler* among the shirts, the stashed gold Krugerrands and crank in the shaving bag, when out of nowhere, to their rescue and relief, came an ominous Chinese drugstore cowboy with a tight smile and a wallet full of official cards. He introduced himself as Wun Mude, from China Sports Service, and gave them each a stiff handshake and a sheaf of diplomatic documents. He rattled a few phrases in Chinese to the brown-suited Red Guards, and the bags were snapped shut and the three journalists whisked past the long line and the immigration officer, and they were outside.

'Always good to know somebody at city hall,' the editor observed. Mude merely smiled and motioned toward a waiting van.

218

The athletes had been arriving from their parts of the world for days, according to their respective countries' budgets. The poorer were to fly in, run, and fly out. The better heeled got there a few days early to acclimatize.

The American runners had been in Beijing for nearly a week, wishing their budgets had been a little less well-heeled. The Oriental food had loosened their lower intestines and the Beijing air had plugged their lungs: 'When you run into the wall in *this* venue,' observed Chuck Hattersly of Eugene, Oregon, when he came in from a light workout, wheezing and spitting, 'you get to see what it's *made* of!'

The Americans were quartered in the modern Great Wall Hotel, complete with elevator Muzak and hot-and-cold running houseboys assigned to each room. The visiting Orientals, the Japanese and Koreans, were in the Beijing Hilton. The Europeans were scattered between. The Chinese were in a large compound dorm with most of the other Third World entries. The day before the race, everybody had arrived except the Tanzanian, Magapius Dasong.

In his tiny double room at the compound, Yang lay exhausted and sleepless after the day's flight in the old Russian turboprop. It had not been the lofty joyride he had expected, this first trip off the earth. The old airplane had been noisy and draughty, the seats confining, and the windows too small. At first he had been thrilled by the great mountains, so steep and terrible looking, but when he examined the range through the field glasses passed him by his father's colleague, he saw that the wild slopes had been tamed. Centuries of hungry toil had chiselled them into steps, thousands of descending agricultural terraces.

Tossing now in his narrow bed, he wished he had never looked. Every time he closed his eyes to try to sleep, he saw those terraced mountainsides, each few feet of retaining wall and few inches of soil the effort of so many hands and years, for another precious ton of corn, another trailer of cabbage.

> *A large state is the lower*
> *reaches of a river –*
> *The place where all the streams*
> *of the whole unite.*
> *In the union of the world*

> The receptive always gets the
> better of the Creative
> by stillness.
> Being still, she takes the
> lower position.
> Hence the large state, by
> taking the lower
> position annexes the
> small state,
> And the small state, by taking
> the lower position
> annexes the large state.

It had always been a peculiar thing to Bling, his first name. His father had called him Ling Wu, after his father the stone mason, and his mother had called him Bill, after her father the missionary. So his name had never really been William.

Yet from his first day of school in Pittsburgh he had been called William by his sixth-grade teacher. By his classmates, Willy Wu, as though it were all one word, an American Indian word perhaps, certainly not half-Irish, half-Chinese – an Indian name for an uncertain wind: Willawoo.

Then when he wearied of Yankee gook wars abroad and left-wing American breastbeating at home and transferred from the University of Pittsburgh back to his birthplace at the University of Beijing, his teachers had called him Bee. Bee Ling Wu. Because he had used the letter B as his first initial on his application. This name had in turn become, to the members of his track team, Bee Wing Lou, thanks largely to the persistence of the only other English-speaking member of the ragtag squad, a girl from Sydney.

'Bee Wing Louie, as yer such a dashing little black-eyed bug,' she had explained with the typical Australian love of wordplay, 'yer more the sprint from-flower-to-flower sort, it looks to me, than a long-runner.'

Indeed, his position on the Pittsburgh team had been in the 100 and the 200 around-the-bend. No world-beater there, either. He had moved to the distances as age and embarrassment forced him out of the dashes. He found a whole new track career in China. Modern Yankee know-how in the form of vitamins, shoes, and training techniques had made him the top 1,500-metre man in all of the eastern provinces. Times that would

220

have been barely mediocre in the States won him in China ribbons and respect. From all but the saucy Aussie.

'Go it!' she would shout at him around the last turn of the 1,500, waving her watch in the air. 'Yer pressin' Mary Decker's time me little Bee Winger, go it!'

And now the American journalists, after he had been introduced to them as Mr B. Ling, were calling him Bling.

Bling Clawsby.

'Have your droll yucks,' he admonished the trio, 'before I tip them you're all KGB agents.'

The photographer shook his head. 'Nobody'll go for it, Bling. Mr Mude told us we have the unmistakable landlord look of American capitalists.'

Mude was the interpreter appointed to the American press for the upcoming special. He was forty and fastidious, with an impeccable Western hairstyle and outfit. For the same reasons that the famous pictures of Marx and Engels were to be taken down for the day of the race, Mude had been advised that it would be acceptable to wear something less jarring to the American public than the grey garb of the Red Menace. Something Western. So Mr Mude had tailored a powder-blue Western outfit, replete with pearl buttons and embroidered longhorns. Taiwan-made cowboy boots glittered from beneath the blue cuffs. A six-shooter tie slide held his neckerchief tight to his throat. He would not have looked out of place on *Hee Haw*.

In the customs terminal at the Beijing Airport, however, there had been nothing funny about his attire. If anything it made him somehow all the more ominous, especially when he waltzed them past the customs guard with one word 'Dipromatic.'

It had been clear from the first that he did not like English. But he had been assigned the odious language, so some test must have indicated aptitude; therefore, he must be qualified; thus he had conquered it.

Hence he could translate – after a stiff fashion – but could not quite communicate. He couldn't chat. He couldn't joke. He could only smile and say 'No,' or 'One cannot,' or 'Very sorry, I fear that is not possible.'

So the journalists had been relieved indeed to come across Bling in the lounge of the hotel, reading a Spiderman comic and listening to a tiny tape machine play 'Whip It Good' by Devo. The journalists had skidded to a gaping stop. Here was a young

Chinese wearing a pair of skinny blue shades, short pants, a crewcut uncut so long it stuck up in random twisted quills. The journalists were impressed.

'Isn't this a splendid surprise?' they applauded. 'A Pekingese punk.'

'Far out,' Bling responded. 'A pack of Yankee Dogs, escaped from the pound. Do have a seat. I can see you are about to buy a poor student a drink.'

After repeated rounds of gin rickeys and ideological argument they enlisted him as a go-between, with an offer of free running shoes and a promise not to reveal his true identity in their story. 'Have no worry,' they assured him. 'No one will ever know that Bling Clawsby has defected to the Orient.'

The deal was struck and Bling was with them from then on. Mude didn't care for this New Wave addition to the retinue, but he tried to make the most use he could of it. In a way, Bling afforded Mr Mude the opportunity to be even more inscrutable. He found he could relegate random questions to Bling. When asked 'How does the sports academy select students?' Or 'Is there legal recourse in China if, say, this crazy bus driver runs over a bicycle?' Or 'Why is China doing this event *any*way?' Mude could pass these difficult questions on with a curt nod. 'Mr B. Ling will explain this you.'

'Explain me this, then, Mr Bling,' the writer pressed on. 'If China wants to put her best foot forward, as you say, then why a marathon? The Chinese entries are going to get *creamed*.'

Bling leaned across the aisle of the rocking bus to answer out of Mude's earshot.

'Contradiction, you have to understand, means something different to the Marxist mind than it means to you peabrains. Lenin claimed that "Dialectics is the study of contradiction in the essence of objects." Engels said, "Motion itself is a contradiction." And Mao maintained that revolution and development *arise* out of contradiction. He saw the traditional philosophy, "Heaven changeth not, likewise the Tao changeth not," as a prop the feudal ruling classes supported because it supported *them*. The so-called "way" was therefore a form of what he termed Mechanical Materialism, or Vulgar Evolutionism, which he considered to constitute a contradiction within the very fabric of the transcendent metaphysical Taoism of the past. Dig? This
222

was the real genius of his early years. Mao did not *judge* the old ways, he merely stoked the contradictions existing within them.'

'Covered himself fore and aft, did he?'

'In a way. In another way, he set up the sequence that was bound to be his undoing. Contradiction may create revolution, but when the revolutionary takes control he tries to eliminate the very thing that brought him to power – dissent, dissatisfaction, distrust of big government. Revolution is a dragon that rises to the top of the pile by eating his daddy. So the revolutionary dragon has a natural mistrust of his own issue – see? – as well as any other fire breathers roaming the rice paddies.'

'Sounds to me like it was *this* dragon's old lady what swallowed him,' the photog remarked. He had been following the latest denouncements in the little English-translation newspapers.

'You mean the Widow Mao and her Quartet? Naw, she's just a foolish old broad happened to inherit the reins. Not enough class or courage or just plain smarts to pull off a conspiracy against old Mao, even on his most senile doddering day. No, what it was was Mao did some bad shit to stay on top of the dragon pile, to some heavy people. Imagine the ghosts of his private hell: all those people he had to liquidate to grease the works of the fucking Cultural Revolution, all those comrades, colleagues, professors, and poets.'

'I thought this guy Mao was what you left Pittsburgh for, Bling. You talk now like he was your typical totalitarian.'

'Contradiction,' Bling answered, turning to look out the window at the endless parade of black bicycles, 'has become the New Way for a lot of us.'

'Is that why you like Devo?' the writer asked. He thought Bling with his funny crewcut and ragged T-shirt had said New Wave. Bling gave him a curious glance.

'I *don't* like Devo. I listen to Devo for the same reason I run – to get an endorphin rush.' He patted his pockets, looking for his comb. 'I run because it hurts.'

The original intention of the meeting was to let the doctors and the press examine the seventy-some participants who would be running tomorrow's race. But what can a doctor know about a marathon man that the athlete doesn't already know about himself? What can a heart specialist say about a thirty-five-year-old phys ed fanatic with a 35-beats-per-minute heartbeat and heels calloused thick as hardballs?

So the physical examination was waived and worried warnings submitted in its place. Of greatest concern was the water.

'Do not suck the sponges. Drinks from race organizers will be on white tables. Private drinks on red tables. Take when you want. Private drinks must be handed in tonight for analysis.'

Chuck Hattersly leaned over to whisper, 'I get it! They're trying to steal our formula for Gatorade.'

'Please don't injure yourself with strain. Take it easy. However, to avoid delaying the traffic and spectators, there will be cut-off points for the slow – '

The shuffling murmur of the room stilled. Cut-off points? No one had ever heard of cut-off points in a marathon. As long as you could put one foot in front of the other, you could run.

'Those who have not reached 25 kilometres by the time of 1:40 will be removed from the race.'

Sitting amidst 60 other Chinese runners, Yang felt knots start in his stomach. He had no idea of his time for 25 kilometres. No notion, even, how *far* that was. From the village to the school? Half that? Twice?

'If you have not reached the 35-kilometre point by 2:20 you will be removed.'

For a moment Yang was cramped with panic. He remembered the cheering crowd at the cemetery. If he were removed he could never return home; better not to start than not to finish! Then it occurred to him that all he had to do was expend his total force to reach that 35-km mark in 2:20; he could *crawl* the remaining distance.

'We also suggest if you begin to feel uncomfortable that you volunteer to drop out.'

'Uncomfortable?' a gnarly veteran from New Zealand muttered. 'Take it easy? The bleeding hell does he think we *run* for?'

'One important thing further. The water in the sponges is for wiping the face. Do not drink it. There will be plenty of drink at the tables. Our deepest suggestion is that you ingest no water from the sponges. Now. I wish you all once again good luck. And look forward to seeing you this evening for the banquet at the Great Hall. Thank you for your attention.'

It had been a peculiar event, lengthy and uncomfortable. And
224

if its thrust and purpose had been somewhat vague, to say the least, no one wanted to prolong it by asking questions. As the runners were queueing up for their buses, the writer, notebook and pen in hand, corralled Chuck Hattersly and inquired reporter-fashion what in his opinion was the upshot, the *kernel* of the long conference.

'Don't,' was Hattersly's immediate summary, 'suck the sponges.'

> When the way of the way declined
> Doctrines of righteousness arose.
> When knowledge and wisdom occurred
> There emerged great hypocrisy.
> When the six family relationships
>   are not in harmony
> There follows filial piety and
>   deep love of children.
> When a country is in disorder,
> There will be praise of loyal ministers.

After lunch there awaited, according to Mr Mude, a plethora of palace and pagodas all deemed mandatory for a first-time visitor to Beijing. The journalists wanted to know if they might go instead to the compound assigned to the Chinese runners. Mude said this afternoon was prescribed rest for the Chinese entries. Then they asked to see Democracy Wall. Mude explained that Democracy Wall no longer existed. Quill-headed free-lunched Bee Wing Bling, feeling looser by the minute among his second-countrymen, explained that the *wall* in fact still existed but was covered now with billboards bragging about refrigerators with egg trays. No more homemade posters of dissent and protest. Mude felt obliged to further explain that those foolish posters had only caused confusion among the people.

'If one has comment, one can write the government bureaux direct.'

'Right,' Bling agreed. 'It's better to cause confusion among the bureaucrats. They're trained.'

'Ah.' Mude swivelled his smile back to the journalists. 'Perhaps you will like to stop at the Friendship Store before continuing to Forbidden City? They have Coca-Cola.'

The journalists would have preferred to scout off on their own but since they were stroking Mude to try to get permission to follow tomorrow's race in a taxi, instead of sitting on their thumbs for two hours at the start/finish with the rest of the press, they had decided to try and keep on his good side.

And if he did not have a good one, to at least stay off his bad.

One sensed that beneath that Western suit and patient Eastern smile an irritability was beginning to bubble. Though Mr Mude never said so, it was obvious to all that whatever affection he had ever held for Mr Bling was now in rapid decline. Whenever he acquired tickets for a tourist attraction he no longer included the scraggly little student. Bling had to fork over his own fen to get in the Forbidden Cities and Summer Palaces. When Bling was finally fenless the journalists forked over for him. This made Mr Mude twitch and fidget in his unfamiliar cowboy clothes.

The tour had taken a turn not to Mr Mude's liking: too many Yankee guffaws at Bling's sardonic commentary on the Beijing scene; too much talk from which he felt excluded, especially track talk.

'You are also a runner, Mr Wu?'

They were coming out of Beihai Park, with its white dome and holiday throngs of colourfully clothed school kids scampering about like escaped flowers. Mude had been mentioning the park's renowned reputation for centuries of quiet beauty; Bling had been filling in with notes of more recent interest that Mr Mude had neglected to mention. Until two years ago, Bling had told them, the park had been closed completely to the general public, the lovely quiet of the lake undisturbed by rented rowboats, the massive gates barred and guarded. No one was allowed in except Mao's wife and her personal guests.

Bling had been explaining what a turn-on it had been, after years of jogging past the prohibited paradise, to one day, out of the blue, have the doors swung wide and be allowed to jog *inside* – when Mr Mude interrupted with that question about running.

'Damn straight I'm a runner,' Bling answered. 'One of your hometown heroes. Three years varsity, Beijing U. Come to a meet sometime, Mude; be my guest.'

'A runner of distance?'

'I've done fives and tens. I hold the school record in the 1,500.'

'Then you must be entered in tomorrow's heroic event?'

226

'Sorry. Tomorrow's heroes will have to run without Bee Wing Lou's company.'

'Surely you must have applied? A running enthusiast residing in Beijing as you do?'

'It's an invitational, Mr Mude . . . remember?'

'Ah, true,' Mude recalled. 'I had forgotten. Too bad for you, Mr Wu.'

Bling pulled down his blue shades to study Mude's face; it was impossible to tell if the mind behind that guarded smile were conniving, condescending, or what.

'Talk them into a 1,500 around the Tien An Men – like the Fifth Avenue mile in New York – *then* you'll see me out there busting my little yellow balls.'

'That would be very enjoyable.'

To get Bling off the hook, the editor asked if it might be possible to take a drive out to the Beijing campus to look over the sports scene, maybe catch a track practice. This time it was Bling who was reluctant and Mude who was suddenly permissive. True, he admitted, he did have preparations to make for the banquet, but saw no reason why they could not drop him off and continue on with Mr Wu to his track practice. Everyone was left stunned by the sudden turnabout, and a trifle uneasy. When they dropped Mude off at the stark brick building he had directed the driver to, Bling became downright unnerved.

'That was the Bureau of Immigration Records!'

'Wonder whose name he's looking up?' the photographer wondered.

'I couldn't say for certain, but I'll bet you all a buck,' Bling said unhappily, 'it turns out to be *Mud*.'

Nobody would cover the bet. The bus ride the rest of the way to the campus was sombre and quiet.

In spite of the bright bustle of students, the campus was as grim as the pot-lid sky sitting heavy over it. One expects lawns on a campus, but most of the grounds were the same packed dirt that surrounded the rest of the city's dwellings, only not as well swept. The rows of grey-green gum trees made the walks and ways dim, like light undersea. The sullen looks of the workers did not help. Bling told them that there had been a lot of strife between students and labourers, who also lived on the sprawling campus. Bicycle tyres slashed. Rapes. Gang fights between workers who considered the students arrogant and lazy and

227

students who saw the workers as the same, only less educated. Without police protection the students would have been in sorry straits. 'Out of a live-in population of about forty thousand, less than eight thousand are students.'

'Sounds like the clods have the scholars unfairly outnumbered.'

'In China,' Bling moped, 't'was ever thus.'

There was no track practice because of tomorrow's race, but three Chinese runners and the Australian girl were prowling the bleak cement gymnasium looking for someone with a key so they could get into the track room. Bling told them how to jimmy the lock and said he thought he'd skip the workout. The editor asked if they might take a look anyway, get some pictures. Reluctantly Bling led them down a dim concrete stairwell to a cracked wooden door in the cellar. The girl was gouging at the keyhole with a chopstick. Bling took over and finally dragged the door open and turned on a light. The room was a windowless cement box with a cot and a tiny desk. An iron rod stuck in the doorframe was draped with a dozen tattered sweatsuits.

'Our locker room,' Bling said. 'Ritzy digs, right? And here' – he pulled a cardboard box from beneath the cot – 'our equipment room.'

The box was piled with shabby mismatched spike shoes, four bamboo batons, a shot, and a discus.

'The javelin is that thing stabbed yonder, airing them sweet-smellin' sweatsuits,' the girl told the journalists.

Back outside, Bling put his blue glasses on and started walking back the way they had come.

'Gives you some idea why China doesn't have such great track times, doesn't it?'

When they got back to the campus gate their familiar bus was gone. In its place was one of the huge black Russian-made limos called Red Flags. It looked like a cross between a Packard and a Panzer. The driver stepped out and bowed and handed them a note and four embossed invitations.

'It's from Mude. He says the bus was required for other tasks, that this diplomatic limousine will take us back to the hotel to dress, then bring us to the banquet at the Great Hall. The fourth invitation is for Mr Wu, and Mude suggests we advise Mr Wu that a place has been reserved for him.'

'Oh, shit,' said Bling. 'Oh, shit.'

Thirty spokes gather around the
hub to make a wheel,
But it is on the circle that the
utility of the wheel depends.
Clay is moulded to form a utensil,
But it is on its emptiness that the
utility of the vessel depends.
Doors and windows are cut to make
a room,
But it is on floor space that the
utility of the room depends.
Therefore turn being into advantage,
and turn nonbeing into utility.

It might be the most beautiful dining hall in the world, certainly the biggest. A Canadian football game could be played comfortably in one of its rooms, with space left a-plenty on all sides for bleachers and bathrooms.

During the day there is always a small crowd outside, gaping at the Great Hall's grandiosity. Tonight, a very large crowd was gathered because two monumental events were occurring: the banquet for the Beijing Marathon, and the State Formal Dinner for President Gnassingbe Eyadema of Togoland. In a land without *M.A.S.H.* reruns or video games this was big potatoes.

The crowd waited on tiptoes behind the line, hoping to catch a glimpse of something exotic – a famous athlete; perhaps the glint of an African potentate's eye. All the limos. Certainly they had to be disappointed by the first passenger exiting from the big black sedan they had allowed through – a spiny-headed Chinese in plain brown sports jacket was all. The next passenger was better, a big occidental stranger with beard, and the next was yet better and bigger. The last apparition rising out of the upholstered depths of the Russian limo – why, he was enough to stretch even the most curious rubberneck to its limits of awe. The man was beyond size or measure, and he carried an optical arsenal of the most convincing proportions crisscrossed across his girth, like bandoliers on one of the bandit giants of old. Many of the onlookers went home immediately after, sufficed.

The foursome was late. The feast had begun. The roar of it could be heard down the marble corridors, drawing them on like the seductive roar of a waterfall. When they at last reached the two ten-foot urns at the door and were passed by the armed guard, they were as dazzled as had been the crowd on the walk outside. A room big as a blimp hangar, with thousands of people at hundreds of round tables, each table manned by dozens of bustling attendants refilling glasses, removing platters, producing new dishes seemingly from the very air.

An usher led them to the table assigned by their invitation, where they found the eight other diners all still waiting politely for their arrival – two middle-aged Africans wearing sombre suits and expressions, two seedy-looking Beijing men in drab Sun Yat-sen, a beautiful oriental woman, two young Chinese runners and their coach. All stood when they approached and shook hands while the woman translated.

The black men were from Tanzania, a coach and trainer. They were sombre because their athlete apparently had not managed to fly out of Tanzania for the race tomorrow; they felt obliged to attend the banquet insofar as a place had been reserved, but they were flying out in the morning, too chagrined by their athlete's absence to attend the race. The seedy pair were from *China Sports*, a limp but adequate little sports rag printed in English. The two young runners were from the same village in a distant province, their faces subtly different from the Beijing faces – flatter, darker, with something almost Gypsy dodging about the eyes. The larger and older of the pair responded to introductions with a dental display that ranked right up there with the rest of the day's sights: he had an extra tooth, right in the middle, and was not at all backward about showing it off. The smaller runner was as shy as his friend was forward, frequently dropping long lashes over his black eyes and buttoning and unbuttoning the sports coat he was wearing. Their coach was studiously aloof.

After the initial *ganbei* of introduction they all sat down for the first course of a meal that would prove to be a marathon in its own right. While they were stabbing at the lead-off oddities with their sticks, the prizes for tomorrow's winners were unveiled on a table in front of the raised dais – ten cloisonné vases, each bigger than the last, and a solid silver trophy that would return to Beijing each year for the new winner. There could be heard all across the room an audible insucking of covetous acclaim. They were very classy prizes.

The speeches then commenced to drone from the dais. They
230

saw Mude had a seat very near the podium. He had changed his attire from Western western to Eastern western – a preppy dark-blue blazer with coat-of-arms. He was introduced and stood to speak. The photographer took Bing's little Panasonic cassette recorder from his shoulder bag. He punched the Record button and set it on the table. It soon became obvious that neither Chinamen nor Roundeyes could understand a word of Mude's address, and the multitudinous roar of small talk rose again from the tables. Mude didn't seem to notice.

The American editor began to interview his Chinese magazine colleagues and the coach. The writer took notes. The photographer busied himself with photographing the exotic dishes as they arrived and whispering descriptions of each into the recorder: if this marathon thing didn't float he might get a cookbook out of it:

GREAT HALL – NIGHT BEFORE RACE

(Much noise of dining; unintelligible speech over loudspeaker in b.g.)

WHISPER NEAR MIKE: . . . tiny tomatoes pickled and arranged in delicate fan, gingered eel, lotus root in oyster sauce, duck neck, radishes carved to look like roses . . .

EDITOR: Whose idea was this race tomorrow?

(Chinese translation back and forth)

FEMALE VOICE: He says it started as a mass movement, the idea. In New China all ideas come from the masses.

EDITOR: Why don't they have better times? Ask him that.

FEMALE VOICE: He says their fastest runner is two hours and thirteen minutes. You will meet him tonight. He is from a minority in Union Province.

EDITOR: What is a minority?

FEMALE VOICE: In China there are many! These two boys are called minorities. From some provinces they speak different languages.

YOUNG MALE VOICE (Bling): Those stars you see on the Chinese flag? They each represent one of the minorities.

WHISPER: Boiled eggs, pickled eggs, eggs soaked in tea, and one one-thousand-year-old fossilized egg for each table, like sinister black jelly with a blacker yolk . . .

EDITOR: Will you ask if China is ready to devote the time and specialization it takes to become world class?

FEMALE VOICE: He says, absolutely.

EDITOR: Was he an athlete himself?

FEMALE VOICE: When he was twenty he had great hopes of going to the Olympics. That was thirty years ago, a time of great turmoil in China.

WHISPER: . . . beans, peanuts, pickled walnuts, fish stomachs and celery *flambé* . . .

MALE CHINESE VOICE: *Ganbei!*

FEMALE VOICE: He says, 'To the health of your country.'

ALL: *Ganbei!*

EDITOR: If one shows athletic talent is he given special dispensation by the government?

FEMALE VOICE: He says, yes.

BLING: Yes, indeedy!

FEMALE VOICE: He says that the person with particular talent will get better food.

BLING: That's why the basketball team has those giants. One eight-foot-eight fucker called the Mongolian Tower! That's quite lofty.

EDITOR: Is there a philosophy . . . I mean, what's the party line on physical fitness?

FEMALE VOICE: He says the party line is to become healthy first and then friendship and then competition.

EDITOR: I knew there had to be a party line. So why, ask him, did they never address the issue of fitness before, because –

BLING: They did address it. Mao made a big point of it. He was a goddamn *health nut*.

EDITOR: I mean was Mao aware of the fitness of the nation?

(*Long Chinese conversation back and forth*)

FEMALE VOICE: In 1953 Chairman Mao noticed China's health standard was low . . . because of disease and poverty. So after the liberation in '53 Chairman Mao decided to make it a special issue.

WHISPER: . . . pickled cherries, pressed duck, shredded ham, mashed molluscs, dugong dumplings, goose ganbeied . . .

MALE CHINESE VOICE: *Ganbei!*

FEMALE VOICE: He says, 'To the sportsmen of China and the U.S.'

ALL: *Ganbei!*

EDITOR: Ask them what they prescribe for an athlete who's injured? Do they use acupuncture?

FEMALE VOICE: He says, 'Yes.'

EDITOR: Can he give me any specifics of athletes who had acupuncture used on them?

FEMALE VOICE: He says he can only give personal experience. He was injured once and cured with acupuncture.

BLING: You know what the most recent study proves? I'll tell you what the most recent study proves: That acupuncture works according to just how fucking educated you are. The more educated, the less it works. *Ganbei* to the ignorant.

WRITER: Better watch that stuff, Bling.

BLING: Know why it's called Mao-tai? I'll tell you why it's called Mao-tai. Mao had it invented when he couldn't get a good mai tai.

WRITER: Bling's fortifying himself for the heartfelt thank-you he's going to give Mr Mude for all this free succour. Good God, look what I found in my soup. A *chicken* head!

BLING: You better keep it. That's the only head you're gonna get in China.

WRITER: Let's see what else –

WHISPER: He's going in again, folks. Look out!

WRITER: Well, here's your basic pullybone.

WHISPER: He's working his way down, folks.

WRITER: Pull, Big Tooth, win a wish.

FEMALE VOICE: He won't know that. He won't, from the south-west –

BLING: She's right. I've never seen a wishbone pulled anywhere but Pittsburgh.

WRITER: Whatcha mean? Look there. His buddy knows. Okay, cuz, you pull.

PHOTOG: Let me get a shot –

ALL: He wins.

WRITER: You win. Ask him what his name is again.

FEMALE VOICE: He says his name is Yang.

EDITOR: Ask him what his time is.

FEMALE VOICE: He says – oh, he is *very* embarrassed; we've made him blush – that he has no time.

EDITOR: No time? Hasn't he ever run a marathon before?

FEMALE VOICE: No. The older fellow says he is a very good runner though.

EDITOR: Why was he invited?

FEMALE VOICE: His friend says because he, Yang, has very good wins in 5,000.

BLING: What was his time in 5,000?

FEMALE VOICE: He says he does not know his time. No times were taken.

WRITER: Ask him – ask him about his family.

FEMALE VOICE: He says he lives with his aunt and uncle near Qufu. And his mother. He says his father is dead.

WRITER: An orphan! Here's our story. The cinderella orphan marathoner! A minority, unknown, shy, out of Outer Mongolia, sails past the pack and takes the gold. Just what I been wishing for. . . .

EDITOR: Very nice. But he was the one that got the wish.

MALE CHINESE VOICE: (*something in Chinese*) *Ganbei!*

FEMALE VOICE: To the Long March!

ALL: *Ganbei!*

EDITOR: To the Long Run!

ALL: *Ganbei!*

BLING: To the MX missile system!

ALL: *Ganbei!*

WRITER: Now you've stepped in it, Bling. Here comes our dude Mude.

FEMALE VOICE: The gentleman of the press says that is Mr Xu Liang coming with Mr Mude. Our fastest runner. He has run in two hours thirteen something.

EDITOR: Two-thirteen! That isn't loafing.

MUDE: Good evening. I would like to introduce you to our Chinese champion, Mr Xu Liang.

ALL: *Ganbei!*

WRITER: He tosses 'em, the champ does.

BLING: And this don't look like the champ's first stop. Hey, Xu Liang! To the Pittsburgh Pirates!

ALL: *Ganbei!*

MUDE: By the way, Mr Wu; I have something for you. Be so kind.

BLING: What is it?

MUDE: Your official packet – your passes and name card and number. You have been invited to participate tomorrow, Mr Wu. To run.

BLING: Oh, shit.

234

EDITOR: Bling? To run tomorrow?

MALE CHINESE VOICE: *Ganbei!*

ALL: *Ganbei!*

MUDE: Gentlemen and ladies, I must take Mr Xu Liang to other tables.

EDITOR: Goodbye.

ALL *Ganbei!*

BLING: Ohhh, shit. . . .

WHISPER: . . . and now the desserts: almond noodles in mandarin orange sweet syrup, glazed caramel apples that are dropped hot in cold water to harden the glaze; no fortune cookies – never any Chinese fortune cookies in China. . . .

Past midnight at the Beijing Airport, a rickety DC-3 fights its way down through a rising crosswind. It was coming in from North Korea with more than a ton of red ginseng and one passenger, on the last leg of a many-legged flight originating in Tanzania.

Magapius woke to find himself unloaded on a windy airstrip. The shadowy workers loading the bundles of ginseng on a truck didn't speak to him, and he felt it would be futile to try to speak to them. He stood beside his suitcase and watched, feeling more and more melancholy. When all the crates were on the truck he stepped forward to ask, 'Beijing?'

The workers stared at him as if he had just appeared. 'I run,' he told them, demonstrating his stride. 'Beijing.' A worker grinned and jabbered, then they all grinned and jabbered. They loaded his bag in the back of the truck. Magapius was about to crawl in after it but the workers insisted otherwise. They made him sit in the cab with the driver. They rode in back.

In the Chinese compound Yang rolled from his cot and tiptoed around his snoring roommate and closed the window. The wind had not wakened him. He had not been asleep.

He looked down the street stretching dimly below his hotel window. The start at Tien An Men Square some ten kilometres to his right, the turnaround some twenty to his left. He did not think about the finish, only about the two cut-off points. He must stay close to Zhoa, who had accomplished this 20-K time before; then he must keep going that fast to the 35-K mark, even if he collapsed ten paces after. He could get up and walk

235

then, if he chose, and return to the square hours behind the ten winners. If the million spectators had all gone home, all the better.

> *A well-shut door needs no bolts,*
> *yet it cannot be opened.*
> *A well-tied knot needs no rope,*
> *yet none can untie it.*
> *A good runner leaves no trail.*

September 27, 1981. Tien An Men Square, Beijing, China. Race scheduled to begin at 11:05 A.M.

10:00. Sky clear, blue, bright. Air sweet and chilled. Crowds already packing the curbs, obedient, quiet. The P.L.A. and police everywhere nonetheless.

10:15. The motorcycle brigade is ranked and ready, resplendent in their white tunics and blue trousers, alabaster helmets and chalk-white Hondas.

10:25. Last of the traffic allowed past before closure, buses jammed with expectant spectators, honking taxis.

10:26. All stop. Quiet. Such a quietness from so many! What attention. What power! And what fidgeting uncertainty as well, in the face of its own power. Men coughing and spitting; women with towels pressed over their mouths. . . .

10:28. The participants jog across the vast square toward the starting line, nervous and colourful in their various outfits, like so many kits rattling in the breeze before launch.

10:35. A regiment of P.L.A. double-times past (they no longer like being referred to as the Red Guard), resembling ill-fitted mannequins wound too tight.

10:54. Balloon-and-banner lifts off, falls back, waggles in the wind, tries again, flapping a long red tail of welcome.

11:00. A sound truck goes by advising everybody to remain calm, and stay behind the lines indicated, and stay quiet. . . .

11:05. Right on the nose a gunshot they're off! No shout, no cheer. One of the blunt khaki jeeps stencilled PRCC precedes the runners along the curb, honking and actually 'dozing into the throng. The American writer jogs to a vantage point and unfolds his chair. Here they come, a Korean in the lead. In the middle of the square the balloon is at last aloft.

Behind all the other runners, the Chinese come by in a pack. The young boy, Yang, is at the very rear. The writer lifts his
236

crooked little finger, reminding the boy of the shared wishbone. Yang returns the salute.

The next turn around, Yang has worked his way up into the pack of Chinese, and it is little Bling who is bringing up the rear, looking as dishevelled as ever in a U of Beijing track singlet, his number on upside down.

'How much farther?' he puffs.

'Only about twenty-four miles,' they call back.

Twenty kilometres straight west out Fu Xing Avenue to the bamboo scaffold erected at Gu Cheng Hu, and twenty kilometres back, then once more around the square to finish. The course will take the runners past many sights of interest – the Forbidden City, the Military Museum of the Chinese People's Revolution, the People's Crematorium, with its sinister plume of yellow smoke . . . and millions and millions of people. This will be the predominant sight, multitudinous faces, yet each face transmitting its singular signal, like tape across a playback head, until the signals make a song and the faces flow into one. All the runners will forever be imprinted with a single billowing black-eyed image: the Face of China. No one else will see this sight.

This face falls when the public address truck informs them that their champion and favourite, Xu Liang, is not among the runners. He was taken ill after his evening at the Great Hall and has withdrawn from the competition. Xu's withdrawal has caused great disappointment among the Chinese runners and worked a great change on Yang's friend Zhoa. Zhoa holds the second-best Chinese time. He is expected to take over, now that the favourite has faltered. The responsibility weighs heavy on Zhoa, Yang can see, affecting his concentration and, in turn, his stride. Yang sees that his head is bobbing too much; this is not like Zhoa. Also there is lateral movement of the arms. Inefficient, inefficient.

When the runners are out of sight there is nothing left for the crowds to gawk at but the journalists, and vice versa. In spite of all their stroking of Mude, they have not been allowed to follow the race. They were informed they could watch the run quite adequately on television on the parked press bus, just like the rest of the world's journalists.

The bus is packed to the door. The American editor stays to argue; the photographer stalks off in a mountainous fit of pique. The writer wanders about the square carrying his chair and seeking inspiration. He finds instead a cluster of Chinese people

237

watching a cardboard box sitting on a folded table. Inside the box is a colour TV with a bouncing picture of the front runners. He unfolds his chair and joins the cluster. The beautiful woman from last night's dinner comes to share his seat and translate the TV announcer for him. He takes his thermos of gin and tonic from his bag and pours a cup. This is more like it! Inspiration might yet occur.

11:35. It's Mike Pinocci from the U.S., followed by Bobby Hodge, Inge Simonsen, and Magapius Dasong. Mike snags a bottle from a drink table, drains half, and passes the rest to the tall Tanzanian.

In the midst of the Chinese runners, Yang watches the back of his friend's neck. Too stiff, too tense, poor Zhoa. . . .

20 km. It's Pinocci and Simonsen and the Tanzanian.

25 km. It's still Pinocci, looking good, strong; and tall, black Magapius Dasong still right behind him looking just as strong. An American coach tries to hand Pinocci a cup of Gatorade but he's too late. The Tanzanian takes it instead. After a sip he comes alongside Pinocci and hands him the cup. The runners grin at each other.

28 km. Pinocci and Magapius Dasong side by side; then Simonsen, struggling a little; then, coming up from the pack, the lanky Swede, Erikstahl.

Nearing 30 km a motorcycle cop shoots past to drive a spectator back toward the curb, and Magapius swerves to avoid the bike and clips Pinocci's heel with his foot. The American trips, rolls across his hip and over his shoulder, and comes back up still running, now third behind the Tanzanian and the Korean, Go Chu Sen. He sticks with the front runners, but his wide eyes reveal the fracture in his concentration.

Magapius lets the Korean pass. He shoots Pinocci a quick look of apology and he falls back alongside.

A stretch of rough road jars something loose in the trailing TV camera. The runners become indecipherable blots of colour for a few miles.

The crowd back at the square is finally showing signs of restlessness. A drumming can be heard – a banging of fists on empty metal, relentless and rhythmless. A military wagon bores through a throng to check it out. . . .

The wind tries to stir up some relief, swirling shreds of paper across the enforced emptiness of the square. The wagon comes

238

driving back, a half dozen scuffed teenagers in custody, one with a bloody ear. All aboard stare stoically ahead, the catchers and the caught.

35 km. The camera is repaired. The picture clears. Pinocci is falling back, favouring his hip, Magapius still steady alongside, leaving Simonsen, the Korean, and Erikstahl to fight for the front. In the Chinese pack Yang realizes he has passed the 35-km cut-off point. He will be allowed to finish. He feels fine. He begins to open up – why not? As he passes Zhoa, his labouring friend exhorts him to go on, Yang. *Chi oh.*

Far, far back, Bling is panting oh shit, shit, shit. He sees he'll never make the 35-km cut-off. That smug mother Mude! Will he ever be delighted to hear Mr Wise-ass Wu was not even capable of finishing.

The Japanese TV crew is disappointed with the crowd action. They're dead as stumps, these Chinamen! A sound man walks to the middle of the street with a bullhorn and tries to get something worked up. At first the crowd is puzzled. Yell! They have nothing to yell.

1:21. Kjell Erikstahl breaks the tape: 2 hours, 15 minutes, 20 seconds. Far from outstanding but, considering the locale, the rigours, the air, it's enough. Close on his heels is Norwegian Simonsen (2:15:51) and third is Jong Hyon Li of the Democratic People's Republic of Korea (2:15:52). Li is followed by his Korean compatriot Go Chu Sen, then Chuck Hattersly in fifth, the only Yank to take home one of the vases. The limping American and the tall, gliding Tanzanian tie for tenth. They embrace at the finish line.

On the final turn around the huge square Yang is suddenly passing runner after runner, to the crowd's delight. *Now* they have something to cheer about. The Japanese sound man gets them going – *Chi oh! Chi oh!* – causing the police to gather in worried, fidgeting packs. Crowds should keep calm. When Yang passes two Italians and two Japanese right in front of them they really get into the idea; *CHI! OH! CHI! OH! CHI! OH!*

Yang is not the first Chinese to finish. He is second behind Peng Jiazheng at 2:26:03. But Peng appears shot at the line, green and gasping, whereas little Yang finishes in a full sprint, arms pumping, looking good, his Gypsy eyes flashing. He's the one the crowd pours across the line to raise on their shoulders.

In Beijing, heroes don't necessarily always finish first.

Later, at the 35-km cut-off, three officials ran into the street with a big red flag to stop Bling. He sped up instead. 'Clear the track, you yellow pigs!' He dodged through them, quickening his stride. The officials gave pursuit, to the crowd's great pleasure. The people began to cheer for this plucky laggard. *Chi oh* indeed. Bling poured it on, yelling back at the receding officials, 'You'll never take Bee Wing Lou alive!'

Luckily they gave up after a block and Bling coasted on home. After he finished he apologized to all concerned, swore he was sorry that he had held up traffic for nearly an extra hour and, no, he didn't really know *why* he had done it.

'Maybe I was motivated by that Red Flag.'

The next day was a rest day for the runners, another mandatory tour for the press. This time, the journalists were told, to the *rural* countryside to see *marvels even more ancient!*

The little bus had stopped on the statue-lined road to Ming's tomb to allow the photographer out for pictures. The writer also dismounted; he was picking up inner rumblings about a Yellow Peril attack. He trotted across the road and back into a pear orchard about five rows, to consult with his colon.

Hunkered among the fallen pears and the waving weeds, he tried to think about the assignment. The team was getting plenty pics and much info, but no story. That's the trouble with the New Policy of the Open Bamboo Curtain – there's too damn *much* info to get a unifying hook into. What was needed to hang this all on was a good old Pearl Buck plot, he was telling himself, or a fresh inspiration; then he looked closer at the handful of leaves he'd torn from the weeds. *Holy shit*, there it was all around him, *acres* of it, waving wild and free. Ming-a-wanna!

He returned to the bus blazing with excitement. He could hardly wait to get through the echoing tombs and chilly temples and back to his private hotel room. It burned in his pockets like money wanting to be spent. There are no headshops in Beijing but plenty pipes, sold as mementos of the Opium War days.

In his room he crammed seeds stems and all in the clay bowl and fired up. He sighed a grateful cloud. By the time his colleagues called at his door to tell him the bus was waiting to take them to the farewell ceremonies at the Peking Hotel, a plot had been conceived, fertilized, and, if he said so himself, well laid. All that was needed now was the hatching.

240

Bling and the writer's journalistic colleagues were at first understandably opposed.

'You're crazy. Worse, you're *high*. What do you think? They're just gonna let us fly out of here with him in a barrel like a souvenir coolie?'

'No, I'm serious. Consider the terrific publicity, the headlines: Shoe Company Smuggles Track Defector Out of Red China. I mean *think* of it. A couple years at Oregon under a good trainer he'll *win* the Boston Marathon! Sell a *zillion* damn shoes! I saw the stats. He went from a 2:06 at 35 km to 2:29 at the finish. That's 4:53 a mile for *the last leg of a marathon*, a world-record pace. The kid's a treasure, I'm telling you, a diamond that will never be cut without the proper training. Consider it. It's in the kid's best interests.'

The editor nodded, considering it, especially the zillion shoes and the dawning oriental market. The photog had reservations.

'Even if the kid goes for it, how would we get him out? You saw the paperwork at that airport. What's he gonna use for a passport?'

'Bling's.'

'Just a *minute!*'

'With little Bling's passport and a scarf around his throat – "the boy cannot talk, comrade; that long run: laryngitis" – he could make it.'

'Just a goddamned minute, what makes you think that little Bling is gonna hand over his passport?'

'Because the mag *pays* little Bling to keep quiet, put on the nice blue warm-ups with the nice hood, and catch the milk plane home to Qufu or wherever.'

'Pays Bling how much?' Bling wanted to know.

'I'd say a thousand Yankee bucks would cover the flight and expenses.'

Now the editor wants to wait just one goddamn minute. Bling was getting behind it, though – 'With another say five hundred for the flight back?' – and the photog was already laying out a mental paste-up for *Sports Illustrated:* shot of kid getting off plane at Eugene, meeting Bowerman at Hayward Field, shaking hands at the state capitol, golden pioneer gleaming in the background. . . .

'Let's have a gander at your passport picture, Bling.'

241

'No less than three thousand Chinese yuan! That's a reasonable compromise, not much more than a thousand bucks!'

'A Chinese Communist Pittsburgh Shylock!'

'How will we make the pitch? We've got to get him off from his coaches – '

'We'll get him to come on our Great Wall tour tomorrow!' cried the photographer, adding another page to his paste-up. 'What do you think, Mr Editor?'

'For starters, Bling doesn't look a thing like him,' the editor observed. 'The eyes are different. The noses. Let's see the passport picture, Bling, because I think that even if you disguised the kid, a customs officer would take one look and – '

He stopped, gawking into the open passport.

'In God's name, Bling; how did you get them to allow a passport photo of you wearing those goofy glasses?'

'They're prescription,' Bling explained.

When they saw the kid in the banquet hall they veered to his table and congratulated him again, each giving him the wishbone pinky handclasp of their growing conspiracy. Bling translated their invitation about the trip to the Great Wall. The boy blinked and blushed and looked at his coach for advice. The coach explained that it would not be possible; all the Chinese runners were scheduled to visit the National Agricultural Exhibition Centre tomorrow. But thank you for so kind.

By the time they got to their table Bling and the writer had cooked up a number of alternative meets where they might make their pitch to the boy in private – Bling would follow him to the bathroom . . . Bling would tell him there was a phone call in the lobby – but it was that master of surprises, Mr Mude, who came forward to further their fantasy.

'The coaches spoke of your thoughtful invitation to our little minority friend,' Mude said as he stopped at their table. Tonight he was wearing a very informal sports jacket, no tie. 'I talked to Mr Wenlao and Mr Quisan about it, and we all think it would make very good media for both our nations. Also, we are told our little Yang has never seen the Great Wall. China owes her young hero an excursion, don't you agree?'

They nodded agreement. Mude asked how their story was progressing. Better and better, the writer told him. Mude chatted a few moments more, then excused himself.

242

'Forgive me, but is that not the Tanzanian that tripped the American? I must go congratulate him. As to our young minority boy, I shall see that all the arrangements are made for your convenience. Good night.'

'Oh, shit,' mumbled the editor when Mude had walked on. 'Oh, shit.'

Mude's mood was still cheerful the next day, his outfit more informal yet – a jogging jacket and Levi's. He stopped the bus whenever the photographer asked. He laughed at Bling's acrid observations on roadside China. He beamed well-being. He knew his assignment had been successful. No bad incidents, and he had learned a good deal about Yankee ways. He was getting with it, as they say. So after their stroll back down from the Great Wall, when Bling asked would it be all right if he and Mr Yang took a little run together before they got in the bus for the long ride back to Beijing – 'to loosen the knots' – Mude responded with his most *with it* expression, a phrase he'd been saving for just such a time:

'All right, you guys. Do your thing.'

Bling was still laughing as he and Yang jogged around the bend out of sight.

The journalists played with the swarms of school kids in the bus lot while Mr Mude smoked with the bus driver. The tourists teemed. And the Great Wall writhed across the rugged terrain like some ambitious stone dragon, bigger than the sandworms of Dune, heavier than the Great Pyramid of Giza.

Not greater, though. Not nearly. As a World Class Wonder the Great Wall is really more awe-inspiring than uplifting. One feels that it had to take some kind of all-prevailing, ill-proportioned paranoia to drive that stone snake across three thousand miles and thirty centuries. The Great Pyramid says, I rise to the skies. The Great Wall says, I keep out the louts. China says, The twentieth century must be allowed to enter! The Wall says, Louts will be *every*where – shooting beer commercials, buying Coca-Cola, strutting their ugly stuff. The twentieth century says, I'm coming in, louts and all, wall or no . . . I'm coming in because Time can't just walk off and leave behind one fourth of all the people in the world, can it now?

The Wall doesn't answer.

It was almost an hour before the two runners came back into

sight, walking. And Bling was no longer laughing. When his eyes met the writer's he nodded and mouthed, 'He'll do it.' Morosely. Somehow the kick had gone out of the conspiracy. Bling put on his blue glasses and climbed in to look out the bus window. Yang took a seat on the other side of the bus, looking at the other side of the road.

The ride back, Mude finally decided, was silent because everybody would be leaving tomorrow. It must make the heart very solemn, leaving Beijing after such short weeks. He embraced them all tenderly when he left them for the final time in the hotel lot. He told them if they ever got fed up with capitalistic landlord mentality to contact their friend Wun Mude in Beijing. He would see that China took them in.

Bling kept quiet up the steps and across the hotel lobby. In the elevator the journalists finally demanded in unison, '*Well?*'

'I'm to pick him up in a taxi when he goes out for his run tomorrow morning. He'll have his papers on him.'

'Far out. The Prince and the Pauper do Peking.'

'What did he say? When you asked . . . ?'

'He told me a story. How his father died.'

'Yeah . . . ?'

'A few years ago there was a thing – a fad, practically – started by members of the intelligentsia who had taken all the shit they could take. Doctors and lawyers and teachers. Journalists, too. They would be found guilty of some crime against the Cultural Revolution and paraded around town with nothing on but a strip of paper hanging from their necks. Their crime would be written on the paper. People – their neighbours, their *families* – would come out and insult them, throw dirt on the poor dudes, *piss* on them! We Chinese are fucking barbarians, you know? We aren't really disciplined or obedient. We've just never had any damn freedom! If we could suddenly go down to our local Beijing sporting goods store and buy guns like in the States, man, there would be lead flying and blood flowing all over town.'

'Bling! What about the kid?'

'A fad, like. Here in Beijing it was doctors. They were catching a lot of crap for catering to the landlord element, treating bourgeoisie heart attacks and so forth. Finally, twenty top physicians, the *cream* of the nation's doctors, man, poisoned themselves by way of protest.'

244

'Some protest.'

'Yeah, well, in Yang's province it was teachers. The kid's father was a professor of poetry. He was condemned to humiliation for teaching some damn out-of-favour tome or other. After enough insults he and a dozen other maligned colleagues walked into the provincial university gymnasium in the middle of a Ping-Pong tournament . . . walked in, lined up, took out their swords, and staged a protest.'

'Like dominoes.'

Bling nodded. 'The man at the end of the line had to do double duty: first dispatch the man in front of him, then do himself. They tried to keep it out of the papers, but there were pictures. And things like that get talked around even in China.'

'Jesus.'

'That anchor man was the kid's father.'

'And that's why the kid went for our plot?'

'That and, of course, the stipend of three thousand huyen . . . that may have had some influence.'

They waited for their Prince and Pauper as long as they dared the next morning. The photographer fiddled with his aluminum camera cases. The writer checked his pockets again to be sure he'd flushed all the wild wanna. The editor paid the phone bill.

They finally ordered a cab.

'I begin to suspect that we've seen the last of Bling, Yang, *and* your thousand clams.'

The editor nodded glumly. 'I wonder if the kid gets a cut?'

'I wonder if the kid even got the *pitch*. Bling may have put a hummer on all of us. Who can tell with these inscrutable pricks?'

The plane was delayed for two hours – emergency work for the flood victims – and they were drinking Chinese beer on the terminal mezzanine when they saw the taxi.

'Hey, look! Here he by God comes!'

'So he does, by God, so he does,' the editor admitted, not too much relieved. 'And, by God, with those glasses and that cap – he *does* look a lot like Bling.'

The photographer lowered his long-range lens. 'That's because it *is* Bling.'

They couldn't get seats together until after the takeoff.

'You did *what* with my money?'

'You heard me. Your three Chinese grand went into young

245

Yang's travel fund to fly him to next year's Nike marathon in Eugene.'

'Wait'll bookkeeping comes across that.'

'Cheer up. He can still defect when he gets to Oregon.'

'But what about you, Bling? Your education, your *career*?'

'When I got back to my dorm room last night I found I'd been moved out, girly books and all. You know who was in my bed, all coiled up like a black snake? That damn Tanzanian. Mude must've liked his style. So I decided it might be time for me to do some myself. Tripping.'

'Listen, Bling. Be straight with us. Did you even *ask* the kid, or is this all a shuck?'

'I will not be tempted by doubt.' Bling sniffed. He pushed the recliner button and leaned back, fingers laced behind his neck. 'Besides, you'll get your money's worth.'

'A thousand bucks for a thirty-year-old Pekingese punk? With times most high school girls can beat?'

'Ah! Good houseboy, me. Wash missy's underdrawers. Velly handy.'

Yang did not wait for the bus from the Qufu airport. He left his bag and his coat with Zhoa. He would get them later at school.

He loped off down the puddled runway, east, in the direction of the village, feeling very happy to be back in the country. The sweepers smiled at him. The workers in the fields waved to him. Perhaps that was the difference: in Beijing there had been no smile of greeting on the streets. People moved past people, eyes forward to avoid contact. Perhaps it was merely the difference between country and city life, not between governments or nations or races. Perhaps there were only two peoples, city and country.

He rattled over the plank bridge crossing the canal and leaped the hedge of brush. Through the damp air he could see the *fengs* rising against the descending twilight, and his grandfather there like a scribble of dark calligraphy on the top, contorting through his ancient exercises.

> *Lofty station is, like one's body,*
> *a source of great trouble.*
> *The reason one has great trouble is that*
> *he has a body. When he no longer*
> *has a body, what trouble will he have?*

246

Thus: he who values his body more than
     dominion over the empire
Can be entrusted with the empire.
And he who loves his body more than
     dominion over the empire
Can be given custody of the empire.
          – Lao-tzu
          Tao Te Ching

                    or

Don't follow leaders,
Watch the parking meters . . .
          – Bob Dylan
          Subterranean Homesick Blues

Little Tricker the Squirrel
Meets Big Double the Bear
–by Grandma Whittier

Don't tell me you're the *only* youngsters never heard tell of the time the bear came to Topple's Bottom? He was a huge high-country bear and not only huge but *horrible* huge. And hairy, and hateful, and *hungry!* Why, he almost ate up the *entire Bottom* before Tricker finally cut him down to size, just you listen and see if he didn't . . .

It was a fine morning, early and cold and sweet as cider. Down in the Bottom the only one up and about was old Papa Sun, and him just barely. Hanging in the low limbs of the crab-apple trees was still some of those strings of daybreak fog called 'haint hair' by them that believes in such. The night shifts and the day shifts were shifting very slow. The crickets hadn't put away their fiddles. The spiders hadn't shook the dew out of their webs yet. The birds hadn't quite woke up and the bats hadn't quite gone to sleep. Nothing was a-move except one finger of sun slipping soft up the knobby trunk of the hazel. It was one of the prettiest times of day at one of the prettiest times of year, and all the Bottom folk were content to let it come about quiet and slow and savoury.

Tricker the Squirrel was awake but he wasn't about. He was lazying in the highest hole in his cottonwood highrise with just his nose poking from his pillow of a tail, dreaming about flying. Every now and again he would twinkle one bright eye out through his dream and his puffy pillowhair to check the hazel tree way down below to see if any of the nuts was ready for reaping. He had to admit they were all pretty near prime. All day yesterday he had watched those nuts turning softly browner and browner and, come sundown, had judged them just one day short of perfect.

'And *that* means if I don't get them today, to*morrow* they are very apt to be just one day *past* perfect.'
248

So he was promising himself 'Just as quick as that sunbeam touches the first hazelnut I get right on the job.' Then, after a couple of winks, 'Just as quick as that sunbeam touches the *second* hazelnut I'll zip right down with my tote sack and go to gathering.' – and so forth, merely dozing and dallying, and savouring the still, sweet air. The hazelnuts get browner. The sunbeam inches silently on – the *fif*teenth! the *twen*tieth! – but the morning was simply so pretty and the air hanging so dreamy and still he hated to break the peace.

Wellthen, the finger just about touches the twenty-*sev*enth hazelnut, when a holy dadblamed goshalmighty *roar* came kabooming through the Bottom like a freight druv by the Devil himself, or at least his next hottest hollerer.

Oh, what a roar! Oh oh *oh!* Not just loud, and long, but high and low and chilling and fiery all to once. The haint hair and the spider webs all froze stiff – it was *that chilling!* – whilst the springs boiled dry and the crab-apples burned black from the hellheat of it. Even way up in Tricker's tall, tall tree the cottonwood leaves turned brown and looked ready to fall still *weeks* before their time. Moreover, that roar had startled Tricker out of his snooze so sudden that he *stuck startled* halfway between ceiling and floor. And hung there, petrified, spraddle-eagled spellbound stiff in midair, with eyes big as biscuits and every hair stabbing straight out from him like quills on a puffed-up porcupine.

'*What* in the name of *sixty cyclones* was *that?*' he asks himself in a quakering voice. 'A dream gone nightmare?'

He pinches his nose to check. The spellbind busts and Tricker drops hard to the floor: *bump!*

'Hmm,' he puzzles, rubbing his nose and his knees, 'it *is* like a dream with a little nightmare noise thrown in – like a plain old floating and flying *dream* dream . . . except when you get real bumps it must be a real floor.'

And right then it cut loose again – 'ROAWRRR!' shaking the cottonwood from root to crown till a critter could hardly stand. Tricker crawls cautious across the floor on his sore knees, and very cautious sticks his sore nose out, and very *very* cautious cranes over to look down into the clearing below.

'Again I say ROARR!'

The sound made Tricker's ears ring and his blood curdle and

249

the sight he saw made him wonder if he wasn't still dreaming, bumps or no.

'I'm BIG DOUBLE from the high ridges and I'm DOUBLE BIG and DOUBLE BAD and DOUBLE DOUBLE HONGRY a-ROARRR!'

It was a bear, a *grizz*erly bear, so big and hairy and horrible it looked like the two biggest baddest bears in the Ozarks had teamed up to make one.

'Again I say HONGRY! And I don't mean lunchtime snacktime littletime hongry, I mean grumpy grouchy bedtime *big*time hongry. I live big and I sleep big. When I hit the hay tonight I got six months before breakfast so I need a supper the size of my sleep. I need a *big* bellyfull of fuel and layby of fat to fire my fulltime furnace and stoke my sixmonths snore a-ROOAAHRRRR!'

When the bear opened his mouth his teeth looked like stalactites in a cavern. When he swung his head around his eyes looked like a doublebarrel shotgun going off at you.

'I ate the high hills bare as a *bone* and the foothills raw as a *rock*, and now I'm going to eat the WHOLE! BOTTOM! and everybody in it ALL UP!'

And with that gives another awful roar and raises his paws high above his head, stretching till his toenails strain out like so many shiny sharp hayhooks, then rams down! And with a evil snarl tears the very earth wide open like it was so much wrapping paper on his birthday present.

In the sundered earth there was Charlie Charles the Woodchuck, his bedroom split half in two, his bedstead busted beneath him and his bedspread pulled up to his quivering chin.

'Hey you,' Charlie demands, in the bravest voice the little fella can muster, 'this is *my* hole! What are you doing breaking into my home and hole?'

'I'm BIG DOUBLE from the HIGH WILD HOLLERS,' the bear snarls, 'and I'm loading the old larder up for one of my DOUBLE LONG WINTER NAPS.'

'Well just you go larding up someplace else, you high hills hollerer,' Charlie snarls back. 'This aint *your* neck of the woods . . .'

'Son, when I'm hongry it's ALLLL Big Double's neck of the woods!' says the bear. 'And I AM HONNNGRY. I ate the
250

HIGH HILLS RAW and the FOOTHILLS BARE and now I'm going to EAT! YOU! UP!'

'I'll run,' says the woodchuck, glaring his most glittering glare.

'I can run *too*-oo,' says the bear, glaring back with a grin that turns poor Charlie's glitter to gloom. Charlie meets the bear's blistering stare a couple ticks more, then *out* from under the covers he springs and *out* across the bottom he tears, ears laid low tail hoisted high and little feet hitting the ground sixty-six steps a second . . . *fast!*

But the big old bear with his big old feet merely takes one! two! three! double-big steps, and takes Charlie over, and snags him up, and swallers him down, hair hide and all.

High up in his hole Tricker blinks his eyes in amazement. 'Yep,' he has to allow, 'that booger truly can run.'

The bear then walks down the hill to the big granite boulder by the creek where Longrellers the Rabbit lived. He listens a moment, his ear to the stone, then lifts one of those size fifty feet as high as his double-big legs can hoist it, lifted like a huge hairy piledriver, and with one stomp turns poor Longrellers's granite fortress into a sandpile all over the rabbit's breakfast table.

'You Ozark clodhopper!' Longrellers squeals, trying to dig the sand out of one of his long ears with a wild parsnip. 'This is *my* breakfast, not yours. You got a nerve, come stomping down here into our Bottom, busting up our property and privacy, when this aint even your stomping grounds!'

'I hate to tell you, cousin, but I'm BIG DOUBLE and ALLLL the ground I stomp is mine. I ate the high hills BARE and the foothills CLEAN. I ate the woodchuck that run and now I'm going to EAT! YOU! UP!'

'I'll run,' says the rabbit.

'I can run *too*-oo,' says the bear.

'I'll jump,' says the rabbit.

'I can jump *too*-oo,' says the bear, grinning and glaring and wiggling his whiskers wickedly at the rabbit. Longrellers wiggles his whiskers back a couple of ticks, then *out* across the territory rips the rabbit, a cloud of sand boiling up from his heels like dust from a motorscooter scooting up a steep dirt road. But right after him comes the bear, like a loaded logtruck coming down a steeper one. Longrellers is almost to the hedge at the edge of the Topple pasture when he gathers his long ears and

251

elbows under him and jumps for the brambles, springing up into the air quick as a covey of quail flushing . . . fast, and *far!*

But the big old bear with the big old legs springs after him like a flock of rocketships roaring, and takes the rabbit over at the peak of his jump, and snags him up, and swallers him down, ears elbows and everything.

'Good as his word the big bum can certainly jump,' admits Tricker, watching bug-eyed from his high bedroom window.

Next, the bear goes down to where Whittier Crick is dribbling drowsy by. He grabs the crick by its bank and, with one wicked snap, snaps it like a bedspread. This snaps Sally Snipsister the Martin clear out of her mudburrow boudoir and her toenail polish, summersetting her into the air, then lands her hard in the emptied creekbed along with stunned mudpuppies and minnows.

'You backwoods bully!' Sally hisses. 'You ridgerunning rowdy! What are you doing down out of your ridges ripping up our rivers? This aint your play puddle!'

'Why, ma'am, I'm Big Double and ANY puddle I please to play in is mine. I ate the ridges *raw* and the backwoods *bald*. I ate the woodchuck and I ate the rabbit. And now I'm going to EAT! YOU! UP!'

'I'll run,' says the martin.

'I can run, *too*-oo,' says the bear.

'I'll jump,' says the martin.

'I can jump *too*-oo,' says the bear.

'I'll climb,' says the martin.

'I can climb, *too-oo*,' says the bear, and champs his big yellow choppers into a challenging chomp. Sally clicks back at him with her sharp little molars for a tick or two, then *off!* she shoots like the bullet out of a pistol. But right after her booms the bear like a meteor out of a cannon. Sally springs out of the creekbed like a silver salmon jumping. The bear jumps after her like a flying shark. She catches the trunk of the cottonwood and climbs like an electric yo-yo whizzing up a wire. But the bear climbs after her like a jet-propelled elevator up a greasy groove, and takes her over, and snags her up, and swallers her down, teeth toenails and teetotal.

And then, it so happens, while the big bear is hugging the tree and licking his lips, he sees! that he is eye-to-eye with a little hole, that is none other than the door, of the bedroom, of Tricker the Squirrel.

'Yessiree bob,' Tricker has to concede. 'You also can sure as shooting *climb*.'

'WHO are YOU?' roars the bear.

'I'm Tricker the Squirrel, and I saw it all. And there's just no two ways about it: I'm impressed – you may have been a little short-changed in the thinking department but when it comes to running, jumping and climbing you got double portions.'

'And EAT!' roars the bear into the hole. 'I'm BIG DOUBLE and I ate – '

'I know, I know,' says Tricker, his fingers in his ears. 'The ridges raw and the hills whole. I heard it all, too.'

'NOW I'm going to EAT – '

'Gonna eat me up. I know,' groans Tricker. 'But first I'm gonna *run*, right?'

'And I'm gonna run *too*-oo,' says the bear.

'Then I'm gonna *jump*,' says Tricker.

'And I'm gonna jump, *too*-oo,' says the bear.

'Then I'm gonna *drink some buttermilk*,' says Tricker.

'And I'm gonna drink buttermilk, *too*-oo,' says the bear.

'Then I'm gonna *climb*,' says Tricker.

'And I'm gonna climb, *too*-oo,' says the bear.

'And *then*,' says Tricker, smiling and winking and plucking at one of his longest whiskers dainty as a riverboat gambler with a sleeve full of secrets, 'I'm going to *fly!*'

This bamboozles the bear, and for a second he furrows his big brow. But everybody – even short-changed grizzerly bears named Big Double – knows red squirrels can't fly – not even red squirrels named Tricker.

'Wellthen,' says the bear, grinning and winking and plucking at one of his own longest whitest whiskers with a big clumsy claw, 'when *you* fly, I'll fly *too*-oo.'

'We'll *see* about that,' says Tricker and, without a word or wink more, reaches over to jerk the bear's whisker *clean out*. UhROAWRRR! roars the bear and makes a nab, but Tricker is *out* the hole and streaking down the treetrunk like a bolt of greased lightning with the bear thundering behind him, meaner and madder than ever. Tricker streaks across the Bottom toward the Topple farm with the bear storming right on his tail. When he reaches the milkhouse where Farmer Topple cools his dairy products he jumps right through the window. The bear jumps right through after him. Tricker hops up on the edge of a gallon crock and begins to guzzle up the cool, thick buttermilk like he hadn't had a sip of liquid for a month.

The bear knocks him aside and picks up the whole crock and sucks it down like he was a seven-year drought.

Tricker then hops up to the rim of the *five*-gallon crock and starts to lap up the buttermilk.

But the bear knocks him aside again, and hefts the crock and guzzles it down.

Tricker doesn't even bother hopping to the brim of the last crock, a *ten*-galloner. He just stands back dodging the drops while the bear heaves the vessel high, tips it up and gradually guzzles it empty.

The bear finally plunks down the last crock, wipes his chops and roars, 'I'm BIG DOUBLE and I ate the HIGH HILLS – '

'I know, I know,' says Tricker, wincing. 'Let's skip the roaring and get right on to the last part. After I run, and jump, and drink buttermilk, then I *climb*.'

'I climb *too*-erp,' says the bear, belching.

'And I fly,' says Tricker.

'And I fly *too*-up,' says the bear, hiccupping.

So *back* out of the milkhouse jumps Tricker and *off* he goes, dusting back toward his cottonwood like a baby dust devil, with the bear huffing right at his heels like a fullblown tornado. And *up* the tree he scorches like a house a-fire, with the bear right on his tail like a volcano. Higher and higher climbs Tricker, with the bear's hot breath huffing hotter and hotter, and closer and closer, and higher and higher till there's barely any tree left . . . then *out* into the fine fall air Tricker springs, like a little red leaf light on the wind.

And – before the bear thinks better of it – *out* he springs hisself, like a ten-ton milk tanker over the edge of a straight-down cliff.

'I forgot to mention,' Tricker sings out as he grabs the leafy top of that first suntouched hazelnut tree and hangs there, swinging and swaying: 'I can also *trick*.'

'ARGHH!' his pursuer answers, plummeting past, 'AAARRG – ' all the way till he splatters on the hillside like a ripe melon.

When the dust and debris clear back, Sally Snapsister wriggles up from the wrecked remains and says, 'I'm out!'

Then Longrellers the Rabbit jumps up and says, 'I'm out!'

254

Then Charlie Charles the Woodchuck pops up and says, 'I'm out!'

'I,' says Tricker, swinging high in the sunny branches where the hazelnuts are just about perfect, 'was never in to *get* out.'

And everybody laughed and the hazelnuts got more and more perfect and the buttermilk just rolled . . .

down . . .

the hill.

Good Friday
– by Grandma Whittier

Dearest Lord Jesus Christ have mercy on this poor confused tormented and just plain scared-silly old soul down on her bony knees in the dark for the first time in heaven knows how long begging bless me and forgive me but honest to betsy Lord i always figured that for one thing you had enough sparrows to keep your eye on and that for another you had done answered this old bird her lifetime's share the time after papa and uncle dicker topple and brother took us kids to the turn-of-the-century worlds fair in little rock and i saw the wild man from borneo running around in a cage all ragged black and half naked with hair sticking out a foot making this crazy low and lonesome sound way down in his chest as he chased after a white chicken and finally caught it right where the crowd had pushed me up against the bars so i couldn't help but see every yellow fang as he bit that chicken neck slick in two then hunkered down there staring directly into my popeyes chewing slobbering and would you believe grinning till i could not help myself but to go and throw up all over him which peeved him so he gave a howl of awful rage and run his hand through the bars at me screeching such a rumpus that the sideshow man had to go in the cage with a buggy whip and a stool and drive him back whining in a corner of the filthy old cage but not before i got my bonnet tore off and had been put in such a state that papa had to leave the other kids with uncle dicker and take me home sick with the shakes so abiding terrible that from that night on through the entire summer i could not be left alone in my room without a burning lamp and even then still had practically every nights rest ruint by these horrible nightmares how this black man not a negro but a wild primitive black man that had been trapped and took from his home and family in the jungles of borneo and was therefore already crazed with savage lonesomeness and hate and humiliation was bound and determined to bust out of that puny little sideshow pen and come after me because of the way i had vomited at the loathesome sight of him and late one autumn
256

afternoon sure as shooting i had just walked little emerson t home from playing in our yard because it was getting towards dusk and on my way from the whittier place coming back towards topples bottom i saw the cane shaking and something coming through the canebrake and heard a kind of choked-off baying moan so chilling i froze cold in my tracks as it came closer and closer till O Lord there he was that big old ball of black hair and that mouth and that chicken flopping in his hand lumbering out of the cane right at me then you can bet i run run screaming bloody murder right acrost the road ruts through the gorse stickers and in that dim light blundered over the edge of a gully and lit headfirst in a pile of junk farm machinery and scrap iron that brother had put there to keep the soil from gullying away so fast and laid there on my back in kind of a coma so as i was still awake and could see and hear perfectly well but could not move so much as a muscle nor mouth to holler for help while tearing through the gorse and dust and blackberries right on down at me here came this wild black head and Loving Jesus as though i wasnt already scared enough to melt now i saw that he was not only going to get me but i wouldn't even be mercifully passed out so i prayed Lord i prayed in my mind like i never prayed before nor till this instant that if i could just die just happily die and not be mortified alive that on my solemnest oath i would never ask another blessed thing so help me Great Almighty God but then i saw it wasn't the wild man from borneo after all it was only the mute halfwit coloured boy that lived with the whittiers cropping hands and as was the occasional custom of the coloureds at that time he had stole a legern pullet from the whittiers coop and the sound i had heard was a mix-up of his cleft pallet moaning the chicken squawking and whittiers old redbone hound bawling after him in a choked-off fashion because mr whittier kept the dog chained to a six-pound cannonball from his navy days that the dog was towing behind him through the brush and i thought oh me i prayed to die and now i am going to lie here paralysed and bleed to death or something and not be mortified after all but then that mute boy seen me hurt at the bottom of the gully and tossed the chicken to the hound and climbed down and picked me up and carried me out of the gully and back through the stickers onto the road just in time for brother happening past to take one look at me all bloody being toted by a goo-gawking black idiot and knock him down with a cane stalk and beat him nearly to death before his daughter

257

my niece sara run to get papa who brought me into pine bluff in the back of uncle dickers wagon with my head a bloody mess yet still wide-open-eyed in mamas lap and the boy roped behind the wagon gaping and gagging at me in the lanternlight waiting for me to tell them but i couldn't speak no more than he could while all the way papa and brother and the other men who joined our little procession kept talking about hangings too good for the inbred maniac he oughta be burnt or worse till they carried me on into doctor ogilvies downstairs parlour and undressed me and cleaned me and doctored my wound as best they could with the doctor shaking his head at papa and mama and my sisters crying and all the time me seeing the lanterns passing back and forth on the porch and hearing brother and the men talking about what they aimed to do to that boy should i not pull through like it looked like i wasnt and then my eyes finally closed and i let out a long last breath and sure enough i died.

It was the queerest thing. I sailed right up out of my body while Doctor Ogilvie was saying, I'm sorry, Topple, she's gone – sailed right over the town through the night right on up to Heaven where the streets were lit with pure gold and the angels were playing harps and the moth I presume did not corrupt. Heaven. But when I started to go through the gates that were all inlaid pearl precisely like they are supposed to be this huge tall angel with an enormous book says to me, Wait a minute, little girl; what's your name? I says Becky Topple and he says Becky Topple? Rebecca Topple? I thought so, Becky; you have been marked by the Blood of the Lamb of God Almighty and you aren't due up here for another good seventy-seven years! The Son of Man Hisself has you down for not less than one entire century of earthly service! You're to be a saint, Rebecca, did you know that? So you got to go on back, honey. I'm sorry. . . .

And sent me sailing back through the clouds and the stars to Arkansas and Pine Bluff and Dr Ogilvie's house all fluttering at the parlour windows with torches and lamps like big angry millers and right down through the roof. I swear it was absolutely the *queerest* sensation, seeing my body in that room with all my folks and family crying and little Emerson T struggling with his papa to get to me, crying Becky aint dead aint dead cant be dead as I just drifted back into my body like so much smoke being sucked back down a chimney and took a breath opened my eyes and sat up and told them that the mute boy had *not*
258

harmed me. No. Quite the contrary. That I'd been fooling around that gully and fell into the scrap iron and he had come along and seen me and *saved* me, thank the Lord (I had my fingers crossed, and said another Thank the Lord to myself) and *I have never bothered you about another single thing since that, Jesus, as I solemnly promised. What was there for me to ask, actually? I have never doubted that angel with the book. Not from that instant to this have I ever faced mortal danger, nor never thought I would have to, either – leastways till nineteen-eighty-something rolled around. And I always figured that by then I would be more than tickled to be getting shut of this wore-out carcass and battered old mug anyhow. So I swear to You with God and that tall angel as my witness that I am not shivering scared here on my knees like some dried-up old time miser pinchin life like her last measly pennies. Because I'm not. What I am asking for is I guess a sign of some kind, Lord; not more time. Running out of time simply is not what I'm scared of. What I am afraid of I can't put a name to yet, having just this day encountered it like finding a new-hatched freak of nature, but it is not of dying. Moreover I am not even sure whether my fear is of a real McCoy danger or not. Maybe the simple weight of years has finally made its crack in my reason like it has in poor Miss Lawn and in loony Mr Firestone with his Communists behind every bush and in so many other tenants at the Towers lots of whom I know are way younger than me – made its cruel crack in my mind so that all these sudden fears these shades and behind-every-bush boogers and all this dirty business that seems to have leaked in are nothin more than just another wild black mistake from Borneo this old white hen is making . . . is what I'm wanting to know, Lord Jesus, is the sign I'm praying for*

I stopped when I heard something way off. Oh. Just that old log train tooting at the Nebo junction. Bringing the week's logging down from Blister Creek. Unless they had changed their schedule sometime since those sleepless nights years ago it meant it was getting near midnight. Good Friday's about to turn into what I guess a body might call Bad Saturday. It sure didn't feel like Eastertime. Too warm. This was the first time Easter would be late enough in April to have Good Friday fall on my birthday since it must of been the first spring after marrying Emery. That first Oregon spring. It was hot and peculiar then, too. Maybe it'd cool some yet, bring down the usual shower on the egg

259

hunt. Still, driving out from Eugene this afternoon I noticed a lot of farmers already irrigating. And the night air dry as a bone. Blessed strange.

I clenched my lips and reminded myself in a calm voice, This isn't strange at all, Old Fool. This is me-and-Emery's old cabin, our old Nebo place. But another voice keeps hollering back, Then why's everything *seem* so hellish strange? Well, it must be because this is the first night away from Old Folks Towers in about a century. No, that don't account for it. I spent last Christmas and New Year's at Lena's and things was no stranger than usual. Besides, I felt it *before* I left the apartment. The moment my grandson phoned this morning I told him I didn't want to go. I says, 'Why, boy, tonight the Reverend Dr W. W. Poll is having an Inspiration Service down in the lobby that I *couldn't miss!*' Having accompanied me a time or two, and knowing that the doctor's services are about as inspirational as a mud fence, he just groans, ugh.

'Sweetheart, think of it as *med*ical,' I says. 'Reverend Poll's sermons are as effective as any of my sleeping prescriptions,' I says trying to kid him away from it.

So I felt it then. He kept at me, though. He's like his grandpa was that way, when he gets a notion he thinks is for somebody else's good. I carried the phone over to turn down *Secret Storm*, making excuses one after another why I can't go till at length he sighs and says he guesses he'll have to tell me the secret.

'The real reason, Grandma, is we're all having a birthday party – a surprise birthday party if you weren't such a stubborn old nannygoat.'

I says, 'Honey, I sure do thank you but when you get past eighty a birthday party is about as welcome a surprise as a new wart.' He says that I hadn't been out to visit them in close to a year, blame my hide, and he wants me to see how they've fixed the place back up. Like for a grade, I thought: another trait of his grandpa's. I told him I was sorry but I did not have the faintest inclination to aggravate my back jouncing out to that dadgummed old salt mine (though it isn't really my back, the doctor says, but a gallbladder business aggravated by sitting, especially in a moving car). 'It was forty years out there put me in this pitiful condition.'

'Baloney,' he says. 'Besides, the kids have all baked this fantastic birthday cake and decorated it for Great-Grandma's birthday; their dear little hearts will be broken.' I tell him to bring them and their dear little hearts both on into my apartment and we'd drink Annie Green Springs and watch the people down in the parking lot. Ugh, he says again. He can't stand the Towers. He maintains our lovely low-cost twenty-storey ultramodern apartment building is nothing more than a highrise plastic air-conditioned *tomb*stone where they stick the corpses waiting for graves. Which it is, I can't deny, but plastic or no I make just enough on my Social Security and Natural Gas royalties to pay my way if I take advantage of Poor People's Housing. My *own* way.

'So I appreciate the invitation, sugar, but I guess I hadn't better disappoint the Reverend W. W. Poll. Not when he's just a short elevator ride as opposed to a long ordeal in an automobile. So you all bring that cake on over here. It'll do us old geezers good to see some kids.' He tells me the cake's too big to move. I says '*too big?*' and he says that they was having not only my party, see, but a whole day-long to-do with music and a service their ownselves and quite a few people expected. A sort of Worship Fair, he called it. 'Al-so,' he says, in that way he used to twist me around his finger, 'the Sounding Brass are going to be here.'

Grandkids always have your number worse than any of your own kids, and the first is the worst by a mile. 'Don't you flimflam *me*, Bub! Not *thee* Sounding Brass.' He says cross his heart; he picked them all up at the bus depot not three hours ago, swallowtails, buckteeth, and all, and they have promised to sing a special request for my birthday, even though they don't usually dedicate songs and haven't done it in years.

'And I will wager,' he says, 'you can't guess which one.' His words some way more extravagant than's even usual for him. I don't answer. I heard it then. 'They are going to sing that version of "Were You There" that you used to like so much.' I say 'You remember *that?* Why, it's been twenty years since I had that record if it's been a day.' 'More like thirty,' he says. He said *al*-so as far as the ride went they had a special bus with a full-size bed in it coming for me at four on the dot. 'So don't give me any more of that bad back baloney. This is your day to party!'

I realized what it was then, to some extent. There was somebody else with him, standing near at the other end of the line so he was grooming his voice for more than just his granny. Not Betsy, nor Buddy. Somebody else.

'In fact it could be your *night* to party as well. Better throw some stuff in a sack.'

After we hung up I was in a kind of dither to think who. I started to turn my programme back up, but it was the ad for denture stickum where the middle-aged ninny is eating peanuts. So I just switched the wretched thing clean off and stood there by the window, looking down at Eugene's growing traffic situation. *Zoom zoom zoom*, a silly bunch of bugs. The Towers is the highest building in all Eugene unless you count that little one-storey windowless and doorless cement shack situated on top of Skinner's Butte. Some kind of municipal transmitter shack is I guess what it is. It was up there just like it stands today the very first time Emerson T and me rode to the top of the butte. We drove if I'm not mistaken a spanking brand-new 1935 Terraplane sedan of a maroon hue that Emerson had bought with our alfalfa sales that spring. Eugene wasn't much more than a main street, just some notion stores and a courthouse and Quackenbush's Hardware. Now it sprawls off willy-nilly in all directions as far as a person can see, like some big old Monopoly game that got out of hand. That little shack is the only thing I can think of still unchanged, and I still don't know what's in it.

I picked up Emerson T's field glasses from my sill and took them out of their leather case. They're army glasses but Emery wasn't in the army; when they wouldn't let him be a chaplain he became a conscientious objector. He won the glasses at Bingo. I like to use them to watch the passenger trains arrive Monday nights, but there isn't much to watch of a Friday noon. Just that new cloverleaf, smoking around in circles and, O, *why*ever had I let him make me say yes? I could still hear my pulse rushing around his words in my ears. I turned the glasses rear-way-round and looked for a while that way, to try to make my heart slow its pit-a-pat (nope, it hadn't been Betsy or Buddy, nor *none* of his usual bunch that I could think of offhand), when, without so much as a by-your-leave or a kiss-my-foot, there, right at my elbow, sucking one of my taffy-babies and blinking those blood-rare eyes of hers up at me was that dadblessed Miss *Lawn!*

'Why Mrs *Whit*tier – '

Made me jump like a frog. Her eyes, mainly. Vin rosé bloodshot. She puts away as much as a quart before lunch
262

somedays; she told me so herself. ' – don't you realize you are looking through the *wrong end* again?' She shuffles from foot to foot in those gum-rubber slippers she wears then, in a breath that would take the bristles off a hog, she coos 'I heard your *television* go off, then when it didn't come *back on* I was worried something might be the *mat*ter . . . ?'

She wears those things for just that purpose, too: slipping. I know for a fact that as soon as she hears my toilet flush or one of my pill bottles rattle she slips into her bathroom to see if my medicine cabinet is left open. Our bathrooms are back-to-back and the razor blade disposal slot in her medicine cabinet lines right up with the razor-blade disposal slot on my medicine cabinet, and if she don't watch out one of these days I'm going to take a fingernail file and put one of those poor bloodshot eyeballs out of its misery. Not actually. We're old acquaintances, actually. Associates. Old maids and widows of a feather. I tell her if she must know I turned it off to talk over the telephone.

'I *thought* I heard it ring,' she says. 'I wondered if it might be Good Book Bob dialling you for dollars again.'

Once KHVN phoned and asked me who it was said 'My stroke is heavier than my groaning.' I remembered it was Job because the Book of Job was the only book of the Bible Uncle Dicker ever read aloud to me (he claimed it was to help me reconcile my disfigurement but I personally think it was because of him constantly suffering from his rupture), and when I answered right and won forty dollars and a brass madonna of unbreakable Lucite Miss Lawn never got over it. If I was in the tub or laid down napping and the phone rang more'n once she'd scoot all the way around from her place in time to answer the third ring, just in case it might be another contest. That's how she thinks of me and of what she refers to as my 'four-leaf-clover life'. Sometimes she comes in and *waits* for it to ring. She swears up and down that I must be hard of hearing because she *always* knocks before she comes in; all I say is it must be with a gum-rubber knuckle.

'Well, it was not Good Book Bob,' I assure her, 'it was my grandson.'

'The *famous* one?'

I just nodded and snapped the field glasses away in their case. 'He's coming in a special bus this afternoon to take his grandmother to a big surprise party everybody's giving her.' I admit I was rubbing it in a bit but I swear she can aggravate a person. 'I'll probably be away to the festivities all evening,' I says.

'And miss Reverend Poll's *special service?* and the doughnuts and the Twylight Towers *Trio?* Mrs Whittier, you must be delirious!'

I told her I was attending an*other* service, and instead of those soggy doughnuts was having a fan*tastic* cake. But I didn't have the heart to Lord it over her about the Sounding Brass, though. Them eyes were already going from red to green like traffic lights. In the entire year and a half she's lived in the apartment next door I believe the only visits she's had from the outside is Jehovah's Witnesses. I says, I *am*, Miss Lawn: dee-*lirious*, and that I was going to have myself a good long hot soak in Sardo before I *popped* with delirium. So, if she would excuse-a *pliz* – and went strutting into the bathroom without another word.

I like Miss Lawn well enough. We went to the same church for years and got along just fine, except her seeming a little snooty. I reckoned that came from her being a Lawn of the Lawn's Sand & Gravel Lawns, a rich old Oregon family and very high society around Eugene. It wasn't till Urban Renewal forced her to follow me to the Towers that I realized what a lonesome soul she actually was. And *jealous* . . . she can't hardly stand how people make over me. She says the way people make over me you'd think I was the only one in the building. I always say, Ah, now, I don't know about that, but I *am* glad people like me. *Well*, she says, they ought to like *me*; I never done anything to make people *dislike* me! I say, All I do is try and be nice and she says, Yeah, but you're *too* nice with them, *gushy*, whether they're good folks or bad; if I had to get friends by being too gushy like that I don't want 'em. Actually, I'm pretty snippy with people, but I say, Yeah, well, if you're gonna make friends you're gonna make 'em by *loving* thy neighbour, not all the time acting like you're passing judgment on him. Besides, I never ran into anybody I didn't think but *was good folks*, you get deep enough down. And she says, Well, when you been around as much as *me* you sure will find different; something will happen someday and you'll find out that there are *some* people who are rotten *all the way down!* 'Then,' she says, 'we'll see how that mushy love-thy-neighbour way of yours holds up.'

Forlorn old frog; what other world could she expect with that

kind of outlook? Like Papa used to say: It's all in how you hold
your mouth. Oh well, I don't know. A little later I called out to
her that there was a bottle of cold wine in my Frigidaire.

I filled my tub just as steaming hot as I could stand and got in.
The Sounding Brass! The last and of course only other time I'd
been fortunate enough to hear them was after Lena left home to
marry Daniel. I got so blue that Emerson drove me back to
Arkansas for a family reunion and on the way back through
Colorado took me to the Sunrise Service at the Garden of the
Gods where the Brass family absolutely stole the show. Afterwards Emery became the Deacon Emerson Thoreau Whittier
and travelled to a lot of religious shindigs. I usually begged off
accompanying him; somebody needs to keep track of the farm,
I'd say. After the house burned and we moved into town I came
up with other excuses. Like Emerson's driving being so uncertain
that it gave me the hiccups. Which it did. But it wasn't just that,
nor just cars. It's anything scurrying around, helter and yon; get
here, get there; trains, buses, airplanes, what-all. Right this
minute my lawyers tell me I am taking a loss of sixty-five dollars
a month on my gas check simply by putting off journeying to
Little Rock to sign some papers in person. But I don't know.
Consider the lilies, I say, they toil not, speaking of which I hear
my Frigidaire door slam as Miss Lawn got over her snit in the
other room, then, the lid of my cut-crystal candy dish, then my
television came back on. The poor old frog. When I finally
finished my rinse and come out in my robe it was still on,
blaring. Miss Lawn was gone, though, as was most of the candy
I'd planned to take to the kids at the farm and *all* the Annie
Green Springs.

I recognized my ride the instant it turned the corner into the
parking lot. Even eighteen storeys down and before I got out
the field glasses there was no mistaking it, a big bus, all glistening
chrome and gleaming white and five big purple affairs painted
on the side of it in the formation of a flying cross. When I got
them into focus I seen they were birds, beautiful purple birds. It
turned and parked in the Buses Only and opened its front door.
I saw get out first what I could tell immediately was my grandson
by his big shiny forehead: *another* trait from his grandpa's side.

Then, behind him, bobble-butting out the bus door, come
that big-mouthed doughball of a character from Los Angeles by

265

the name of Otis Kone. Otis is a kind of full-grown sissy and has always rubbed me the wrongest of any of my grandson's gang. For instance the way he stood there, looking at the Towers like he might buy it. He had on a little black beanie and around his rump he had strapped a belt with a scabbard. He pulled out a big long sword and flashed it around his head for the benefit of all. About the only good I can say about Otis is that he always goes back to Southern California as soon as our rains start in the fall, and stays there till they stop. Which is to say he stays away most of the year, praise the Lord. Watching him parade around Devlin with that sword I says to myself, Uh-huh, *that's* who was giving me the willies from the other end of the phone!

Then, out come this other fellow. A big fellow, draped in white from crown to toe like an Arab. Was he something! I strained through the glasses to see if I knew him but his face was all a-swirl. In fact, it seemed that he was *wrapped* in a kind of slow swirl. He come out of that bus and sailed about like he was moving fast and slow at the same time, pausing in midair to reach back for somebody else then swirling around again, opening like a flower as he lit down. I saw he had a little child who was also dressed in white but only in short pants and shirt with nothing over his head. It was quite apparent then that both of them were of the black race. He set the little child on his shoulder and followed Otis with his sword and my grandson with his forehead into the building, out from beneath my sight. But you could imagine it: Miss Prosper the nurse and receptionist craning over the top of her *Organic Gardening*, the rest of the lobby loafers looking up from their games and so on. I bet you didn't hear so much as a checker move.

I just had time to get the last clippie out of my hair before there came two quick knocks at my door, then one, then two more.

'Let me in queeck, Varooshka; they are on to us! Ve must atomize the feelm!'

It was of course that nitwit Otis. I shudder to think what would have happened had he pulled that at Mr Firestone's door by mistake. I opened as far as the chain would let me and seen it was just a wooden stage sword painted silver. He was wearing some patched-up baggy pants and the fly not even zipped. 'Sorry,' I says, 'I gave all my rags to the mission,' and made like to slam it before I said, O I *am* sorry. They laughed at that.

266

'Happy Birthday,' Devlin says, hugging me. 'You remember Otis Kone?'

I took Otis's hand. 'Sure.' I gave it a good squeeze, too. 'Sure I remember Otis Kone. Otis comes up from California every summer to try and get my goat.' To which Otis says, 'It's not your goat I'm after, Granny,' wiggling his eyebrows, then made to reach for me. I spronged his fat little fingers with a clippie harder'n I meant. He howled and duckfooted around the hall like Groucho. I told him to get his pointed head in out of the hall before somebody called the Humane Society. He slunk past so low I had to laugh in spite of myself. He is a clown. I was about to apologize for ragging him when the third fellow glided into sight.

'Grandma, this is my longtime friend M'kehla,' Devlin says, 'and his son Toby.'

'Mrs . . . ?' he asks. I tell him it's Whittier and he bows and says, 'It's Montgomery Keller-Brown, Mrs Whittier. The name M'kehla was . . . what would you say, Dev? a phase?' Then he smiles back at me and holds out his hand. 'Everyone has told me about Great-Grandma. I'm very honoured.'

He was even grander than through the field glasses: tall, straight-backed, and features like the grain in a polished wood, a rare hardwood, from some far-off land (though I could tell by his voice he was as country southern as I was). Most of all, though, with a set to his deep dark gaze like I never saw on another earthly being. I found myself fiddling at my collar buttons and mumbling howdy like a little girl.

'And this man-child,' he says, 'is called October.'

I let go the hand, feeling relieved, and looked to the little feller. About five years old and cute as a bug, squinting bright up at me from behind his daddy's robe. I lean down at him. 'Was that when you was born, honey? October?' He don't move a hair. I'm used to how little kids first take how I look, but his daddy says, 'Answer Mrs Whittier, October.' I say, 'It's all right. October don't know if this ugly old woman is a good witch who's going to give him one of her taffy-babies or a bad witch gonna eat him up,' and stuck my false teeth out at him. That usually gets them. He eases out of the shrouds of his daddy's robe. He didn't smile but he opened his eyes wide enough so I suddenly seen what it was made them so strangely bright.

'Toby is the name I like best,' he says.

'Okay, Toby, let's get some candy before that Otis consumes it all.'

We all come in and I got refreshments. The men chattered about my apartment and low-income housing before they got around to what they had come about, the Worship Fair. I let little Toby look through the field glasses while my grandson showed me a little programme of what was going to be happening. I said it looked like it was going to be a real nice affair. Otis dug down into one of his big pockets and come up with a handbill of his own that said ARE YOU PREPARED? with a picture of him in a priest's outfit. He was looking up at the sky through the tube out of a roll of toilet tissue, his mouth saying in big black letters 'THE CHICKENWIRE PARACHUTE IS COMING.' I knew it was just more of Otis's nonsense but I folded it up, put it in my overnight bag, and told him I was *always* prepared. And that I notice *he* is, *too*, and reach down like to zip up his baggy old pants. He turns his back to do it himself, ears red as peppers. *Some*body's got to teach these city kids, I tell Mr Keller-Brown, and he laughs. My grandson hefts at my bag and says, 'Unh, who do you usually get to carry your purse?' I told him, 'Don't razz a woman about her essentials,' and if he didn't think he was stout enough to handle it I bet little Toby could. The little boy put the glasses right down and came and started to lug at the purse. I says, 'Aint we the good little helper, though?'

Mr Keller-Brown smiles and says, 'We work on being the good helper, don't we, Tobe?' and the little fellow nodded back.

'Yes, Daddy.'

I couldn't help but gush a little bit. 'What a change from most of the little kids you see being let go hog wild these days, what a gratifying change.'

The main elevator was still being used to clear out the collection of metal they found when they opened poor Mr Fry's apartment, so we had some wait for the other one. I said I hoped we didn't miss the Brass family. Devlin says we got plenty of time. He said did I know that Mr Keller-Brown was part of a gospel singing group himself? I says, Oh? What are you called? Because I might have heard them on KHVN. Mr Keller-Brown says they were called the Birds of Prayer but he doubted I'd heard them, not on AM.

The elevator arrived with Mrs Kennicut from 19 and the two Birwell sisters. I told them good afternoon as I was escorted on
268

by a big black Arab. You could have knocked their eyes off with a broomstick. Otis gave them each one of his handbills, too. Nobody says a thing. We went down a few floors, where a maintenance man pushed on carrying a big pry bar much to Mrs Kennicut's very apparent relief. He don't say anything either, but he hefts his pinch bar to his shoulder like a club. So nothing will do but Otis take out his sword and hold it on his shoulder, too.

We slid on down, packed tight and tense. I thought Boy, is *this* gonna cause a stink around me for months to come – when, from below, I felt this little hand slip up into mine and heard a little voice say, 'It's crowdy, Grandma. Pick me up.' And I lifted him up, and held him on my hip the rest of the ride down, and carried him right on out through that old lobby, black curls, brown skin, blue eyes, and all.

I seen some rigs around Eugene – remodelled trailers and elegant hippie buses and whatnot – but I never saw anything on wheels the beat of this outfit of Mr Keller-Brown's. Class-y, I told Mr Keller-Brown, and was it ever. From the five purple birds on the side right down to a little chrome cross hood ornament. Then, *inside*: I swear it was like the living room of a travelling palace: tapestries, a tile floor, even a little stone fireplace! All I could do was gape.

'I just helped minimally,' he explained. 'My wife is the one that put it together.'

I told him he must have quite *some wife*. Otis puts in that Montgomery Keller-Brown did *indeed* have quite some wife, plus his wife had quite some father, who had quite some bank account . . . which might have helped minimally as well. I watched to see how Mr Keller-Brown was going to take this. It must be touchy enough for a Negro man to be married to a white girl, then if she's rich to *boot*. . . . But he just laughed and led me toward the rear of the rig.

'Devlin told me about your back. I've got a chair here I think might suit you, a therapeutic recline-o-lounger.' He pushed back a big leather chair. 'Or there's the bed' – then ran his hand over a deep purple wool bedspread on a king-size bed fixed right into the back of the bus.

'Fiddlesticks,' I says. 'I hope it *never* gets to where I'm not capable of sitting in a chair like a human. I'll sit here awhile, then maybe I'll lay on that bed awhile, as my fancy takes me!'

269

He took my arm and helped me into the chair, my face burning like a beet. I pulled my dress down over my legs and asked them what they were waiting on, anyhow. I could feel twenty storeys of wrinkled old noses pressed to their windows as we drove out of the lot.

Me and my grandson gossiped a bit about what was happening with the family, especially Buddy, who seemed to be getting in two messes with his dairy business as quick as he got out of one. Up front, Otis had found a pint bottle of hooch from one of his big baggy pockets and was trying to share it with Mr Keller-Brown at the wheel. Devlin saw the bottle and said maybe he'd better go up and make sure that addlehead doesn't direct us to *Alaska* or something. I told him, Phooey! I didn't care if they drunk the whole bottle and all three fell out the door; Toby and me could handle things! Devlin swayed away up to the front, and pretty soon the three men were talking a mile a minute.

The boy had his own little desk where he had been piddling with some Crayolas. When Devlin left he put the Crayolas back in the desk and eased out of the seat and sidled back to where I was. He took a *National Geographic* out of the bookcase and made like to read it on the floor beside my chair. I smiled and waited. Pretty quick sure enough his big blue eyes came up over the top of the book and I said peek-a-boo. Without another word he put the book down and crawled right up into my lap.

'Did Jesus do that to your face?' he asks.

'Why, don't tell me you're the only boy who never heard what Tricker the Squirrel done for the Toad?' I says and went into the tale about how Mr Toad used to be very very beautiful in the olden times, with a face that shined like a green jewel. But his bright face kept showing the bugs where he was laid in wait for them. 'He would have starved if it wasn't for Tricker camouflaging him with warts, don'cher see?'

He nodded, solemn but satisfied, and asks me to tell him another one. I started in about Tricker and the Bear and he went off to sleep with one hand holding mine and the other hanging onto my cameo pendant. Which was just as well because the therapeutic recline-o-lounger was about to kill me. I unclasped the gold chain and slipped out from under him and necklace both.

I backed over to the bed and sunk down into that purple wool very near out of sight. It was one of those waterbeds and it got

me like quicksand, only my feet waggling up over the edge.
Very unladylike. But wiggle and waggle as I might I could not
get back up. Every time I got to an elbow the bus would turn
and I would be washed down again. I reminded myself of a fat
old ewe we used to have who would lose her balance grazing on
a slope and roll over and have to lay there bleating with her feet
in the air till somebody turned her right side up. I gave up
floundering and let the water slosh to and fro under me while I
looked over the selection in Mr Keller-Brown's bookcase. Books
on every crazy thing you ever heard of, religions and pyramids
and mesmerism and the like, lots with foreign titles. Looking at
the books made me someway uneasy. Actually, I was feeling
fine. I could've peddled a thousand of these waterbeds on TV:
'Feel twenty years younger! Like a new woman!' I had to giggle;
all the driver would have to do was look in that mirror and see
the New Woman's runny old nylons sticking spraddled into the
air like the hindquarters of a stranded sheep.

And I swear, exactly while I was thinking about it, it seemed I
felt sure enough a heavy dark look brush me, like an actual
touch, Lord, like an actual physical presence.

The next I know we were pulling into the old Nebo place.
Devlin was squeezing my foot. 'Thought for a minute you'd
passed on,' he teased.

He took my arm to help me out of bed. I told him I'd thought
so for a while, too, till I saw that familiar old barn go by the bus
window. 'Then I knew I wasn't in no Great Beyond.'

The bus stopped and I sat down and put on my shoes. Mr
Keller-Brown came back and asked me how my nap was.

'I never had such a relaxing ride,' I tell him. 'Devlin, you put
one of these waterbeds in your convertible and I just might go
gallivantin'.' Mr Keller-Brown says, Well, they were going to
drive to Los Angeles to sing Sunday morn and he would sure be
proud to have me come along. I told him if things kept going my
way like they had been I just might consider it. Little Toby says,
'Oh, *do*, Grandma; do come with us.' I promised all right I
would consider it just as Mr Keller-Brown scooped him up from
the recline-o-lounger, swinging him high. I see he's still got a-
holt of my pendant.

'What's this?' Mr Keller-Brown asks. He has to pry it from
the little tyke's fingers. 'We better give this back to Mrs Whittier,

Tobe.' He hands me the necklace but I go over and open the little desk top and drop it in amongst the Crayolas.

'It's Toby's,' I told them, 'not mine.' I said an angel came down and gave it to Toby in his dreams. Toby nods sober as an owl and says Yeah, Daddy, an angel, and adds – because of the cameo face on it was why, I guess – 'A *white* angel.'

Then Otis hollers, 'Let's boogie for Jesus!' and we all go out.

We'd parked kind of on the road because the parking area (what *used* to be Emerson T's best permanent pasture) was full to overflowing – cars, buses, campers, and every sort of thing. The Worship Fair was going like a three-ring circus. There was people as thick as hair on a dog sitting around, strolling around, arguing, singing. A long-haired skinny young fellow without shoes or shirt was clamping a flyer under every windshield wiper, and a ways behind him another longhair was sticking CHRIST'S THE ONE to the bumpers and sneaking off the flyers when the first kid wasn't looking. The first one caught the second and there then ensued a very hot denominational debate. Otis went over with his sword to straighten it all out and pass out some flyers of his own.

Across the orchard I could see they'd built a stage on the foundation where the house used to stand. At the microphone a girl was playing a zither and singing scripture in a nervous shaky voice. Devlin asked me if I knew the verse she was singing and playing. I says I thought the singing vas verse than the playing, but it vas a toss-up.

Back behind the stage we found Betsy and the kids. The kids wanted to give me my presents right off but Betsy told them to wait for the cake. The men went off to take care of getting the next act onstage and I went off with Betsy and the kids to look how their garden already was coming up. Caleb led Toby on ahead through the gate, hollering, 'I'll show *you* something, Toby, that I bet you don't have in *your* garden.' And Betsy told me that it was a mama Siamese, had her nest in the rhubarb.

'She just has one kitten. She had six hidden out in the hay barn but Devlin backed the tractor over five of them. She brought the last one into the garden. He's old enough to wean but that mama cat just won't let him out of the rhubarb.'

We strolled along, looking how high the peas were and how the perennials had stood the big freeze. When we got to the

272

rhubarb there was little Toby amongst the leaves hugging the kitten and grinning for all he was worth.

'That's the first time I seen the little scoot smile,' I told Betsy.

'Toby can't have our kitten, can he, Mom?' Caleb asks. Betsy says if it's all right with his folks it was most decidedly all right with her. I said with all the traffic maybe we'd better leave the kitty in the garden until he asks *his* mama. The smile went away but he didn't turn loose. He stood there giving us a heart-tugging look. Betsy said he could carry it if he was careful. 'We'll ask M'kehla,' she says.

All the rest of the afternoon Toby hung on to that cat for dear life, Caleb worrying at him from one side and the anxious mama cat from the other.

Sherree took me in to show me her new curtains and we all had some mint tea. We could hear things out at the stage getting worked up. We moseyed back just as an all-boy chorus from Utah was finishing up. People had commenced to push in towards the stage so's it was pretty thick, but the kids had saved me a nice shady spot with a blanket and some of those tie-dyed pillows.

I didn't see Devlin or Mr Keller-Brown, but that Otis, he was impossible to miss. He was reeling around in front of the stage making a real spectacle of himself, getting all tripped up in his sword, which was worked round between his legs, hollering Hallelujah and Amen and Remember Pearl Harbor. And somebody had spray-painted across the rump of his baggy pants: 'The Other Cheek'. I told Betsy he hadn't better turn that other cheek to *me* if he knew what was good for him.

The announcer was one of the local ministers. After the all-boys from Utah he asked if we couldn't have a little quiet and a little respect – he said this right at Otis, too – 'a little respect for one of the all-time great gospel groups of all time: The Sounding Brass!' I says good, just in time, and sits me down on one of them pillows.

It started just like in Colorado Springs; a gong was rung backstage, soft and slow at first, then faster and faster and louder and louder. It's very effective. Even Otis set down. The gonging rose and rose until you thought the very sky was gonna open and, when you thought you couldn't stand it a moment more, made one last hard loud bang and they came running on stage and went right into 'Ring Them Bells', the world-famous Sounding Brass.

At first I thought we all had been tricked! The Sounding Brass? These five old butterballs? Why, the Sounding Brass is tall and lean with natural red hair that shines like five halos, not these sorry old jokes. Because I mean to tell you the men didn't have a hundred scraggly old white hairs divided between the four of them! Plus the woman was wearing a wig looked like it had been made out of wire and rusted. And I'm darned if she didn't have on a minidress! I could see the veins from fifty feet away.

I finally just shook my head; it was them, all right. All their movements and gestures were exactly those I remembered. But it looked like they'd been set to moving and then forgot the grease. And their voices, they were just *horrible*. I don't mean old – I know a lot of older groups who sing fine, creaks, whistles, and all – I mean *thin, hollow*, like whatever had been there had been scraped away and left five empty shells. I recall reading how they'd had a lot of income tax problems; maybe that done it. But they were surely pathetic. They finished a couple of songs and people give them a little hand of pure charity. Then Jacob Brass stepped to the microphone.

'Thank you and buh-*less* you all,' he says. 'Now, the next number . . . well, we *hear* from *reliable sources* that it is the *favourite* of a very fine lady out there having her birthday on this beautiful spring day. *Eighty-six years young*. So puh-*raise* the Lord this Good Friday song is especially *ded*-icated to our Good Friday Birthday Girl, Mrs Rebecca Whittier!'

I wanted to dig a hole and crawl in it. And let me tell you: if they sounded bad on their faster numbers they now sounded downright pitiful. To make matters worse that dad-blamed Otis got going again. They'd sing, 'Were you there . . . when they nailed Him to the cross?' and Otis would answer back, 'Not me, youse mugs! I was in Tarzana drinking Orange Juliuses I can prove it!' loud enough the people got to laughing. Which of course only encouraged him.

'Pierced Him in the *side?* Ech. I wasn't there *then*, either. I don't even go t' roller derby.'

The Brass family was so peeved by the laughter that to the secret relief of all they stalked offstage as soon as they finished two choruses, absolutely furious.

274

Betsy says she's sorry my favourite number got messed up and I say me too, but little Toby says, very seriously, that it'll be all right, because *here* comes *his* folks. *Then* did the crowd hoop and holler! The Birds of Prayer was the other end of the stick from the Brass family. They pranced out all in purple, Mr Keller-Brown and another big black fellow with a beard, and three pretty little coloured girls. The fellow with the beard played organ and sung bass, and Mr Keller-Brown played those big native drums and kind of come in now and then, talking to them. The three coloured girls sung and played guitars and shook tambourines. After the Brass family they were like a breath of fresh air. My grandson comes through the crowd toward us, bouncing up and down to the rhythm.

'How'd you like your dedication?' he asks, taking a pillow alongside me so's he can reach the devilled eggs. I tell him it was fine but not a *candle* to them kids singing up there now. He grins, his lips all mustard. 'So you like the Birds better'n the Brass?' A bushel, I say, that they were as good as anything I ever heard on KHVN. But I thought somebody said Mr Keller-Brown's wife was one of the group? He says, 'She is. That's her on the left.' And before I thought I says, 'But what about our little – ' I stopped before I said 'blue-eyed', but I'd said enough. My grandson shrugged and Betsy put a finger to her lips, rolling her eyes over at the little boy sitting there petting his kitty.

I could have bit my stupid tongue off.

Then the next thing that happened was after sundown. After the main of the crowd drove away or drifted off, a bunch of us walked down to the ash grove for my cake. Mr Keller-Brown had pulled his bus down there and the kids had set up a table in front of where the cake was waiting. They sung 'Happy Birthday, Great-Grandma' while Quiston scampered around with a box of matches trying to keep all those candles lit.

'Here!' says I. 'You kids help Grandma blow 'em out before we start the woods a-blaze.'

There was Devlin's three, Quiston, Sherree, and Caleb, and Behema's Kumquat May, and Buddy's Denny and Denise, and the usual passel of Dobbs kids all circled close to be first at the cake. Quite a cluster. I seen little Toby way in the back outside this ring of glowing faces. He was still holding that cat.

'Let Toby in there, Quiston. This many candles gonna need all the breath we can muster. Okay, everybody? One . . .

two . . .' – with all of them drawing a lungful except Toby there, his chin resting between the ears of that Siamese kitty, both of them looking right at me, expressions absolutely the same – 'blow!'

When I could see again, his daddy was standing right where he'd stood, lighting a Coleman lantern. He'd changed out of his purple jumpsuit into his most spectacular outfit so far.

'Goodness me! Aren't you something! You're almost as pretty as this cake.'

Actually, the cake looked like one of them lumpy tie-dye pillows whereas his robe was an absolutely beautiful affair, purple velvet and gold trim and wriggling front and back with some of the finest needlepointing I ever saw – dragons, and eagles, and bulls you could practically hear snorting. He thanked me kindly and did a slow swirl with the lantern held up hissing above him.

'You must've locked your little woman home with needle and thread for about six months,' I says. I'd had a glass of sherry with Betsy before and was feeling feisty.

'Nope,' he says, starting to ladle out paper cups of punch for the kids. 'It only took three months. And I made it.'

'Well, my, *my*,' I says, aiming to tease him was all, 'I never seen anything so delicate done by a man.'

The kids all laugh again but he took it some way wrong and the laugh died off too quick. Instead of responding to my rib he went right back to handing out that punch. To try to smooth over my foolishness I says, 'Go on. I bet your wife *did too* make it.' By way of apology. But before he could accept my effort Otis stumbles up and butts across the front of us to take a Dixie cup.

'Oh, I'll vouch for M'kehla's wife, Grandma, she doesn't make *any*thing.' Otis pours the cup about half full of brandy before he adds, 'Any more.'

The quiet got even quieter. I thought he was going to look two holes in the top of Otis's head. But Otis keeps sniffing his nose down in his booze like he don't notice a thing.

'My first Christian communion and from a Dixie cup,' he moans. 'How rural. At my Bar Mitzvah we drank from at *least* clear plastic.'

After his success aping the Brass family, Otis had got worse and worse, singing and reciting and cutting up. Yet everybody had took it in good humour. Devlin told me once that Otis was

276

like he was because he'd been given too much oxygen at birth, so nobody generally took offence at what he said. But you could tell Mr Keller-Brown was aggravated, too much oxygen or whatever. He reached over and snagged the paper cup out of Otis's hand and threw it hissing into the fire.

'Is this your first communion, Mr Kone? We'll just have to get something more fitting for your first communion.'

I noticed back by the fire his wife's sister stood up from where she'd been talking with my two grandsons and Frank Dobbs.

Mr Keller-Brown turns from Otis and hands me the punch ladle. 'If you'll take over, Mrs Whittier, I'll see if we can't find Mr Kone a more appropriate vessel.'

The sister comes hurrying over and says, 'I'll get it, Montgomery – ' but he says, No, he'd do it, and she stops on a dime. Otis reaches for another cup mumbling something about not to trouble and he says No, it's no trouble and Otis's hand stops just the same way. He still hasn't looked up to Mr Keller-Brown's eyes.

The kids are beginning to get upset, so I say, 'Why, if Mr Kone gets a glass to drink out of, Mr Keller-Brown, oughten *I* get a glass to drink out of?'

Little Sherree, who is a Libra and a smart little peacemaker in her own right, joins in and says, 'Yeah, it's Great-*Grand*ma's birthday.' And the other kids and Toby, too, says yeah, yeah, Grandma gets a glass too! Those eyes lift off Otis and move to me.

'Certainly,' he says, laughing off his temper. 'Forgive me, Mrs Whittier.' He winked to me and jerked his thumb back at Otis by way of explanation. I winked and nodded back to indicate I knew precisely what he meant, that many's the time I wanted to wring that jellyroll's neck myself.

He went into the bus and the kids went back at the cake and ice cream. I never could stand having people fight around me. I've always been handy at oiling troubled waters. Like when I was living with Lena: Devlin and Buddy would get in terrible squabbles over whose turn it was to mow the lawn. While they were fussing I'd go get the lawn mower and mow away till they came sheepfaced out to take over. (More handy than straightforward, to be honest.) So I thought the storm was past when Mr Keller-Brown come back out with three dusty brandy glasses and shared some of Otis's brandy. I blew at the dust and

277

filled mine with the kids' punch and all of us clinked glasses and toasted my birthday. Otis said that he would sympathize with me, being eighty-sixed quite a number of times himself. Everybody laughed and he was down from the hook. Five minutes later he was running off at the mouth as bad as ever.

I opened my little pretties and doodads the kids had made me and gave them all a big hug. Buddy rolled some logs up to the fire. We sat about and sung a few songs while the kids roasted marshmallows. Frank Dobbs stamped around playing the mouth harp while the big black fellow with the beard patted at Mr Keller-Brown's drums. Devlin strummed the guitar (though he never could play worth sour apples) and the fire burnt down and the moon came up through the new ash leaves. Betsy and Buddy's wife took their kids up to the house. Mr Keller-Brown took Toby into the bus, him still hugging the kitty. He brought out a jar of little pellets that he sprinkled into the embers. Real myrrh, he said, from Lebannon. It smelled fresh and sharp, like cedar pitch on a warm fall wind, not sickening sweet like other incense. Then he brought out some pillows and the men settled down to discussing the workings of the universe and I knew it was time for me to go to bed.

'Where's that giant purse of mine?' I whispered to my grandson.

He says, 'It's in the cabin. Betsy has made the bed for you. I'll walk you up that way.' I told him never mind; that the moon was bright and I could walk my way around this territory with a blindfold on anyway, and told them all good night.

The crickets were singing in the ash trees, happy that summer was here. I passed Emerson's old plough; somebody had set out to weld it into a mailbox stand and had apparently give up and just left it to rust in the weeds, half plough and half mailbox. It made me sad and I noticed the crickets had hushed. I was taking my time, almost to the fence, when he was suddenly in front of me – a sharp black pyramid in the moonlight, hissing down at me.

'Backdoor! Don't you never come backdoorin' on me or my little boy *again*, understand? *Never!* Y' under*stand?*'

Of course I was petrified. But, truth to tell, looking back, not utterly surprised. For one thing I knew immediately who it was behind that black pyramid and that hissing gutter drawl. For another, I knew what he was talking about.

'The motherfuckin necklace I let pass 'cause I say "She old. She just old. She don't know." But then to pull the same shit about the motherfuckin *cat* . . . that's back *door!*'

Two big hands from somebody behind grabbed both sides of my head, forcing me to look up at him. Fingers came all the way around over my mouth. I couldn't holler or turn aside or even blink.

'White angel white mother angel, my *ass!* I show *you* white angel!'

And then O sweet Saviour it was like he pulled back the dark blouse of his face. Two breasts came swirling out toward me dropping out and down until the black nipples touched my very eyeballs . . . giving suck . . . milking into me such thoughts and pictures that my mind knew at once not to think or look. Let them slide, I said in my mind, sli-i-ide . . . and I made a picture of rain falling on a duck. This duck splattering around must have come as a shock to him because he blinked. I felt the invisible hands drop from my head and I knew there hadn't been nobody behind me.

'So don' let me catch you – '

The duck run out a great long neck and quacked. He fumbled and blinked again.

'I mean y' better don' try no secret influencs on my *son* again, is all I wanted to tell you. Y' understand? A dude, a father's got to look *out* for his *own*. You understand?'

And was gone back in the bush before I could catch my breath to answer. I hotfooted right on up to the cabin *then* I hope to tell you! And without slowing one iota pulled the shades took two yellow pills got in bed and yanked the covers up over my head. I didn't dare think. I recited in my mind all the scripture I knew, and the words to 'My Country 'Tis of Thee' and 'O Say Can You See'. I was into bread recipes before they took effect.

Just like praying for something, Lord, I don't like to take a pill for sleeping unless it's absolutely necessary. Often's the night I laid awake till dawn listening to the elevators go up and down the Towers rather than take one of these blessed pills. They always make me sleep too long and leave me feeling dopey as a dog for days. Don't even let you dream, usually. But now I found myself dreaming like a fire broke out! It was those thoughts and pictures I'd been given suck with. I hadn't shed them after all. I'd just covered them over like sparks in a mattress. Now they were blazing to life in icy flames, revealing a whole different version of life, and death, and Heaven. Mainly it was this shadow thing – sometimes it was an alligator, sometimes it was a panther or a wolf – rushing through my world and snapping off pieces, all the weak namby-pamby limbs, like snapping off Devlin's hands playing the guitar, or Frank Dobbs's leg while he was striding around, or my tongue from saying little oil-on-the-water fibs. Miss Lawn it lopped off absolutely. And Emerson T, and most of my past. Then it moved ahead, a dark pruning shadow snipping through the years ahead until only the bare cold bones of a future was left, naked, with no more fibs, nor birthday cakes, nor presents and doodads. For ever and evermore. Standing there. And out of this naked thing the heat begins to drain, till the ground was as cold as the soles of its feet and the wind the same temperature as its breathing. It still *was* because it was a true thing, but it was no more than the rock or the wind. And all it could do was stand there gawking into eternity, waiting, in case God might want to use it again. Like an old mule or the ghost of a mule, its meaning spent, its seed never planted and wouldn't have grown anyway because it is a mule, a trick of God.

It saddened me to my very marrow. It seemed I could hear it braying its terrible bleak lonesomeness forever. I wept for it and I wished I could say something, but how can you offer comfort to one of the bleak tricks of God? It brayed louder. Not so bleak, now, nor far-off sounding, and I opened my eyes and sat up in bed. Out the window I saw Otis under the moon, howling and running in circles, way past wishing he'd blown the dust out of *his* brandy glass. Devlin and the others were trying to get him, but he still had his wooden sword and was slashing at them.

'Keep your place. It wasn't me not this wienie *he had no call!* Devlin? Dobbsy? Help me, old chums; he's put the glacier on your old – *he had no justifications I'm already pruned!*'

First begging for help then whacking at them when they came close, screaming like they'd turned into monsters.

'He's trimming me, boys, dontcha see? Me who never so much as – *he had no right you black bastard all I was was just foolish!*'

And get so wound up he'd scream and run right into the fence around the chicken yard. He'd bounce off the fence and hew the men back away from him then he'd howl and run into the wire
280

again. The chickens were squawking, the men hollering, and Otis, Lord Jesus, was going plumb mad. *This isn't just foolishness*, I told myself; this is simon pure unvarnished *madness!* He needs *help*. Somebody to phone somebody. Yet all I could do was watch like it was more of my same cold dream rushing about in the moonlight and chicken feathers, until Otis got his sword snaffled in the wire and the men swarmed on him.

They carried him thrashing and weeping to the house, right past my cabin window. As soon as they were gone from sight I was up out of that bed. Without a further thought on the matter I put on my housecoat and slippers and struck out toward the ash grove. I wasn't scared, exactly. More like unbalanced. The ground seemed to be heaving. The trees was full of faces, and every witch-doctor and conjure-man story I ever heard was tumbling up out of my Ozark childhood to keep me company, but I still wasn't scared. If I let myself get the slightest bit scared, I suspicioned, I'd be raving worse than Otis under the curse of Keller-Brown.

But he wasn't sticking pins in dolls or such like that. He was sitting calm in his therapeutic recline-o-lounger reading one of his big books by the light of the Coleman lamp, a big pair of earphones on his head. Through the bus windows I could hear there was a tape or record or some such playing, of a bunch of men's voices chanting in a foreign tongue. His mouth was moving to the words of the chant as he read. I slapped on the side of the bus stairwell.

'Hello . . . can I come in a minute?'

'Mrs Whittier?' He comes to the door. '*Sure*, man. Come in. Come on in. I'm honoured. Honest.'

He gives me his hand and seems genuinely happy to see me. I told him I had been thinking and if there'd been a misunderstanding I wanted to be the first – But he cuts right in, apologizing himself, how he'd acted abominable and inexcusable and hang on a second. Please. Then held up a big palm while he swirled around to flip a switch on his phonograph. The speakers went off but the tape still turned on the machine. I could hear a tiny chorus chanting out from the earphones on the recline-o-lounger: *Rah. Rah. Rah ree run*. Like that. . . .

'I'm glad you come,' he says. 'I been feeling *ter*rible for the way I acted. There was no excuse for it and I apologize for getting so heavy on you. Please, come on in.'

I told him it was understandable, and that was why I was there. I started to tell him that I had never said anything about the little boy having the kitten without his mom's consent when I glanced back to the waterbed. She wasn't there but the little boy was, lying propped up on a pillow like a ventriloquist doll, his eyes staring at a glass bead strung from the ceiling. He had on his own pair of earphones, and the bead twisted and untwisted.

'Well, I get to apologize first,' I told Mr Keller-Brown. That that was why I'd come. I told him that he'd been com*plete*ly correct, and that I had no right telling his child those kind of whoppers and *deserved* a scolding. The chant went something like *Rah. Rah. Tut nee cum.* Mr Keller-Brown says okay, we've traded apologies. We chums again? I said I guess so. *Rah. Rah. Tut nee eye sis rah cum RAH* and that bead turning slow as syrup on its thread. He says he hopes I'll still consider riding down to LA with them; they'd be honoured. I say it's too bad it ain't to Arkansas; I need to go to Arkansas – for legal business. He says they go to St Louis after Oklahoma City and that's near Arkansas. I says we'll see how I feel tomorrow; it's been a big day. He says good night and helps me back down the steps. I thank him.

At the bus window waving, his face gives me no clue whether he believed it or not. Everything suddenly turned ten times brighter as I felt him withdraw that terrible pruning shadow and return it to its sheath. Now forget it, I told myself, all, and made a picture of the rain stopping and the duck flying off.

I walked through the bright moonlight at the edge of the ash grove. The look of things was headed back to normal. There were crickets in the trees, nothing else. The ground ran level and the night was calm. I had just about convinced myself that it was all over, that it was all just a widder woman's nightmare, nothing more, nothing worse, when I heard the mama Siamese meowing.

The kitten was stuffed under some ash roots and covered with big rocks. I could barely move them. You were right, I told the mama; you should've kept him in the rhubarb. She followed crying as I carried it up to the cabin. I kept talking to her as I walked, and fingering the poor stiffening little kitty to see if it was cut or broke or what. And when I found it at the furry throat I was reminded of the time I was picking pears in the

282

dusk as a kid of a girl in Penrose, Colorado, and reached up to get what I thought was sure a funny fuzzy-feeling pear, when it suddenly uncurled and squeaked and flew away and I fell off the ladder with bat bites all over my hand . . . was what I thought as my fingers recognized the cameo and chain knotted around its neck. O Lord, I cried, what have I got into now? And tossed it under the cabin porch without even trying to break that chain. Then I come inside and took another pill out of my bag and got right down on my knees for a sign.

And a dumb old rooster just crowed. Okay. Okay then. *If not a sign Lord Jesus to make me certain then how about the strength to act like i am for it looks to me like i am left with no choice but to go ahead along a fortress or harbour Amen Lord amen –*

(to be continued)

Now We Know How Many Holes It Takes to Fill the Albert Hall

In the waning days of 1968, for some reason never very specific and now nearly obscured by time, the prime movers from the Dead Centre made arrangements with the Beatles at Apple to send over to London a sampling of psychedeloids.

A kind of cultural lend-lease, heads across the water and all that.

There were thirteen of us in all – hippies, hoopies, and harpies; Hell's Angels and their hogs; a few serious managers with lots of plots and proposals . . . one prankster without plan one.

I was happy to be getting out of the U.S. That book about me and my Kool Aid cronies had just come out and I felt the hot beam of the spotlight on me. It burned like a big ultraviolet eye. The voltage generated by all this attention scared me a little and titillated me a lot, and I needed a breather from it before I became an addict, or a casualty. *Stand in this spotlight, feel this eye pass over you. You never forget it. You are suddenly changed, lifted, singled out, elevated and alone, above any of your old bush-league frets of stage fright, nagging scruples, etc. Self-consciousness and irresolution melt in this beam's blast. Grace and power surge in to take their place. Banging speed is the only thing even close. Drowsing protoplasm snaps instantly to Bruce Lee perfection – enter the dragon. But there's the scaly rub, right? Because if you go around to the other end of that eye and look through at the star shining there so elevated, you see that this adoring telescope has a cross hair built in it, and notches in the barrel filed for luminaries: Kennedy . . . King . . . Joplin . . . Hemingway. . . .*

Anyway, we headed to London, flying high (as Country Joe put it) all the way. As the DC-8 began to hum down through the thick English fog, everybody realized that after our transatlantic antics a customs check was almost certainly coming up, and what couldn't be flushed had better be swallowed.

Up to the bustling British customs table we floated, a big-eyed
284

baker's dozen from America, in leather and furs and cowboy hats and similar fashionable finery. The weary officer sighed sorely at the sight, then politely searched us for three hours, even the cylinders of the two Harley-Davidsons. It was well into the afternoon by the time our fleet of taxis headed for London, escorted through the wrong-side-of-the-road traffic by Angels Old Bert and Smooth Sam Smathers on their two huge choppers. It was clammy grey twilight by the time we all arrived at Apple.

There was a small flock of the faithful at the door, waiting with that radiant patience of reverent pilgrims. Frisco Fran, a long blond mama of thirty-five, with a feeling for Old Bert and Old Bert's new Harley, and a $6,000 mink coat over her T-shirt and greasy jeans, looked at the little gaggle of fans on the Savile Row steps, then up at the crisp white office building, and observed, 'I feel like I'm going to see the Pope, or something.'

In the outer lobby a chubby receptionist welcomed us with a cheeky wink for the men and an embossed invitation for each of us. She looked like Lulu in *To Sir, With Love*. After a confirming call from higher up, she let us into lobby #2, where all the rock & roll managers greeted each other – Yanks, Limeys, even a visiting Frog – embracing and slapping five and jiving each other rock-&-roll-wise. This got us through lobby 2's door into the crimson-carpeted keep of lobby #3, where George Harrison finally came down to shake everybody's hand and escort us into the very core of the Apple organization – endless offices, wandering halls with gold records on all the walls, a huge recording studio in the basement that looked like Disney had designed it for Captain Nemo and hired Hugh Hefner to decorate it – finally to a doorless doorway upstairs opening on to a large room that we could use as our digs, we were told, during our stay. All eyes popped at the accommodations. The room was full of food: roasted pigs suckling apples, smoked turkeys, cheeses, breads, cases of champagne and ale stacked to the ceiling . . . for the big Apple Christmas party coming up, we were told. Old Bert immediately dropped his ratty bedroll to the floor and booted it beneath a table full of glazed goose and stuffing.

'Looks like home to me,' he proclaimed.

Ringo dropped in for 'arf a mo' to welcome us, and once we thought we caught a glimpse of Paul down the hall, though some said it wasn't Paul, that Paul was in New York getting engaged.

But he *was* bright-eyed, lovable, and barefoot so it might have been Paul. Also, he was small.

'They're all so . . . so . . .' – Spider, a tall ex-UCLA-track star gone hip and hairy and thirty, searched for the precise word – '*diminutive*.'

'They're all the size I thought Ringo was,' Smooth Sam added.

'I know,' said the mama in mink, eyes shining with tender solicitude. 'It makes me want to hold an umbrella over them, or something.'

We didn't see John until later, at the famous Apple Christmas Debacle. What happened that night has been run down in a bunch of books, both pro-Yank and anti, so no one else needs to go into that. I only want to give you the setting for Lennon's entrance, for drama's sake . . .

As the day drifted toward the festive eve ahead, we drifted out of our little food-filled office to stroll the Christmasy London streets and drink stout in the pubs – work up an appetite for the feast to come. When we ambled back to 3 Savile Row and past the pack of cheeky fans that cluttered the steps with their little autograph books (they *all* looked like Lulu) and through lobbies #1 and #2 to the hallowed lobby #3, we found that another coterie of Yanks had established a beachhead right in the middle of the lush crimson carpet. What kind of pull they had used to bore this deep into Apple I couldn't imagine, because they were even scruffier than we were. There were half a dozen big bearded dudes with ragged grins, a bunch of naked noisy kids, and one woman – a skinny redhead on the sinewy side of thirty sporting a faded blue dress of hillbilly homespun with matching hicky twang.

'We're the Firedog Family,' she informed us. 'We come here to see the Beatles all the way from Fort Smith, Arkansas. I had this dream me and John was running side by side through the electric-blue waters of the Caribbean and he looked at me and says "Come Together." "Ticket to Ride" was playin'. We was naked. We was on acid. We ran right out of the water right up into the sky. And my given name is Lucy Diamond. Let's chant again, children.'

The pack of kids stopped fussing and settled themselves obediently in a circle and began chanting.

'*John and Yo-ko Ring-go too-ooo. John and Yo-ko Ring-go too-ooo. . . .*'

286

The woman snaked across the carpet to the rhythm, all knees and elbows and freckles. 'We *know* they is in the building. One of the kids was running in the hall and seen them carrying a big red sack. This chant will bring us together.'

Her eyes fluttered shut a moment at the divine prospect, then she stopped dancing and gave us a look faded as her blue dress.

'Y' know, don't you, that the Beatles is the most blessed people on earth? They are. For instance, how many times have you been coming down with the blues and heard a Beatles tune come on the radio and thought to yourself, "God bless the Beatles". Huh? That's exactly what I said when I saw *Yellow Submarine* after my last abortion. "God bless the Beatles." And how many folks all over the world have done the same thing more or less, blest the Beatles? So, you see – they're all saints. Blessed saints. I mean *who* on this miserable earth, in this day and age, who can you name that has been blest more times than the Beatles?'

We couldn't think of a soul. We were hungry and tired and not very interested in playing Name the Saints. When the door was finally opened to us and we left lobby #3 the kids were still chanting '*John and Yo-ko Ring-go too-ooo*' and the woman was swaying and the bearded dudes were nodding to the beat. We walked up the hall to our assigned room without a word, stomachs grumbling, only to find the food had been completely removed. Nothing left but the smell. It seemed like a hint. Grumpily, Old Bert gathered his bedroll from beneath the empty table.

'Blessing them's all right, but I don't guess you have to get right up in their faces to do it.'

'Yeah,' Frisco Fran agreed. 'Let's cut.'

Back down in the main sanctum the night's crowd was gathering – toffs in worsted flannel and sandalwood cologne, birds in bright beads and bouffants by Vidal Sassoon, executive types in tie-dyed Nehru shirts and Day-Glo tennies – and the champagne was flowing. Old Bert decided a little snack might be nice before leaving. His nose told him the grub couldn't be far away. He sniffed up to a parted door where a natty lad in a plaid weskit was positioned as guard.

'Whatsye, myte?' Bert had picked up a nice cockney accent in the afternoon pubs. 'That I grabs me a drumstick for the road?'

'Cawn't, I don't think,' the boy answered, nervous and vague.

287

'Supposed to save it for after. The invited, rather. You understand – for later.'

'We *are* invited, old sport.' Bert produced the card we'd been issued. 'And maybe we ain't staying till later. *Further*more' – he jerked a thick-knuckled thumb over his shoulder, indicating a place in the past – 'I ain't ate since the airport.'

The boy looked at the thumb with all that carbon and grease still under the thumbnail from reassembling the bikes, and at the leather wristband with its battered studs, and at the big, vein-laced forearm with those terrible tattoos of knives and nooses, and it appeared to me that he was about to see his way clear to advancing Old Bert an early taste of turkey. But just then one of the tie-dyed higher-ups sidled by in long muttonchops and a snide smile. He was eating a macaroon.

'Don't give it to them, Clayburn,' this colourful creature advised through a long bony nose as he chewed his cookie. 'I don't care how much chanting they do.' Then, very foolishly, he added, 'They're nothing but leeches and mumpers anyway.'

'What was that, myte?' Bert asked with a wide grin, turning slowly from the turkey to what promised to be juicier fare. 'What did you sye?'

'I said, "Leeches and mumpers."'

Pow! The executive went somersaulting backward all the way to the wall, where he slowly slid down in a pile against the baseboard and lay there, like a rumpled rainbow. The room suddenly polarized, all the Englishmen springing to one side of the carpet to surround their clobbered countryman in an instant display of British pith, all the Yanks to the other.

'Anybody else,' Bert asked the group glaring at us from across the room, 'thinks we're leeches or mumpers?' – in a challenge so specific that everybody knew it would have to be answered or none of the home team would ever be able to look the statue of Admiral Nelson in his steely eye again. I took off my watch and put it in my pocket. The music stopped. The two factions tightened and gathered, readying for the rumble.

It was into this smouldering scene, right between these two forces about to clash, that John Lennon came, in a red Santa Claus suit and a silly white beard.

'Awright, then,' he said, not loud but very clear, and reasonable, and unsmiling, that thin, bespectacled face pale yet intensely bright, polished by more time spent beneath the blast

of that high-voltage beam than any face I have ever seen, the thin hands coming out of the white fur cuffs to hold back the two sides of the room, like Moses holding back the waters –
'That's enough.'

And it was. The rumble didn't erupt. He stopped it, just like that. Old Bert was so impressed that he apologized at once to everyone, even bent down to help the young executive brush the bloody coconut crumbs out of his muttonchops. Everybody laughed. A cork popped. The music resumed. Yoko emerged from behind John, as though cloned from his yuletide image, in matching beard and red Santa suit with a big red sack over her shoulder. She began passing out gifts. Blond Mama Fran decided to take off her mink and stick around awhile after all. Spider began to eye the nervous Lulus. The caterers swept in with trays of sliced meats and pickled crab apples. The party went on.

Oo blah dee.

After New Year's Day, I returned to London with my family. We took a flat in Hampstead and I tubed daily to Apple to work on a spoken-word record that was to be called Paperback Records. It never happened. Fell apart. Administrative shake-ups. I didn't mind. It was a fun time, hanging around the action in the Apple orchard in those days when the bounty was still unblighted.

I saw John Lennon every once in a while after that first night – on the roof watching the sky, in the halls, playing the piano in the studio, at Albert Hall for his over-hyped 'Alchemical Wedding' when he crawled into a big bag with Yoko for forty uncomfortable minutes of public humping while the packed and petulant house hooted and whistled and called out things like ''Ow's the revolootion goin' then, John?' – but never again saw anything as bright and clear and courageous as when he stepped between the two sides at the Christmas party.

He was something.

When he said 'Peace,' even the warring angels listened.

But this isn't a nickel valentine to a dead superstar. What this story is really about is not so much John Lennon as about all the stuff his passing stirred up around our farm, effluvia both bygone and yet to be, tangible and chimeral . . . mainly about these three visitations I had that week of his death, like the three ghosts from *A Christmas Carol.*

The first came the day before the killing, Sunday evening,

289

while we were waiting for my mom and Grandma Whittier to come out for supper. This spectre was the easiest to comprehend and deal with. In fact, he was almost classic in his immediate comprehensibility; versions of this spook have probably been around since the first campfire. He poked his bearded kisser in out of the night, all shaggily a-grin. He had a bottle of screw-top Tokay in his right hand, a battered black boot in his left, and a glint in his gummy eyes that could have been bottled and displayed in the Bureau of Standards: the Definitive Panhandler Come-on Glint.

'Greetings the house!' he called through a curtain of phlegm. 'This is Bible Bill, ol' Bible Bill, come in the name of the Main Redeemer, praise Him. Anybody home?'

I didn't have to give it a second thought. 'No,' I said.

'Dev? Brother Deboree? Greetings, brother, greetings!' He held forth the Good Book and the bad wine. 'Compliments of Bible Bill, these – '

'No,' I repeated, pushing right on past the offerings. I put one hand on his chest and held the door open with the other, pushing. Behind him, I could make out an entourage of shivering teenagers, unhappy in the December wind. Bill wasn't pleased with the prospect of getting shoved back out in it, either.

'Dev, don't be like this, dammit all! I promised these kids – '

'No.' I pushed.

'Give it up, dude,' one of the teenagers said to him. 'Can't you see you're bugging the man?'

'But *kin*folks – '

'But my butt,' another kid joined in. 'Let's go.'

With me pushing and them pulling we moved him back to the Toyota they'd come in, him hollering, 'But *cousins! Brothers! Comrades!*' and me hollering back, 'But *no! No! No!*'

The second visitation was a little more complex. For one thing, he was likeable. He showed up the next morning while I was out in the field with Dobbs, fixing the fence where the cows had broken through during the night. Whenever it's real cold Ebenezer likes to lead her herd in an assault on the barnyard, hoping to break into the hay sheds (for cussedness and comfort more than food), and it was real cold. The ruts and tracks raised by their midnight raid were still hard as iron. Dobbs and I were long-johned and overalled and leather-gloved and still too cold to be able to effectively hammer in staples. After a half-hour's

290

work we would have to head to the house for a gin and tonic to warm us up. After the third try, we haywired a hasty patch and came in for good.

I saw him standing by our stove, bent to the open door, moving his hooked hands in and out of the heat the way a man does when they're numbed so stone hard he's afraid to thaw them back to feeling. I left him alone. I peeled out of my overalls and boots and mixed Dobbs and me a drink. The guy never moved. When Betsy came downstairs she told me she had let him in because he was obviously about to freeze to death and didn't seem the slightest bit worried about the prospect.

'He says he's got something for you.'

'I'll bet he does,' I said and went over to talk to him. His hand was as hard as it looked, a calloused claw, beginning to turn red with the heat. In fact he was turning red all over, beginning to glow and grin.

He was about thirty-five or forty, like Bible Bill, with a lot of hard mileage in his eyes and scraggly hair on his face. But his hair was the colour of berries on a holly bough, the eyes sharp and green as the leaves, merry. He said he was called – no lie! – John the Groupie, and that we had met once fifteen years ago at the Trips Festival, where I had given *him* something.

'I got good and turned on,' he confided with a big limber-shouldered shrug, 'and I guess I never been able to get turned off.'

I asked him what in the dickens was he doing this far north at Christmastime with nothing on but ventilated sneaks and knee-less jeans and a Sunset Strip pink pearl-button shirt? He grinned and shrugged his carefree shrug again and told me he'd caught a ride with a hippie kid outta LA over the Grapevine, and the kid said he was headed all the way to Eugene, Oregon, so John the Groupie says, well, what the hell . . . never been to Oregon. Ain't that where Old Man Deboree hangs his hat? Maybe I'll go check him out. Met him once, you know, over a tab or two, ho ho.

'Besides,' he added, trying to get that big red claw down a hip pocket, 'I got something here I knew you'd want.'

This made me back off two steps, I didn't care how carefree his shrug or merry his eye. If there was one thing I had learned in Egypt, it was Don't take nothing free, especially from ingratiating types who come on 'My friend *please* be accept this wonderful geeft, my nation to yours, no charge' – pressing into your palm a ratty little scarab carved out of a goat pellet or something, a little hook by which the hustler can attach himself to you. And the less you want the goddamned thing he forces on you the more attached he becomes.

'I got right here,' John the Groupie announced proudly, holding out a wad of white paper, 'Chet Helms's *phone number*.'

I told him I had no need for Chet Helms's phone number, that I had never needed Chet Helms's phone number, even during Chet Helms's San Fran Family Dog promoter days, hadn't even seen Chet Helms in ten years!

John stepped close, becoming intimate.

'But I mean this isn't Chet Helms's *answering* service, man,' he made me to realize, delicately holding forth the little chit like it might have been a spindle of the purest Peruvian. 'This is Chet Helms's *home* phone number.'

'No,' I said, holding both hands high and away from the offered morsel, which I wanted about as much as I wanted a goat turd or a hit off Bible Bill's bottle. 'No.'

John the Groupie shrugged and put it down on the coffee table.

'In case you get eyes for it later,' he said.

'No.' I picked it up and put it back in his hand and folded the freckled fingers over it. 'No, no, no. And I'll tell you now what I have to offer: I'll give you something to eat and I'll let you sleep in my cabin, out of sight. Tomorrow I'll give you a coat and a hat and put you back on I-5, on the southbound side, with your thumb out.' I fixed him with my sternest scowl. 'My God, what a thing to do – just showing up at a man's place, no invitation, no sleeping bag, not even any damned socks. It's not courteous! I know it's inhospitable to turn a wayfarer out like this, but goddammit, it's discourteous to be tripping around unprepared this way.'

He had to agree, smiling. 'Like I said, I never been able to get turned off the trip. I guess I do get turned *out* a lot, though, ho ho hee.'

'I don't want to hear about it,' I kept on. 'All I want you to know is I'm offering warmth and sustenance and a way back to Venice Beach if I *don't* have to listen to you run any numbers on me, savvy?'

He put the paper back in his pocket. 'I savvy like a mother-fucker, man. Just point me to this outasight abode.'

Like I say – likeable. Just your basic stringy, carrot-topped, still-down-and-it-still-looks-up-to-me acidhead flower child gone to seed. Probably no dope he hasn't tried and, what's more, none he wouldn't try again. Still grooving, still tripping, he didn't give a shit if he was barefoot in a blizzard. I left him rolled up in two cowhides, thumbing through the latest *Wonder Warthog* while the pine flame roared and rattled in the rusty little cabin woodstove like a caged Parsi firedemon.

When he wandered back up to the house it was dark. We had finished supper and were on the other side of the room watching *Monday Night Football*. I didn't turn but I could see Betsy in the mirror setting him a place. Quiston and Caleb had been duck hunting the day before, and we'd had two mallards and a widgeon for supper, stuffed with rice and filberts. A whole mallard and two half-eaten carcasses were left. John ate the mallard and picked all three carcasses so clean that red ants wouldn't have bothered over the leavings. Plus a whole loaf of bread, a pot of rice big enough for a family of Cambodian refugees, and most of a pound of butter. He ate slowly and with bemused determination, not like a glutton eats but like a coyote who never knows how long it might be before the next feast so he better get down all he can hold down. I kept my eyes on the game, not wanting to embarrass him by letting on I was watching.

It was the Dolphins against the Patriots, the fourth quarter. It was an important game to both teams, as they fought for a playoff berth, and a tense series of downs. Suddenly Howard Cosell interrupted his colourful commentary and said a funny thing, apropos of nothing discernible on the screen. He said, 'Yet, however egregious a loss might seem to either side at this point in time, we must never lose sight of the fact . . . that this is only a football game.'

A very un-Howard-Cosell-like thing to say, I thought, and turned up the sound. After a few moments of silence Howard announced over the play-action fake unfolding on the field that John Lennon had been shot and killed outside his apartment in New York.

I turned to see if John the Groupie had heard the news. He had. He was twisted toward me in his seat, his mouth open, the last duck carcass stopped midway between tooth and table. We

293

looked into each other's eyes across the room, and our roles fell away. No more the scowling landowner and the ingratiating tramp, simply old allies, united in sudden hurt by the news of a mutual hero's death.

We could have held each other and wept.

The weather broke that night. It rained awhile, then cleared. The sun sneaked through the overcast after breakfast, looking a little embarrassed for the short hours it had been getting away with during this solstice time. Betsy bundled John up and gave him a knit cap, and I drove him to the freeway. I let him off near the Creswell ramp. We shook hands and I wished him luck. He said not to worry, he'd get a ride easy. Today. I saw somebody stop for him before I had gotten back across the overpass. On the way home I heard a report on *Switchboard*, our local community-access programme, that there was no need to call in to try to scam rides today, that everybody was picking everybody up, today.

When I got home the phone was ringing. It was a Unitarian Minister from San Francisco who was trying to put together some kind of Lennon memorial in Golden Gate Park, needed some help. I thought he was calling to ask me to come speak or something – deliver a eulogy. I started saying that, sorry, much as I'd like to I just couldn't make it, I had a fence to fix and kids' Christmas programmes to attend and so forth . . . but he said, oh no, he wasn't wanting that kind of help.

'What is it you need, then?' I asked.

'I need some organizational help,' he said. 'I've never done anything like this before. I need to find out about permits and the like. So I was wondering if you might know how I could get in touch with Chet Helms? The guy who did all those big be-ins? You happen to have Chet Helms's phone number anywhere?'

Many such memorable scenes from the last decade and a half of our onreeling epic have been underscored by the Beatles music: 'With a Little Help from My Friends' was playing when Frank Dobbs and Houlihan and Buddy helped hold my acified atoms together one awful night. During my six-month sojourn in the outer reaches of the California penal system, I used a Beatles record as my mantra, a litany to lead me safely through the Bardo of Being Busted. The record was 'All You Need Is Love'. I listened to it so many times that I came to count the number of times the word 'love' is used in the mix. It was 128 times, as I recall.

Now, as I run my eyes over these three ragged runes of Christmastime in the Eighties, looking at them for whatever message or augury they might offer, I cannot help but view them to the accompaniment of Guru Lennon's musical teachings.

The lesson learned from Bible Bill and his ilk is simple. I already had it pat: Don't encourage a bum. Attention is like coke to these bottomless wraiths – the more they get the more they want.

The epiphany taught by the visitation of John the Groupie is simple enough on the surface: Don't forget the Magical Summer of Love in the Chilly Season of Reagan. I think even John the Limey would have agreed with this interpretation.

What complicates the lesson is that in its wake washes up the third apparition.

This final visitor is still a mystery to me. I knew how to deal with Bible Bill. I know now how I should have dealt with John the Groupie. But I still don't know what to do do about my third phantasm, the Ghost, I fear, of Christmases to Come: Patrick the Punk.

He was on the road alongside my pasture, shuffling along in army fatigues and jacket and carrying a khaki duffel over his shoulder. I was headed to town to pick up some wiring and exchange a video tape. When I saw him I knew there was no place he could be headed but mine. I stopped the Merc and rolled down the window.

'Mr Deboree?' he said.

'Get in,' I said.

He tossed the duffel in the back and climbed in beside me, heaving an unhappy sigh.

'Fuckin Christ, it's cold. I didn't think I'd make it. My name is Patrick.'

'Hi, Pat. How far have you come?'

'All the way from New York State on a fuckin Trailways bus. Took every nickel I had. But fuck, you know? I mean I *had* to split. That East Coast – shit, all they want to do is fuck you over or suck you dry. I'm dry, Mr Deboree. I'm broke and I'm hungry and I haven't been able to sleep in three days from this fuckin' poison oak.'

He was only a few years past voting age, with a soft unblinking stare and a grey mould of first whiskers on his chin. The whole right half of his face was covered with white lotion.

'How'd you get poison oak?'

'Running through the woods from this murderous old bitch in Utah or Idaho or someplace.' He dug a Camel out of a new pack and stuck it in his swollen mouth. 'She thought I was trying to rip off her fuckin' pickup.'

'Were you?'

He didn't even shrug. 'Hey, I was terminally drug with that fuckin' bus. Who can sleep with all that starting and stopping? Bums and winos, maybe, but not me.'

I still hadn't resumed driving. I realized I didn't know what to do with him. I didn't like having him in the car with me – he stank of medicine and nicotine and sour unvented adrenalin, of rage – and I didn't want to let him stroll onto my place.

'I came to see you, Mr Deboree,' he said without looking at me. He seemed in a kind of shock. The Camel just hung there.

'What the hell for? You don't know me.'

'I've heard you help people. I'm fucked and sucked dry by those vampires, Mr Deboree. You've got to help me.'

I started to drive, away from the farm.

'I never read *Sometimes a Cuckoo Nest*, but I seen the flick. I did read what you said in the *Whole Earth Catalogue* about believing in Christian mercy. Myself, I'm an antagnostic, but I believe everybody has a right to believe in mercy. And I need some, Mr Deboree, you can fuckin believe that! I'm no wino bum. I'm intelligent. I've got talent. I had my own little C & W group and was doing real good for a while, but then, them fuckin vampires – I mean, man, you know what they – ?'

'Never mind. I don't want to hear. It'll just depress me. If you'll promise to spare me your tale of woe I'll buy you lunch in town.'

'Lunch isn't what I had in mind, Mr Deboree.'

'What exactly did you have in mind?'

'I'm an artist, not a mooch. An experienced singer/songwriter. I need a job with a good little country-and-western group.'

O, dear God, I thought, as if I knew a country-and-western group, or as if any group would want to take on this whey-faced zombie. But I kept quiet and let him ramble on in general about the shitty state of everything, about all the fuckin psychedelic
296

sellouts and nut-cutting feminist harpies and brain-crippling shrinks and mother-raping bulls who run this black fuckin world.

It was a week or so after the Lennon killing, a day yet before the winter solstice, so I tried to listen to him without comment. I knew he came as a kind of barometer, a revelation of the nation's darkening spiritual climate. Still, I also knew that, as black as it might be, the Victory of the Young Light could always be expected after the darkest time, that things *would* get better in, and I told him so. He didn't look at me, but I saw the side of his mouth move to make a smile, or a sneer. The expression was unpleasant, like an oyster lifting a corner of a slimy lip from a cold cigarette, but it was the first that had crossed his puffy puss and I thought maybe it was a hopeful sign. I was wrong.

'Get better? With seventy per cent of the nation voting for a second-rate senile actor who thinks everybody on welfare should be castrated? Hell, *I* been on welfare! Food stamps too. It's the only way a legitimate artist can survive without selling out to the fuckin vampires. Fuck Jesus, if you knew the rotten shit I been through, with that bastard bus driver and that trigger-happy bitch in Idaho and now this fuckin poison oak – '

'Listen to me, punk,' I said, gently. For I figured that anybody who doesn't have anything better to do than travel 4,000 miles to try to get a fat old bald retired writer who he hasn't even read to get him a job as a singer in a country-and-western band that doesn't even exist is in dark straits indeed; so I decided to give him the benefit of some of my stock wisdom. 'Don't you know you got to change your mind? That the way you're thinking, tomorrow is gonna be worse than today? And next week worse than this and next year worse than last? And your next life – if you get another one – worse than this one . . . until you're going to simply, finally, go out?'

He leaned back and looked out the window at the passing Oregon puddles. 'Mister, I don't give a fuck,' he said.

So I gave him three bucks and let him off at a Dairy Queen, told him to get something to eat while I did my shopping. For the first time his eyes met mine. They were pewter grey, curiously large, with lots of white showing all the way around the pupil. To certain oriental herbalists, the white of the eye showing beneath the pupil means you are what they call *sanpaku*, 'a body out of balance and bound for doom.' I concluded that

297

Patrick's curious eyes must indicate a kind of ultra-*sanpaku*, something beyond just being doomed.

'You're coming back to get me, aren't you?'

Something both doomed and dangerous.

'I don't know,' I confessed. 'I'll have to think about it.'

And handed him his duffel. As I pushed it out the door at him, I felt something hard and ominous outlined through the canvas. It gave me pause.

'Uh, you think you'll need more than three bucks?' I felt compelled to ask. He had turned and was already walking away.

It had felt about the size and shape of an army .45. But, Christ, I couldn't tell. I didn't get much wiring purchased, either. I couldn't decide whether to leave him at the Dairy Queen, or call the cops, or what. I kissed off the electrical shop and went on to the video rental to trade in 'Beatles at Shea Stadium' for a new tape, then I circled back by the Dairy Queen. He was already out on the curb, sitting on his duffel, a white paper bag cradled under his chin as though to match the chalky swatch on his cheek.

'Get in,' I said.

On the way back to the farm he started coming on again about the hard-hearted Easterners, how nobody back there would help him whereas he had always helped others.

'Name one,' I challenged.

'What?'

'One of these others you've helped.'

After some thought he said, 'There was this little chick in New Jersey, for example. Real sharp but out of touch, you know? I got her out of the fuckin hypocritical public junior high and turned her on to a *true* way of living.'

Made me mad again. I turned around and drove the little bastard back to the freeway. That evening when I came back from dropping my daughter off at her basketball practice, there he was, hunching along Nebo Road with his duffel over his shoulder, heading towards the farm.

'Get in,' I said.

'I wasn't going to your place. I'm just looking for a ditch to sleep in.'

'Get in. I'd rather have you where I can keep an eye on you.'

So he ate supper and went to the cabin. He wouldn't let me build a fire. Heat bothered his rash, and light was starting to

298

hurt his eyes. So I turned out the light and left him lying there. While we were watching our video tape I couldn't help but imagine him, stretched out down there in the black and cheerless chill, eyes still wide open, not scratching, not even brooding, really, just lying there.

The movie we were watching was *Alien*.

The next day Dobbs and I loaded up the pickup for a dump run to Creswell and I went down to stir Patrick up.

'You better bring your bag,' I told him. Again he gave me that you-too-huh-you-fuckin-vampire look, then lifted his duffel from the floor and sullenly swung it up to his shoulder. The harsh right-angle object was no longer outlined through the khaki.

He was so peeved at being hauled away he barely spoke. He got out while we were at the dump unloading and wouldn't get back in.

'Don't you want a ride to the freeway?' I asked.

'I'll walk,' he said.

'Suit yourself,' I said and backed the rig around. He stood in the mud and gravel and Pampers and wine bottles and old magazines, the duffel at his side, and watched us pull away, his round grey eyes unblinking.

As I jounced out of the dump I felt those cross hairs on the back of my neck.

The next day he phoned. He was calling from the Goshen Truck Stop, just down our road. He said his poison oak was worse and he was considerably disappointed in me, but he was giving me another chance. I hung up on him.

And last night my daughter said she saw him through the window of the school bus, sitting on his duffel bag in the weeds at the corner of Jasper Road and Valley. She said he was eating a carrot and that his whole face was now painted white.

I don't know what to do about him. I know he's out there, and on the rise.

Dobbs and I went carousing this afternoon with ol' Hunter S. Thompson, who's up to do one of his Gonzo gigs at the behest of the U of O School of Journalism. We stopped at the Vet's Club to help him get his wheels turning in preparation for his upcoming lecture – his 'wiseman riff' he called it – and we talked of John Lennon, and Patrick the Punk, and this new legion of dangerous disappointeds. Thompson mused that he didn't

299

understand why it was people like Lennon they seemed to set their sights for, instead of people like him.

'I mean, I've pissed off quite a few citizens in my time,' the good doctor let us know.

'But you've never disappointed them,' I told him. 'You never promised World Peace or Universal Love, did you?'

He admitted he had not. We *all* admitted it had been quite a while since any of us had heard anybody talk such Pollyanna pie-in-the-sky promises.

'Today's wiseman,' Hunter claimed, 'has too much brains to talk himself out on that kind of dead-end limb.'

'Or not enough balls,' Dobbs allowed.

We ordered another round and mulled awhile on such things, not talking, but I suspected we were all thinking – privately, as we sipped our drinks – that maybe it was time to talk a little of that old sky pie once more, for all the danger of dead ends or cross hairs.

Else how are we going to be able to look that little bespectacled Liverpudlian in the eye again, when the Revolutionary Roll is Up Yonder called?

The Demon Box: An Essay

'Your trouble is – ' my tall daddy used to warn, whenever the current of my curiosity threatened to carry me too far out, over my head, into such mysterious seas as swirl around THE SECRETS OF SUNKEN MU or REAL SPELLS FROM VOODOO ISLES or similar shroudy realms that could be reached with maps ordered from the back of science fiction and fantasy pulps:

' – is you keep trying to unscrew the unscrutable.'

Years later another warning beacon of similar stature expressed the opposite view. Here's Dr Klaus Woofner:

'*Your* trouble, my dear Devlin, is you are loath to let go your Sunday school daydreams. Yah? This toy balloon, this bubble of spiritual gas where angels dance on a pin? Why will you not let it go? It's empty. Any angels to be found will not be found dancing on the head of the famous pin, no. It is only in the dreams of the pinhead that they dance, these angels.'

The old doctor waited until his audience finished snickering.

'More and more slowly, too,' he continued. 'Even there. They become tired, these dancing fancies, and if not given nourishment they become famished. As must everything. For the famine must fall eventually on us all, yah? On the angel and the fool, the fantastic and the true. Do any of you understand what I'm talking about? Izzy Newton's Nameless Famine?'

Dr Woofner was still asking this straight at me, black brows raised, giving me the full treatment (like a cop's flashlight, somebody once described the analyst's infamous gaze). I ventured that I thought I understood what he was talking about, although I didn't know what to call it. After a moment he nodded and proceeded to give it a name:

'It is called, this famine, *entropy*. Eh? No ringing bells? Ach, you Americans. Very well, some front-brain effort if you please. Entropy is a term from conceptual physics. It is the judgment passed on us by a cruel law, the Second Law of Thermodynamics. To put it technically, it is "the nonavailability of energy in a closed thermodynamic system." Eh? Can you encompass this, my little Yankee pinheads? The *non*availability of energy?'

Nobody ventured an answer this time. He smiled around the circle.

'To put it mechanically, it means that your automobile cannot produce its own petroleum. If not fuelled from without it runs down and stops. Goes cold. Very like us, yah? Without an external energy supply our bodies, our brains, even our dreams . . . must eventually run down, stop, and go cold.'

'Hard-nail stuff,' big Behema observed. 'Bleak.'

The doctor squinted against the smoke of his habitual cigarette. A non-filter Camel hung from his shaggy Vandyke, always, even as he was on this night – up to his jowls in a tub of hot water with a nude court recorder on his lap. He lifted a puckered hand above the surface as though to wave the smoke away.

'Hard nails? Perhaps. But perhaps this is what is needed to prick the pinhead's dream, to awaken him, bring him to his senses – *here!*'

Instead of waving, the hand slapped the black water – *crack*. The circle of bobbing faces jumped like frogs.

'We are only here, in this moment, this leaky tub. The hot water stops coming in? Our tub cools down and drains to the bottom. Bleak stuff, yah . . . but is there any way to experience what is left in our barrel without we confront that impending bottom? I think not.'

About a dozen of my friends and family were gathered in the barrel to receive this existential challenge. We'd been driving down the coast to take a break from the heat the San Mateo Sheriff's Department was putting on our La Honda commune, bound for Frank Dobbs's ex-father-in-law's avocado ranch in Santa Barbara. When we passed Monterey I had been reminded that coming up just down the road was the Big Sur Institute of Higher Light, and that Dr Klaus Woofner was serving another hitch as resident guru. I was the only one on board who had attended one of his seminars, and as we drove I regaled my fellow travellers with recollections of the scene – especially of the mineral baths simmering with open minds and unclad flesh. By the time we reached the turnoff to the Institute, I had talked everybody into swinging in to test the waters.

Everybody except for the driver; somewhat sulky about the

302

senseless stop anyway, Houlihan had elected to stay behind with the bus.

'Chief, I demur. I needs to rest my eyes more than cleanse my soul – the wicked curves ahead, y'unnerstand, not to mention the cliffs. You all go ahead: take some snapshots, make your, as it were, obeisance. I'll keep a watch on the valuables and in the event little Caleb wakes up. *Whup?* There he is now.'

At the mention of his name the child's head had popped up to peer through his crib bars. Betsy started back.

'Nay, Lady Beth, you needn't miss this holy pilgrimage. Squire Houlihan'll keep the castle safe and serene. See? The young prince dozes back down already. Whatcha think, Chief? Thirty minutes for howdies and a quick dip, forty-five at the most? Then ride on through the fading fires of sunset.'

He was wishful thinking on all counts. The little boy was not dozing down; he was standing straight in his crib, big-eyed to see the crew trooping out the bus door to some mysterious Mecca, and it was fading sunset by the time we had finished our hellos at the lodge and headed for the tubs. It was long past midnight before we finally outblasted the regular bathers and could congregate in the main barrel where the king of modern psychiatry was holding court.

This was the way Woofner liked it best – everybody naked in his big bath. He was notorious for it. Students returned from his seminars as though from an old-fashioned lye-soap laundry, bleached clean inside and out. His method of group ablution came to be known as 'Woofner's Brainwash'. The doctor preferred to call it Gestalt Realization. By any name, it reigned as the hottest therapy in the Bay Area for more than ten years, provoking dissertations and articles and books by the score. There are no written records of those legendary late-night launderings, but a number of the daytime seminars were taped and transcribed. One of the most well known sessions was recorded during the weekend of my first visit. It's a good sample:

DR WOOFNER: Good afternoon. Are you all comfortable? Very good. Enjoy this comfort for a while. It may not last.

(*The group sprawls on the sun-dappled lawn. Above is the acetylene sky. Down the cliffs behind them is the foamy maw of the Pacific. In front, seated at a shaded table with an empty chair*

303

opposite him, is a man in his late sixties. He has a bald pate, peeling from sunburn, and an unkempt billygoat beard. A cigarette droops from his mouth and a pair of tinted glasses sits slantwise on his nose.

(He removes the glasses. His eyes move from face to face until the group starts to squirm: then he begins to speak. The voice is aristocratically accented, but an unmistakable edge of contempt rings under the words, like the clink of blades from beneath an elegant cloak.)

DR W: So. Before I inquire if there is a volunteer who is willing to interface with me, I want to clarify my position. First, I want you to forget all you have heard about 'Super Shrink' and 'Charismatic Manipulator' and 'Lovable Old Lecher', etc. I am a catalyst; that is all. I am not your doctor. I am not your saviour. Or your judge or your rabbi or your probation officer. In short, I am not responsible for you. If I am responsible for anyone it is for myself – perhaps not even that. Since I was a child people told me, Klaus, you are a genius. It was only a few years ago that I could accept what they said. This lasted maybe a month. Then I realized that I did not much care for the responsibility required to be a genius. I would rather be the Lovable Old Lecher.

(The group giggles. He waits until they stop.)

So. I am not Papa Genius but I can play Papa Genius. Or Papa God, or Mama God, or even the Wailing Wall God. I can take on the role for therapy's sake.

My therapy is quite simple: I try to make you aware of yourself in the here-and-now, and I try to frustrate you in any attempt to wriggle away.

I use four implements to perform this therapy. The first is my learning and experience . . . my years. Second is this empty chair across the table, the Hot Seat. This is where you are invited to sit if you want to work with me. The third is my cigarette – probably irritating to some but I am a shaman and this is my smoke.

Finally, number four is someone who is willing to work with me, here and now, on a few dreams. Eh? Who wants to really work with the old Herr Doktor and not just try to make a fool of him?

BILL: Okay, I guess I'm game. *(Gets up from the lawn and takes the chair; introduces himself in a droll voice.)* My name is
304

William S. Lawton, *Cap*tain William S. Lawton, to be precise, of the Bolinas Volunteer Fire Department. (*Long pause, ten or fifteen seconds.*) Okay . . . just plain Bill.

W: How do you do, Bill. No, do not change your position. What do you notice about Bill's posture?

ALL: Nervous . . . pretty guarded.

W: Yes, Bill's wearing quite an elaborate ceremonial shield. Unfold the arms, Bill; open up. Yah, better. Now how do you feel?

B: Butterflies.

W: So we go from the stage armour to stagefright. We become the anxious little schoolboy in the wings, about to go on. The gap that exists between that 'there' in the wings and *here* is frequently filled with pent-up energy experienced as anxiety. Okay, Bill, relax. You have a dream that we can work with? Good. Is it a recent dream, or is it recurring?

B: Recurring. About twice a month I dream of this ugly snake, crawling up me. Hey, I know it's pretty trite and Freudian but –

W: Never mind that. Imagine that I am Bill and you are the snake. How do you crawl up me?

B: Up your leg. But I don't like being that snake.

W: It's your dream, you spawned it.

B: All right. I am the snake. I'm crawling. A foot is in my way. I'll crawl over it –

W: A foot?

B: Something, it doesn't matter. Maybe a stone. Unimportant.

W: Unimportant?

B: Unfeeling, then. It doesn't matter if you crawl over unfeeling things.

W: Say this to the group.

B: I don't feel this way toward the group.

W: But you feel that way toward a foot.

B: I don't feel that way. The snake feels that way.

W: Eh? You're not the snake?

W: Say to us all what you're not. 'I'm not a snake, I'm not – ?'

B: I'm not . . . ugly. I'm not venomous, I'm not cold-blooded.

W: Now say this about Bill.

B: Bill's not venomous, not cold-blooded –

W: Change roles, talk back to the snake.

B: Then why do you crawl on me, you snake?

W: Change back, keep it going.

B: Because you don't matter. You're not important.

– I am important!

– Oh, yeah? Who says?

– Everybody says. I'm important to the community. (*Laughs, resumes the affected voice.*) Captain Bill the firefighter. Hot stuff.

w: (*taking over snake's voice*) Oh, yeah? Then why is your foot so cold? (*laughter*)

B: Because it's so far from my head. (*more laughter*) But I see what you're getting at, Doctor; my foot *is* important, of course. It's all me –

w: Have the snake say it.

B: Huh? A foot *is* important.

w: Now change roles and give Mr Snake some recognition. Is he not important?

B: I suppose you are important, Mr Snake, somewhere on Nature's Great Ladder. You control pests, mice and insects and . . . lesser creatures.

w: Have the snake return this compliment to Captain Bill.

B: You're important too, Captain Bill. I recognize that.

w: How do you recognize Captain Bill's importance?

B: I . . . well, because you told me to.

w: Is that all? Doesn't Captain Bill also control lesser creatures from up on the big ladder?

B: Somebody has to tell them what to do down there.

w: Down there?

B: At the pumps, crawling around in the confusion . . . the hoses and smoke and stuff.

w: I see. And how do these lesser creatures recognize you through all this smoke and confusion, Captain Bill, to do what you tell them?

B: By my – by the helmet. The whole outfit. They issue the captain a special uniform with hi-viz striping on the jacket and boots. Sharp! And on the helmet there's this insignia of a shield, you see –

w: There it is, people! Do you see? That same armour he marched onstage with – shield, helmet, boots – the complete fascist wardrobe! Mr Snake, Captain Bill needs to shed his skin, don't you think? Tell him how one sheds a skin.

B: Well, I . . . you . . . grow. The skin gets tighter and tighter, until it gets so tight it splits along the back. Then you crawl out. It hurts. It hurts but it must be done if one is to – wait! I get it!

306

If one is to grow! I see what you mean Doctor. Grow out of my armour even if it hurts? Okay, I can stand a little pain if I have to.

w: Who can stand a little pain?

B: Bill can! I'm strong enough, I believe, to endure being humbled a little. I've always maintained that if one has a truly strong 'Self' that one can –

w: Ah-ah-ah! Never gossip about someone who isn't present, especially when it is yourself. Also, when you write the word 'self' you would do better to spell it with a lower-case *s*. The capital *S* went out with such myths as perpetual motion.

And lastly, Bill, one thing more. What, if you would please tell us, is so important over there –

(*lifting a finger to point out the vague place in the air where Bill has fixed his thoughtful gaze*)

– that keeps you from looking *here*?

(*bringing the finger back to touch himself beneath an eye, razor-blade blue, tugging the cheek until the orb seems to lean down from his face like some incorruptible old magistrate leaning from his sacrosanct bench*)

B: Sorry.

w: Are you back? Good. Can you not feel the difference? The tingling? Yah? What you are feeling is the Thou of Martin Buber, the Tao of Chung Tzu. When you sneak away like you are divided, like Kierkegaard's 'Double Minded Man' or the Beatles' 'Nowhere Man'. You are noplace, nothing, of absolutely no importance, what*ever* uniform you wear, and don't attempt to give me a lot of community-spirited elephant shit otherwise. Now, out of the chair. Your time is up.

Woofner's tone was considered by many colleagues to be too sarcastic, too cutting. After class, in the tub with his advanced pupils, he went way past cutting. In these hunts for submerged blubber, he wielded scorn like a harpoon, sarcasm like a filleting knife.

'So?' The old man had slid deeper beneath the girl and the water, clear to his mocking lower lip. '*Der Kinder* seem to be fascinated by this law of bottled dynamics?' His sharp look cut from face to face, but I felt the point was aimed at me. 'Then you will probably be equally fascinated by the little imp that inhabits that vessel – Maxwell's Demon. Excuse me, dear – ?'

He dumped the court recorder up from his lap. When she surfaced, gasping and coughing, he gave her a fatherly pat.

' – hand me my trousers if you would be so kind?'

She obeyed without a word, just as she had hours earlier when he'd bid her stay with him instead of leaving with the Omaha Public Defender who had brought her. The doctor towelled a hand dry on a pant's leg, then reached into the pocket. He removed a ballpoint pen and his cheque-book. Grunting, he scooted along the slippery staves until he was near the brightest candle.

'About one hundred years ago there lived a British physicist named James Clerk Maxwell. Entropy fascinated him also. As a physicist he had great affection for the wonders of our physical universe, and it seemed to him too cruel that all the moving things of our world, all the marvellous, spinning, humming, ticking, breathing things, should be doomed to run down and die. Was there no remedy to this unfair fate? The problem gnawed at him and, in British bulldog fashion, he gnawed back. At length he felt he had devised a solution, a *loophole* around one of the bleakest laws on the books. What he did was ... he devised this.'

Carefully cradling the chequebook near the flame so all could see, he began to draw on the back of a cheque, a simple rectangular box.

'Professor Maxwell postulated, "Imagine we have a box, sealed, full of the usual assortment of molecules careening about in the dark . . . and inside this box a dividing partition, and in this partition a door . . ."'

At the bottom of the partition he outlined a door with tiny hinges and doorknob.

'"And standing beside this door . . . a demon!"'

He sketched a crude stick figure with a tiny stick arm reaching for the doorknob.

'"Now further imagine," said our Professor, "that this demon is trained to open and close this door for those flying molecules. When he sees a hot molecule approaching he lets it pass through to this side"' – he drew a large block H on the right half of the box – '"and when he sees a cold, slow-moving molecule our obedient demon closes the door, containing it on this, the *cold* side of the box."'

Mesmerized, we watched the puckered hand draw the C.

308

'"Should not it then follow," Professor Maxwell reasoned, "that as the left side of the box got colder the right side would begin to get hot? Hot enough to boil steam and turn a turbine? A very small turbine, to be certain, but theoretically capable of generating energy none the less, *free*, and from within a closed system? Thus actually circumventing the second law of thermodynamics would it not?"'

Dobbs had to admit that it seemed to him like it ought to work; he said he had encountered such demons as looked like they had the muscle to manage it.

'Ah, precisely – the muscle. So. Within a few decades another fascinated physicist published another essay, which argued that even *granted* that such a system could be made, and that the demon-slave could be compelled to perform the system's task without salary, the little imp still would not be without expense! He would need muscles to move the door, and sustenance to give those muscles strength. In short, he would need *food*.

'Another few decades pass. Another pessimist theorizes that the demon would also have to have light, to be able to see the molecules. Further energy outlay to be subtracted from the profit. The twentieth century brings theorists that are more pessimistic still. They insist that Maxwell's little dybbuk will not only require food and light but some amount of education as well, to enable him to evaluate which molecules are fast-moving and hot enough, which are too slow and cool. Mr Demon must enrol in special courses, they maintain. This means tuition, transportation to class, textbooks, perhaps eyeglasses. More expense. It adds up. . . .

'The upshot? After a century of theoretical analysis, the world of physics reached a very distressing conclusion: that Maxwell's little mechanism will not only consume more energy than it produces and cost more than it can ever make, *it will continue to do so in increase!* Does this remind you of anything, children?'

'It reminds me,' my brother Buddy said, 'of the atomic power plants they're building up in Washington.'

'Just so, yah, only worse. Now. Imagine again, please, that this box' – he bent again over the picture with his ballpoint, changing the *H* into a *G* – 'represents the cognitive process of Modern civilization. Eh? And that this side, let's say, represents "Good". This other side, "bad".'

He changed the *C* to an ornate *B*, then waggled the picture at us through the steam.

'Our divided mind! in all its doomed glory! And ensconced right in the middle is this medieval slavery, under orders to sort through the whirling blizzard of experience and separate the grain from the chaff. He must deliberate over *every*thing, and to what end? Purportedly to further us in some way, eh? Get us an edge in wheat futures, a master's degree, another rung up the ladder of elephant shit. *Glor*ious rewards supposedly await us if our slave piles up enough "good". But he must accomplish this before he bankrupts us, is the catch. Und all this deliberating, it makes him hungry. He needs more energy. *Such* an appetite.'

His hand had drifted down to float on the surface, the chequebook still pinched aloft between thumb and finger.

'Our accounts begin to sink into the red. We have to float loans from the future. At the wheel we sense something dreadfully wrong. We are losing way! We must maintain way or we lose the rudder! We hammer on the bulkhead of the engine room: "Stoker! More hot molecules, damn your ass! We're losing way!" But the hammering only seems to make him more ravenous. At last it becomes clear: we must fire this fireman.'

We watched the hand. It was gradually sinking, chequebook and all, into the dark waters.

'But these stokers have built up quite the maritime union over the past century, and they have an ironclad contract, binding their presence on board to our whole crew of conscious faculties. If Stokey goes, everybody goes, from the navigator right down to the sphincter's mate. We may be drifting for the rocks but there is nothing we can do but stand at the wheel, helpless, and wait for the boat to go . . . down.'

He held the vowel, bowing his voice like a fine cello.

'O, my sailors, what I say is sad but true – our brave new boat is sinking. Every day finds more of us drowning in depression, or drifting aimlessly in a sea of antidepressants, or grasping at such straws as *psycho*drama and re*gression* catharsis. Fah! The problem does not lie in poo-poo fantasies from our past. It is this mistake we have programmed into the machinery of our *present* that has scuttled us!'

The book was gone. Not a ripple remained. Finally the court recorder broke the spell with her flat, cornbelt voice.

310

'Then what do you advise we do, doctor? You've figured somethin', I can tell by the way you're leadin' us on.'

That voice was the only thing flat she'd brought from Nebraska. Woofner leered at her for a moment, his face streaming moisture like some kind of seagoing Pan's; then he sighed and raised the chequebook high to let the water trickle out of it.

'I'm sorry, dear. The doctor has not figured anything. Maybe someday. Until then, his considered advice is to live with your demon as peacefully as possible, to make fewer demands and be satisfied with less results . . . and above all, mine students, to strive constantly to be *here!*'

The wet chequebook slapped the water. We jumped like startled frogs again. Woofner wheezed a laugh and surged standing, puffy and pale as Moby Dick himself.

'Class dismissed. Miss Omaha? A student in such obviously fit condition shouldn't object to helping a poor old pedagogue up to his bed, yah?'

'How about if I walk along?' I had to ask. 'It's time I checked on the bus.'

'By all means, Devlin.' He grinned. 'The fit and the fascinated. You may carry the wine.'

After getting dressed, I accompanied the girl and the old man on the walk up to the cottages. We walked in single file up the narrow path, the girl in the middle. I was still in a steam from the hot-tub talk and wanted to keep after it, but the doctor didn't seem so inclined. He inquired instead about my legal status. He'd followed the bust in the papers – was I really involved in all those chemical experiments, or was that merely more *San Francisco Chronicle* crap? Mostly crap, I told him. I was flattered that he asked.

Woofner was quartered in the dean's cabin, the best of the Institute's accommodations and highest up the hill. While the court recorder detoured to get her suitcase, the doctor and I continued on up, strolling and sipping in silence. The air was still and sweet. It had rained sometime since midnight, then cleared, and pale stars floated in puddles here and there. The dawn was just over the mountains in the east, like a golden bugle sounding a distant reveille. The colour echoed off the bald head bobbing in front of me. I cleared my throat.

'You were right, Doctor,' I began, 'about my being fascinated.'

'I can see that,' he said without turning. 'But why so much?

311

Do you plan to use the old doctor's secrets to remove a rival in the nut-curing business?'

'Not if I can help it.' I laughed. 'The little while I worked at the state hospital was plenty.'

'You wrote your novel on the job, I heard?' The words puffing back over his shoulder smelled like stale ashtrays.

'That's where I got all those crazy characters. I was a night aide on a disturbed ward. I turned in all my white suits the moment I had a rough draft done, but I never lost the fascination.'

'Your book must have reaped certain rewards,' he said. 'Perhaps you feel some sort of *debt* toward those crazy people and call it fascination?'

I allowed that it could be a possibility. 'But I don't think it's the people I'm fascinated by so much as the puzzle. Like what *is* crazy? What's making all those people go there? I mean, what an interesting notion this metaphor of yours is, if I've got it right – that modern civilization's *angst* is mechanical first and mental second?'

'Not *angst*,' he corrected. 'Fear. Of emptiness. Since the Industrial Revolution, civilization is increasingly afraid of running empty.'

He was breathing hard but I knew he wasn't going to stop for a rest; I only had another couple dozen yards left before we reached his cabin.

'And that *this* fear,' I pressed on, 'has driven us to dream up a kind of broker and install him in our brain so he can increase our accounts by – '

'Minds,' he puffed. 'Into the way we think.'

' – minds . . . by monitoring our incomes and making smart investments? He *can't* be any smarter than we are, though; we created him – and that *he* is the main snake-in-the-grass making people crazy, not all that psychology stuff?'

'That psychology stuff is . . . like the stuff the *Chronicle* writes . . . mostly crap.'

I followed in silence, waiting for him to continue. The wheezing breaths turned into a laugh.

'But, yah, that is my metaphor. You got it right. He is the snake in our grass.'

'And no way to get him out?'

He shook his head.

'What about the way he got in? What would happen if you hypnotized somebody and told them that their dream broker was no more? That he got wind the bank auditors were coming and committed suicide?'

'Bank failure would happen.' He chuckled. 'Then panic, then collapse. Today's somebody has too much invested in that dream.'

We were almost to his cabin. I didn't know what else to ask.

'We *are* experimenting,' he went on, 'with some hybrid techniques, using some of Hubbard's Scientology auditors – "Clears", these inquisitors call themselves – in tandem with John Lilly's Sensory Deprivation. The deprivation tank melts away the subject's sense of outline. His box. The auditor locates the demon and deprogrammes him – clears him out, is the theory.'

'Are you clearing any out?'

He shrugged. 'With these Scientology *schwules* who can tell? What about you? We have a tank open all next week. Just how fascinated are you?'

The invitation caught me completely by surprise. Scientologists and deprivation tanks? On the other hand, a respite from the bus hassles and the cop hassles both was appealing. But before I could respond the doctor suddenly held up a hand and stopped. He tilted his hairy ear to listen.

'Do you hear a gang of men? Having an argument?'

I listened. When his breathing quieted I heard it. From somewhere beyond the hedge that bordered the cottages arose a garbled hubbub. It did sound like a gang of men arguing, a platoon of soldiers ribbing each other. Or a ball team. I knew what it was, of course, even before I followed the doctor to an opening in the hedge; it was Houlihan, and only one of him.

Against the quiet purple of the Big Sur dawn, the bus was so gaudy it appeared to be in motion. It seemed to be still lurching along even though its motor was off and Houlihan wasn't in his driver's seat. He was outside in the parking lot among the twinkling puddles. He had located some more speed, it looked like, and his six-pound single jack. Then he had picked out a nice flat space behind the bus where he could waltz around, toss some hammer, and, all for himself alone and the few fading stars, talk some high-octane shit.

'Unbelievable but you all witnessed the move – one thirtieth of a sec maybe faster! How's *that* you sceptical blinkies? for

313

world champion sinews and synapsis. But what? Again? Is this champ never satisfied? It looks like he's going for the backward double-clutch *up* and over record! Three, four – count the revolutions – five, six . . . which end first? In which hand? . . . eight, nine – *either* hand, Houlihan, no deliberation – eleven twelve thir*teen kafwamp yehh-h-h*. . . .'

Flipping the cumbersome tool over his shoulder, behind his back, between his legs – catching it deftly at the last instant by the tip of the dew-wet handle. Or not catching it, then dancing around it in mock frustration – cursing his ineptness, the slippery handle, the very stars for their distraction.

'A miss! What's amiss? Has the acclaim pried open our hero's as it were *vanity*? Elementals will invade through one's weakest point. Or has he gone all dropsy from a few celestial eyes staring?' – bending and scooping the hammer from its puddle to spin it high again and pluck it out of a pinwheeling spray. 'Nay, not *this* lad, not world-famous Wet . . . Handle . . . Hooly! No pictures, please; it's an act of devotion. . . .'

I'd seen the act plenty times before, so I watched the doctor. The old man was studying the phenomenon through the hedge with the detached expression of an intern observing aberrant behaviour through a one-way mirror. As Houlihan went on, though, and on and on, the detachment changed to a look of grudging wonder.

'It's the demon himself,' he whispered. 'He's been *stoned* out of his box!'

He stood back from the hedge, lifting his brows at me.

'So it is not quite *all Chronicle* crap, eh, Dr Deboree? Eviction by chemical command? Very impressive. But what about the risk of side effects?' He put his hand on my shoulder and looked earnestly into my eyes. 'Mightn't such powerful doses turn one into the very tenant one is trying to turn out? But, ach, don't make such a face! I'm joking, my friend. Teasing. These experiments you and your bus family are conducting deserve attention, sincerely they do – '

It was over my shoulder that his attention was directed, though. The court recorder was coming, carrying a small green suitcase and a large pink pillow.

' – but at another time.'

He gave me a final squeeze good night and promised that we would resume our consideration of this puzzle the very next opportunity. In the tubs again this evening? I nodded, flattered and excited by the prospect. He asked that I think about his invitation in the meantime – sleep a few quiet hours on it, yah? Then he bustled off to join the girl.

I pushed my way through the hedge and headed across the lot, hoping I could get Houlihan geared down enough to let me sleep a few quiet *minutes*. Fat chance. As soon as he saw me coming he whinnied like an old firehorse.

'Chief! You're bestirred, saints be praised. All 'bo-*warrrd!*'

He was through the rear window and up into his seat with the motor roaring before I could make it to the door. I tried to tell him about my appointment with the doctor but Houlihan kept rapping and the bus kept revving until it beckoned its whole scattered family. Too many had been left behind before. They came like a grumpy litter coming to a sow, grunting and complaining they weren't *ready* to leave this comfortable wallow, wait for breakfast.

'We're coming right back,' Houlihan assured one and all. 'Positively! Just a junket to purchase some brake fluid – I checked; we're low – the merest spin back to that – it was a Flying Red Horse if I recollect rightly – hang on re-*verse pshtoww!* now I ain't a liar but I stretch the line. . . .'

Drove us instead up a high-centred dirt road that llamas would have shunned and broke the universal miles from the highway but coincidentally near the hut of a meth-making buddy from Houlihan's beatnik days. This leathery old lizard gave the crew a lot of advice and homemade wine and introduced us to *his* chemical baths. It was a day before Buddy returned from his hike to borrow tools. It was nearly a week before we got the U-joint into Monterey and welded and replaced so we could baby the bus back down to civilized pavement.

It was a whole decade before I kept my appointment with Dr Klaus Woofner, in the spring of 1974, in Disney World.

A lot of things had changed in my scene by then. Banished by court order from San Mateo County, I was back in Oregon on the old Nebo farm with my family – the one that shared my last name, not my bus family They were scattered and regrouped with their own scenes. Behema was communing with the Dead down in Marin. Buddy had taken over my Dad's creamery in Eugene. Dobbs and Blanche had finagled a spread just down the road from our place, where they were raising kids on credit. The bus was rusting in the sheep pasture, a casualty of the Woodstock campaign. A wrong turn down a Mexican railroad had left nothing of Houlihan but myth and ashes. My father was a mere shade of that tower of my youth, sucked small by something medical science can name only, and barely that.

Otherwise, things seemed to be looking up. My dope sentence and my probation time had been served and my record expunged. My right to vote had been reinstated. And Hollywood had decided to make a movie of my nuthouse novel, which they wanted to shoot in the state hospital where the story is set. They were even interested in me doing the screenplay.

To firm up this fantasy I was limousined up to Portland by the producers to meet the head doctor, Superintendent Malachi Mortimer. Dr Mortimer was a fatherly Jew of fifty with a grey pompadour and a jovial singsong voice. He sounded like a tour guide when he showed the hospital to me and the high-stepping herd of moguls up from Hollywood. Hype of moguls might be better.

As I followed through the dilapidated wards, memories of those long-ago graveyard shifts were brought sharply back to me – by the sound of heavy keychains jangling, by the reek of Pine Sol over urine, especially by the faces. All those curious stares from doorways and corridors gave me a curious feeling. It wasn't exactly a memory but there was something familiar about it. It was the kind of tugging sensation you get when you feel that something is needed from you but have no notion what it is, and neither does the thing needing it. I guessed that maybe it was just information. Over and over I was drawn from our parade by looks so starved to know what was going on that I felt obliged to stop and try to shed some light. The faces did brighten. The likelihood that their sorry situation might be exploited as the set for a Hollywood movie didn't seem to disturb them. If Superintendent Mortimer decided it was all right, then they had no objections.

I was touched by their trust and I was impressed with Mortimer. All his charges seemed to like him. In turn he admired my book and liked the changes it had wrought in the industry. The producers liked that we liked each other, and before the day was over everything was agreed: Dr Mortimer would permit use of his hospital if the movie company would foot the bill for a much-needed sprucing up, the patients would be paid extras, I would write the screenplay, the hype of moguls would pull in a heap of Oscars. Everyone would be fulfilled and happy.

'This baby's got big box written all over her!' was the way one enthusiastic second assistant something-or-other expressed it.

But driving back to Eugene that evening I found it difficult to hold up my end of the enthusiasm. That tugging sensation continued to hook at me, reeling my mind back to that haunted countenance at the hospital like a fish to a phantom fisherman. I hadn't confronted that face in years. Or wanted to. Nobody wants to. We learn to turn away whenever we detect the barbed cast of it – in the sticky eyes of a wino, or behind a hustler's come-on, or out the side of a street dealer's mouth. It's the loser's profile, the side of society's face that the other side always tries to turn away from. Maybe that's why the screenplay I eventually hacked out never appealed to the moguls – they know a loser when they have to look away from one.

Weeks passed but I couldn't shake that nebulous nagging. It put a terrible drag on my adaptation efforts. Turning a novel into a screenplay is mainly a job of cutting, condensing; yet I felt compelled to try to say not only more but something else. My first attempt was way long and long overdue. I declined the producers' offer to rent me a place up near the hospital so I could browse around the wards and maybe recharge my muse. My muse was still overcharged from that first browse. I wasn't ready to take another. For one thing, whatever it was that had got me so good was still waiting with baited looks; if it got me any better I feared it was liable to have me for good.

For another, it seemed to be communicable, a virus that might be transmitted eye to eye. I was beginning to imagine I could detect traces of it in friends and family – in fretful glances, flickers of despair escaping from cracked lids, particularly in my father's face. It was as though something picked up from the hospital had passed on to him, the way the fear inside a fallen rider can become the horse's. It was hard to believe that a mean old mustang raised on the plains of west Texas would inexplicably develop a fear of emptiness. He had always been too tough. Hadn't he already outlasted all the experts' estimates by nearly five years, more from his own stiff-necked grit than from any help they had given? But suddenly all that grit seemed gone,

317

and the sponge collar that he wore to keep his head up just wasn't doing the trick any more.

'What'd this Lou Gehrig accomplish that was so dadgum great?' was the sort of thing he had taken to asking. 'No matter how many times you make it all the way around the bases, you're still right back where you started – in the dirt. That's no accomplishment.'

He swept the sports page from his lap and across the lawn, exposing the withered remnant of his legs. I had dropped by and caught him out on the backyard lawn chair, reading the newspaper in his shorts.

'I'm sick of home plate is what it is! I feel like a potted plant.'

'Well, you ain't no tumbleweed any more,' my mother said. She was bringing another pot of coffee out to us. 'He's working up to buying that used motorhome down the street is what it really is – so I can drive him to the Pendleton Roundup.'

'Maybe he wants to go to Mexico again,' I said. Buddy and I had rented a Winnebago some years before and taken him on a hectic ride over the border. I had wanted him to come on at least one of those unchartered trips that he used to warn me against. He came back claiming that the only thing he'd got out of it was jumping beans and running shits. I winked at my mother. 'Maybe he wants to go into the jungle and look for diamonds, like Willy Loman.'

'Uh-huh,' Daddy grunted. The sudden sweep of the papers had tilted his head; he was pushing it straight with his hand. 'Maybe he don't, too.'

'Another cup of mud?' my mother asked to change the subject.

I shook my head. 'One cup of that stuff is plenty; I've got to work tonight.'

'How you coming with it?' my dad wanted to know.

'Slow,' I said. 'It's tough to get the machine up to speed.'

'Especially when you ain't run the thing in a dozen years.' He had his head steady enough to get me with his old, stiff-thumb-in-the-ribs look. 'If you expect to have that movie out in time to benefit from *my* opinions, you better crank 'er up to speed pretty damn quick!'

It was the look that flashed a second later, after the stiffening went out, that got me. I finished my coffee and stood up. 'That's where I'm headed out to right now,' I said. 'To crank 'er up.'

318

'Better not head too far out,' he growled, reaching for another section of the paper. 'I'm liable not to wait for you to get back.'

Mom met me at my car. 'They have him on tap for another one of those spinals Saturday,' she said. 'He hates the nasty things, and they scare the dickens out of me.'

'Spinals aren't dangerous, Mom: I've seen dozens of them.'

'Ever think that might be why he wants you to be around, you knothead!'

'Take it easy, Mom, I'll be around,' I promised. 'Thanks for the mud.'

So when Dr Mortimer called the following Thursday to invite me to join him at the annual convention of psychiatric superintendents, I told him I'd better stay home and keep at our project.

'But it's in Florida this year!' he explained through the phone. 'At the Disney World Hotel! The movie people will pick up your tab.'

Again I declined. I didn't mention my father. 'I'm a little stuck with the script,' I explained.

'They said they thought a trip like this might help unstick you. This year's entertainment is The Bellevue Revue. I saw them two years ago in Atlantic City. Positively hilarious. I bet you could pick up some fresh angles from those Looney Toons. Also, the keynote speaker? They've dug up the author of that beatnik bible, *Now Be Thou*. You've perhaps heard of him? Dr Klaus Woofner?'

I said yes I had, and that I'd be interested to hear what he was talking about these days – 'But not right now.'

'They've got you a ticket waiting at the Portland airport: United to Orlando at three thirty.' Mortimer sounded as excited as a kid. 'A free trip to Disney World, you lucky dog – think of it!'

I told him I would; I had a good twenty-four hours to make up my mind. 'I'll phone you tomorrow morning and let you know what I decide.'

'I'm sure it'll be a load of laughs,' he urged. 'Honestly try to make it.'

I said I was sure, too, and that I honestly would, though I had no intention whatsoever of driving a hundred and fifty miles to Portland, then flying all the way to Florida, not even to hear old Woofner huff and puff.

The next morning I didn't feel quite as firm about it. The night had cranked me backwards and left me feeling uncertain. I had shitcanned most of my old draft and made a fresh start, and the new stuff was already looking old. A little break away from it looked more and more inviting. On the other hand, a drive to Portland in my wishy-washy condition would be a task. By the time it was getting late enough that I had to make the call to Mortimer, one way or the other, I was in the middle of a quandary. I decided that I had best consult the *I Ching* for an answer; the oracle has helped me clear up more than one wishy-washy quandary. I had just carried the book to the breakfast table when the dogs announced the arrival of a car. Betsy opened the door for a well-dressed young man with a monotone voice.

'Good morning, Mrs Deboree. I'm Dr Joseph Gola. Dr Mortimer sent me down from the hospital to pick up your husband.'

'Pick up my husband?'

'And drive him back to Portland. Dr Mortimer was afraid there could be a problem getting gas.'

That weekend was the peak of the Arab oil embargo. Governor McCall had motorists buying gas on odd or even days, according to the last digit on their licence plates, and there were still reports of craziness at the pumps.

'The patients call me Joe,' he introduced himself. 'Joe Go.'

Joe Go was a young Irish-Italian, wearing a hopeful expression and a St Jude the Obscure pin for a tie clasp. He was very soft-spoken. After he accepted a chair and a cup of coffee, he shyly asked about the picture-covered book in front of me.

'It's just an *I Ching*,' I explained, 'with its cover collaged with photographs. I was about to ask it whether to go or not to go. Then you showed up. I better pack my suit.'

'Better pack the book too,' he said with a grin. 'In case we need to ask about coming back.'

Betsy was completely taken by his altar boy innocence. While I packed she kept bringing him coffee with blueberry muffins and big smiles. The kids on the other hand had nothing but frowns for Doctor Joe. After all, *they* had never been to Disney World – not to Disneyland in Anaheim, even. If innocent young company was what was needed in Florida, couldn't I take one of them along? They each made their bid a few times, then moped off in protest, all except for little Caleb. The ten-year-old
320

remained at the table in his long Grateful Dead nightshirt and his longing face. He yearned to go as much as his brother or sisters, but it wasn't Caleb's style to mope off and maybe miss something else. He was the only one that came outside to wish us farewell, too.

'Remember to bring us something back from Disney World, Dad,' he called from the porch, his voice brave. 'Something neat, aw-right?'

'Aw-right,' I called back as I climbed into the car. I waved but he didn't wave back – he couldn't see me through the Lincoln's tinted safety glass. The thing was big as a barge. I told Doctor Joe he'd better back it out instead of trying to turn around between our blueberries. 'They're hard enough to keep alive.'

He started down our drive in reverse, twisting out his door to try to miss the deepest holes. I buckled my seatbelt and rolled with the bouncing. After a night of getting nowhere on my own, I found I liked the idea of being picked up and carried away. I was leaning back to try the cushy headrest when, from out of nowhere, something yanked me straight up and wide-eyed, something deeper than any of our chuckholes.

It was that same tugging sensation again, to the tenth power – still as enigmatic and even more familiar, like a dream so meaningful that it jolts you awake, then you can't remember what it was about. It only lasted a second or two before it faded, leaving me dumbfounded. What the hell was it? Simply the thought of going back up to that hospital and having to face that face again? Some kind of hangfire out of the past bounced loose?

'What's the best way back from here?'

It took a moment to realize the young doctor was asking me the best way back to Portland. He'd come to the end of our driveway.

'Well, I go that way if I'm in a hurry.' I pointed up the hill. 'Or down through Nebo and Brownsville if I've got time for a peaceful cruise.'

He backed around headed downhill. 'We've got plenty of time,' he said, and reached over to open a leather case that was waiting on the seat between us. It looked like an old-fashioned sample case for patent medicines. Neatly arranged between the dividers was an extensive selection of those miniature bottles of brand liquors, dozens of them.

'It looks like things have changed since I was connected with the mental health business,' I observed.

'Some ways yes, some ways no,' he said, choosing a tiny Johnny Walker. 'Less restrictions, more medications. Still no cures. Help yourself.'

Conversation was sparse. The young man was more of a one-liner than a talker, and I would have been content to keep quiet and go over the mystery of that thing that had hit me back in the blueberries, or go to sleep. But with the help of the long drive and the medicine kit we gradually got to know each other. Doctor Joe had rebounded into psychology after flunking out of the field of his true interest: genetics. Both the Latin and the Gaelic sides of his family had histories of mental disease, not to mention a lot of crazy poets and painters and priests. Joe said he had inherited a lot of bad art, blind faith, and troubling questions. Also, he said he was going to the convention for the same reason I was – to see Dr Klaus Woofner. He said he had been a fan since his undergrad days at Queens.

'I've read every little thing written by him, plus that huge pile of shit about him. They called him everything from the Big Bad Wolf to Old Sanity Klaus.'

He gave me a look of hopeful curiosity. We were on a stretch of empty two-lane through the gentle pasturelands above Salem, the cruise control set at a drowsy forty-five.

'The old goat must have been some sort of hero, yeah? to get so much shit started?'

Yeah, I nodded. Some sort of hero. I closed my eyes. Could the old goat get it finished was what I was curious about.

The Lincoln's horn woke me. We were in an insane jam of cars all trying to gas up before the weekend rush. The hospital was less than a mile away but we couldn't get through the snarled intersection where the gas stations were. Cars were lined up bumper-to-bumper for blocks. Joe finally swung about and took a wide detour around the tangle. By the time we got to the gate at the hospital grounds, the dashboard clock showed we had less than a half hour before flight time. What's more, the drive up to the main building was blocked by a police car slanted into the curb. We couldn't get around it.

'Grab your bags!' Joe switched off the Lincoln right where it sat. 'Maybe Mortimer's still on the ward.'

He sprinted off like a track star. I picked up my shoulder bag and my suitcase and followed groggily after him, reluctant to leave the big car's torpor. But that surprise at my morning *Ching* should have forewarned me; this was not going to be a peaceful cruise. When I rounded the squad car I encountered a tableau that stopped me in my tracks.

The car was still idling, all four doors open. At the rear a stout state trooper and two overweight police matrons were trying to bring down an Unidentified Flying Object. The thing was far too fast for them, a blur of noise and movement, whirling in and out of the haze of exhaust, hissing and screeching and snarling. Honking, too, with some kind of horn-on-a-spear. It used this spear to slash and honk at the circle of uniforms, holding them at bay.

Two burly hospital aides came loping to help out, a sheet stretched between them dragnet fashion. Reinforced thus, the herd charged. The UFO was silenced beneath half a ton of beef. Then there was a high, sharp hiss followed by a beller of pain and the thing whirled free again. It scurried right through the legs all the way around the herd into one rear door of the car and out the other, twittering curses in some language from a far speedier dimension. By the time the pursuers had circled the car, their quarry was arrowing down the drive for the open gate. The herd was already slackening their halfhearted chase – anybody could see that there was nothing earthly capable of catching up – when, to everybody's astonishment, the arrow missed that huge two-lane opening by a good five feet and crashed full tilt into the cyclone fence. It spronged back, spun erratically a moment on the gleaming green, then went down a second time under the welter of uniforms. There was a final piteous little *squank* from beneath the pile of lawn, then nothing but heavy puffing and panting.

'Come on!' Joe had returned and jerked me out of my gawk. 'Don't worry. You couldn't hurt that little cyclone with fifty fences.'

He led me through a lobby full of carpenters, past the elevator, and up a long, echoing ramp. The ramp levelled off to a metal door. Joe unlocked it and I found myself back on Dr Mortimer's ward. Everything was in upheaval for the Hollywood renovation, new stuff and old piled in the halls. Mortimer wasn't in his office. Neither was his secretary. We hurried past the staring patients to the nurse's station at the ward's intersection. The duty nurse and the secretary were both there, sharing a box of Crackerjacks.

'Omigod!' the nurse exclaimed as though caught. 'Dr Mortimer just left.'

'Left for where!'

'The lot . . . Possibly the airport.'

'Joannie! You get on the phone to the main gate.'

'Yes, Dr Gola.' The secretary hurried back to the office.

'Miss Beal, you try the CB in the lobby, in case he's still at the motor pool. I'll run down to the lot.'

The nurse trotted off, Crackerjacks rattling in the pocket of her white cardigan. Joe sprinted back the way we'd come, leaving me alone in the fluorescent buzz.

Well, not exactly. Robed spectres were trolling back and forth past the windows and open half door of the nurse's station, casting looks in at me. I turned my back on them and sat down on the counter, pretending to peruse a back issue of *OMNI*. As the minutes hummed past I could feel eyes picking at my neck. I traded *OMNI* for a copy of *National Enquirer*, rattling the big pages. The hum seemed to caramelize right over the noise of the paper like a clear glaze. Spells in the blueberries. U.F.O.s on the lawn. Now this. I am in no condition for this. Then the glaze was shattered by a screech at the Admissions Door.

' – fascist snotsucking shitmother *pigs!* Don'cha know *who*soever wields the Diamond Sword of ACHALA *wields burning justice?* Where's my cane you ignorant assholes and don't whisper to me Cool it! Like, you're so hip? So with it? Don'cha know this messing with blood sacraments in the name of revolution must fucking *cease?*'

The high twittering hiss had been slowed but it was still sharp; the words chopped through the impacted air like an axe through ice.

'*Down* with dilettantes who mouth dopey slogans and muddy the flow of change! May the lot of you be slit butthole to bellybutton by the *diamond edge of ACHALA Lord of Hot Wisdom*, whose face is *bloody fangs*, who wears a *garland of severed heads*, who turns *Rage to Accomplishment*, who is clad in *gunpowder* and *glaciers* and *lava*, who saves *honest tormented spirits* from filth-eating fascist pig *ghosts!* In His name I curse you: NAMAH SAMANTHA VAJRANAM CHANGA!'

324

It sounded like some militant soprano Gary Snyder tongue-lashing a strip miners' meeting. I joined the others in the hall to see what it was that could sound so pissed-off and poetic all at once.

'MAHROSHANA SHATA YA HUM TRAKA HAM MAM!'

It was a girl, still years and inches short of legal age or full growth, bony and bone-coloured, skin, hair, eyes, clothes, and all. There was a checkerboard pattern up her front from the crash with the Cyclone fence, but no cuts, no purple bruises. The only colour in the whole composition was a green swatch down the side of her close-cropped head, probably from the scuffle on the lawn. She fingered the air before her a moment, like a cave lizard, then lunged.

'Give me my fucking stick you faggot!'

'No you don't, Lissy.' The biggest-butted aide held it high out of her reach. 'This could be a weapon in hostile hands.'

I saw that the spear had originally been the kind of lightweight staff used by the Vision Impaired. The white paint was all but gone from the battered aluminium, and it had been thonged from tip to handle with feathers and beads, like an Indian spear. Just in front of the handle was lashed the staff's main mojo – a rubber squeeze-toy head of Donald Duck, his angry open bill forward and his rubber sailor cap within thumb's reach. This was how she had been able to swing the thing and quack it at the same time.

'Give it give it *give it!*' she screeched.

'I won't won't *won't!*' the aide mocked, parading ahead like a fat-assed drum major with a baton. The girl took squinting aim at the plump target and kicked; she missed as wide as she had missed the gate. She would have fallen if the matron hadn't been gripping her arms.

'What about my glasses then? Am I going to deathray somebody with my fucking glasses? I'm fucking legally *blind*, you stupid shits! If I don't get my glasses immediately every turd of you is gonna fry! My whole fucking family are *lawyers*.'

This threat hit home harder than all the other curses together. The parade stopped cold to talk it over. The aide who had gone in search of higher authorities came panting back with the news that the ward seemed empty of doctor and nurse alike. After a whispered debate they decided to relinquish the specs. The state

325

trooper removed them from a Manila envelope and handed them to her. The matrons loosened their grip so she could put them on. The lenses were like shot glasses. As soon as they were settled on her nose she swung around snarling. Out of that whole hallful of gaping spectators she focused on me.

'What are *you* gawping at, Baldy? You never seen somebody on a bum trip before?'

I wanted to tell her as a matter of fact I had – been on some myself – but the ward door clashed open again and in bustled Joe, the nurse, and Dr Mortimer. The nurse was carrying a two-way radio. She saw the congestion in her halls and waded right in without breaking stride, swishing it clear with the antenna. She stopped in front of the girl.

'Back so soon, Miss Urchardt? You must have missed us.'

'I missed the elegant facilities, Miss Beal,' the girl declared. 'Wall-to-wall walls. Bathtubs you could get drowned in.' A lot of the sharp sting had gone out of her tongue, though.

'Then let's not hesitate to enjoy one. Dr Mortimer? Would you phone Miss Urchardt's father while I admit her? The rest of you, go about your business.'

At his office Dr Mortimer passed the task right on to his secretary and hurried Joe and me toward the ramp door. We could hear the phone start ringing before he got it closed. He leaned back in.

'That's probably the senator now, Joannie,' he called. 'If he wishes to speak to his daughter, tell him she's in the Admissions Bath. If he wishes to speak to me, tell him he'll have to call Orlando, care of the Disney World Hotel. Ask for Goofy.'

Then locked the door behind us. He giggled all the echoing lope down the ramp. 'Ask for Goofy, Senator; ask for Goofy.'

With the help of a ticket agent, a later longer flight finally got us through the night to the sticky Florida sunshine. The rent-a-car cost us double, because of the fuel shortage, we were told, but the room for three at Disney's monstrous pyramid cost us only about half the regular rate, and for the same reason. The gum-chewing peach behind the desk told us we were lucky, that triples was took months in advance, usually.

I asked if a Dr Klaus Woofner had checked in yet. She glanced at her book and told me not yet. I left my name and a message for him to call our room as soon as he arrived. 'Or leave word if we're out,' Mortimer added, herding us upstairs to stow our bags. 'Time's a-wasting, boys. I intend to see it all.'

On the monorail to the park Dr Mortimer divided the package of free ticket books that had been provided us by the movie producers, more thrilled by the minute. He really did intend to see everything, we found out. He ran Joe and me ragged for hours. I finally balked at Small World.

'I want to phone the hotel, see if anybody's heard anything about Woofner.'

'And *I* want,' Joe added, 'to buy one of those beadwork botas.' We had seen a bunch of foreign sailors drinking out of wineskins on the Mississippi Riverboat Ride, and Joe had been covetous ever since.

'I suspect they're not available here, Joe,' the doctor suspected. 'I hate to get separated – '

'Joe can ask around while I phone. We'll check for you every half hour – at, say the Sky Ride ticket booth?'

'I guess that will be all right,' the doctor singsonged, right in time with 'It's a small world af-ter all,' and hurried away toward the music.

Joe asked around and I phoned. Nobody had heard anything about Woofner or wineskins, either one. On the Sky Ride we were able to enjoy Joe's samples in the privacy of our plastic funicular. We alighted to find that there are ticket booths at each end of the ride. When the doctor wasn't at one end there was nothing to do but climb back aboard and highride back to the other. We spent a good part of our afternoon this way, without another glimpse of Dr Mortimer. Once, though, Joe thought he might have seen Dr Woofner.

'The guy with the nurse?' Joe pointed a tiny Tanqueray bottle at the funicular that had just passed us. 'Could that be our hero? He appears old and bald enough.'

I craned around to look. An old man and a blond nurse were seated on each side of a folded wheelchair. He wore dark glasses and a too-big Panama hat. For a second something about him did remind me of Woofner, some severe slant to the shoulders, some uncompromising hunch that made me wonder if I wanted to meet up with the the ornery old gadfly as much as I thought I did, then a breeze flipped the hat off. The man was old and bald all right, nary a hair from his crown to his chinless neck, but he wasn't much bigger than a child. I laughed.

'Not unless he's turned into a Mongoloid midget,' I said. 'These dwarf drinks must be affecting your vision, Joe.'

When we docked I phoned the hotel nevertheless. No doctor by that name had checked in. There was a message from one named Mortimer, though. He had returned, reserves exhausted – would see us before the evening's programme.

The Sky Rides had depleted Joe's reserves, too, so we spent the rest of the afternoon more or less on the ground. It was exactly like Disneyland in Anaheim except for one striking addition: the Happy Hippos. This was a temporary exhibit set up in Adventureland, near the Congo boat dock. A low fence had been erected outside a tent, and a pair of full-grown hippos lounged in a makeshift puddle in the enclosure.

These brutes were nearly twice as big as those mechanical robotamuses on Disney's Wild Jungle River Ride, awesome tons of meat and muscle, fresh from the real wild. Yet they dozed complacent as cows in their knee-deep puddle, beneath an absolute downpour of insults. Kids bounced ice cubes and balled-up Coke cups off their bristled noses. Teenagers hollered ridicule: 'Hey Abdul how's yer tool?' A Campfire Girl probed at the wilted ears with her rubber spear from Frontierland until an attendant made her stop. Every passerby had to stop and express contempt for this pair of groggy giants, it seemed. The chinless dwarf from the Sky Ride even got in his licks; he took a big sip of Pepto-Bismol, then motioned his nurse to wheel him up close so he could spew a pink spray at them.

Inside the tent was the exhibit's film, produced by UNESCO, Made Possible by a Grant from Szaabo Laboratories, rear-projected on three special screens donated by Du Pont. As the right and left screens flashed slides of drought-stricken Africa, the centre screen would show parched hippos being winched from the curdled red-orange mire of their ancestral wallows. These wallows were drying up, the narration informed us, as a result of a lengthy dry spell plus the damming of rivers to provide electricity for the emerging Third World.

After an animal was successfully winched up from his bog he would be knocked out with a hippo hypo, forklifted onto a reinforced boxcar, and released, hundreds of miles away, into a chainlink compound full of other displaced hippos awaiting relocation. The compound looked as desolate as the regions

328

they'd just been evacuated from, swirling with flies and thick orange dust.

'During the initial weeks of the project,' the voice of the narrator told us, 'the hippos made repeated charges against the compound's fences, often breaking through, more often injuring themselves. We were eventually able to quell these assaults by introducing into their drinking water a formula especially designed by our laboratories – making them, comparatively, much happier hippos.'

'Compared with what?' I heard Joe's one-liner from the dark. 'Each other?'

The shadows were long when we emerged from the film, the sun sinking between the spires of Cinderella's Castle. I had pretty much lost interest in the convention, but Joe felt he should make an appearance. Besides, now his reserves were completely exhausted. So we took the old-fashioned choo-choo around to the gate, where we boarded its modern monorail counterpart.

We had to wait while our engineer had a cigarette outside on the landing. A restless musing filled the car while we waited. Hidden machinery hummed. People slumped in the chrome-and-plastic seats. Out the open doors of the car, the Florida sky was airbrushed full of crimson clouds, just like Uncle Walt had ordered, and the indistinct sounds and voices of the park waved softly in and out on the evening breezes. Annette Funicello's recorded greeting at the entrance gate could be heard clearest: 'Hey there hi there *ho* there,' she chanted like a cheerleader. 'We're as happy as can *be*, to have you here *today* . . . hip hip hoo-*ray!*'

None of the waiting passengers seemed inclined to be led into the cheer. In the seat in front of us a family rode, six of them. The husband sat alone, his back to us, his muscled arms spread over the red plastic seatback. Across from him, facing us, his family fussed and stewed. His wife had dark circles under her eyes and at her Rayon armpits. In her lap his toddler whimpered. On one side of her his first-grader whined and on the other his sixth-grader sucked her thumb. Across the aisle his teenager slouched and bitched.

'The kids at school will not be*lieve* we never went on Pirates of the Caribbean!'

'Hush, honey,' the mother said wearily. 'We were out of tickets. You know that.'

'We could have bought more,' the teenager maintained. The other kids wailed agreement. 'Yeah! we could have bought *more!*'

'We were also out of money,' the mother said.

'We didn't even get to see the Enchanted Tiki Birds. The kids at school simply will not *believe* it!'

'That we were out of money? Well, the kids at school had better believe it. And you better give it a rest if you know what's good for you – *all* of you!'

And all the while the father sat without comment, not moving, just the muscles in his forearms and his big workadaddy hands, gripping the back of the seat. I noticed he'd been able to get his wrists and knuckles clean for this occasion, but there was still carbon under the fingernails, the indelible tattoo left by the other fifty-one weeks of his year working a lathe in Detroit, or changing tyres in Muncie, or scrabbling coal in Monongahela.

'In a recent worldwide survey,' Annette's voice continued in a more serious vein, 'it was found that twice as many people desire to go to Disney World than to any other attraction on earth. That's pretty impressive, don't you all agree?'

Nobody nodded agreement, not even the kids. Before we could hear more our driver returned to his controls; the doors hissed shut and the big tube hummed away toward our hotel. The hands continued their gripping and ungripping of the seat-back, trying not to let it show how hard it was getting to be, this business of keeping a grip.

Joe and I exchanged looks. The poor guy. Hadn't he done everything you're supposed to? Laboured hard? made a home? raised a family? even saved enough for this most desired of all vacations? But it wasn't working. Something was wrong somewhere, and hanging on was getting harder all the time.

We never saw his face. They filed off forward of us at the hotel. As they left Joe shook his head:

'Just the tip of an enormous iceberg,' he said, 'heading toward a titanic industry.'

I had no idea just how titanic until I saw the exhibits. While Joe rushed off to make his appearance at industry parties, I roamed the crowded exhibition hall, amazed at all the latest
330

devices and potions designed to care for and control the upcoming hordes unable to care for or control themselves. Teenagers rented from the local high school were our guides through a vast maze of displays. They demonstrated long-snouted pitchers that could get nourishment down the most intractable throat. They showed us how new Velcro straps could strap down a big strapping lad as well as the bulky old buckle cuffs. They invited us to test the comfort of urine-proof mattresses, pointing out the slotless screwheads that held the bedframe together: 'to keep them nuts from eating the screws.'

There were unrippable pyjamas with padded mittens to prevent the hallucinator from plucking out an offending eye. There were impact-dispersing skullcaps for the clumsy, disposable looparound mouthpieces for the tongue gnashers, lockfast maxi-Pampers for the thrashing incontinent, and countless kinds of medication reminders that beeped and buzzed and chimed to remind the forgetful.

The vast majority of the booths were manned by the many pharmaceutical laboratories supported by this industry. Most of these displays lacked the visual pizazz of the hardware shows. Pills and pamphlets just aren't as interesting to look at as restraining chairs featuring built-in commodes with automated enemas. The Szaabo display was the exception, attracting far the largest audience of all the booths. Company designers had mocked up a large cocktail lounge complete with plastic plants and free peanuts and waitresses in miniskirts. Above the bar was a big-screen TV monitor that played actual tapes of the company's products in action. Conventioneers could eat peanuts and drink and cheer like a Monday Night Football crowd as they watched big hyperactive hellraisers get wrestled down and turned meek as mice with a shot. I wondered if the display designers get the idea from the hippo show, or vice versa.

The trouble was once you got into the popular Szaabo lounge, it was next to impossible to get back out through the crush of the boisterous crowd. Harder than that to snag one of the free drinks. I was buffeted back and forth through the smoky clamour until I found myself near an exit along the far wall. It was marked for Emergency Use Only. I felt my smarting eyes and burning throat qualified so I pushed the lockbar and peeked out. To my great relief I saw I had found not only a private balcony

331

with fresh air and a view of the sunset, but a tray of unclaimed martinis.

I squeezed through and heard the big door shut behind me over the noise. I grabbed the push bar but I was too late. 'Let it lock,' I decided, releasing the bar. 'I can get by on olives if I miss the banquet.'

I noticed these olives were skewered on clever little S-shaped silver swizzles, supposed to look like the Szaabo logo. It was also etched on the martini glasses, in red and yellow, like the crest on Superman's chest. About halfway through the tray I raised one of the glasses in a toast – to Szaabo Labs, original layers of those tiny blue eggs of enlightenment. Remember when we used to think that every egg would hatch cherubs in every head and that these fledglings would feather into the highest-flying Vision in mankind's history? Remember our conspiracy, Szaabo? You make 'em; we'll take 'em – as far as the Vision can see. Who's left to carry the colours of our crusade now? Where's the robin-egg-blue banner of the Vision of Man now? In the hands of one little girl, that's where, some titless wonder who can see about as far as she can pee, and *she's* been captured, probably by now quelled with one of your latest designer formulas and watching a rerun of *Happy Days*, comparatively happy herself.

But, like Joe says, compared to what?

By the time the drinks were drained and the olives eaten, the din on the other side of the door had gone down considerably. For a keepsake I dropped the last glass in my shoulder bag with my *Ching* and my leftover ticket books and tried the door. I was able to attract one of the waitresses by rattling the tray between the bar and the metal. She let me back in, apologizing all over herself for not hearing my signal earlier; it had been just too dern *noisy*. I gave her the tray and a ten spot and told her not to worry – I hadn't been signalling earlier, anyhow.

The Szaabo bar and the convention hall were both almost empty. Everybody was off getting dressed for the evening's main event. I swung one more time by the main desk and saw my message to Woofner still folded in his box. The fresh peach behind the desk told me so many folks'd been asking she was curious *herself* what'd come of this missin' doctor.

Up in our room Dr Mortimer was trying to find an answer to the same question. He was pacing to and fro in front of the

332

telephone table in his rumpled tux and untied tie, talking into the receiver in a loud singsong German. I discerned he was a little drunk. When he saw me he put his hand over the receiver and shook his head forlornly.

Joe was also dressed for dinner, more rumpled than his boss and lots drunker. He was tilted back on a wastepaper basket. 'You're burned bright as a beet,' he said squinting at me. He held out the miniature bottle of Beefeater he was drinking. 'Use some of this on your head. White wine's best but gin'll do.'

I shook my head, explaining I had come to expect olives with my gin. Joe finished the bottle and dropped it between his legs into the wastebasket. I heard it clink against other bottles. He looked at his boss pacing foolishly with the phone, then started singing, 'Who's afraid of the big bad wolf, the big bad wolf, the big bad wolf . . .'

Mortimer got the point and finally hung up. 'I know you're both disappointed' – he sighed – 'but it may be just as well. According to some of my colleagues our big bad wolf has long ago lost his fangs. And who wants to sit through a dull gumming? The programme will be just fine, regardless. We've got last year's minutes, and the Bellevue Revue, and Dr Bailey Toocter from Jamaica has already volunteered to fill in as keynote with his – what did he call it, Joe?'

'Therapeutic Thumb harp,' Joe answered. 'Soothes the savage breast.'

It was just as well with me, too. I had realized as much locked out on the balcony – that I'd been wishful dreaming. Only a pinhead fool would hope to find the wild and woolly Big Sur of bygone days in the Florida torpor. I stepped over Joe's legs to the closet where my grey suit hung.

The dinner was held in an elegantly appointed wedge-shaped hall, its point focusing on the raised dais. Dr Mortimer was seated at this head table between the square-jawed Dudley DuRight who was to be the evening's master of ceremonies and a wild-headed black man in a coral pink tuxedo. First served, they had already finished eating. Dudley was sober and serious about his evening's role – he kept checking backstage, reading messages, going over his handful of notes – while the black man and Mortimer whispered and giggled like carefree schoolgirls. On the table in front of their plates was a hinged wooden box inlaid with mother-of-pearl butterflies. I assumed it was the thumb harp.

Joe and I were about three tables back, still picking at our lobster Newberg but already into our third bottle of Johannesburg Riesling. I admitted to Joe that he was right; the cold wine *was* relieving to the outside of my burned head as well as the inside. I didn't mention the main relief I was feeling – that I would not have to face my old mentor after âll. I wasn't disappointed and I found I was rather pleased with that fact. I saw it as a significant stride. If you feel that nothing is owed you, then you owe nothing. I leaned back with my chilled Riesling and newfound wisdom, prepared to enjoy a peace I had not enjoyed for months. Screw the nuts and to hell with the heroes. As far as I was concerned, the change to the thumb harp was just what the doctor ordered.

But when Dudley got up and took the mike and launched into a grandiloquent introduction of the great man who was to speak to us, I wondered if anybody had told him about the change.

'A legend!' he proclaimed. 'A star of Sigmund Freud's magnitude, of Wilhelm Reich's radiance, of Carl Jung's historic brilliance! A pillar of fire burning before most of us were born, yet still listed in the Who's Who of *Psychology Today!* Still considered a giant in the contemporary field – a *giant!*'

This didn't seem to describe the dreadlocked Dr Toocter, not even the thumb harpist himself, now frowning perplexed up at the MC. Indeed, all seated at the main table were turned toward the master of ceremonies in wonder. It was nothing like my amazement, though. When our speaker rolled in from the curtain wings, I saw it was the hairless dwarf from the Sky Ride after all.

The tall blonde nurse had changed from her nurse's uniform into a beige evening gown, but her patient was wearing the same dark glasses and rumpled shirt and slacks, as though he'd never left the chair. She wheeled him to the podium through an uncertain flurry of clapping, then helped him stand. When she was sure he had a good grip on the podium she wheeled the chair back off, leaving him swaying and nodding in the spotlight.

He was not merely hairless; he was partially faceless as well. The corner of his upper lip and much of the lower had been pared away, all the way down his chin, and the scar covered with flesh-coloured make-up. This was why he had looked to me

334

like some kind of long-lived Down's syndrome this afternoon. And without his hat the Florida sun had burned his head even brighter than it had mine. He was a blazing Day-Glo purple everywhere except the painted scar. This hand-sized swatch looked like the only island of natural flesh on a globe of synthetic skin, instead of the other way around. The clapping had been over for a long minute before he finally cleared his throat and spoke.

'Who's who,' he murmured, shaking his head. '*Das ist mir scheissegal*. Who's who.' Then the voice lifted a little. 'That's what you really want to consider, yah? Who was, who is, who *will be* who, when next season's list is published?'

The accent was thicker and the speech halting. It would never be the fine instrument of old, but there was still a ring to it.

'How about we consider instead who is correct. Der Siggy Freud? All those interesting theories? like how anal retention becomes compulsive repetition and causes some sort of blockage what he called *petrification?* Und how this blockage could be dissolved with enough analysis, like enough castor oil? Please, mine colleagues, let us speak truthfully, doctor to doctor. We have all observed the application of these theories. Interesting though they may be, we all know that they are for all practical purposes useless in the psychiatric ward. Castor oil would be more effective, and Sigmund would have been more useful had he written romances for a living. The romantic ideal can be useful in the world of fiction; in the world of medicine, never. Und we are all medical men, yah? We must be able to distinguish medicine from fiction. We must be able to know what is psychological results and what is psychological soap opera, never mind how the one is so discouraging while the other is so fascinating. You are all just as capable as I am of knowing who is really who and what was really what, so you all *must* have suspected what I am trying to tell you before now: that Sigmund Freud was a neurotic, romantic, coke-shooting *quack!*'

When he said this he slapped the podium a sharp crack. The effect on the convention crowd would not have been greater if he'd said Albert Schweitzer was a Nazi, then fired a Luger at the ceiling. He swept his black-goggled gaze about the hall until the air subsided.

'Old daydreamer Carl Jung mit his sugar-glazed mandala? Willy Reich teaching orgasm by the numbers? All quacks. Yah,

335

they were all very good writers, very interesting. But if you are a woodcutter, let us say, and you purchase a woodsaw – what does it matter how interesting the sawmaker writes about it? If it does not saw good it is not a good saw. As a woodcutter, you should be the first to detect the cheat: it won't cut straight! So take it back to that lying sawmaker, or paint a sunset on it, or throw it in the river – but don't pass the crooked wood on to your *customers!*'

He paused to reach down and pick up Dr Toocter's wadded napkin. He bowed his head to dab at the sweat that had begun to glisten on his neck and throat. He waited until his breathing calmed before he looked back up.

'Also, you are bad woodcutters for more reason than you invest in bad saws. You are afraid to go into the forest. You would rather invent a tree to fit your theory, and cut down the invention. You cannot face the real forest. You cannot face the real roots of your world's madness. You see the sore well enough but you cannot heal it. You can ease the pain, perhaps, but you can't stop the infection. *You cannot even find the thorn!* Und so' – he lifted his shoulders in a deprecating shrug – 'that is the reason why I have flown to speak to you here tonight, even here, in the very heart of the festering American dream: to point out to you that thorn. Miss Nichswander?'

She was already rolling out the blackboard. When it was secured behind the dais she took a stick of chalk from her jewelled handbag and handed it to her boss. He waited until she was out of sight through the curtains before he turned back to us.

'Okay, some concentration if you please.' The hand began pushing the chalk around the slate rectangle. 'I will explain you this only once.'

It was the same annotated sketch from ten years before, only honed far finer, with more bite to it. I smiled to think of those who had been worried about getting a dull gumming this evening. The old wolf was maimed and mangy, but still plenty sharp. His history of James Clerk Maxwell and the laws of thermodynamics was more extensive, his drawing more detailed. The demon had acquired a set of horns and a very insolent sneer. And the seams of the whole concept had come together so ingeniously that he could move the metaphor back and forth at will, from the

336

machine to the modern mind, hot and cold to good and bad, smooth as a stage magician.

'This problem of nonavailability was grasped by only a few during Maxwell's day: William Thomson, Lord Kelvin; Emmanuel Clausius. Clausius understood it best of all, perhaps; he wrote that, while the energy of the universe is constant, entropy is always on the increase. Only a handful of the smartest, back then. Today every illiterate clod with an automobile is beginning to get it; every time he sees the price of petrol go up, he sees his world go a little emptier, and a little more mad. So you educated doctors ought to be able to see it. Of all people, you must have seen the signs. Your ward rollbooks should trace the trend; as the power shortage increases, enrolment in your institutions follows along? What are your most recent statistics? One American in five will be treated for mental illness sometime during their lifetimes. What? Did I hear someone say it is now one in four? Ach, don't you see? You are no longer the gentlemen curators of some quaint Bedlam, displaying such mooncalfs as once were accounted rare. You are the wall guards over increasing millions. In ten years it will be one out of three; in thirty years one out of *every*one – millions and millions, and rundown walls in the bargain.'

He paused again to catch his breath, swaying with the effort. I noticed Joe was swaying slightly in concert as he stared, like a bird watching a cobra.

'Still, you are true to your duty. You walk your watch, chin high and diplomas shouldered for all to see, though you are secretly certain that if the rabble decides to rush the walls, that roll of paper will be as useless against them as Freud's theories. You are up on that wall armed with only one weapon with any proven firepower. Can anyone tell the rest of the class what that weapon is? Eh? Any guesses? I shall give you a hint: Who is paying the bill for this august gathering?'

No hands went up. The whole hall was spellbound. Finally the old man gave a disgusted snort and unrolled the napkin for all to see: embossed around the border, like a record of registered cattle brands, were all the logos of the convention's sponsors.

'Here's who!' he declared. 'The pharmaceutical companies. Their laboratories manufacture your weapon – drugs. They are the munitions dealers and you are their customers. This gathering is their marketplace. Each of those displays downstairs was designed to appeal to your need up on that wall, to convince you that *their* laboratory can provide you with the most modern ammunition – the very latest in the high-powered tranquillizers! painkillers! mood elevators! muscle relaxants! psycho *del*ics!'

This last category could have been aimed at the table where Joe and I sat, but with those black glasses it was impossible to be sure.

'That is all you have in your arsenal,' he went on softly, 'the only armament known to work on both the demon and the host: a few chemicals – though the host has become a horde, and the demon, he is legion. A few feeble spears and arrows, dipped in a temporary solution to which that horde will soon become immune. Miss Nichswander?'

The blond was already coming through the drapes to retrieve the blackboard. She wheeled it away without a word. The drapery closed behind her, leaving Woofner sucking thoughtfully on his piece of chalk. It was the only sound in the room – not a shuffle or cough or clink else.

'I apologize,' Woofner said at length. 'I know that at this point in the programme one is expected to follow up his diagnosis of the disease with a prognosis for a cure. I am sorry to have to disappoint you. I do not have a cure for your problems up on that wall, and I refuse to offer temporary solutions. I should have made it clear to begin with that I bring you no salvation. All I can do is bring you to your senses, here, in the present. Und if you find that the pressure of this here-and-now is too much for you to bear, ach, then – ?' He wagged his head derisively. 'Then it is quite an easy task to simply step over the wall and join the happy hippos.'

If most of his audience was left in the dark by his closing metaphor, this time at least I was certain: it was a parting shot at none but me. He must have recognized me at my table during his talk and at the hippopotamus tank both, probably even on the Sky Ride. His shoulders sagged and he drew a long ragged breath; he was hunched so low that the sound whistled loudly through the mike. His whole body appeared to shake with the effort, like some kind of holy ruin about to collapse before a gale. Then he took off the pitch-dark glasses; the contrasting beam that burned forth was a shock. The temple roof might have been in ruin but the altar still held its fire, blue as the arc from an electric welder, and as painfully bright. Don't look away

338

if he turns it on you, I told myself. Try to meet it. Sure. Try matching eyes with skull-necklaced Kali. At the first searing touch I bent and focused on the congealing butter sauce around my lobster shell, for whatever unguent the oil might offer.

'So? That is that, yah? Yah, I think so. I thank you all for your attention. *Guten Abend und auf wiedersehen*! Miss Nichswander?'

When I looked back up she was wheeling him through the velveteen slot.

The Bellevue Revue couldn't understand why their crazyhouse hilarity received even less laughs than it deserved, which was damned little. My leftover lobster was funnier than they were; I was sorry when the waiter took it away. After the banquet broke up, however, the conventioneers set about dispelling the heavy pall the best way they could, by trying to make light of it. The remainder of the evening was spent drinking hard and listening to a lot of lampoons of the Woofner address. His heavy accent made him easy prey to parody. The joking got so uproarious in the wide-open hospitality suite the La Bouche Laboratories had reserved that kindhearted Dr Mortimer fretted the old man might hear.

'All this ridicule, this loud laughing – what if the poor fellow happened to come by? It could be injurious to someone in his condition.'

'This isn't laughing,' Joe said. 'This is whistling in the graveyard.'

It was long after midnight before the revellers wore it out and Mortimer got everybody quieted down enough to listen to Dr Toocter play his harp. It was the perfect soporific. Within minutes people were yawning goodnights and stumbling off toward their rooms.

As much as I'd drunk I was sure I'd drop straight off when I hit the bed, but I didn't. The air of our room seemed too close, the pitchy dark full of racket. The air conditioning throbbed brokenly and Mortimer snored along. I was so tired and dehydrated I could barely think, not even about Woofner. I'll think about him tomorrow. I'll look him up in the morning for a quick hello, then get on the first thing I can find flying west. Tonight all I want is a little sleep and a lot of liquid.

On one of my trips to the bathroom to refill my water glass, I met Joe coming out carrying his. He frowned at me from the crack of light.

'Christ, man, do you really feel it that bad?'

'Not quite,' I said. 'But I feel it coming.'

Joe took me by the arm and pulled me into the bathroom and shut the door. He gave me a big pink tablet from his shaving kit.

'Remedy number one,' he prescribed, 'is to duck it. Before it hits.'

I took the pill without asking any questions.

After that I got up only once more, to get rid of some of that liquid. The room was still black but still at last. The broken throbbing had been fixed and Mortimer's bed was quiet as a church. It seemed I had just lain back down when he shook me awake and told me it was Sunday.

'Sunday?' I squinted at the light. My head hammered. 'What happened to Saturday?'

'You looked so wasted we decided to let you rest,' Joe explained. He was drawing open the drapes. In the cruel light my two roommates looked pretty wasted themselves. Mortimer said I must be hungry but there would be time for a bite of breakfast before our flight; we'd better hurry.

I didn't feel hungry or rested either. I just had a cup of airport coffee and bought a box of Aspergum to have in my shoulder bag – the hammering in my head promised to get louder. Boarding the airplane I confided to Joe that whatever I had ducked seemed to be swinging back for another shot. He sympathized but said that big pink pill had been his last. He gave me a peek in his sample case, though; he'd managed to buy a quart of black rum from one of the Cuban maids.

'Remedy number two: if you can't duck it, try to keep ahead of it.'

It was a long sober return flight even with the rum. While Mortimer slept, Joe and I drank steadily, trying to keep ahead of the thing. The rum was gone before we got to Denver. Joe looked at the empty bottle mournfully.

'Yuh done somethin' t' the booze, Hickey,' he muttered in a thirties dialect. 'What yuh done t' da booze?'

The mutter was for my benefit, but Dr Mortimer was roused from his doze by the window.

'What's that, Joe?'

'Nothing, Doctor.' Joe slid the bottle out of sight. 'Just a line

340

that came to me from O'Neill's *The Iceman Cometh*. It's in the last act, after Hickey's given them all "The Word", so to speak, and one of the barflies says something to the effect of "The booze ain't got no kick t' it no more, Hickey. What yuh done t' da booze?"'

'I see,' Mortimer answered, and dug his head back into the little airplane pillow. He saw about as well as anybody did, I guessed.

With the help of Aspergum and overpriced airline cocktails I was still in front of the thing when we landed in Portland, but it was closing fast. The banging in my skull heralded it like the rising toll of a storm bell. Mortimer phoned his wife from the airport to have her meet him at the big Standard station on the edge of the hospital grounds. He said he simply did not have the energy to check on the ward just now. Joe said he would do it. Dr Mortimer gave Joe a grateful smile but allowed as how the nuts had been cracking right along without either of them for two days and nights now; another night probably wouldn't hurt.

'Besides, our guest has to be driven home,' he added. 'Unless he'd like to lay over a night with us. Devlin? It would give you an opportunity to study the set sketches the producers sent up.'

'Yeah, why don't you?' Joe put in. 'You can check out my collection of bad religious art from Ireland.'

I shook my head. 'I promised I'd be back. My dad was scheduled for a spinal this morning. I thought about phoning from Denver,' I said, 'but you know how it is.'

They both nodded that they did and no more was said about it.

We dropped Dr Mortimer off at the gas station. His wife was nowhere in sight, but we might not have seen her; there was still a jam of cars stretching around the corner of the block both ways. Joe began to fret as soon as the looming complex of the hospital came into sight. 'I think I ought to swing in, anyway,' he said. 'We can make a quick round while they're gassing us up at the motor pool.'

He braked to make the turn and the guard at the gate waved us on. He pulled to the NO STOPPING curb in front and motioned the aide sweeping the lobby to come out.

'Mr Gonzales? Would you mind driving this bomb around back and filling it up?'

Gonzales didn't mind a bit. Grinning at his good fortune, he gave Joe the broom and took the wheel. Joe shouldered it and marched around to my door.

'Come on,' he implored, 'you can stand it if I can.' He even added an enticement. 'Maybe I can scrounge up another pink pill.'

I could see he was needing the company; the hopeful glow had gone out of his eyes, leaving a gloomy smudge. I caught the strap of my shoulder bag and followed him toward the lobby, resolved to stand it.

The lobby was empty and completely changed. The renovation was nearly finished and the workers had knocked off for the weekend. There was gleaming new tile on the floor and fresh white paint on the walls. The veteran squad of khaki couches had been discharged and a replacement of recruits waited in close-order file, still in their plastic shipping bags. All the venetian blinds had been removed from the windows, and the wooden window frames replaced by chrome. It glistened in the harsh sunshine streaming through the big windows.

The only thing about the lobby that was the same was the fluorescent lights. They still buzzed and fluttered even in the shadeless sunlight. They made me think of the ward above. And this suddenly made my resolve start to flutter like the chilly light in those long tubes. I backed out when the elevator door opened.

'I'll wait down here,' I had to tell Joe. 'Maybe I'll finish that *Ching* you interrupted the other morning.'

'Right,' Joe said. 'So you can find out whether to go or not to go to Florida.' He handed me the broom. 'Find out for me too, why don't you?'

The elevator took him up and left me standing there, knowing that I had let him down. I leaned the broom against the wall and went to the drinking fountain and spit out my last piece of Aspergum. I tried to rinse out the taste but it wouldn't go away. It tasted like pennies, or a lightning storm in the making. I walked to the receptionist's deserted desk. Two of the buttons on her switchboard were blinking. As I watched, they both stopped. Calls were probably being relayed to another board during renovation.

I managed to get an outside line and dial my parents' house. I listened to it ringing at the other end. Maybe they were still at the hospital. Maybe something had happened. I should have tried earlier. I had lied about Denver. I hadn't thought of calling from there at all.

I tried awhile to ring Information for the number at the clinic, but I couldn't decipher the complicated switchboard. I finally gave up and walked to the couches. I took a seat in the one at the front of the rank, right at the windows. New louvred sun shades waited along the baseboard. They would replace the old blinds. Now the sun boomed in dead level, like cannon fire.

I got up and went around to the couch at the rear. It was still in the sun but I managed to pull it over into the bar of shade from one of the windowframes. I sat down in the narrow shadow and closed my eyes.

Joe was gone a long time. The sun angled along. I had to keep scooting the plastic to stay behind that shadow. I slumped back and folded my arms, hoping I might appear calm and relaxed should a guard happen past. I just about had the flutter in my breath under control when a thumping crash right at my feet made me jump a mile. My shoulder bag on the couch had been spilled by my fidgeting – the thump was the *I Ching* hitting the floor; the crash was the martini glass I'd swiped from Szaabo.

I tried to make fun of myself: Whadja think, one of the guys in white gotcha with his butterfly net? I was leaning to gather up the spilled stuff when I saw something that got me worse than any net ever could. It was on the front cover of the book, one of the pictures taken years before – of a little boy in pyjamas looking over the rail of a crib at the back of a cluttered bus. God Almighty had *that* been all there was to it? Nothing but a spell of *déjà vu!* a commonplace phenomenon triggered by that glimpse of Caleb standing on the porch in his nightclothes? It seemed to be that simply: the image on the porch had resonated with the photograph of that other time I traipsed off to see this mysterious Wolf Doctor. Always one of my favourite of Hassler's bus pictures. That's why it's front page centre in my collage. A ringing moment from the past, and it happened to find a corresponding note in the present. This could account for all these shadows that have been haunting me. Reverberations. The nuthouse reverberations. Woofner repeated. Separate splashes in the same pond, the ripples intersecting. Resonating waves, that's what it is, clear and simple –

yet . . .

there must be something more to it than surface waves to get you so good. It stirs too far down, rolls from too far away. To roll that far, wouldn't the two moments have to share something deeper as well? some primal heading? some upwelling force from a mutual spring that drives the pair of times to join forces and become one many times more lasting than either original time alone, a double-sided moment that can roll powerfully across years and at the same time remain fixed, permanently laminated in a timeproof vault of the memory, where the little boy stands longing yet, in unfading Kodachrome, in flannel pyjamas and Grateful Deadshirt both, on the porch at the farm and holding to the crib rail at the back of the bus, eyes shining forever brave down that dim and disorderly tube –

and yet . . .

it isn't the longing. Or the bravery. It's the trust. If Dad leaves a speed demon to babysit, the very act must signify it's aw-right, right? If he says a visit to Disney World is a Big People's business trip, then that's that. Trust doesn't fume off in a pout, like big brother Quiston, or wheedle like May or Sherree; but it does expect to have something brought back. It does expect to reel in something if it casts far and often and deep enough, like those faces on the ward. It does expect to slide in someday to more than a plate of dirt if it rounds bases enough. It expects these things because these things have been signified. That's what gets you.

Especially if you're one of those that's been doing the signifying.

So the discovery that I was having *déjà vus* did not bring me any ease. It only clarified the fearful murk that had been nagging me into something far more haunting: guilt. And when I closed my eyes to shut out the little face looking up from the book on my lap, I found my head crammed full of other faces waiting their turn. What was my mother going to say? Why hadn't I phoned? Why wouldn't I lend poor Joe a little support a while ago after all of it he's afforded me the last two days? Why can't I face those faces upstairs? I know now that it isn't my fear that chains me back. It's the bleak and bottomless rock of failure, jutting remote from the black waters. Onto this hard rock I am chained. The water pounds like blame itself. The air is thick with broken promises coming home to roost, flapping and clacking their beaks and circling down to give me the same as

Prometheus got . . . *worse!* Because I sailed up to those forbidden heights more times than he had – as many times as I could manage the means – but instead of a flagon of fire the only thing I brought back was an empty cocktail glass . . . and I broke that.

I clenched my eyes, hoping I guess to squeeze out a few comforting drops of remorse, but I was as dry as the Ancient Mariner. I couldn't cry and I couldn't do anything about it. I couldn't do anything about anything, was about what it came down to. All I could do was sit by myself on my godforsaken reef of failure, clenching my eyes and gnashing my teeth in morbid self-recrimination.

This is what I was doing when I realized I was no longer by myself.

'*Squank!*'

She was leaned over the back of the couch, her twin telescopes within inches of my face. When I turned she reared away, wrinkling her nose.

'Tell me, Slick: are you wearing that expression to match your breath, or are you this lowdown for real?'

When I regained myself I told her that this was about as real as it got, and as lowdown.

'Good,' she said. 'I hate a phony funk. Mind if I join you? I'll even share your troubles . . .'

She came around without waiting for an answer, tapping her way to a place beside me.

'So. How do you explain this hangdog face?'

'I swallowed more than I can bite off,' was all I told her. I didn't think this myopic little freak would understand more, even if I could explain it.

'Just don't spit up on me,' she warned. She leaned around to get a closer look at my face. 'Y'know, dude, you look kind of familiar. What do they call you besides ugly?' She stuck out a skeletal hand. 'I'm called the Vacu-Dame, because I'm out in deep space most of the time.'

I took the hand. It was warm and thin, but not a bit skeletal. 'You can call me the Véjà Dude.'

She made a sound like a call-in beeper with a fresh battery. I guessed it was supposed to be a laugh. 'Very good, Slick. That's why you look so familiar, eh? Very clever. So what's with all the pictures stuck on that book in your lap? Photos of your famous flashbacks?'

'In a way. The pictures are from a bus trip I took once with my gang. The book's an ancient Chinese work called *The Book of Changes*.'

'Oh, yeah? Which translation? The Richard Wilhelm? Let me have a look at it, so to speak.'

I handed her the book and she held it up to her face. I was beginning to suspect that this freak might understand more than I thought.

'It's the English edition. That's what I used when I first started throwing the *Ching*. Then I thought I'd try using Wilhelm in his original German. I wanted to see if it helped the poetic parts. I found such a veritable shitload of difference between the two that I thought, "Shit, if it loses this much from German into English, how much must've been lost from ancient Chinese to German?" So I decide to hell with it all. The last *Ching* I threw I threw at my degenerate Seeing Eye dog for turning over my wastepaper basket looking for Tampons. The sonofabitch thought I was playing games. He grabbed the book and ran outside with it, and by the time I tracked him down he'd consumed every page. He was a German shepherd. When he found something written in his ancestral tongue he just couldn't put it down. What's all this glass underfoot, incidentally? Did you drop something or did I just miss a Jewish marriage? I don't care for dogs but I *love* a good wedding. It gives the adults an excuse to get soused and let all the dirty laundry hang out. Is that where you're bringing such a booze breath back from, Ace? A big wedding?'

'I'm bringing it back from Disney World, believe it or not.'

'I believe it. On the Red Eye Rocket. Here, you better put your fancy book away before I see a dog.'

When I tried to reach around her for my bag I bumped her staff. It tipped and fell before I could grab it.

'Watch it!' she shrilled. 'That's my third eye you're knocking in the broken glass!'

She picked it up and turned around to stand it behind the couch, out of danger. Then she leaned close again and gave me a fierce frown. 'You're the one broke it too, ain't you? No wonder you got such a guilty look on you, cursed with such a clumsy goddamn nature.'

For all her frowning, I couldn't help but grin at her. She didn't seem as fierce as she looked, really. She might not have realized she was frowning all the time. She wasn't as hopelessly homely as she first appeared, either, I decided. Or as titless.

'Speaking of curses,' I said, 'what was that one of yours the other day? It was formidable.'

'Oh, *that*,' she said. The frown vanished instantly. She drew her knees up to her chin and wrapped her arms around her shins. 'It isn't mine,' she confessed. 'It's Gary Snyder's, mostly, a poem of his called "Spel Against Demons". You want to know why I happened to memorize it? Because one time I spray-painted the entire thing. On a football field. Remember when Billy Graham held that big rally in Multnomah Stadium a couple of years back?'

'You're the one who did that?'

'From goal line to goal line. It took nineteen rattle cans and most of the night. Some of the words were ten yards big.'

'So, you're the famous phantom field-writer? Far damn out. The paper said the writing was completely illegible.'

'It was dark! I've got a shaky pen hand!'

'You were plenty legible the other afternoon,' I prompted. I wanted to keep her talking. I saw her cheeks colour at the compliment, and she started rocking back and forth, hugging her knees.

'I was plenty ripped is what I was,' she said. 'Besides, I recite better than I handwrite.'

She rocked awhile in thought, frowning straight ahead. The sun was almost out of sight in the ridgeline across the river, and the light in the room had softened. The chrome trim was turning the colour of butter. All of a sudden she clapped her hands.

'*Now* I remember!' She aimed a finger at me. 'Where I know your melancholy mug from: the dust jacket of your goddamn novel! So far-damn-out to *you* too!'

She started to rock again. It wouldn't have surprised me to see her put her thumb in her mouth.

'I'm something of a writer myself,' she let me know, 'when I'm not something else. Right now I'm an astral traveller on layover. Too far over, too, after two days of Miss Beal's Bed and Breakfast.'

I told her she didn't look nearly as far laid over as the others I saw up there. This made her blush again.

'I cheek the tranqs,' she confided. 'I never swallow anything they give me. Watch – '

She felt around between her ragged deck shoes until she found a big shard of glass. She tossed it to the back of her mouth and swallowed. She opened wide to show nothing but teeth and tongue, then a moment later spat the shard tinkling across the new tile.

'Want to know the reason they hauled me in here? Because I dropped three big blotter Sunshines and went paradin' around the rotunda at the capitol. Want to know why I got so ripped? I was celebrating the completion of my new novel. Want to know the name of it?'

I told her that as a matter of fact I would like to know the name of her novel. I couldn't help but feel that somebody was getting their leg pulled, but I didn't care. I was fascinated.

'I called it *Teenage Girl Genius Takes Over the World!* Not too shabby a title, huh?'

I conceded that I'd heard worse, especially for first novels.

'First your ass! This is goddamn third. My first was called *Tits & Zits* and my second is *Somewhere Ovary Rainbows*. Shallow shit, those first two, I admit it. Juvenile pulp pap. But I think *Girl Genius* has got some balls to it. Hey, let me ask you something! My publisher wants to reprint the first two and bring all three out as a package. But I'm not so sure. What's your thinking on that plan, as one novelist to another?'

I didn't know what to think. Was she on the level or lying or crazy or what? She sounded serious, but that could have been like the frown. I couldn't get over that feeling of a pulling sensation on my leg. I avoided her question with one of my own.

'Who's your publisher?'

'Binfords and Mort.'

If she'd named off some well-known New York house like Knopf or Doubleday I'd have started shovelling pantomime manure. But Binfords & Mort? That's a speciality house for high-class historic stuff, and hardly known outside of the Northwest. Would she pick such company to lie about? Then again, would they pick her?

'I think you could do worse than follow the advice of Binfords and Mort,' I averred, trying to probe her eyes. I couldn't get past the glass. I'd have to try another test.

'Okay, Girl Genius, I've got one for you.'

348

'It'll have to be quick, Slick. I think my chariot has just arrived.'

A black sedan had indeed just pulled up at the NO STANDING curb. She must have heard it. An ambitious-looking young legal-type flunky got out and started for the lobby door.

'Quick it is,' I said. 'I'd like to know what's *your* thinking – just off the top of your I.Q. – on the Second Law of Thermodynamics?'

If I hoped to see her thrown by this, I was disappointed. She got very deliberately to her feet and stood in front of me. She bent her face down until it was almost touching mine. The thin lips were starting to stretch at the corners. The eager pad of driver's footsteps stopped a few feet away but neither the girl nor I turned.

'Melissa?' I heard him say. 'Everything's cleared, Sweetie. Your father wants us to go to the Leaning Tower and order a couple giants – a pepperoni for him. He'll join us as soon as he gets rid of that damned delegation from Florence's fishing industry – they're still singing the blues about the salmon regulations. How does Canadian bacon sound for the other one? It's smoke cured . . . ?'

The lenses never wavered from me. But the lips continued to stretch, wider and wider, until it seemed her whole head might be split in half by her grin. The blush raged across her cheeks and neck, and her eyes flashed around their crystal cages like giddy green parakeets. She finally cupped her hand so we were shielded from the driver's eyes.

'Entropy,' she whispered behind her hand, like a resistance fighter passing a vital secret under the very nose of the enemy, 'is only a problem in a closed system.' Then she straightened and spoke up. 'What's more, a singing fisherman from Florence sounds better to me than a singed pig from Canada. How about you, Slick?'

'Much better,' I agreed.

She nodded curtly. The scowl snapped back into place. Without another word she turned on her heel and stalked unaided past the waiting flunky, across the lobby, and straight out the door toward the sedan, majestically, or as majestically as possible for a knobby-jointed maybe-crazy half-green-haired nearly-completely-blind girl-thing from another dimension.

349

'If you're ever in Mt Nebo,' I called after her, 'I'm in the book!'

She kept going. The flunky caught up to her but she disdained his help. She nearly stumbled when she stepped off the curb, but she caught the rear fender and felt her way to the door handle and got in. It was then I realized that, in her show of majesty, she'd left her cane.

They were pulling away as I ran out. I waved the feathered staff, but of course she couldn't see me. I thought of honking the thing after them but they were already to the gate, and the traffic was loud.

Besides, I knew it was the very sort of something I was supposed to bring back. It was absolutely neat. Caleb would love it. He would take it to school, show it off, brandish it, twirl it, honk it. His classmates would admire it, covet it, want one of their own. On their next trip to the Magic Kingdom they would look for them at all the Main Street souvenir shops, ask after them in all the little information kiosks . . .

Then, one bright blue airbrushed morn – a marvel of demand and supply! – there they'll be.

Last Time the Angels Came Up

'I'm so damn proud to *be* here today,' yells Mofo.

It was the first thing I heard when I got back from Florida three days ago and found them all here, and I've heard him holler it at every lapse and lull ever since, changing only the italics: 'I'm *so* damn proud to be here today' or 'I'm so damn proud to be *here* today . . .'

'Me too,' agrees the little one named Big Lou. 'And I'll be just as proud when I'm gone. If the heat leaves us go in peace I'll be proud and pleased both.'

It's currently against the law to ride motorcycles in the state without crash helmets. They'd been hassled by one state trooper after another, all the way from the California/Oregon border.

'They fuckin better,' says the three-hundred-plus-pounder called Little Lou. 'I'm tired of taking shit off these uniformed faggots. Especially when they's only-est one of them to thirty of us. Might's right, ain't it?'

'Fuckin A,' answers Big Lou.

'I know for a fact that the Reverent Billy Graham says that right is might. So might is got to be right by *miles*, right? Thirty to one?'

'Seems right to me,' says Big Lou, stretched out on his belly down in the yard, six-foot-six and a sixth-of-a-ton of dusty meat and leather. 'But the only-est thing I know for fact is that, since San Fran, I got miles and miles of piles.'

Then, a moment later, that measured laugh. It comes hammering up from the yard and the concrete apron in front of my shop where numerous Harleys are undergoing various repairs. I can't tell if it's a laugh about Big Lou's rhyme, or about another comment about me up here typing, or what.

'Say I'll tell ya what *I've* got,' says the heavy voice I've come to recognize belongs to that one called Awful Harry: 'I got brakes by Christ I didn't even know I had!'

Then goes roaring a doughnut and braking and raising an awful pillar of dust in my driveway to prove his point.

'See that? Brakes! This morning when I'm coming back out

from the mechanic and sees this little chickie here hitchhiking, I locked 'em up. I mean locked 'em the fuck *up!* When I finally stops I looks behind me and all I sees a strip of rubber running a quarter mile back to her standing there with her little pink tummy hanging out. Aint that right, Chickie Bird?'

Chickie Bird doesn't answer but Rumiocho squawks his 'Right on!'

'Hear that?' Harry rasps. 'He says "Right on." The fuckin bird's hipper'n all you pukes. Hey, Parrot? I'd *steal* your ass if you didn't belong to friends o' the *fam*-bly har har har . . .'

Although Awful Harry isn't the biggest of the brood, he's potentially the baddest. He told me he was a security guard five days a week, keeping things tame in a Marin County shopping mall, so he requires five times as much wildness on the weekends as his Angel's recompense and right. He isn't tall but he's heavy and hard. When he walks he swings a hard heavy gut around in front of him with the efficient ease of a sumo wrestler. When he talks he comes off halfway halfwitted, except for his eyes betraying a malicious mocking intelligence. A quickness. In his intimate moments he admits to being a four-point student for the first two terms of his one unfinished year at Cal . . . claimed he kissed it off because the academic pace was too *pokey* for him, sneered up at me rattling out the window – 'Is *that* all the faster you can type up there?'

Mickey Write comes driving in eyes the scenes goes driving right back out.

The reporter from *Crawdaddy* that I completely forgot was coming calls from the airport to say she has arrived. She will be driving right out as soon as she rents a car, get right into our in-depth interview. I tell her not likely, fill her in on the unforeseen scene and warn her what to expect. Oh, great she *loves* it, can't wait, hopes they won't leave before she finds her way out. I'm able to picture her by sound, by the plumage of her voice over the wire, preened like a pea hen, fluttering with excitement. I give her directions to Mt Nebo and she flutters off, instructing me to watch out and sit tight till she arrives.

In a way I can do both. By now I can picture the scene without getting up, just by the sounds: Tinkering at the bikes, barking after the stick . . . the mama hen clucking her brood with her across the lawn so they can examine the famous hitchhiking Chickie Bird who's lying under the apple tree with

352

the portable record player balanced on the provocative pink
midriff which set up the scene yesterday on the cabin porch
that eventually got my strung-out and strung-over jail partner,
Rampage, punched by hard and heavy Harry.

I hear the record end. I hear the needle kick automatic back
to the start of the 45. I hear Janis Joplin screech *Piece o' My
Heart* for the six-hundredth time in the last seventy-two hours, it
seems. . . .

Their hot black shuttle car comes swinging in the drive, no,
goes past the drive squeals a stop, backs up and then comes
swinging in the drive . . .

Remember: Psalm 73; the dosed ducks; the gate left open the
cows crazy in the blueberries, Ebenezer charging the Harley; the
crumpled opalescent horn; Dobbs and Rampage to the rescue
and the surreptitious evacuation of the women and kids . . .

Beneath the curtain, Awful Harry sits down on the lawn
beside the girl, gets leaned comfortable against the apple tree so
he can concentrate on the extensive collection of *Mad* mags he
brought in his fancy saddlebags. I remember Old Bert saying
Harry was an anthropology major.

The hen and chicks, scratching and pecking around.

Tyres spitting gravel, the black shuttle heads off to town to
pick up the trailer they've decided to rent. The dust provokes a
din of coughing and spitting . . . the hen squawking for cover.
Harry sees me and waves his magazine and starts to get up. I sit
back down. The sound of a typewriter is a powerful repellent . . .

'Hey, Lucifer!' It's Old Bert up from his snooze, hollering at
the youngest prospect. 'Go get everybody ready to roll. We
been fuckin hangin around here buggin these people three fuckin
days. It's time we got in the wind.'

Pinktummy has finally put on another record, electrically
enhanced Beatles claiming the Magical Mystery Tour is coming
to take us a-way. But when it's finished, nothing happens. Just
the Fool on the hill with his eyes turning 'round . . .

Bootheel in the gravel. The tall stooped guy with the cast on
his leg goes lurching by toward the toilet, dour.

The paper shears on my desk looks like a weapon.

That measured laugh, always the same length, precisely the
amount of hammering it takes to pound one ten-penny nail into
a dry pine plank.

Hanging from the highest limb of the apple tree are the three

God's Eyes Quiston and Caleb made out of yarn at Camp Nebo. The eyes aren't moving a wink in the thick hot air, but they likely see the world spinning around as well as any Fool's.

Turns out they can't roll quite yet. They've got to wait for the black car to get back with the trailer. Why? Something about they've decided they are going to have to haul the bike of the guy that laid 'er down coming off the freeway, the president. His hog. Back to Frisco. His head is hurting and he's going to fly. Lengthy bitching and back-rapping about this: 'Ya say fly mumble mumble he's gonna *fly?* Candy ass I calls it mumble grumble. I don't give a fuck he *is* president!'

More tinkering. Random exclamations through the heatwaves: 'Duty calls!' 'A-men!' 'I'm gonna rip off that bitch you don't keep her dressed!' . . . voices from a time-impacted playground, the kids never heard the bell ending recess, now they have all become man-sized and whiskered and hung over.

'Truck it! The word for the day is "Truck it!"'

Because the trailer idea fell through – too much hassle to hook a tow-rig to the black shuttle's rear bumper. Now the plan is to use Joe Blow's credit card to rent a refrigerated truck and truck the extra bikes home. Why a refrigerated truck? All I can think is it's to keep the cruel summer heat off the wounded machines, but that doesn't make any sense . . .

The prospect called Reject peeks in to ask, 'You seen Old Bert?' I tell him not in a while and he goes farting off. Yesterday's chili.

'I'm so damn proud! To be here! To-day!' – followed by that sharp, insinuating snigger, more a planing, now, than a hammering. I picture pine chips falling in white curls around black boots.

Somebody knocks on our big farm bell. I yell out my window 'That bell's an alarm bell! For fires! Nothing to be played with.'

'With us,' Harry hollers back from the other direction, '*any*-thing's to be played with.'

A loud *chongk!* It's a hunting knife being thrown against the pumphouse.

I hear Dobbs's voice from down at the cabin porch. He's reading from Grandma Whittier's big Bible, very loud, about all the trouble Paul had with the Corinthians twenty centuries ago. If I was him I'd tone down and consider the trouble Rampage had only yesterday.

One of the Harleys pops to life, roisterous and husky, a machine in rut. The black car revs, honks twice, leaves. Another bike is stomped awake.

'Hey, everybody! let's hear it for seriousness.'

Everybody; 'Hawr hawr hawr . . . !'

Visiting Jenneke, that Danish delight, up from her rest, standing in the cookhouse doorway half-naked but with such a toothache that nobody dares come on to her, yet . . . glares at it all shaking her head – never seen barbarism like this in Copenhagen.

The tall guy with the cast comes lurching back, buckling his belt. Dobbs hollers up from the cabin, 'Hey tell us the tale of your accident?'

Without halting his lurch the guy says, 'Screech. Crash. Hurt. Hospital.'

Jenneke decides to put on a short kimono and take some of her stale pastry down to feed the ducks.

'I'm so damn *proud* . . . to be here . . .'

More bikes are racketing now, the majority of them, grunting, coughing, roaring – 'Let's go go *go-o-o!*' Then they all shut down. It's Awful Harry that's holding them up. His brakes after all. Completely fucked.

The black car is back with the trailer. *What* refrigerated truck? Nobody told *them* about no fuckin refrigerated truck.

Dobbs comes strolling up, drops in on me, shaking his head at all the starting and stopping out my window. 'They're like a rock band getting ready to play: tuning up and jerking off and rattling around trying to find the right key for so long that sometimes it comes close to music.'

'Never close enough,' I say, but I have to concede to myself: the bastards *are* trying to find the key, true enough. Maybe even the right one. Rusty gates might be unlocked by all this rattling and *damn* we'd hate to miss that . . .

The black car splits again, sans trailer.

'You tell me tough shit? When I aint got no fuckin brakes and my front end's fucked up and I'm strung out and you tell me tough shit? Well fuck you!'

'Hey it was tough shit for me when I went down in that fuckin blizzard in Reno last Easter with my bad arm, but *I* didn't get no truck ride home. So fuck you, *too!*'

Silence follows the flare-up, then the tinkering, then the sound of the knife against the pumphouse again.

The afternoon stretches out. There's a breeze moving the God's Eyes at last. The guy that I think is the acting president is sitting under the tree holding his head with both hands.

A meadowlark calls, bright and incongruous. More yells from the greasy concrete:

'Hey you know what?'

'Hey you know what I don't *give* a shit is what.'

'Hey you know what?'

'Yeah, I know what . . . I want one of those downers is what.'

'*Who* got some downers? *Who?*'

'Who shits through feathers?'

'Hey you know what? I'm so *damn* proud . . .'

'I slid down the snow to the other lane and fuckin near got hit by a *diesel*, too!'

'. . . to *be* here . . .'

'Who's got a yellow? I need a mellow yellow.'

'. . . *to*-day!'

The girl for the interview shows up, her East Coast attire provoking whistles and howls. 'Take off them *ray-ud* pants!'

The knife hits the pumphouse. You can tell it doesn't stick that often.

'Hey, where's Varmint-boy? Let's bug the Varmint some more.'

'Yeah, where is that weird little Varmint dude?'

'Bug the Varmint! Bug the Varmint!'

'The Varmint's already bugged out,' Dobbs yells from the cabin. 'Headed for the hills this morning while you guys weren't watching, bow and arrow and all.'

'*Ahhh*,' everybody says.

The knife hits the pumphouse.

'Hey, Lucifer! Run up to the store and get us something while we're waiting.'

'Yeah, some *pussy*.'

'Yeah! Hey you up there in them, red pants' – boredom is beginning to stiffen into horniness – 'why don'cha interview *me?*'

'O, cook, cook, *cook* that ol' dog!'

They've got Reject masturbating Stewart. A roar of applause congratulates the ejaculation.

'Hey you know what? I can do better'n that.'

'Right on, Little Lou! Do it! Do it!'

'Cook! Cook! Get it, dog!'

'Yea! I won!'

'You won my dick! Reject pumped out a good half a quart more than you.'

'So what? You want quantity or you want quality? I made him shoot all the way to that piece of wood. If you're talkin quality I can jack off circles around Reject and you both!'

'Lucifer, get us some warshwater.'

'Hey, Lucifer!'

'Where the hell is he? I want my hands warshed.'

'He's getting Bert a beer. Reject, see if you can find a hose.'

'I know what! Let's sit that chick with the toothache over there and see if Stewart can hit her in the mouth.'

'Yeah! There you go! Cook!'

The black car again, like a dispatch runner back and forth from the front.

Jenneke bends over to feel the temperature of the pond. Even sixty yards away her ass shines like a beacon through the thin kimono.

'Hey you know what? I could go for some smorgasbord.'

More talk of leaving and worry about the State Troopers. They've managed to locate one helmet and Awful Harry has it on, out in the goat pen. He's down on all fours battling Killer the goat. Jenneke the animal lover strides around, hands on her hips, glowering and joggling.

'Mmmboy let's hang around another day,' somebody suggests on the basis of Jenneke's boobs.

'Mmmboy let's fucking not! I aint no oral surgeon.'

'Hey where's Old Bert? We're getting ready to roll anybody seen Old Bert?'

Going to pee I find Bert and Harry's hitchhiking ladyfriend drying off after a shower. The 45 portable is sitting on the dryer – 'Take a . . . take another little piece of my har-ar-art . . .'

Bert grins at me. 'Be outta here in a hot second,' he says, sheepish. Old Bert's the only one I know any more. Everybody else crippled or busted or snuffed. Bert used to be president, says now he'd rather ride than ride herd. ' – we just had to rinche off the cum.'

Back up in the office I hear more bikes starting. Harry comes walking across the yard, bare-bellied, swinging his arms wide out like his ribs hurt. Maybe old Killer tagged him one.

Now Bert is kicking his old chopper over. Same one he took to London, years ago. The girl puts the record player in the black car then shuffles around, uncertain. Awful Harry rolls his big luxury model out of the garage, declares he's got brakes again. The girl looks from Old Bert's old bike with its skimpy seat, to Harry's new Electro-glide with elaborate leather cushions and sissybar. Harry shakes his head at her.

'Oh no you don't, bitch! He balls you, he hauls you.'

She climbs on behind Old Bert and wraps her sunburned arms around his waist. He grins up at me.

More popping, roaring, backfiring, churning brown dust and blue smoke . . . stalling and stalling . . . then, all at once, they are leaving, whooping and roaring, rolling in a long detonating wave out our dirt road to the pavement, west, rap-bap-bapping up the grade toward Mt Nebo, then out of sight, south, echoing their way through the smoky afternoon.

'Right off!' Rumiocho squawks when the last one is gone.

A civilization begins to drift back over the farm, like the settling dust. The silence is a thunderclap of relief.

Me, I'm gonna go change out of these boots and back into my moccasins.